Daughters of Artemis

L. M. Townsend

ISBN 0-9744121-3-9
Second Printing 2003
Cover design by Anne M. Clarkson
Cover photo used with permission from
Mag. Gerhard Poellauer

Published by:
Dare 2 Dream Publishing
A Division of Limitless Corporation
Lexington, South Carolina 29073

Find us on the World Wide Web
http://www.limitlessd2d.net

Printed in the United States of America

Dedication and Acknowledgements

Gosh, it's already been a year since The Amazon Queen was published! I can't believe it.

This book again is dedicated to Crow, to Sarina, and to "Tai'" for all of your love and support and encouragement every day - I thank you with all of my heart.

I also want to dedicate this book to my grand-parents, Ann and Walter Heidenreich. Thank you for always believing in me - Grandpa, I did it! I really, really did it - and I know that you can hear my thoughts and feel my love for you, even as I can still feel you loving and guiding me from the other side. Your "Poppy" is a real author now. ☺

Grandma, thank you for your continued love and encouragement and support every single day of my life. I couldn't have done this without that - and without you. Thank you for not only being my Grandma, but my friend, too.

I want to thank my mom for teaching me to be a strong woman - just like her and like the Amazons. Again, I wouldn't have done this without that strength you gave me. I want to thank Sam and Anne, too - for believing in me and my work enough to take a chance in publishing me - you really have made my life-long and much cherished dream come true. Thank you both so very much for that.

Blessed Be!

Special Thanks

A very special thank you goes out to the very gracious photographer and archeologist who gave Ms. Townsend and Limitless his permission to use the extraordinary photo which graces the cover of this book.

Cover photo by *Mag. Gerhard Poellauer*, the founder of the Amazon Research Subscriber Network. He is an Austrian archaeologist and historian who has been engaged in the research of the Amazon history for more than 15 years.

Amazon Research Subscriber Network

A-9020 Klagenfurt, AUSTRIA

Website:
http://www.myrine.at/Amazons/index.html

e-mail:
GPoellau@myrine.at

Original photo of the doorway at Karpu Kale, believed to be the last refuge of the Amazons.

Prologue: In the Beginning was the Sword ...

Skeletal fingers of lightning rent the black sky as if it were rotted silk. Thunder crashed, shaking the earth below. Then the rain came, fat crimson drops, splattering the Amazon city. Again the lightning snaked down from the angry sky. Thunder cracked sharply and the gore-splashed buildings of the Amazon city toppled into ruins.

Far away, the sound of horses' hooves striking the earth drowned out the sound of a child, wrapped in the arms of a stranger, crying for her mother.

Thunder came again, shaking the earth open, a wide chasm from which emerged a woman so beautiful, it hurt mortals' eyes to look upon her. She strode into the ruined Temple of the Amazons and wrenched the Sword of Artemis from the hand of the statue. The statue fell across the altar as if reaching for what had been stolen from it, and broke into pieces.

The woman smiled in triumph and held the gleaming silvery Sword aloft. The lightning descended again, striking the Sword, wrapping itself around the hilt and yanking the Sword from the woman's hand into the heavens where it disappeared from sight.

"Treachery! Betrayal!" she howled with rage and pain as she began to transform. Her legs grew together and scales covered her lower body. Her hair rose up, a nest of hissing serpents striking at the empty air. Her face became a hideous skull-like mask, her swollen tongue lolling between sharp fang-like teeth. Slowly the earth began to pull her back down. She sank back into the chasm, which closed over her yowls of fury.

Far away, the lost child cried out in the night from her strange bed for a mother who would never return ...

The priestess awoke from the nightmare, trembling. The cold sweat which had broken out during the evil dream chilled her as she looked around her cosy house behind the Temple of the Amazons. She sighed.

"The Child of Promise," she whispered as the dream began to fade away from her memory. She had recognised the curly-haired, dark-eyed daughter of Thalia and Queen Aradia as the child from her dream. "The Sword of Artemis ... the Salvation of the Amazon Nation ... must be kept safe ..."

The priestess slowly sank back into a deep and dreamless sleep until dawn.

Chapter I: Sword of Artemis

A woman stood in the centre of a crossroads. Her long, dark coppery hair blew in the rising wind as her eyes, the colour of violet petals, surveyed the scene before her, trying to take in the horror and failing as tears kept mercifully blurring her vision.

All three roads as far as the eye could see were lined with crosses. But these crosses were not empty - oh, no. Far from it. Bodies still adorned these gruesome reminders of the Amazons' destruction, for these were the mouldering remains of Amazons. Skeletons, mostly, still dressed in the rotting remains of Amazon armour. Each skull seemed to silently scream at the horror they had become - still hanging there nearly a decade after the battle of Chadesia, where the Kaskan Army had cruelly decimated the Amazon Nation ... the Amazons, betrayed by their former sisters, the Gorgons, lost that day...

The woman looked up as dark storm clouds roiled overhead, thunder rumbled, and a breeze swirled dead, dry leaves over the ground. The leaves which skittered across the converged roads sounded like so many whispers and the weary woman imagined those whispers to be recriminations for her seeming desertion of her people.

Slowly, she began to walk down one of the roads, stopping at the foot of one of the crosses as the memories she had fought to bury suddenly erupted in a blaze of unexpected emotion, triggered by the sight of a body hanging from one of the crosses, an Amazon amulet still dangling from the skeletal neck. Tears welled in the woman's eyes as she reached up and pulled the amulet free. As she gazed at the object in her hand, she noticed an offering placed lovingly at the foot of the cross. Bending, she picked up the flowers with her free hand; they crumbled into dust, blown away by the growing wind.

The woman was Aradia, the queen of this dead host and she had been gone for the decade which had passed, leaving her sisters to their fate, but it had not been by her own choice.

Her mind wandered back to a memory she had tried to close out, but failed ...

Heavy iron chains, manacled about her wrists weighed down more than just her body; her very soul felt the cold iron, cutting and chafing as much as her raw wrists felt them. They couldn't even let her wear her own clothing. Filthy and battle torn as it was, it would have been a great deal more comfortable than this ridiculous, revealing Greek-like thing - what was it called? Oh, yes a chiton. *Her arms and legs and one breast were bared to the rocks and offal thrown by the "citizens" of Roma who had lined up to watch the parade. She was spit upon, to the accompaniment of the foul invectives shouted by those illustrious citizens, most of which was nothing but a blurry roar in Aradia's head. Yet the Amazon Queen walked, her head up and her shoulders as far back as the weight of her chains would allow. Aradia's eyes never left the back of her captor, Aurelian, General of the Roman Army. Those violet eyes which had once been warm and loving in their gaze now held no emotion, for Aradia had hardened her heart and it was now as if it were encased in ice. She had lost too much to ever allow herself to feel anything ever again - except for maybe a vague desire for vengeance, but even that ... she was too soul-weary to contemplate it.*

Aradia was sold to the Gladiator Arena. Aurelian had mistakenly thought the exotic appeal of an Amazon would make a lot of money for him - but Aradia didn't care to appeal to the masses of Rome - she killed because it was instinct to kill anyone who attacked her. Well-honed instinct, bred and trained into her from her birth. In truth, Aradia wouldn't have minded dying. It would have been an easy escape from this hated place, but she couldn't fight her body's natural desire to survive, and so she dispatched her opponents with a look of disgust to the booing masses of blood-thirsty Romans.

And then one night, Aradia escaped the Gladiator barracks with the aid of an unknown benefactor. A cloaked figure had awakened her, pointing to the open cell door. Aradia blinked once then shook her head.

"Why?" she asked.

"I need you elsewhere," was the whispered reply. The cloaked figure fought off the guards, dispatching them with ease. As Aradia shook off the sleep stupor, the nightmarish quality of the last decade also left her. The ring of clashing steel assaulted her ears and instinctively she sought a weapon to join the battle for her own freedom, but her mysterious saviour waved her away with a grin.

"Go, go!" she hissed and Aradia grabbed the ragged woolen blanket from the mean straw pallet which had served her for a bed these last years. She fashioned a makeshift cloak against the night's chill and ran.

The cloaked figure pulled back the hood, revealing a beautiful woman. She spared a glance at Aradia's escape, then turned her attention back to the guards with a cold smile, dispatching them to whatever hell they had earned for themselves before fading from the sight of the other, clamouring captives in the Gladiator's cell.

Aradia had run until her breath burned in her chest that night. She rested for only a short time, fearing the Roman hounds at her back before taking flight once again. As she returned to her people, she watched the moon wane, then wax several times, all the while her senses were re-sharpening themselves to the dangers of the road, the foremost being her imagined pursuers. It had been a nightmare journey of several new moons, but at last she made her way home, only to be greeted with death ... Death of her sisters, death of hope, death of the Tribe, all ...

"Dead," said Aradia, dully, kicking the plate of rotting fruit left as an offering at the foot of one of the crosses. "What the Tartarus good is *this*?". She looked again at the amulet still in her hand then back up at the skeleton on the cross whose blonde hair still blew in the wind. "Thalia ... how did this come to be?" Aradia looked down the rows of crosses, her mind unable to encompass the horror of the catastrophe. "Why are you still up there, why are all of you still up there?" she cried out, agony ripping at her very soul. Aradia dropped her head in defeat, but her eyes caught something on the ground - Thalia's broken sword half-buried in the brush at the foot of the cross. She fell to her knees and picked up the sword. For a brief moment, Aradia allowed the tears of grief to fall, then looked back up at the grisly remains of her once-second in command.

"Your sword, shattered as my hope ... as broken as the Amazon Spirit ..." said Aradia, her voice breaking. She raised her eyes to the gathering dark clouds and cried out in agony. "Why? Great Artemis, where were you when your daughters were slaughtered and left as so many trophies for our enemies to gloat over? Where were you when our Nation was destroyed? Where were you when I was captured and put on display like some animal in a circus? Why did you let this happen, Mother? *Why*?"

As if in answer, a loud crack of thunder sounded and lightning illuminated the sky, the afterimage appearing to Aradia's narrowed eyes as the glowing image of a sword against the background of the dark clouds. Aradia's eyes narrowed further, as she sought to understand the vision.

She rose to her feet, tucking the broken sword into her belt. Suddenly, her heightened senses alerted her to a body approaching. She took cover in the heavy, overgrown brush by the side of the road as a small, cloaked figure approached the cross of Thalia. The figure knelt briefly, then rose, pushing back the hood of the cloak, revealing a young girl of about twelve birth-seasons, leaving a fresh offering at the foot of Thalia's cross. Aradia silently emerged from her hiding place, at first unnoticed by the young girl. Startled, the girl saw Aradia standing there and tried to run, but Aradia grabbed her arm firmly, stopping her.

"What are you doing here?" said Aradia. She looked up at the crosses. "This is no place for a child."

"You startled me. I thought you were - " said the girl, defiantly.

"Kaskan? If I were, you'd be dead," said Aradia, harshly.

"No - not Kaskan. One of them," said the girl, raising her eyes to the cross. "I come here to honour my mother as best I can ..."

At the sound of galloping horses, the girl pulled Aradia quickly back into the brush as a Kaskan patrol thundered by. A moment passed and both Aradia and the girl emerged from their hiding place.

"Bloody, gods-be-damned - those were *Amazon* horses!" said the girl through gritted teeth. "If only I had been old enough to fight! I would have stood by my mother - we would have killed *all* of those Kaskans! I would -"

"You would be hanging right next to her," said Aradia, quietly, looking up at Thalia's remains again. "They should have been given the proper rites long before this."

"Didn't you just see the patrol? It's death to even be caught leaving an offering," said the girl.

Aradia looked sharply at the girl, as if just recognising her. "And yet you defy the Kaskans to honour the Amazon dead ..." she said, softly.

"I am Saraea, daughter of the Amazon Thalia, and when the queen returns and the Amazon Nation rises again - " said the girl, defiantly.

"What did you say?" said Aradia, startled.

"The old shamaness, Mhari, has prophesied that the Queen would return and then the Amazons will rise again," said Saraea.

"Mhari lives?" said Aradia, grabbing the girl's shoulder. Saraea nodded. "Do any of the others?" Saraea looked at the woman, warily, refusing to answer. Frustrated, Aradia shook her a little, as if trying to shake the answer loose from the young girl's set lips. "Answer me - did any of the other

Amazons survive ... this?" Aradia gestured to the rows of crosses.

"If you want to know such things, you should talk to my uncle, Silas - who are you, anyway?" said Saraea, eyeing the woman, suspiciously.

"I am the Amazon Queen," she replied, smiling bitterly at the irony of this statement. She looked at the young girl, who was gazing up at her in awe. Then the child lifted her chin, proudly offering her queen an Amazon salute. Aradia feeling hopeful for the first time in long over a decade, saluted her back.

)O(

Aradia sat at a wooden table, eyeing the girl, Saraea who sat across from her, staring, caught in the throes of "hero-worship". The cottage was cosy if smallish. Saraea's uncle, Silas brought a plate of food to Aradia, setting it down before her and gesturing for Saraea to move and give their visitor some peace in which to eat. The gesture was ignored and Silas sighed, taking the remaining chair at the table and sitting himself. Aradia started to ravenously tear into the food, then remembered herself.

"Sorry - it's been a while since I've been around people," said the queen.

"The road is a harsh place," said Silas, sympathetically.

"There are worse - much worse," said Aradia, tossing the piece of bread in her hand back onto the plate.

"Like where?" asked Saraea, eagerly.

"Never mind, Saraea. You go on up to bed now," said Silas.

Saraea ignored Silas until Aradia, frowning, gestured to her to obey. Grinning, the girl offered another Amazon salute and scampered up the ladder to the loft.

"That girl is headed for trouble," said Aradia shaking her head.

"She's stubborn - got it into her head that she's an Amazon - like her mother - my sister," said Silas with a sigh.

"You're Thalia's brother," said Aradia.

"Yes," said Silas. "Saraea was with me when Thalia and the others went up against Yarg. I've had her ever since."

"What of the others?" asked Aradia, thoughtfully.

"What others?" said Silas, suspiciously.

"The other Amazon children - where are they?" asked Aradia.

"Dead," said Silas, quietly. "After Yarg crucified the captured Amazons, he went through the Village and killed most of the women and girl children to ensure he hadn't missed any Amazons. Saraea was spared only because we had been away at the time of the battle and I convinced them that she was my own daughter."

"No - the Amazon children would have been well-hidden and well-protected. They must be somewhere," said Aradia rising.

"They were all killed," insisted Silas, eyeing the broken sword tucked into Aradia's belt. "And the rest of us are little more than slaves, working our fields only to feed the Kaskan army."

Aradia began pacing, her eyes narrowed. "No - not all have been killed - the old shamaness, Mhari, still lives," she said. She looked at Silas, trying to catch his eyes. "Or so Saraea told me."

Silas hesitantly looked from the sword to Aradia's face and back again, avoiding her eyes.

"Saraea was mistaken - old Mhari is the Village tale-teller - she makes up stories to amuse the children and - " he began.

Aradia, frustrated, pulled the sword from her belt and held it against his chest as if to run him through with the broken blade.

"Is *this* your problem?" she asked.

"Yarg has outlawed all weapons - only his warriors are permitted to carry blades - even a broken one could mean trouble ..." Silas said, stoically. Aradia released him.

"I don't obey Kaskan law," she said, replacing the sword.

"Then you'll end up ... out there," said Silas, with a quick nod towards the grisly row outside in the pouring rain.

"No, I don't think so. I need to see Mhari - and I need to find the children," said Aradia, resuming her pacing, her frustration growing by the moment.

"Even if the old woman speaks true, you wouldn't be able to get near them - they would be too well-hidden and that hiding place too well protected," said Silas.

Aradia whirled around, grabbing Silas by the throat. "You *know* Mhari speaks the truth and you know where the children are," she said. "Now, are you going to take me to her?"

Silas, eyes wide, reached up and pushed Aradia's tattered sleeve, revealing a tattoo on her arm. His eyes met Aradia's and slowly he nodded. Aradia released him.

"You are ..." he began, swallowing hard.

"Yes," said Aradia.

Silas nodded again, looking defeated. He looked up toward the loft, then sat wearily at the table, his head in his hands.

"There were survivors," he said. "They're holed up in the woods. The rest of the Amazon children are with them."

"All but Saraea?" asked Aradia pointedly.

Silas looked up at her, pain evident in his face. "I loved my sister. I love her daughter as if she were my own. She's all I have left of Thalia."

Aradia nodded in understanding and sympathy. "I loved Thalia, too - she was my second -in-command. Saraea was so young - she doesn't really remember her mother, does she?"

Silas shook his head. "No, she's only heard the stories. I'm afraid for her. Her hatred of the Kaskans is so great. I'm afraid that one day her thirst for revenge will ..."

"Get her killed," Aradia finished for him. "She should be taught - "

"No!" Silas cried, leaping to his feet. Then he looked at Aradia, pleadingly. "Please - she's all I have left. I can't lose her, too."

"As Thalia's daughter, she has a right to- " began the Amazon queen.

"I said no - she has the right to live long enough to grow up," said Silas, firmly.

"Grow up under the Kaskan yoke? Live under Yarg's tyranny - and Rome's? Is that really what you want for her?" asked Aradia, angrily.

"I'm only trying to protect her," said Silas, shaking his head. "As I have done for the last ten years."

"You're trying to protect her from death," said Aradia, quietly. "There are worse things than dying, Silas - like living as slaves to our enemies. I should know."

Silas was silent for a moment contemplating. He looked again at Aradia's face, the lines created by the last decade of hell making her look somehow more noble and wise. He sighed again, knowing that this time was coming for a long time - as Mhari had prophesied - did not make his decision any easier, but he knew that it was the right one for Saraea.

"You're right," he said, defeated. "I know where the Amazon survivors are hiding."

"Tell me of these survivors - are you sure they're Amazons and not Gorgons?" said Aradia, her eyes narrowing.

"No, they're Amazons," replied Silas. "I patched up as many of the wounded as I could and gave them what food I had - and they left. Mhari stayed behind - to help look after Saraea, I suspect - and to keep watch - for you."

"I need to speak with Mhari," said Aradia, more gently now.

"In the morning - it's late. And after ... I'll take you to your people," Silas said.

)O(

Yarg, the Kaskan leader sat at a table in his tent admiring a beautiful shimmering sword. The blade shone like pure polished silver. The pommel was in the shape of two crescents flanking a circle which represented the phases of the Triple Moon. A *labrys* - or double-headed battle-axe - was etched in the centre of the circle which represented the full moon.

The beast of a man rose and swung it experimentally, smiling at the feel and sound of it as it "whooshed" through the air. At that moment, another man entered the tent and saluted, staying in his position of obeisance as Yarg sat back down at the table, roughly planting the beautiful sword in the dirt floor of the tent. Then he acknowledged the subordinate with a grunt, proceeding to eat the food on the table. The man arose, swallowing his disgust at his leader's table manners - or, rather, lack thereof. Yarg sat, slurping his wine, ignoring the bits of food which fell into his beard, and finally, wiping his greasy hands on his shirt before looking up at the other man with a loud "wet" belch.

"Well? What is it?" said the Kaskan chief.

Bowing and holding out a rolled parchment, the man spoke. "A dispatch from Rome my lord."

"Well? What's it say? And skip all that official greeting crap from the Imperial bastard - just get to the meat of it, will you?" said Yarg.

The man unrolled the parchment and quickly scanned it before speaking, occasionally glancing up at Yarg, nervously.

"My lord it seems the Amazon has escaped," he said, barely controlling the trembling in his voice.

Yarg looked at him, calmly, but the man knew all too well that calm was often a disguise for something darker and far more frightening than his leader's usual bellowing. Men tended to die more when Yarg was "calm".

"Seems? Well has she or hasn't she?" said the Kaskan chief, still quietly.

"She has, my lord," said the man, resigning himself to whatever the Fates decided. Yarg spoke again, his voice still dangerously quiet. "That so?"

"Yes My lord. The Emperor asks that we keep an eye out for her in case she comes back here. He wants her back alive."

Yarg threw his head back and laughed. The man released his fear in tentative relief. Death would not have him today, it seemed.

"Yes I'm sure he does," said the Kaskan chief. "Can't have a magnificent trophy like the Queen of the Amazons get the better of the Emperor of Rome - might just make him look like the fool he is. He will of course have to make an example of her."

"Yes, My lord. Shall I assign more men to patrol?" asked the minion.

Yarg eyed the sword glinting in the light from the tent lamps and rose, pulling it out of the dirt. He gazed at it as if mesmerized.

"No I don't think that will be necessary," he said. "We have something she wants, I think. She will come to us and she will bring the rest of the surviving Amazons. Then we'll finish the job we started ten years ago." He looked out of the tent flap to the lines of crosses and grinned. "The Emperor can have what's left of her when I'm done."

"Yes my lord," said the man, again bowing low to the ground in salute. He left Yarg still staring transfixed at the sword.

Suddenly, there was a flash of light and another stood before the Kaskan chief. He was stunningly beautiful to look upon, with wavy jet black hair to his shoulders. His skin was as smooth as marble and as golden as the sun. His eyes were piercing and black and when he moved, the play of well-defined muscles rippling under his white silk tunic was evident. His mouth was cruel, if a bit petulant, like the spoiled child he was, for this was Ares, god of war, the favoured child of Hera and Zeus.

Ares watched Yarg, frowning with some concern over the mortal's apparent fascination with the sword.

"Don't get too attached - I have plans for that blade," said the god, not quite breaking the spell the sword had over the Kaskan chief.

"Ares," said Yarg, acknowledging the god, but never taking his eyes from the sword - which now glowed in the god's presence.

"It does have a certain attraction to it doesn't it?

Unfortunately, I can't let you keep it."

"Huh?" said Yarg, tearing his dull, muddy eyes away from the sword.

"Remember? I had you get that for someone else," said the war god. "Someone who will use it to put me in the top god position."

Yarg found his eyes irresistibly drawn back to the glowing sword. "Who?

"Never mind that," said Ares, sharply. "You just keep it safe for now. What ever you do, do not let the Amazons get it back. If you do my sister gets her full powers back and she's not real happy with me right now. Messing with her Amazons kinda puts her in a bad mood."

Yarg again with effort, tore his gaze away from the sword to look at the god of war. Then laughed. "You have no scruples whatsoever - I like that in a god," he said. "No I won't let it get into Amazon hands. In fact I'm going to use it to destroy those unnatural women once and for all."

Ares raised one eyebrow and sighed. "I hate trusting this to a mortal," he said, sadly. "Just remember -- guard it with your life or I will have your head."

Ares disappeared in a flash, leaving Yarg to continue admiring the sword.

)O(

Saraea stood at the door and knocked until it was opened by a woman who quickly pulled the girl inside. She looked both ways out in the street, then went in, closing and barring the door behind them.

She turned to the girl, frowning sternly. "You grow too bold, Girl -- coming here in broad daylight," she scolded, shaking her head.

"She's back," said Saraea, grinning. "The queen is back, Mhari, just like you said."

"Where?" said the older woman, smiling in delight.

"She's at our house. Oh, Mhari, she's ... she's... so ... "

"Yes, yes, Child," said the older woman, patting the young girl on the shoulder.

"She sent me to bring you to her," said Saraea. "She wanted to come to you herself, but ..."

"It's a little too dangerous for the Amazon Queen to be seen here, I know," said the woman. She began going about the house, putting things into a basket then donned her cloak. "Well, let's go. Even old Mhari doesn't keep our Queen waiting."

Mhari and Saraea walked quickly toward Silas's house, but were still accosted by two Kaskans. One grabbed Mhari's basket.

"Hey what's in here?" he said.

The second grabbed Saraea, who squirmed and struggled to get away from him.

"Hey, Cutie, what are you doing?"

Saraea answered by stomping on his foot and elbowing him in the gut. He let go of her with a grunt of pain, while his companion laughed at him.

"You gotta watch the women in this village - they've been corrupted by those Amazons. Probably don't even know how to act like real women," said the first, pawing through Mhari's basket. Saraea started toward him, but was gently restrained by Mhari, who merely smiled at the two.

"Now gentlemen," she said. "My granddaughter here is a very proper young lady - you can't expect her to understand your ... attentions ... as the *compliment* I'm sure you intended."

"Yeah - *compliment,"* said the second Kaskan, still glaring at Saraea. "What are you two doing out here at this time? You should be in the fields now."

"My father is sick. I went to fetch Granny for him," said Saraea, tossing her head, defiantly.

"Yeah, just medicines in here," said the first, handing the basket back to Mhari. "You can go."

"Wait," said the second as the women started to leave. They stopped, looking at each other in dread. "You're Silas's girl aren'tcha?" Saraea nodded. "So that's why he didn't report for work this morning? He's sick?"

"Yes," said Saraea, impatiently.

"What's wrong with him?" asked the first Kaskan. "Not plague is it?"

"If I knew what was wrong, I wouldn't have had to get Granny would I?" said Saraea, smiling sweetly.

Both Kaskans stepped back quickly.

"Go on then," said the first. "Tell Silas when he's better to report to the field supervisor."

Saraea nodded as Mhari leaned up and whispered to the second Kaskan, the one who had grabbed Saraea. He blushed and waved them away. The two walked rapidly toward Silas's house, Mhari grinning.

"What did you say to him?" whispered Saraea.

"Why I just told him if he had trouble getting women to come and see old Mhari rather than grabbing a young girl off the street. I'll brew him a love potion guaranteed to give him a 'real' woman," said Mhari.

Saraea rolled her eyes, and giggled, as they arrived at the door of Silas's house.

The door opened and Mhari stepped in, followed closely by Saraea. Aradia was sitting on the floor by the hearth, working on the broken sword. She looked up and smiled, rising to her feet and making her way to the two in one graceful move. She embraced Mhari with a kiss on the cheek.

"Granny, I - " Aradia began, then broke into sobs while Mhari held her, patting gently.

"Hush, Child - it's alright now," said the old shamaness.

Aradia gently disentangled herself from Mhari's embrace. She looked at her and saw tears in the older woman's bright blue eyes. They both laughed, hugging again as Saraea looked on, wide-eyed, watching the exchange. Silas entered the room, nodding a greeting to Mhari before addressing Aradia.

"We'll leave for the forest after dark," he said, nodding at the sword Aradia had left leaning against the hearthstones. "How's that coming along?"

Aradia turned and retrieved the sword. A "scar" was visible where the broken blade had been roughly mended.

"Well, I could do a better job with a proper forge, but it will do," she said. "It will never be the same, though."

"None of us will, Child," said Mhari. "But that blade will be stronger than ever for your care - just like the Amazons."

Saraea approached, a little shyly and reached out to touch the sword. "That's .. that's my mother's sword, isn't it?" she asked.

Aradia gingerly handed the sword to the girl, carefully placing her hands on the hilt, making adjustments in the girl's grip. Saraea held the sword aloft, gazing at it with a kind of awe. Aradia, took it back from her, gently placing it back against the hearthstones.

"I have something for you," said the girl, running up the ladder to the loft.

"Silas, you have done well with her. But now ... it's time for - " said Mhari, gently.

Silas nodded, sadly. "I know. Aradia and I have talked. Saraea needs to be with her mother's people now," he said quietly.

"Silas, I promise you, Saraea shall be as my own daughter," said Aradia, solemnly. "Thalia was my Second in Command, and she would have taken over as queen if it had been I who ..."

"Thalia would have been queen?" asked Silas.

"As will her daughter," said Aradia, nodding. "Saraea shall be trained as my successor, a princess in her own right, providing - "

"Providing what?" said Saraea, a leather sheath in one hand, halfway down the ladder, holding on with the other hand, staring at them.

"Providing that, when you come of age, you are found worthy of the task and choose accept the responsibilities that go with it of your own free will," said Aradia.

Saraea looked to Mhari as she hopped the rest of the way off of the ladder and walked towards Aradia. "You knew?"

"Yes, Child," said the shamaness.

"What must I do to be found worthy?" asked the girl, looking to Aradia.

"After your training and initiation, we will know - it really isn't anything you do - but who you are and the choices you make which will tell us if you are the one to be queen after me," replied Aradia.

"I will do my best," said the girl, solemnly.

"Yes, I know you will," said Aradia, looking toward the shuttered windows. "It's nearly time."

Saraea handed her the sheath. "I don't know if this was my mother's or not - I found it .. out there," said the girl.

Aradia retrieved the sword from the hearth and slid it into the sheath. "Yes, almost a perfect fit. Thank you," she said. Aradia fastened the sheath to her belt, again glancing at the shuttered window. Silas nodded, picking up his pack and shouldering it.

"It's time," he said, looking at Saraea, sadly.

)O(

Four cloaked, hooded figures made their way silently through the trees. One of them stopped to listen and motioned to the others to stop as well.

Suddenly, several Amazons appeared as if by magic from their hiding places amidst the trees and the group was surrounded by Amazon swords.

"Who are you?" asked the Amazon leader.

Aradia pushed back the hood of her cloak, then threw back her head, emitting a distinctive battle cry. Quickly, the Amazons sheathed their swords and dropped to their knees before her.

"My Queen - we thought you were - " began the leader.

"You were wrong, Thraso," said Aradia.

"Apparently so, my Queen," said Thraso.

The others - Saraea, Mhari, and Silas - also pushed back their hoods.

"Get up, all of you - is groveling in the dirt what the once-great Amazon Nation is reduced to now?" said Aradia.

One by one, the Amazons began to rise.

"Your Majesty, there is no more Amazon Nation," said Thraso, still kneeling.

Aradia angrily reached down and pulled Thraso roughly to her feet. "How dare you?" she seethed through gritted teeth. "If even one of us survives, the Nation lives - or are you renouncing your place in the Nation, Thraso?" Silence from their leader was the example the rest of the Amazons followed as Aradia looked around. "Any of you - do you wish to renounce your Initiation vows? Are you still Amazons?"

There was a quiet murmur among the group as Saraea stared wide-eyed and Mhari smiled proudly at Aradia. Thraso, head bowed, remained silent.

"Tell me - do I have any sisters here? Or do they all still hang on crosses, trophies to our enemies?" said Aradia, looking around yet one more time.

A collective yell from the Amazons confirmed their loyalty to Queen and Nation as Aradia released Thraso.

"And what do you say, Thraso? Are you still an Amazon?" asked Aradia, so quietly only Thraso could hear her.

"My Queen, I - " began Thraso. She lifted her head and looked around at the Amazons, then looked at Aradia and smiled slightly. "I am an Amazon, my Queen."

Aradia smiled brightly and pulled Thraso into a tight hug, holding her close for a moment, then releasing her.

"Welcome home, my Queen," said Thraso, returning the hug.

"Where - exactly - is 'home'?" asked Aradia.

"We'll take you there, my Queen, but ... um ... " Thraso looked uncomfortably at Silas.

"I'll head back now," said Silas, taking the thinly veiled hint.

Aradia clasped Silas's arm. "Be safe, my friend. Artemis watch over you till we meet again. You will always have the gratitude of the Amazons," said the Queen.

Saraea, suddenly realising what this meant, ran up to Silas and hugged him, hard.

"Uncle - can't you come with us?" she said.

Silas gently disengaged himself from her arms.

"Saraea, no man is permitted to dwell among the Amazons - you know that," said Silas.

"But I thought ... since you ... Oh, Uncle - I can't just go and leave you to the Kaskans. When they find both Mhari and me missing, you will be in trouble!" said Saraea, tears in her eyes.

"Shh ... Little One, it'll be fine - you'll see," said Silas, looking to Aradia for help.

"Saraea, we have to go. Silas will be fine - the Kaskans won't be here much longer," said the Queen.

"So it's true? We will win back our land from them?" Thraso asked the shamaness.

"There is a more important prize to be won - and another enemy to defeat, even greater than Yarg ... " said Mhari, her eyes looking far off.

"Rome," said Aradia, grimly.

"Even more powerful than the Emperor," said the shamaness.

"Who, Granny?" asked Aradia.

"I can't ... quite ... see ... " said Mhari, shaking her head.

"Never mind - we have to go - " began Aradia.

"An ally will come to us from an unexpected place ... and perhaps an enemy from one we trust ... it's gone," said the shamaness, frowning.

"Old-Mother, you see the past," said Thraso, gently. "We have already been betrayed by our own, the Gorgon Tribe. And a man has done us the service of raising and protecting one of our daughters." She nodded to Silas.

"Well, we shall have to see," said Mhari, with a sigh.

Silas released Saraea. "Go on, now - I'll see you soon," he said.

Tearfully, Saraea stepped back and gave Silas the same salute she gave to Aradia. Aradia smiled slightly and nodded at the girl as Silas turned and disappeared into the trees. The Amazons began walking, Aradia and Thraso side by side, Saraea hanging back a bit with Mhari.

"Are we really going up against Yarg and his men?" asked Thraso.

"Yes," replied Aradia.

"How? They are so many - and backed by Rome - and we are now so few. How, my Queen?" said Thraso.

"We are not so few, Thraso. Have we not sisters from the Celtic Isles to the Eastern Steppes?" said Aradia.

"Well, yes, but - " said Thraso.

"Tonight we send out the call to all the remaining Tribes in the Nation," said Aradia.

"But my Queen - " protested Thraso.

"And enough of this 'my Queen' and 'your Majesty' - as my Second in Command, you will call me by my name - Aradia," said the queen.

Thraso stopped walking and stared at Aradia. "Why - your Second, my ... um, Aradia?"

"Unless, of course, you prefer to challenge me," said Aradia.

Thraso resumed walking, shaking her head. "Blessed Artemis, no! I mean ...yes, my ... um, Aradia. I'm honoured to be your Second, but I have no wish to challenge you," she said.

"Good," said Aradia, smiling at her new Second. "I have no wish to fight you, Thraso. We have enough fighting ahead of us."

"When do we start?" asked Thraso.

"Tonight. I want our sisters down off those crosses and their souls on their way to the Goddess by dawn," said Aradia, firmly.

"My Queen - I mean, Aradia," said Thraso, frowning. "Those of us who have tried to recover them now hang with them. How - ?"

"Yarg won't know what hit him," said Aradia, smiling wickedly.

)O(

Yarg lay in bed, asleep, clutching the sword to him like a "teddy bear." A flash of light marked Ares's appearance and the god roughly shook Yarg awake, somewhat annoyed that his flashy appearance was not noted by the sleeping Kaskan chief.

"Yeah - what? Oh, it's you," said Yarg, sitting up slowly.

"You might want to see this," said Ares, strongly resisting the temptation to simply blast this ignorant pig into Tartarus.

Ares walked over and lifted the tent flap to reveal flames lighting up the predawn sky. All but about six crosses were missing - and on those six hung the Kaskan patrol. With a roar of rage, Yarg was up out of bed, the sword still clutched in his hand.

"What the -?" bellowed the chief.

"Looks like Aradia's back," said the god, gratified to see some reaction from Yarg.

Yarg stared out of the tent flap in disbelief. "Gods be damned ... *women*! How did they--?"

"You wouldn't be the first man to underestimate the Amazons, Yarg," said Ares in mock sympathy.

Yarg growled and pushed past Ares out to the crossroads, dragging the sword behind him.

"They won't get away with this!" said the Kaskan chief with a growl.

Ares sighed. "There you go again," said the god, annoyed. "I'm warning you Yarg. Do not disappoint me. Don't underestimate Aradia - I don't. She has a fire in her eyes that I haven't seen in a woman since ... " Ares smiled sadly. "Well, in a very long time."

"Fine-I'll see her eyes are delivered to you when I get a hold of her," said Yarg, scowling at the flames.

At last the god reached his tolerance limit. His dark eyes literally flaming, he reached out and backhanded the huge man, sending Yarg reeling back, to land on his ample backside. "I am really beginning to wonder if you're the right man for this after all," said Ares, shaking his head as Yarg struggled to his feet.

"What do you mean by that?" said the Kaskan chief, brushing off the blow as he dusted himself off.

"Well, first you involved Rome - and you have no idea how much trouble that has caused me," said the god of war, darkly. "Now this - and look at the way you treat my sister's sword!"

Yarg looked down and saw the sword dragging in the dirt. Quickly he picked it up and tucked it into a sheath at his side.

"You just keep your sister off my back. I'll take care of the Amazons," said Yarg.

"Just don't disappoint me again Yarg - Tartarus is nothing compared to what I can dish out," said Ares, disappearing in a brilliant flash, leaving Yarg to stand and watch his men trying to put out the Amazon pyres and pull the patrol down off the crosses. A guard approached him saluting.

"My lord-General Aurelian is here," he said as the Roman General approached.

"A bit of trouble tonight, Yarg?" said Aurelian.

Yarg grunted. "Nothing I can't handle."

"The Emperor has sent me along with a unit of soldiers to recapture the Amazon," said Aurelian, looking about the Kaskan camp. "He believes she will come here. From the looks of things, she has already arrived."

Yarg glared at the Roman. "Nah - just some troublemakers from the village," he said. "I was just getting ready to send some of my men to - "

"That won't be necessary," Aurelian interrupted. "I have already posted sentries within the village walls. I have also assigned some men to patrol the perimeter and the outlying area."

Yarg grunted and returned to his tent, slapping the flap closed behind him. Aurelian turned, and silently watched the Kaskans trying to put out the fire. His face illuminated by the flickering flame was unreadable to the Kaskans, but they knew the look on their chief's face as he had stormed away from the General. Roman or not, most of them figured Aurelian had better watch his back.

)O(

"The village" of the Amazons was little more than a circular clearing in the forest. Aradia stood on a large boulder in the centre of the clearing. She looked around approvingly at the sturdy houses built up in the trees. There was an the elaborate rope system of ladders and pulleys for travelling through the treetops and hauling supplies up to the houses. She gazed around at the inhabitants of the village surrounding her. They ranged from elders to very young children. Most were young girls Saraea's age or a little older. These had been the children a small group of warriors had taken here to this place in the woods and hidden away, protecting them while their mothers and sisters and aunts - even some of their grandmothers fought and died to protect them and the way of life they wanted for these girls.

Earlier that evening, Aradia sat at the table in the treehouse swiftly built for her in this Amazon Village of treehouses with a basket. She gently lifted a string of beads with a large coloured stone as a pendant and held it up. Another like it - the one she had collected herself from Thalia's remains, was hanging about her neck now.

"Ainippe," she said, laying the amulet in her hand down upon the table. She withdrew another beaded necklace. "Areto," she said, laying it next to the other. Wiping away tears, she withdrew several necklaces from the basket and named each one, until she was interrupted by a knock on the door. Composing herself quickly, she called, "Enter!"

Mhari, accompanied by Saraea and Thraso came in. Aradia smiled in delight, rising to embrace the wisewoman.

"Granny," the queen said, hugging her fiercely, as the grief for her fallen sisters threatened her composure.

"Now, Child - don't give in - not just yet - time enough for mourning later - after the work's done," Mhari told her. "You retrieved their Initiation amulets, I see - good girl."

"Yes," Aradia said, releasing the older woman. "So many ... gone."

"And so many still here, Child," Mhari said, removing her cloak and hanging it on a peg in the wall. "It is those you must be thinking of now - the ones all these - " Mhari swept her hand towards the amulets on the table, "gave their lives for."

Aradia reflected briefly on the sacrifice of those whose final journey to the Goddess had been completed this night. A wry grin crossed her lovely face as she thought about the difficulty the Kaskans would have putting out the pyres. The Amazons had used the crosses themselves, but they had been fashioned from the resinous trees native to this region. The Amazons had also used the traditional fire blossoms whose oil was pleasantly fragrant, but also highly volatile. The bodies of the Amazons were dry bones and it would take little time for them to be consumed by the purifying and liberating flames. No, they would not be able to put out the fire until her sisters' remains were gone.

Mhari and Saraea now stood on either side of Aradia. Thraso stood behind her and a little to the side, in the position of the Second in Command.

"Sisters, it is good to be home," said Aradia.

An Amazon stepped forward. "Home? You call *this,"* she swept her arm about to indicate the tree village, "Home? Our *home* is occupied by those Kaskan pigs!"

"For now," Aradia acknowledged with a nod. "But you have done well here, Sisters."

"Well?" said the Amazon, angrily. "How can you say that? We are barely surviving. We live on what we can hunt and forage. We are a hunted people and must hide like animals. What we had before - our land, our homes, our horses, our crops - all gone. And you say we are doing *well*?"

"You are alive," said Aradia. "You are relatively free. And," she looked around. "We have something to build on here. I have hope - something I never thought I'd feel again."

Another Amazon stepped up and spoke. "What of our land, Your Majesty? What of vengeance for our fallen sisters? What of the treachery of the Gorgons?"

"One thing at a time Sister," said Aradia, gently. "Tonight, we began the journey to re-build our Nation - our fallen sisters' souls now soar free to the Goddess."

The Amazons cheered and the one who confronted Aradia nodded in acknowledgment, seemingly satisfied for the moment and stepped back.

"The next step is to drive the Kaskans from our homeland," said Aradia, bringing a smile to that Amazon's face as again, the Amazons cheered. "But first ..." Aradia held out her hand and Saraea handed her a ram's horn. She smiled and gestured with one hand. The rhythmic beating of Amazon drums started up. "We call together all the Tribes of the Amazon Nation. Together, we as Amazons and as Sisters,

Daughters of Artemis, together, we will fight our enemies and take back what is ours."

Aradia lifted the horn to her lips ... and blew.

As the morning mist drifted through the mountains and valleys, the sound of the ram's horn and the drums carried and was joined by others, in a massive relay across the lands.

Amazons toiling in fields stopped their labours and listened. Not one of them ever thought to hear the call of the horn and the drums again and had resigned themselves to their fate. Almost. Throwing down their tools, they hastened to gather weapons and amulets long ago hidden away in secret places where no man would think to look for such things.

Alone and in groups the Amazons left their existence and made their way over the mountains and seas and into the forest where their lives began again. Their souls, answering the ancient Amazon call soared. Within weeks, thousands of reborn Amazon Warriors stood ready.

And Aradia, now wearing the regalia of an Amazon Queen, stood before them on a wooden platform which had been built in the centre of the clearing. Again Mhari and Saraea stood on either side of her and Thraso as second in command "had her back." Aradia looked around at the gathered Amazons, thousands strong, yet still only a remnant of the once great Amazon Nation.

Some were warriors but not nearly enough for the difficult task before them. Most were untried girls, bearing weapons far too big for them. Sadly she shook her head. She looked at their eager young faces, their shining eyes all focused on her and then smiled proudly. She then realised that she had never felt prouder of being an Amazon. Aradia gave them all an Amazon salute and they roared a cheer to their queen, saluting her back. She raised her arms and there was silence.

"My sisters look around at yourselves," said Aradia, gravely. "You see the entire Amazon Nation - we are all that's left."

The Amazons murmured sadly, but Aradia smiled brightly

at them and continued.

"We represent every tribe in the nation. The call went out and every one of you responded. You should be very proud of yourselves, for you represent the heart of the Amazon spirit - honour, integrity, and sisterhood. Today, my sisters, Artemis smiles upon her favourite daughters!"

The Amazons again offered a roaring cheer, intermixed with wolf howls, birdcalls, and other animal sounds according to the different tribal traditions represented. Thraso leaned forward, smiling.

"She smiles upon the Amazon Queen too - just look what you've accomplished," she said.

The village had expanded, the Amazons were better dressed, better armed, and better fed, but most important, they were very happy and very proud.

Aradia, smiling back at Thraso, replied, "You gave me a solid foundation to build on. This village is a testament to your leadership skills, my friend."

"Mine?" said Thraso, surprised.

Aradia nodded gravely. "You started with nothing - no food, no shelter - and the threat of the enemy behind every bush and tree," she said. "That you survived at all, let alone what you began to build here, makes me very proud of you."

"But - I was still so relieved when you came back and took over," said Thraso.

"I know - but that, too, is the sign of a leader," said Aradia, smiling at her friend. "I chose well when I made you my Second."

Suddenly there was a commotion and two Amazons roughly hauled a third up to the platform, shoving her to her knees before Aradia. She was a girl only a little older than Saraea.

"What's this?" asked Aradia.

"We caught this Gorgon trying to sneak into the village," said one of the Amazons.

"Who's at your post now?" asked Thraso, looking

worriedly at Aradia.

"It's alright, Majesty - we detained her until our relief arrived," said the second Amazon.

Aradia nodded. "Very good," she said. She looked down at the girl at her feet. "Who are you?"

"I am Julisa, My Queen," said the Gorgon girl.

"How dare you call her that?" said the first Amazon, raising a hand to strike Julisa, but Aradia grabbed her wrist and stopped her.

"Never strike a sister Amazon in anger," said the Queen, firmly.

"Sister Amazon?!" cried the second Amazon. "She's one of those traitorous Gorgons!"

"Julisa, what were you doing coming here?" asked Aradia.

"I heard the call - I answered," replied the girl, simply and quietly. "I was coming to join you."

"More likely to spy," said the first Amazon, bitterly.

"No, I swear it," said Julisa. "It's true, I am of the Gorgon tribe. But ... " Julisa bowed her head.

"But what child?" said Mhari, gently helping the girl to her feet.

"I am ashamed of what my people did," said Julisa. "They betrayed the rest of our Nation to the Kaskans. I was too young at the time to say anything, But ... I am an Amazon, not a Gorgon!"

Aradia turned to Thraso. "Thraso, send a detachment of warriors out to comb the area - make sure there are no others with her," she said, then turned to Julisa. "You - come with me. Thraso, dismiss them and then come to my house."

)O(

Aradia sat in a chair against the wall, facing the door.

Julisa stood, facing her. Mhari also sat in a chair by the other wall to the right of Aradia. Saraea stood beside Aradia's chair, watching the proceedings.

"You have posed quite a dilemma for me, young woman -

how do I know I can trust you?" asked Aradia.

"You don't," said Julisa. "And I don't blame you for not trusting - what my people did is unforgivable."

"Yes it is - but now, I have to do something with you. I don't want to kill you outright -" Saraea gasped, but Aradia continued as if not hearing her heir. "But I cannot allow you to roam freely here, either. For your safety as well as that of the Amazons."

"Your Majesty, please don't send me back there - I would rather you killed me than that," pleaded Julisa.

"Why is that?" asked Aradia.

"Our leader, Athtar - she is mad," said Julisa. "She doesn't know what she's doing, allying us with the Kaskans - they hate us as much as they hate all Amazons."

"How is it that you, a young girl, see this when your leaders do not?" asked Mhari.

"I don't know - but it's obvious to me that when the Kaskans are done with us, it will be Gorgon corpses on crosses," said Julisa.

Aradia looked thoughtfully at the girl for a few moments, then nodded. "Yes, you are correct in that," she said. "Just as when Rome is finished with Yarg, the Emperor will destroy him."

"How do you know all that?" asked Saraea.

"I just do," said Aradia. "The emperor fears what he cannot control - and what he fears he seeks to destroy. And he fears the Amazons because he knows no man will ever control us. And as soon as Yarg and the Kaskans are no longer useful to him, he will seek to destroy them, too."

"Unless we do it for him," said Saraea, her eyes narrowed. *"Tanti* - Aunt, let me carry my mother's sword into battle against the Kaskans!"

"I wish I could, but you don't yet know how to use a sword," Aradia said with a rueful smile.

"Then teach me - please," said Saraea, eagerly.

"That's not something you can learn in a few hours," said

Aradia. "Besides, Saraea, you are my successor - I can't let you fight - not yet, not until you have the training you'll need to come out alive."

"But - " began a disappointed Saraea.

"Saraea, I said no," said Aradia, firmly. "Besides, I have another task for you. From now on, you are to stay with Julisa - do not let her out of your sight - understood?"

"Yes. But - " the girl persisted.

"No buts - I am entrusting not only her safety to you, but until I can be sure she can be trusted, the entire Amazon Nation's safety is your hands," said Aradia, grimly.

Saraea smiled, proudly. "Oh - I understand, *tanti*," she said. "Come, Julisa - are you hungry?"

Both girls left Aradia's house together. Aradia rose and began to pace.

"Mhari, I'm getting soft - I should have just killed the girl and been done with it," she said, worriedly.

"Why didn't you?" asked Mhari.

"I don't know," said Aradia, shaking her head. "Something about her makes me believe her - and yet something else tells me she's not who she would have us believe. I just don't know what to think."

"Well, Child, you know I've always taught you to go with your instincts," said Mhari.

"Yes, I know - but what if I'm wrong?" said the queen with a sigh. "I just told Saraea that she's my successor and then left the two of them alone - if Julisa means us harm, she has her 'target' right there with her."

"Well, if it helps any, I believe the girl - I don't think she means us any harm - just the opposite, in fact," said the shamaness.

"It helps a lot, Granny. Thank you," said Aradia, smiling at the older woman.

"Anytime, Dear," said Mhari, returning the smile. "And now *my* instincts tell me that something else is bothering you - and has been these past weeks. What is it?"

Aradia sighed deeply and sat back down at the table where the dead Amazons' amulets still lay. "Why am I alive and they," Aradia indicated the amulets, "are not? Do you know how easy it would have been to just ... let one of them kill me in that arena? But I didn't. Why? I don't understand it."

"Evidently, the Goddess had other plans for you, Child," said Mhari, softly."Like this - these girls here - they needed you. You are the answer to their prayers. Do not feel remorse for surviving, Child. That's just pain foolishness - and silly, misplaced pride. That's not what I taught you."

"No, I can't look around at all those faces looking to me to lead them, protect them and care for them and really feel sorry for living. I know that I am needed here and that's why I live still," said Aradia. "I just don't understand what it was that drove me to do so when I thought the Amazon Nation was gone. It was like that whole time was spent asleep, a nightmare; then one night ... I just woke up. I still wish I knew who that woman was and why she chose to rescue me."

"I have a feeling that one day, you will know, my Child," said Mhari.

"Yes," said Aradia. "The day she comes and names her price for saving me. I only hope I have the means to pay it."

Mhari's reply was interrupted by a knock on the door and Aradia called "Enter!" Thraso came into the house.

"My...um, Aradia - there's trouble," she said.

"What kind of trouble?" asked Aradia.

"Romans," replied her Second. "A general by the name of Aurelian and hundreds of Roman soldiers ... are you alright?"

Aradia had grown pale. "Aurelian is here?"

"You know him, this Roman?" asked Thraso.

Aradia's mind wandered back to her first direct encounter with Aurelian.

"You are going to fight in the arena for me. An Amazon should bring in quite a revenue in wagers alone," said Aurelian.

That's what you think, *Aradia thought to herself, though*

she remained silent. Aurelian whirled around and looked at her.

"Oh you will *fight, Aradia," he said, grinning at her. The only indication that she was aware of his words was a slight, involuntary shiver. "If you do not, I will find another use for you, one you may not like as well."*

"Unfortunately," replied Aradia. "Where is he?"

"In the Kaskan camp," replied Thraso. "He's posted his men all over the Village and has patrols in the all of the outlying areas. What are we going to do, Aradia?"

"Do?" said the queen, a cold smile stretching her lips, but not quite reaching her eyes. "Why, we're going to take back what belongs to us - and send a message to Rome that the Amazons are no mere trophies - we are a Nation in our own right and one to be reckoned with."

)O(

Yarg stood before his assembled troops, Aurelian beside him. The Romans were in formation beside the Kaskan army. Suddenly, they heard a piercing cry which froze their blood - the Amazon battle cry. The Romans stood, awaiting their general's orders, but the Kaskans broke from the disciplined formation, grabbing up weapons and turning to face the threat. They were not expecting what they saw. Instead of a handful of ragged, desperate women finally gone mad, rushing to their destruction, the Kaskans faced a massive army of women. They grimly made ready to fight, even as Aurelian shouted orders to the Roman troops, fighting to make himself heard over the din of the screeching Amazon battle cries, coming at them from all sides.

The two armies met the onslaught, but the Amazon warriors poured over their defences like ants over a honeycomb, wading into their ranks, an irresistible and deadly tide to which the unprepared and outnumbered Romans and Kaskans fell with alarming swiftness.

Interspersed with the Amazon warriors were villagers,

unable to bear the Kaskans' oppression any longer and heartened by the Amazon attack. They had picked up their tools as weapons and joined the throng of Amazons as the women had attacked.

Silas himself faced off with Yarg. He had heard the commotion and, grabbing a carpenter's adze from his workbench he'd run out to the battle. Yarg was fighting with the Sword of Artemis. The confrontation was brief. Silas didn't get a single hit. Yarg sliced off the razor-sharp head of the adze, leaving only a jagged, splintered stick before plunging the blade into Silas's mid-section and dragging it upward to the sounds of cracking bone and gurgling breath. Blood poured out, making the hilt slippery and the Sword slid from Yarg's grasp. Silas fell screaming, the blade still lodged in his body, as Yarg roared in derisive laughter.

"Saraea ... !" was Silas's last word as he succumbed to death. Yarg took a step towards the fallen Silas to retrieve the Sword.

Suddenly, Saraea was there out of nowhere, standing between her fallen uncle and the porcine warlord. Julisa was nowhere to be seen, and all around them, the Amazons and villagers were fighting Kaskans and Romans alike, oblivious to all but their own individual battles of life and death.

Saraea stopped and looked at the Kaskan leader laughing at her uncle's demise. With a strength she didn't know she had, the girl reached down and grabbed the sword from her uncle's still form and held it to Yarg's chest. Yarg merely laughed harder.

"What do you think you're doing, little girl?" he taunted. "You think you know how to use that? Come on, then - run me through!"

The Sword was audibly thrumming with power, a high buzzing like a hive of bees but Saraea seemed not to hear it as the Sword became merely an extension of her arm, the hilt molding to fit her small hand.

"You like nailing women to crosses and killing little

children?" asked Saraea, quietly, her eyes never leaving the giant before her.

"As a matter of fact, I do," sneered Yarg.

The only reaction from Saraea was a narrowing of her eyes over the flames of rage which sprang up in them. "Wrong answer, Pig," she said, coldly.

She swung the sword with a strength and an expertise no untrained girl should have and planted it deeply in the Kaskan's chest. He looked down, his eyes bulging in disbelief at the blood pouring out of him and over Saraea's small hands. Saraea, her face still expressionless, spoke quietly.

"When you get to Tartarus, tell the Kaskan pig who killed my mother hello. I'm just sorry it wasn't me who killed him, too."

Yarg fell, and the sword still clutched in Saraea's hand pulled free of him. He felt his life pouring out of him with his blood as the object of his obsession became the instrument of his death. He reached out with one hand as if trying to recapture the Sword which now receded further and further away from his grasp. As he wheezed his last breath, his vision dimmed. The last thing he saw in life was the gleaming silver Sword.

The girl shook her head as if just waking up, then horrified, saw the blood on her hands. She looked over to her prone uncle. In his hand was an Amazon amulet - he had been making it for her Initiation, since her mother wasn't there to do it for her. Saraea reached down and took it, looking at it in awe and then looking to her uncle with love and grief pouring from her. Tears sprang to her eyes and she ran from the battlefield, still clutching the Sword of Artemis.

Aradia and Thraso, back to back, fought Romans. Aurelian was on horseback, watching his men fall to the greater force of the Amazons. Shaking his head, the General finally sounded a retreat. Both Kaskans and Romans ran from the battlefield as the Amazons and Villagers cheered triumphantly.

A shimmering light appeared and a woman so beautiful it almost hurt one's eyes to look upon her walked out of it. Aradia gasped and started to kneel, but Artemis, smiling, prevented her.

"No, my Dear - you said so yourself - my daughters will never again kneel in the dirt - not to anyone," said the goddess.

"Lady, we won," said Aradia.

"You won this battle, Aradia, only because my sword is once again in the hands of an Amazon - however young she may be," said Artemis.

"Your sword? But ... Yarg had it," said Aradia.

"Yes - and then he got it, right where it could do the most good," said the goddess, stepping back to reveal the bodies of Yarg and Silas lying near one another.

"Oh ... oh, no ... not Silas!" cried Aradia.

"This man means something to you, Daughter?" asked Artemis.

"Yes - he was a good man and a friend to the Amazon Nation," said Aradia, sadly.

The goddess smiled and nodded. Slowly, Silas sat up, looking around, dazed.

"Then let him continue to befriend my daughters," said the goddess, smiling.

"Thank you, Lady. Saraea would be - " began Aradia.

"I'm afraid the damage has been done there," said the goddess, frowning.

"What do you mean?" asked Aradia.

"Saraea has my sword - it was she who killed Yarg," said Artemis.

"What!? I forbade her to - " began Aradia.

"Yes, you did - but she came here anyway," said the goddess. "Now she is grieving and angry - and she has my sword."

"We have to find her," said Thraso.

"Yes, you do - before my brother does. Otherwise ..." said the goddess, closing her eyes and shaking her head before fading from sight.

)O(

In the middle of the forest, far beyond the clearing where the Amazons had built a new home, Saraea sat on a rock staring at the sword as if in a trance. Ares stood behind her, though she in her grief and horror - and rage - was oblivious to his presence. He watched her for a moment, then smiled and nodded before fading from sight. In the trees, some distance from Saraea, Julisa stood, also watching the scene. When Ares was gone, Saraea lowered her head, weeping. Julisa nodded once, and then transformed into the woman who had once helped Aradia escape from the Romans.

She realised that this child would bear close watch and decided it would be best if the Amazons got to her ... before someone else did ....

Chapter Two: Guardian of the Sword

Athtar, Queen of the Gorgons paced in her hut in the Gorgon village. She had heard of the battle and now she was worried.

"Damn Yarg!" she muttered to herself. The Amazons were not supposed to win. She still couldn't figure out how they had defeated the Roman troops which had stood with the Kaskans.

"Damn Aurelian - why in Hades did he retreat?"

"Because he's a very good general. He's not willing to lose men he doesn't have to - especially when he can come back with those same men and fight a battle he can actually win." Athtar looked up to see Ares standing before her, grinning. Cursing, she drew her sword.

"Who are you? How dare you come in here - this is Amazon territory!" she cried. Ares laughed and pushed the sword away.

"I'm your best friend right now, Athtar - and by the way, this is no longer 'Amazon' territory - the other Amazons have disowned the Gorgons," said Ares. He looked at the queen, taking in her cruel beauty. She was a veritable snow queen. Her hair was so blonde it was almost white and her eyes were a pale, icy blue, but her gaze was intense as she glared at him, her lips curled almost in a snarl.

"What do I care what they think?" she asked, her voice low and dangerous.

"You should care very much," said Ares. "They have the Sword of Artemis."

"I thought Yarg ..." she began, her eyes widening in alarm momentarily. Then she remembered herself. "Who *are* you?"

"I am Ares," said the god, bowing slightly. "Yarg ... yes, well, he *had* the Sword, but he's dead - killed by a little girl. A little *Amazon* girl and with the Sword of Artemis."

For a brief moment, he thought saw a flash of fear in Athtar's eyes, then it was gone.

"Well, this ... complicates things," she said, resuming her pacing. Once again Ares laughed.

"You could say that," he said, approaching the pacing queen. "The Amazons will be seeking their revenge against the Gorgons - you betrayed them to Yarg. What made you do that, Athtar? Your hatred of all men is well known - and let's face it, Yarg was the epitome of all that make men so ... detestable."

"He had the Sword," said Athtar with a shrug. "He would have destroyed us as well as the others - I had to look out for my own."

"Ah, but if you had allied with your sisters, you may have beaten him," said Ares.

"He had the Sword," Athtar repeated, looking squarely at Ares. "Which, by the way, he said *you* gave him - so we both backed a loser."

"*Touché*," said Ares, with a smile. "But Athtar, I know why *I* backed him. Why did you? There has to be more to it that mere self-preservation - come on, a *child* took him out with the very Sword he was supposed to be protecting."

"I told you - he had the Sword of Artemis," said Athtar.

"And?" said Ares, looking intently into her eyes.

"And I ... wanted it," said Athtar, unable to tear her eyes from the god's.

"Ah, now we have the truth - and truth is very important between friends," said Ares, softly. He stepped closer to the Gorgon Queen. "So I will tell you an ironic truth - that sword was always intended for you."

Athtar looked at him, her face betraying nothing, then she laughed, bitterly. "I betrayed the Amazons for nothing," she said.

"Well, that all depends," said Ares.

"On what?" said Athtar.

"On whether or not you can get that Sword from them," said Ares. "Because if you can, then you will be invincible - almost a goddess in your own right. All the Amazons would bow to you as their queen. Not one of them would dare raise a hand against you then."

"That's true," said Athtar, musing. "Wait a minute - you're a god. Why can't you get it from them?"

"It's a little complicated," said Ares, frowning. "As long as an Amazon possesses that sword, my sister has the power to stop me from doing anything against the Amazons. I can send troops to attack them but I am powerless to sway the battle my way. As long as that sword is in the wrong hands, I am unable to do anything to the Amazons." He reached out and took Athtar's hands in his own and kissed the tips of her fingers, one at a time, slowly, then turned them over and kissed the palms. He looked up into her eyes and his dark gaze was compelling. Athtar closed her eyes as he pulled her close, still holding her hands in his firm grip.

"In the right hands, though - *these* hands," he said, kissing them once again. "We could be an invincible team."

"Hmmm ... and what do you get out of all this, Ares?" asked Athtar, her eyes snapping open.

Ares backed slightly away and looked at her, one eyebrow raised. He smiled and leaned in to kiss her. "Satisfaction," he said.

Athtar shoved the god roughly away.

"You have got to be kidding me," she said, walking away from him. She whirled around to face him again. "No, Ares, there's more to this than that. What else is in this for you?"

Ares sighed and shook his head. "You see what I mean?" he said. "I can't even deceive an Amazon now." He laughed at his own joke. Athtar remained silent, looking at him coldly. "Alright - Yarg was a bigger mistake than even I expected. He went to the Emperor for troops against the Amazons. Aurelian captured Aradia and sold her to the Gladiator Arena."

"So?" said Athtar.

"So, Aradia is some fighter," said Ares, shaking his head. "She wouldn't give the people a show - just killed every opponent they sent up against her, no fanfare, nothing - just slaughter."

"Good for her," said Athtar. "Although I am surprised she didn't just give in and let herself be killed - most Amazons don't last in captivity."

"Yeah, I know," said Ares. "Unfortunately, she escaped."

"That explains how the Amazons defeated Yarg," said Athtar, nodding. "That shamaness, Mhari - meddlesome old woman - she was spreading rumours that Aradia would return, giving the Amazons in hiding a lot of false hope."

"Evidently, it wasn't false," said Ares, frowning in displeasure. "Aradia is back - and she has called all the Tribes of Amazonia together - except, of course, the Gorgons."

Athtar snorted derisively. "Of course not," she said. "We heard the call, naturally - who couldn't? My women know which side of their bread is buttered."

"At any rate," Ares continued. "She had help - evidently, she caught the attention of a very old rival of mine. A minor goddess by the name of Medusa; very dangerous."

"I've never heard of Medusa," said Athtar.

"Most people haven't. She was around long before Rome," said Ares. "Aradia's lack of showmanship got her relegated to the Provinces. Some pissant little village whose name I can't remember built their arena over one of her old shrines. Evidently, Aradia's kills there acted like some sort of massive blood sacrifice and now Medusa is awake."

Athtar shrugged. "So - what does that have to do with me?" she asked.

Ares glared at her. "Medusa is very dangerous."

"To you maybe," said Athtar.

"To everyone," said Ares gravely. "My sister doesn't know what she's doing, allying herself with that ... being."

"What do you mean - Artemis is allying with this Medusa - against you?" said Athtar.

"Medusa is a dangerous entity," said Ares. "If she gains enough power, death and destruction will reign throughout the world until every living creature is gone and the earth is a wasteland."

"There is more that you're not telling me. Truth between ... ah, 'friends', remember?" said Athtar. Ares sighed and looked directly into her pale blue eyes. "Ah, wait, I think I see." A slow smile spread over Athtar's face.

"Do you, Athtar? Do you, indeed?" said Ares, softly.

"Oh, yes, Ares," said Athtar. "You aren't the least bit worried about death and destruction spreading across the world - as long as *you're* the one spreading it. You just don't want this Medusa stepping on your toes."

"You see just a little too clearly," said Ares, his hand sliding up to Athtar's throat. She flinched slightly as he began to squeeze, then the hand relaxed. Ares shook his head and stepped back. He smiled sheepishly. "I really must learn to watch my temper."

"Yes, you must," said Athtar, coldly. "If you want my help."

Ares smiled. "I knew I could count on you," he said, fading from Athtar's presence as a warrior entered the hut.

"Your majesty," she said bowing to Athtar.

"What is it Myrina?" snapped Athtar.

"I'm sorry to bother you - I heard voices - I just wanted to make sure ..." began the warrior.

"What? That you were not going as mad as others say that your queen is?" said Athtar with a sigh.

"No, of course not, My Queen," said Myrina, frowning.

"Of course not," repeated Athtar, resuming her pacing. "You have heard that Aradia is back?"

"Yes," said Myrina, grimly. "And that Yarg is defeated."

"He's dead, not just defeated," said Athtar, her nostrils flaring.

"Your Majesty, if I may make a suggestion?" said Myrina.

"Yes?" said Athtar.

"The Roman General, Aurelian is still about the village," said Myrina, her eyes narrowing. "Perhaps an alliance with Rome at this time may be beneficial."

"An alliance with Rome is never beneficial to anyone but Rome," said Athtar, shortly.

"Yes, Your Majesty," said Myrina, bowing again.

"No, not Rome - but perhaps ..." said Athtar, thoughtfully. "Leave me now, Myrina - and ready my horse. I have an errand."

"Yes, Majesty - your guards will be - " began the warrior.

"No," said Athtar, shortly. "I must do this myself."

"Majesty, are you ... certain? With Aradia back, the Amazons will be - " Myrina again began.

"Do not question me, Myrina," said Athtar, coldly. "I can easily find another to lead my army - or do it myself."

"As you say, Majesty," said Myrina, leaving to carry out her orders as Athtar turned and glared at the wall.

)O(

In the Amazon Tree Village, another queen was pacing in her house. Mhari sat watching her, an amused smile playing about the corners of her mouth.

"Just what is so damned funny?" said Aradia, stopping and looking at the old shamaness.

"She will be back, Aradia," said Mhari. The queen sat down with a sigh.

"I won't ask how you know that, Granny," she said.

"I can see out the window," said Mhari. Aradia jumped to her feet and went to the window, peering out. She saw Thraso leading both Saraea and Julisa up to the rope ladder to her house.

"Thank Artemis!" said Aradia, going to the door. Then she stopped. "Where's the Sword?" She waited until the three climbed up the ladder and entered the house.

"Saraea," she said, hugging the girl close to her for a moment. "Are you okay?" she asked, looking critically at the young girl.

Saraea nodded, then sat wearily at the table, putting her face in her hands and weeping. Aradia looked to her second in command.

"What happened?" she asked. Thraso shrugged.

"Julisa came and led me to her," said the Second in Command.

"Thank you, Julisa," said Aradia, nodding acknowledgement to the girl. "Saraea, where is the Sword?"

The girl looked up at her, her face wet with weeping and shrugged. "I don't know," she said, defiantly. Julisa looked at her, alarmed, but remained silent.

"How can you not know, Saraea? Did you drop it somewhere?" asked Mhari.

"Yes, I think I did," said Saraea, quietly.

"Where?" asked Aradia, grabbing her shoulders and roughly pulling the girl to her feet. "Saraea, do you have any idea what that Sword can do?"

The girl smiled, bitterly. "Oh, yes," she said, softly. "It kills men."

Aradia released the girl who slid back into the chair, still smiling up at her. "Saraea," she said softly. "Silas is alive."

For a moment, the girl's smile left her, then it returned. "Don't try to deceive me - I saw him," she said, bitterly. "That pig Yarg killed him, but I avenged Silas."

"Silas is alive, Saraea," said Mhari. "Would you like to see him?"

"I did see him, Granny - he was covered in blood and his eyes were - " began the girl.

"Saraea, enough," said Aradia sharply. "He is alive, by the grace of Artemis."

"He's a man - why should she bother about him?" asked Saraea with a shrug.

"What is going on with you, Girl?" asked Aradia.

"Nothing, Aunt," said Saraea. "Yarg killed Silas and I killed Yarg."

"You were only able to kill Yarg because you held the Sword of our Goddess," said Aradia. "Now I need to know where it is so we can keep it safe and out of the wrong hands."

"Whose to say whose hands are the wrong ones, Aunt?" asked Saraea.

"I am, Girl," said Aradia, angry now. "Are you going to tell me where the Sword of Artemis is?"

"How can I when I don't know?" asked Saraea.

"Very well," said Aradia. "Go to your room until I can figure out just how to make you remember."

Saraea stood and walked to her room in Aradia's tree-house. Julisa followed reluctantly. "She knows, alright," said Aradia with a sigh.

"Indeed she does," said Mhari, uneasily. "Yet, I still think you were a bit harsh with her, Aradia. She has suffered - "

"We all have," said Aradia, sharply. "Some of us more than others. Well, at least she's back. Now we can concentrate on finding that sword. Thraso, I want a platoon combing the area where Saraea was found. We have to get to the sword before anyone else does." Her eyes narrowed as Thraso sketched a salute and left the tree-house.

"Aradia, I think it is crucial that Saraea see Silas as soon as possible," said Mhari.

"So do I," agreed the queen. "Unfortunately, Aurelian has a bloody Legion camped all around the village. I just don't know how to get around them without getting her and anyone who escorts her there captured - or killed."

"Hm. That is a problem," said Mhari. "Of course, I could take her."

"No you cannot," said Aradia. "You don't think the Romans saw her kill Yarg? She's sure to be recognised."

"Aradia, you didn't see her kill Yarg - I think it likely that most of the men fighting were as absorbed in their own battles as you were," said the shamaness.

"Not Aurelian," said Aradia, frowning in thought. "He saw everything."

"How can you be so sure?' asked Mhari.

"Because I know him," said Aradia with a sigh.

"How well do you know this man, Aradia?" asked Mhari,

gently.

"Well enough to hate him," said Aradia, her voice low and dangerous. "I had time to learn him during the last ten years, Mhari. He's a cold bastard, though I have no doubt he will be emperor before much longer, and then woe to us all."

Aradia's violet eyes took on a glazed affect. Mhari had known the queen all her life, save the decade she had been away and the shamaness had never seen Aradia so prone to "spells" of despair and melancholy. She knew that the younger woman had been through hell and back. Still it saddened her to see the haunted look which was now in Aradia's eyes whenever she thought no one was watching her.

"Aradia," she said and the queen turned her head slowly to look at her.

"I'm sorry - I was somewhere else for a moment," said Aradia.

"I know - and it didn't look like a very nice place at all," said Mhari, rising and going to her. "Send word to Silas to come here - or a more neutral meeting place, since these poor women will kill any man on sight now."

"'Poor women'? Oh, please, Mhari," said Aradia. "We have Roma practically crawling up our ... well, anyway, they're whining about staying in this beautiful village!"

"They want to go home, Aradia," said Mhari, gently, though secretly she agreed with the queen.

"Will they never realise that this is home?" said Aradia. "Yeah, I miss my house - I missed it for ten years; I miss Thalia - Blessed Artemis, but I miss her." The queen's eyes took on a different sort of faraway look, one of wistful memory, until tears broke the memory and Aradia looked again to Mhari. "I miss it all, but it's gone now - and we have to concentrate on re-building, not just getting back what once was - because there's no getting it back. Ever."

"They are young, Aradia, raised on tales of our former glory and riches," said Mhari. "They hear tales of the Gorgons' wealth and power - "

"The Gorgons have naught but Roman crumbs dropped by that pig Yarg - and not even that now," said Aradia, wearily.

"That's true," said Mhari. "And there is also the fact that their queen is mad."

Aradia laughed, mirthlessly.

"Many here could say the same," she said, shaking her head. "What is it that is said, 'Whom the gods wish to destroy, they first drive mad'? Perhaps that is Artemis's way of punishing one who betrayed her daughters."

"I think our Great Mother is more merciful than that, certainly," said Mhari, appalled at the sentiment.

Aradia smiled at her old mentor. "I don't know, Mhari," she said. "I have had much in life to cause doubt in the mercy of any god."

"At any rate, Artemis would never lift a hand against any Amazon - even a Gorgon," said Mhari. "She is our patron - our Great Mother. She cannot harm her own."

"What is that, Mhari? Some kind of 'god rules'?" said Aradia with a chuckle.

"Look around you, Aradia," said Mhari, her voice solemn, but her blue eyes twinkled. "Everything has a pattern a cycle - an order, if you will. Perhaps the gods do have rules which they, too, must follow."

"That actually makes sense," admitted Aradia. "So, how do we find our 'Mother's' Sword, Old-Mother?"

"We look for it, Child," said Mhari.

)O(

Athtar rode as deep into the forest as her horse could carry her, until the trees grew so close together that the horse's girth would no longer fit between their wide trunks. She dismounted and began to walk deeper still. Here the forest was tangled and wild. Thick vines, some even as thick as Athtar's waist, hung from the limbs of the gnarled old trees which withered under the constant twilight created by their taller, stronger brethren.

Athtar could feel the vines, writhing around the trees, dipping their heads to brush her brow, her slender neck, her shoulders, like a lover's caress.

She stumbled through the tangled foliage, having left any thought of a trail far behind. This was ancient, primordial forest, some said seeded by the goddess's own hand. Athtar needed no trail, however. She followed her instinct until she came to a cave. There, she stripped off her clothing and entered the dark cavern, feeling the damp chill along her skin. She walked deeper in through the winding cave corridors until she heard the sound she had been listening for. A sibilant host of voices now spoke to her as cool, smooth bodies began to wind their way up her bare legs.

"What do you seek here?" came the whispers she heard through the sizzling sounds in her mind.

"I seek the one known as Medusa," said Athtar, her own voice echoing through the cavern.

Suddenly, she felt the writhing bodies begin to undulate and vibrate at the same time, and a woman appeared before her. She almost too beautiful to look upon, her hair as black as a moonless night. Her skin was white like the moon, though, and iridescent. Her eyes were silver and cast a soft glow in the blackness of the cave, illuminating the serpents which now clothed Athtar from her head to her ankles.

"Yesss?" said Medusa. "Why do you seek me out?"

"To worship," said Athtar. Suddenly, she no longer felt sensual pleasure in the serpents' writhing. Athtar began to feel the oppressive force of the silence as they ceased their sounds and began to squeeze their bodies around her limbs. Her chest felt heavy and she struggled for breath, unable to move or even speak, her eyes locked onto the beautiful Medusa.

"Why?" asked Medusa.

"You are a goddess," gasped the Gorgon Queen. "I offer ... worship."

"Worship? You do not know me, Athtar," said Medusa, her voice sharp and clear in the silence of the cave.

"No ... but I wish to," said Athtar, struggling yet immobile against the crushing weight of the serpents covering her bare body, the very smoothness and coolness chilling her blood.

"Be careful what you ask me for, for I guarantee you shall receive it," said Medusa, her voice barely above a whisper. The goddess stepped closer. "What do you offer? I see no sacrifice in your hands - you come to me naked as a newborn. Am I to assume that you are yourself the sacrifice?"

Athtar again tried to struggle against her living bonds, sharp fear piercing her soul at the same time a serpent's fangs pierced her skin just above her breast. The serpents began to writhe, undulating their way off of Athtar's body and slithering into the dark recesses of the cavern as Medusa came ever closer. Medusa put out one slender white hand and caressed Athtar's shoulder.

"Ssssooo cold," whispered the goddess, both hands on Athtar's shoulders. Athtar felt frozen, indeed, unable to move or to speak. She felt the blood from her wound trickling slowly down her breast until a crimson drop depended precariously from her nipple. Medusa leaned forward, her tongue trailing down Athtar's breast, lapping the blood which trickled there. Then darting out swiftly, it caught the drop before it fell.

Athtar began to tremble, but still could not move of her own will as Medusa raised her head. The goddess's gaze held Athtar in thrall and the Gorgon queen could still neither move nor speak under the spell.

"Bitter," said Medusa. "The taste of your treachery is bitter in your blood. You would seek to deceive me, Athtar, but I can taste the desires of your cold heart. You want the Sword. And you shall have it. But remember my warning."

Medusa disappeared and Athtar found that she could move again. She tried to run, but dropped to floor of the cave, as if boneless. She pulled herself up by her arms and tried to crawl, but her legs were gone, her lower body transformed into that of a serpent. She cried out in horror, then began to weep, her eyes spilling tears which would never again cease to flow.

Slowly, she pulled herself forward to opening of the cave, dragging her serpent's body behind her.

The darkness gave way to shadows as she approached the mouth of the cave, horrifying shadows of herself which Athtar could not bear to see. She kept her eyes forward, but then saw a sight almost as horrifying as her transformation. A great, three-headed serpent now guarded the opening of the cave, rearing back and hissing at her approach, three forked tongues flicking ominously, fangs glinting in the half-light of the ancient forest behind the fearsome creature.

"Go back," said one of the heads, its voice a mere whisper.

"You may not pass," said another.

"Go back, deep into the cave and there you will find your treasure," said the third. Suddenly, the serpent transformed into three old women and they began to walk slowly towards Athtar. Athtar backed away, her lower body slithering. She discovered the strength in her tail and rose up, hissing at the three old women. They cackled and kept coming nearer, Athtar backing away from them, her fear of the crones inexplicable to her. Suddenly, she turned and moved swiftly deeper into the cave.

She made her way past the coiled serpents who had first greeted her, deeper and deeper. Her eyes, still pouring copious tears down her cheeks, began to take in the deep gloom of the cave and soon she could see, despite the inky blackness. At last she came to a room deep within the earth which housed the cave. She saw the Sword of Artemis, casting its own light and her shadow against the walls of this room. She moved towards the sword and took it into her hands, her eyes gleaming in the dark. Then she began to make her way back to the three old women.

"They will not stop me now," she said as she moved even more swiftly, her new body becoming more and more comfortable until she forgot how it felt to have legs or to move any other way.

"Get out of my way," she said to the women. They merely laughed again and stood before the mouth of the cave.

"You are the guardian of the sword now, Athtar," said one.

"And we are your guardians," said another.

"None shall pass us," said the third, and the three transformed back into the serpent and turned to face the forest outside of the cave.

With a hiss, Athtar swung the sword, cleaving the three heads from the serpent, but in their place, three more sprang up, the severed heads withering and blowing away as dust. The Serpent turned to face Athtar.

"You must go back now," they said as one. "Go deep into the cave and guard the sword there, even as we guard it - and you - here."

Athtar looked at the creature, then at the sword. Then slithered back into the recesses of the cave, weeping bitter tears which stung her face and steamed when they hit the stone floor of the cave.

)O(

Thraso led the platoon into the forest and ordered them to spread out. The women began crawling through the brush while a smaller group stood as sentries to warn of any approaching enemy.

"Here!" cried one of the searchers. Thraso strode over to where she knelt in the leaves. She bent forward and parted the low-hanging willow fronds which brushed earth beneath them and peered into the shady coolness under the tree. There she saw the leaf cover had been scraped away and then hastily pushed back over the dirt.

"Think she buried it?" asked the searcher, brushing her sweat-dampened curls off of her forehead.

"Maybe," said Thraso, frowning. "This is where Julisa said she found her, crying. Let's dig a bit and see what we find."

The two women scraped the fallen leaves and dirt away and saw the fresh, damp soil had indeed been disturbed, but the area was too small to conceal the Sword of Artemis. Thraso looked to the other Amazon, then shrugged.

"What do you think?" she asked her.

"I think we should dig," said the woman, continuing the scrape at the soil. Thraso pulled out a dagger and began to dig. The women unearthed the amulet Silas had been clutching when Yarg killed him.

"What is that?" asked the Amazon. Thraso pulled it out and shook the dirt off. It was beautiful, a perfect quartz crystal with polished amethysts and small black feathers threaded on the leather cord on either side of the quartz.

"An Amazon amulet," replied Thraso, tucking the find into a pouch which hung from her belt.

"Whose, I wonder?' asked the other Amazon as both women rose to their feet. Suddenly, a large green snake rose up from the pile of leaves, disturbed by the Amazons' search. It reared back, poised to strike. Both women froze as the snake's head swayed back and forth, its forked tongue flicking rapidly at them.

"Don't move, Marpe," said Thraso, casting her eyes about for a way to escape the snake.

"Don't worry," said Marpe, still as a stone. Suddenly, something whirred past Thraso's head and smacked the snake in the head. Both women took the opportunity to bolt while the snake struck at the honeybee which had crashed into it. The bee flew off, leaving the snake to slither back into the pile of leaves which the women had disturbed.

"That was too close," said Marpe.

Thraso frowned. "I have never seen such a serpent here before - and we have lived here for over ten years - nor have I ever seen a bee act so strange," said the warrior. "They are not usually out this time of year."

"Thank Artemis that one has its own schedule," said Marpe with a shudder.

"Yeah - thank someone, anyway," said Thraso with a sigh. She looked around at the others, still searching. "I really don't want to go back empty-handed, but I just don't think the sword's here."

Suddenly, one of the sentries signalled that someone was approaching. The Amazons stopped their search and took to the trees, climbing swiftly. Thraso watched from a broad limb, barely breathing as Myrina and about ten of her warriors entered the clearing where the Amazons had been searching for the sword.

Gorgons, she thought. *Oh please Lady - let the Amazons keep their heads and not attack!*

Thraso saw Myrina and stifled a gasp. Before the Battle of Chadesia, they had been friends. Now she saw that Myrina bore the Second in Command badge, even as she herself did. The Gorgons spread out and began searching through the trees. Thraso held her breath for a moment.

One of the Gorgons stepped up to Myrina.

"No sign of her here, either, Myrina."

Myrina frowned and started towards the willow tree where Thraso and Marpe had found the amulet. Suddenly, Thraso dropped from her perch and stood before Myrina.

"You don't want to go in there," said Thraso.

The Gorgons drew their weapons, but Myrina stopped them. "Why not, Thraso?"

"Snake," said Thraso. "A big one. One of our young girls lost something and while we were looking for it, we disturbed its nest. One of my Amazons and I barely escaped."

"She's lying!" cried one of the Gorgons. "They probably hid the body in there!"

"Silence!" said Myrina, never taking her eyes from Thraso. "A snake - awake at this time of year, Thraso?"

"Like I said, we must have disturbed its nest," said Thraso. ""Believe me or don't - up to you."

Myrina continued to gaze at Thraso, then bent and picked up a stick. She nodded her head once in the direction of the willow and Thraso shrugged and followed, feeling the weight of eyes upon her back. The two women parted the willow fronds and Myrina saw the coiled serpent, evidently asleep, then backed out, pulling Thraso with her.

She looked at the Amazon anew, then smiled slightly.

"That snake is deadly," said Myrina. "In Hesperia, they kill many people. I wonder how it got here?"

"I don't know," said Thraso.

"You didn't have to warn me," said Myrina, softly.

"Yes, I did," said Thraso. Myrina chuckled, but it was without mirth.

"I suppose you did," she said with a sigh. "I should kill you - our people are at war with one another."

"Aradia hasn't declared war against the Gorgons," said Thraso. "And I could just as easily kill you, Myrina."

"Then my women would slaughter you," said Myrina.

"Not necessarily," said Thraso.

She whistled and the Amazons dropped from the trees, surrounding and outnumbering the Gorgons. Thraso looked squarely at Myrina.

"Do you want to fight? Because I don't."

"No, oddly enough, Thraso, I don't," said Myrina. "Though Athtar will be sorely displeased with me that I did not just kill you outright."

"I'm sorry, Myrina," said Thraso, placing one hand on the other woman's shoulder. "It shouldn't be like this. Our people should be united against the common threat of Rome."

"Thraso, you know that will never happen. Your people will never trust mine to not betray you again," said Myrina. "And your people have the Sword of Artemis - and Athtar wants it, so there will never be peace between us," said Myrina.

Thraso looked sadly at Myrina. "Never?" she said, her hand dropping from Myrina's shoulder. Myrina caught the hand and held it.

"If it were up to me ..." said Myrina.

"But it isn't," said Thraso, pulling her hand away. Myrina looked at her, sadly and shook her head.. "So, what do we do now?"

"We walk away," said Myrina, signalling the Gorgons, who sheathed their weapons and walked away, back into the forest in the direction from which they had come.

Marpe ran up to Thraso.

"You okay?" she asked.

"Yeah," said Thraso, quietly.

"Shouldn't we go after them?" asked another Amazon.

"No, we need to get back and report to Aradia," said Thraso.

The Amazons made their way back to the tree village and Thraso dismissed them to their homes. Wearily, she climbed the ladder to the queen's house and knocked on the door.

"Enter!" called Aradia. Thraso came in to find Aradia alone, sitting at the table with the basket of Amazon amulets before her.

"Is this a bad time?" asked Thraso, sitting across from her.

"No, it's never a bad time for you, Thraso," said Aradia, looking up and smiling at her. "You're back early. No luck, huh?"

"That depends, We ran into some Gorgons. And, we found this," Thraso said, pulling the amulet from her pouch and handing it to the queen. "It was buried under the tree where Julisa said she found Saraea."

"Gorgons?" said Aradia. "What happened?"

"It was Myrina - she's wearing Athtar's Second badge," said Thraso. "They seemed to be looking for something - or someone."

"You think it was the Sword?" asked Aradia.

"No," said Thraso. "There was a snake - a big one - where Marpe and I found the amulet. I warned Myrina away from there and one of the Gorgons said something about us burying 'the body' there."

"You spoke with Myrina?" asked Aradia, looking sharply

at Thraso.

"Yes, I did," said Thraso.

"How did you keep the Amazons from attacking the Gorgons?" asked Aradia.

"I had told them from the beginning this was a peaceful mission and they were to engage no one we encountered, though I confess I expected Romans before Gorgons," said Thraso with a shrug. "Aradia, I couldn't let her get bit - I'm sorry. We were pretty close at one time. I guess I let my feelings get in the way of my judgement."

"No, Thraso, I'm glad you did what you did," said Aradia. "It shows you have honour. What did Myrina say?"

"Just that there could never be peace between the Amazons and the Gorgons as long as we have the Sword of Artemis," said Thraso. "Even if the Amazons could learn to trust the Gorgons again, Athtar wants the sword."

"Is that all she said?" asked Aradia.

"Pretty much," said Thraso.

"Thraso, 'pretty much' doesn't cut it; I need to know exactly what she said so I know what do," said Aradia.

"She said she didn't want to fight even though Athtar would be very displeased with her for that and that if she were in charge, things would be different," said Thraso. "Another thing, Aradia - that snake - she recognised it from the Gorgon homeland, Hesperia. She said they killed a lot of people there."

"Interesting," said Aradia, thoughtfully. "I wonder why she risked her queen's wrath? Athtar's temper is well known, even in Rome."

"Like I said, we were friends once - and I did warn her about the snake," said Thraso. "Perhaps she figured ... a life for a life."

"Perhaps," said Aradia, picking up the amulet. "I saw Silas making this for Saraea. I wonder how it got under the tree."

"What about these?" asked Thraso, indicating the basket

on the table.

"I wanted to take them to Artemis's Temple, along with the sword - when we find it," said Aradia.

"What if we don't find it?" asked Thraso.

"We have to," said Aradia, rising and pacing. "The alternative is unthinkable."

"If Athtar gets her hands on that sword, it will mean the end of the Amazons," said Thraso, grimly nodding in agreement.

"Hm," said Aradia, fingering the amulets in the basket. "I'm not altogether sure it isn't our end already, Thraso."

Thraso frowned, and looked into the basket. "It sure looks like a lot," she said. "I think I have a better idea for those than the Temple, though."

Then she arose and left the treehouse. Curious, Aradia rose and stepped outside on the platform which encircled the house. She saw Thraso step up on the wooden dais in the centre of the village. Thraso took the horn and blew, summoning all of the Amazons to the meeting place. Within minutes, the village was full, the Amazons milling about with barely any room to stand.

Thraso looked up to Aradia and called out, "Aradia, bring the basket down."

Frowning, but still curious, Aradia, hefted the heavy basket, attaching it to a rope pulley and lowering it before climbing down the ladder herself. She unhooked the basket and carried it to Thraso on the dais. Mhari came out of her own house and watched from her platform. Saraea, too, came out of her room and stood on the platform just vacated by Aradia.

"What are you up to?" she said, quietly. Thraso merely smiled at her.

"Sisters," she called out to the Amazons, who immediately grew silent. "In this basket are the amulets of those who died to save our Nation. You, me, and our queen - we are the legacy they left behind. We are the recipients of their selfless sacrifice. Our queen wears the amulet of one of our fallen sisters to honour her. I believe that each of us should also wear one of these amulets in their honour, to show that even though they are gone, their spirits remain with us, always and their sacrifice shall never be forgotten."

The Amazons cheered and the roar was deafening. Aradia looked into the basket and realised that the Amazons standing before her far outnumbered the amulets in the basket. She looked at Thraso and smiled.

"Thanks," she said.

"For what?" said Thraso, beaming back at her.

"For reminding me why I'm here," said Aradia. "Not for these," she swept a hand over the basket of amulets, then nodded towards the crowd of gathered Amazons. "But for these. You've inspired me, Thraso. I have an idea of my own for these women."

Thraso looked at the queen, her curiosity piqued, but said nothing waiting for Aradia to speak first.

"Sisters," Aradia called out, her voice silencing the Amazons once again. "The loss of the sisters who once wore these amulets was great. Yet, our numbers are now even greater - so great, in fact, that before even half of you receive one of these amulets, the basket will be empty. And so, what I propose is this - a Tournament, with these amulets as prizes, so that our greatest warriors will bear the honour of carrying on the names of our lost sisters. These amulets will prove a reminder, as Thraso said, that though their souls have moved on, their spirits remain with us always."

There was a brief murmur, then the cheering of the Amazons became deafening. The Amazons seemed to love the idea - save for one. Saraea scowled, then stomped back into her room, slamming the door so hard that the little house shook. Aradia and Thraso were oblivious to the momentary tantrum, but Mhari had glanced at the girl on the platform of the Queen's house and saw, to her dismay, the anger in the child's eyes.

The Queen and her Second in Command brought the basket of amulets back up to Aradia's house. There they were met by the shamaness.

"Inspired idea, Ladies," said Mhari, smiling slightly.

"Yeah, it was," said Aradia, smiling at Thraso.

"Unfortunately, you may not find it so popular in your own house, Aradia," said the shamaness with a sigh.

"What do you mean?" asked Aradia with a frown.

"Your ward," said Mhari. She told the queen what she had seen.

"What am I going to do with her?" asked Aradia, sighing and shaking her head.

"She's just at a difficult age, Aradia," said Thraso, sympathetically.

"You've had experience with this, Thraso?" asked Aradia.

"We were left with the children," said Thraso, shrugging. "They all go through a difficult time sooner or later - just try to imagine twenty or so of them all at the same time." Aradia chuckled and shook her head.

"No thanks - one at a time is enough for me," said the queen. "I just don't think I'm going to have the patience for this, though. Maybe I should have another Amazon - one with daughters of her own - to -"

"No, Aradia," said Mhari, shaking her head. "You mustn't give up on Saraea so easily. She's a good girl. I see the potential in her. The worst thing you could do is to give her away."

"I have no intention of giving up - or giving her away," said Aradia. "She's Thalia's daughter."

"She's *Saraea*," said Mhari, firmly. "If you keep that in mind, more than half your problems with her will be solved."

"Mhari's right, Aradia," said Thraso. "You need to show Saraea that she is important to you for herself, and not just as Thalia's daughter. In order to do that, you need to spend some time with her, getting to know *Saraea*."

"*What* time?" chuckled Aradia. "Seriously, you have both

opened my eyes. It's true, I took her in out of loyalty to Thalia at first. Now I need to let her know that she is more than just a responsibility to me. I still don't think I'm 'mother material', but thank you."

"You'd best get started," said Mhari, inclining her head towards the door of Aradia's house. Aradia smiled again and bade both women good-bye. She entered her house, lugging the basket of amulets and setting it on the table.

"Saraea?" she called. "Saraea?" She walked to the door of Saraea's room and tentatively knocked.

"Enter," came the reply. Aradia pushed open the door and saw the girl lying on her narrow bed, a large tabby cat sprawled over her and purring as Saraea absently stroked its long, soft fur.

"Where's Julisa? And where did that cat come from?" asked Aradia.

Saraea shrugged and sat up, gently moving the cat from her chest to her lap. "I don't know where Julisa went - she said she had to go to the privy, but she hasn't come back yet," said the girl, dully. "The cat just came in through the window."

"She's beautiful," said Aradia, approaching and rubbing the cat under its chin. The cat purred louder, its green eyes half-open and lifted its chin for the queen's attention. "Looks like you have a pet, Saraea."

The girl's eyes widened and her lips hinted at a smile.

"She can stay with us?" Saraea asked hopefully.

"Of course - for as long as she chooses to," said Aradia. "You'll have to name her - and feed her, of course."

"Of course," said Saraea.

"Listen, I need your help with something," said Aradia, sitting on the bed next to Saraea.

"The sword again?" said the girl, her eyes narrowing in suspicion.

"Naturally, Saraea, when - *if* - you remember where the Sword of Artemis is, I would expect you tell me," said Aradia, as patiently as she could manage. "But no, that's not what I'm talking about."

"It isn't?" said Saraea.

"No it isn't," said Aradia. "I need your help with a new project - something which I believe will be very important in the history of our people."

"What?" asked the girl, almost breathless with excitement.

"A tournament," said Aradia.

Saraea's eyes narrowed and her jaw set squarely. "I heard," she said quietly.

"You don't look too happy about it," said Aradia.

"Will you give my mother's amulet away, too?" asked Saraea, fingering the object resting against Aradia's tunic. Aradia clutched at the amulet.

"Thalia's? Oh, great goddess, no!" said Aradia. Saraea pulled her small hand back as if it were burned. She looked at Aradia with narrowed eyes, her nostrils flaring.

"You've taken my mother's amulet - and her sword - and you may try to take her daughter, but you are *not* my mother!" she cried, leaping to her feet, the cat jumping gracefully to the floor. The girl jumped out the window to the broad limb below and clambered to the ground, running as soon as her feet hit the earth. The cat followed her out the window and down the tree. Aradia went to the window, She whistled, capturing Thraso's attention and gestured for the Second in Command to follow the girl. Thraso nodded once and took out after Saraea, two more Amazons accompanying her.

Saraea ran as fast as she could to the clearing in which she had taken refuge after the battle. She went to the large rock and searched about until she found a thick fallen tree branch. Using the branch and another fair-sized rock, she levered the large stone up and peered underneath, gasping at what she saw.

"Oh, no!" she cried. There was nothing there. Suddenly, Saraea sensed movement behind her. She turned, horrified to see two Kaskans leering at her.

"Well, what's this? Little Amazon girl?" said the first

Kaskan, grinning.

Terrified into speechlessness, Saraea let the rock drop with a thud, puffs of dust rising around her ankles. She swallowed hard and pulled her little trail knife from her belt, brandishing it towards the Kaskans.

"L - leave me alone," she said.

The Kaskans laughed. After the disastrous battle which killed their leader, the Kaskans had scattered and were now little more than highwayman, making a living by robbing travelers on the road and pillaging small villages. They preyed upon those weaker and a young girl, Amazon or not, qualified in their small minds as weaker.

"Ho, Ho! The little Amazon has a knife!" said the first one. "An Amazon without a sword? Maybe she's not an Amazon after all, what say you, Holic?"

"Heh, heh, I got a sword for 'er," said Holic, thrusting his pelvis forward.

Saraea felt disgust through her terror. "Kaskan pigs," she said through gritted teeth.

"That so?" said Holic, his piggy eyes narrowing. "Come on, Czaba - let's show 'er!" Both men approached as Saraea stood her ground, still holding the small knife.

"Yeah, show me - come any closer and I'll - " she began.

"Saraea!" The girl turned her head at the sound of a familiar voice and dropped her knife in shock.

"Silas?" she said, her voice barely a whisper. She was frozen now, the large rock between her and her uncle, the Kaskans approaching. Saraea didn't know which way to run.

"You men - leave my niece alone!" Silas yelled. He lifted a hunting bow and knocking an arrow, aimed it toward the menacing Kaskans.

"You can only hit one of us at a time," Holic yelled back, drawing a sword, Czaba following suit.

"Which one of you is volunteering to be first?" said Silas, calmly.

"Come on - I'll gut you both," said Saraea, taking courage

from the "ghost's" protective presence.

"Pah, she ain't worth it, Czaba," said Holic, sheathing his sword. Czaba looked from his companion to the Amazon girl to her uncle and decided to agree. He sheathed his sword and both men walked off, back into the trees from which they had come. Silas lowered the bow and put the arrow back into his quiver.

"Are you ... are you a ghost?" asked Saraea.

"No, Saraea, I am very much alive - thanks to Artemis, so I'm told," said Silas, accepting the girl's eager embrace.

"I thought ... Aradia and Mhari told me, but ... I saw you, Uncle," she said, her tears flowing freely.

"I know, I know," said Silas, gently stroking the child's long dark hair.

Thraso emerged from the trees and found them like that. She stayed the other two Amazons who would have rushed Silas in a mistaken attempt to "rescue" Saraea and approached the two.

"Thank Artemis," said the Amazon Second.

"I do every day," chuckled Silas. "You need to be aware, you have Kaskans in your forest - they just attacked Saraea - or would have."

"But you saved her," said Thraso, smiling. "I will tell Aradia and post extra patrols to try to round them all up."

"Hey, Thraso, what's a man doing hunting on Amazon lands?" yelled one of the other Amazons. "We should kill him for a poacher!"

"No," said Thraso. "This man is a friend to the Amazons - he has Aradia's permission to hunt here."

"No man is friend to Amazons," muttered the other Amazon. Her companion nudged her.

"Isn't that Silas, Thalia's brother?" she asked.

"Yeah," said her friend peering more closely. "He's the one Artemis raised from the dead - I was there."

The two approached the group behind the rock.

"Silas," said the first Amazon. "I want to apologise - I

didn't recognise you. Thalia was a friend. Her brother is no less."

"Thank you," said Silas, nodding in acknowledgement.

"Uncle, I want to go back to the village with you," said Saraea, entreatingly.

"Saraea, that's not possible," said Silas. "Conditions have ... improved somewhat, under Roman rule, but the village is no place for an Amazon."

"I am not an Amazon," said Saraea, quietly.

"Maybe not yet, but you will be after your Initiation," said Silas. "I'm sorry, Saraea. I had made an Initiation amulet for you ... since your mother ... well, anyway, it must have been lost in the battle."

"Oh!" said Saraea, looking up at him. "That's okay, Uncle."

"Perhaps Aradia will make you another ..." said Silas.

"Yeah - she knows all about amulets, doesn't she - she wears my mother's," said the girl, bitterly.

"Saraea, Aradia wears that amulet to honour your mother," said Thraso.

"It should be mine," said the girl.

"Based on what?" asked Thraso. "You knew your mother for two years. Aradia knew and loved her for ten times that many years. Silas here has more 'right' to that amulet than you have."

Surprised into silence, Saraea merely clung more tightly to her uncle and refused to look at Thraso.

"Come on Saraea, you have to go back with them now," said Silas, gently disengaging her arms from his waist. "Thraso, would you please ask Aradia to arrange a time and place where we can meet? We have some very important matters to discuss."

"Of course," said Thraso. Saraea looked up at her, triumphant. *Silas will tell Aradia and all the Amazons to treat me better - or he'll take me home,* she thought.

"Meet me back here with her answer tomorrow at

moonrise - and watch out for the Kaskans," said Silas, turning to go.

"Wait!" cried Saraea, once again clinging to him. "Won't you please take me back with you?"

"Saraea, I already told you no," said Silas, firmly. "You stay with the Amazons now. And be a good girl."

"*Me* be good?" said Saraea. "What about them? Can't you see that I'm a prisoner? Aradia sent her hounds out after me and - "

"Saraea, enough," said Silas wearily. "You are almost a grown woman now - I can't take care of you anymore. You need to be with your mother's people now."

"You are my mother's own brother - you are her 'people' as much as anyone," protested Saraea. "Silas, you are all I have left of her!"

Torn, Silas started to speak, then looked at Thraso, who saw the tears beginning to form in his eyes. She raised an eyebrow and his nod was all but imperceptible to the Amazon Second.

"Come on 'Prisoner'," she said with a sigh. Thraso took the girl by the arm and gently, but very firmly guided her away from Silas.

"Silas!" Saraea continued to scream after him as Thraso and the other two women dragged her back towards the Amazon village. One of the Amazons finally took pity on Silas and gagged her until they reached Aradia's house. The Amazons released her at the foot of the rope ladder and left Thraso to get her back up to the house.

"Climb," said Thraso. "And don't try to be cute - I am in no mood to go chasing off after you again."

"You should have just left me, then," said Saraea, sullenly.

"You wish," said Thraso, grinning and swatting her backside, playfully. "Now get up there and face the music."

Saraea looked at Thraso, then up the ladder and finally around the village.

"Don't you even think about it - get up there," said Thraso, giving her a little shove. Saraea glared at Thraso, then began to climb. Aradia came out of the house and silently watched her, grabbing her hand and pulling her the rest of the way up.

"Do I need to board up your window or can you be trusted not to go jumping out of it anymore?" she asked, looking directly into the girl's eyes. Thraso came up behind Saraea and waited.

"No, I'm not going to go jumping out of the window," said the girl, rolling her eyes. Aradia grabbed the girl's face in one hand and held it.

"Okay, maybe this is partly my fault," said Aradia, looking intently at the girl. "I didn't set any ground rules. I'm going to correct that right now. From now on, you do not leave this house except to eat and use the privy - and then only with an escort."

"For how long?" asked Saraea, quietly. Aradia looked at Thraso who held up five fingers behind the girl.

"Five days - and nights," said Aradia, releasing the girl. "On the sixth day, you will begin training with the other girls your age."

"Training?" said Saraea, puzzled.

"For the sword, staff, bow and arrows - whatever you feel most comfortable with will be your primary weapon," said Aradia.

"What if ... what if I don't want to be a warrior?" asked Saraea.

"Every Amazon must learn at least the basics of fighting," said Thraso. "Would have come in handy this afternoon when you ran into those Kaskans, wouldn't it have?"

Aradia looked at Thraso, one eyebrow raised, then looked back at Saraea. "Go on in now - you need to feed your cat," said Aradia.

"She came back?" said Saraea, smiling a bit.

"Just before you did," said Aradia as the girl went into the house. She looked at Thraso after the child was gone.

"Kaskans?"

"Yes, we came up on them - Silas chased them off before they did any real harm," said Thraso. "He wants to meet with you - says he has some things to discuss with you."

Aradia nodded. "Yes, I was hoping to meet with him, too," she said. "Thraso, I want you to - "

"Assign more patrols to round up any Kaskan stragglers - I already did that on my way back here," said Thraso.

Aradia looked at her only mildly surprised. "Excellent," she said. "Now, we just need to find the Sword - and Julisa. She's been missing since this morning."

Thraso sighed. "Maybe she went back to the Gorgons," she said. "Or maybe, she's who Myrina and the Gorgons were looking for and they found her?"

"That's not impossible - there are a lot of Amazons here now - it's very possible that some may be Gorgons," said Aradia, thoughtfully.

"How would we know?" asked Thraso. Aradia looked at her, surprised, then lifted both of her sleeves. On each arm was a tattoo. "This one," she said pointing to her left, "denotes that I am queen. This one," she pointed to her right arm," tells my Tribe. Come on Thraso - you mean to tell me that you don't have a Tribal mark?"

Thraso looked down, unable to speak for a moment. "I wasn't old enough when ... when my mother was killed in the Battle of Chadesia. Afterward, those of us who were left decided that if we were captured it might be better if we didn't have them at all," she said quietly.

"That makes sense," said Aradia nodding thoughtfully. "That was very wise, actually. I was lucky - the Romans wanted me known as an Amazon. I saw Kaskan captives being carved up and burned - mutilated to remove their Tribal marks. Most of them died from infection."

"Capture was something we feared every day of our lives until your return, Aradia," said Thraso, shuddering. "Anyway, there was no one left who actually knew how."

"Mhari knows," said Aradia. "But I will leave that up to you and the others to decide. It's your skin, after all."

"No, I want one," said Thraso, fierce pride springing up as tears in her eyes. "I just never thought it would be possible to have one. It seemed that was something else lost to us."

"Very well," said Aradia, smiling gently. "I will arrange it with Mhari. Send out the announcement that all who have been Initiated may receive the mark - and Thraso, between you and me, make it *sound* mandatory to those you don't know well enough. That ought to weed out any Gorgons in disguise. I'll be needing it done before the Tournament so that we can see which Tribes are being represented."

Thraso smiled and left to do as her queen bade her.

Chapter Three: Spirit of The Sword

Aradia walked to Saraea's room and knocked. The girl called for her to enter and Aradia did so, sitting on the bed beside her. *She doesn't look anything like Thalia - that should help me realise that she is not simply her mother's daughter,* thought the queen.

Saraea had long, straight dark hair and intense dark brown eyes. She was tall and leggy and slender to the point of near frailty. That was true of most of the village children; they worked hard in the fields most of their young lives and reaped little of the harvest.

Saraea had changed from her Amazon leggings and belted tunic to her village skirt and blouse.

"Bet you're glad you weren't wearing this when you shimmied down this tree?" said Aradia, smiling at her. The cat wound her way around the queen's ankles and Aradia bent and lifted her to her lap.

Saraea shrugged, her head down, her long hair hiding her face. "I guess Thraso told you, huh?" she said.

"Told me what?" asked Aradia, petting the cat.

"That I asked Silas to take me back with him," said Saraea.

Aradia raised one eyebrow. "No, she didn't," said the queen. "Why did you do that?"

"Because I don't want to be an Amazon anymore," said the girl and Aradia could hear the misery in her voice.

"Well, that's a switch," said Aradia. "But I understand."

"You do?" asked Saraea, looking up at her surprised. Aradia stopped petting the cat and began to braid the girl's hair to get it out of her eyes.

"Of course I do," she said. "This isn't like you thought it would be, is it?"

"No," said Saraea. "I thought ... I thought ... I honestly don't know what I thought it would be like. When I killed Yarg, I felt awful. He was a terrible man - he was our enemy, but when I saw his blood on my hands, I ... I guess my mother would be very disappointed in me, wouldn't she?"

The girl looked up at Aradia, a terrible and painful desperation in her eyes.

"Oh, no - quite the opposite, she would be very, very proud of you," said Aradia, smiling gently.

"Really?" said Saraea, a tiny smile hinting at the great weight just lifted from her small shoulders.

"Oh, yes," said Aradia, her eyes taking on a bittersweet wistfulness as she thought about Thalia. "Your mother was a warrior, but she didn't like killing either; she hated it. She said war was a waste of life. And she's right. But Saraea, we only fight to survive. We do not wage war for conquest or glory. Those are men things, not Amazon things. Being an Amazon means so much more than being a warrior."

"Like what?" asked Saraea.

Aradia thought for a moment, then rose to her feet. "I'll show you," she said. "Come on - oh, you may want to change back into trousers; I understand there are some pretty wicked snakes about. Get dressed and meet me in the village centre."

Aradia climbed down the rope ladder and strode over to the drill field. Thraso was there with a large group of women, building and expanding the area in preparation for the Tournament. Aradia called her over and Thraso grinned and left the group, jogging over to her queen.

"It's coming along," she said, wiping her damp brow.

"It is indeed, said Aradia, obviously pleased with the progress. "Listen, you know which women are the most vocal about moving back to the old place, don't you?"

Thraso rolled her eyes and nodded. "There are only about a dozen or so, but they're *vocal* alright," she said.

"Get them together and gathered in village centre and I'll meet you there," said Aradia.

"What do you have in mind?" asked Thraso.

"We're going on a field trip," said Aradia. "I'm planning a two-fold lesson on what it means to be an Amazon."

Thraso nodded and ran off to comply while Aradia made her way to Mhari's house. She knocked and entered at Mhari's call, greeted first by the heady scent of incense. Aradia smiled at the memories the scent invoked.

"Mhari, I'm taking a group to the old town," said Aradia. "I wanted to ask you to join us, if you're not too busy?"

"Ah, the old home place," said Mhari. "I don't know which would be worse, the climb to my old limbs or the sight to my old heart."

"Granny, are you alright?" asked Aradia.

"Oh, yes, Child," said the shamaness, smiling at the queen. "Just old and very tired."

"Mhari, you'll never be old," said Aradia, smiling fondly at her.

"Oh, yes, Aradia, I already am," said the shamaness, with a sigh. "I will accompany you back to the old place. I haven't been there since the battle. I imagine with Yarg dead, the Kaskans will have abandoned it by now and hopefully gone back to their own land."

"Not necessarily," said Aradia, grimly. She told Mhari what Thraso had said of the stragglers who had accosted Saraea.

"My, my - and Silas just happened to be out hunting? That's interesting," said the shamaness, looking troubled.

"Well, I had sent Thraso and a couple of warriors out after her, so she was never in any real danger," said Aradia, with a shrug.

"No, she wasn't," said Mhari, absently. "And she now knows that Silas is alive."

"Mhari, she asked Silas to take her back to the village with him. She told me she doesn't want to be an Amazon anymore," said Aradia.

"Only natural after what's happened," said Mhari, nodding. "Will you give her a choice?"

"Of course she has a choice," said Aradia frowning.

"Does she, Aradia?" said Mhari. "You said yourself she

couldn't go back to the village - she would be recognised. Can the Amazons afford to keep her if she doesn't go through Initiation?"

Aradia thought for a moment before answering.

"Mhari, I am committed to making a place for all women, Amazon or not, who need a refuge, a safe place to be just themselves," said Aradia. "Even if Saraea doesn't choose Initiation, there are other ways she can contribute to the Amazons."

"I am proud of you, Aradia," said Mhari, smiling.

"Yes, well, before we can help others, we have a lot of work to do right here. This trip is the first step," said Aradia. "I'm taking the more vocal protesters - and Saraea - back. I'm hoping they will prove me wrong when I tell them we can't move back, but I don't expect that will happen."

"You may be surprised," said Mhari. "And so may they. We won't know until we get there. So why don't we get started?"

The women met in a group in the village centre. There was entire platoon of warriors, laden with camping equipment, volunteering to accompany the group back to their old home, which had been taken by the Kaskans. Some chose to go out of nostalgia, some out of curiosity, but most wanted to protect their queen and their other sisters from any Kaskans still in the area. Thraso would remain behind since the queen was going to be gone for a few days.

The group made their through the forest. Aradia was amused to see Saraea's cat following them in the tree tops overhead. Saraea looked around as the trees grew taller and even closer together than in the Amazon Tree Village. As they moved further away from the village in which she had been raised, Saraea began to feel different, somehow. It wasn't anything she could explain with words, but the feeling was definitely there, mingled with excitement at seeing the Amazons' old home and trepidation at the thought of meeting any more Kaskans.

It took three days to get through the forest. Along the way, Saraea learned how to sleep in the trees without falling out. She learned how pitch a tent and how to build a fire. She learned a little about snaring small game and how to skin, clean and cook what she had caught. The other Amazons were eager to teach a "little sister" and Aradia watched her growing trail skills with interest.

As they neared the heart of the forest, the hunters reported to Aradia with some concern that game was becoming scarce. They found no evidence that a snow leopard or some other large predator was about and there was no explanation to tell them just why the smaller animals had been scared off.

"Never mind that for now," said Aradia. "We have enough journey rations to get us through the forest. We can solve this later. Just keep everyone close together - no wandering off or scouting in groups of less than four."

They passed by a cave in the very heart of the great old forest and Saraea shuddered, drawing closer to Aradia as they passed the great yawing darkness of its mouth. Aradia felt a warmth at that act like she had never felt before, placing a comforting arm around the girl's shoulders in a quick, impulsive hug, before releasing her and putting her hand near the hilt of her sheathed sword. The cave made them all feel uneasy and they passed it as swiftly as possible.

At last they came to edge of the forest. The Amazons climbed the tall trees and surveyed the flat open fields between the forest and the hills where the Amazons had formerly lived. The way looked clear and the women climbed down and met at the edge of the woods where the thinning trees gave Saraea pause; they were almost visible here and it made the girl nervous.

"Okay, we're going to be exposed going across, but so will anyone else who comes here," said Aradia. "Any questions before we cross?"

"Um, what happens if we meet any Kaskans?" asked Saraea.

"Then you and Mhari get out of our way while the warriors pound them into the earth," said one warrior, grinning fiercely.

Saraea nodded, somewhat relieved and stayed close to Aradia and the shamaness as they made their way across the empty fields where Amazons had once grown crops and grazed cattle and horses. Saraea saw some wild horses frolicking and grazing in the distance near the hills which were the Amazons' destination.

"Oh, aren't they beautiful?" she said, wistfully. "Amazon horses."

"Yes, they are," said Aradia, looking at the creatures with a sense of longing herself. "Let's keep going - those are wild horses and they can be dangerous."

The group moved on, wary of all movement in the grass, for they had been warned of snakes by Marpe and Thraso before they set out. They made their way across the fields to the hills. The sun was beginning to sink, so they pitched camp at the foot of the hills.

"Where is the old city of the Amazons, Aradia?" asked Saraea.

"At the top of these hills," replied the queen as the two sat before the fire. "Just beyond these hills is the valley which we once called home."

"It feels different here," said Saraea, looking up at the stars in the moonless sky.

"Different how?" asked Aradia.

"I don't know," said Saraea frowning in thought. "I feel ... more. It's like a snake that sheds its skin. I feel like that, I think. Sort of new all over."

"Interesting analogy," said Aradia, smiling gently at the girl. "But I understand what you mean. If you choose Initiation, the rite conveys the same sort of feeling. It is a re-birth of sorts."

Saraea looked down. "I said some things the other day - " she began.

"Saraea." Aradia interrupted her with a gentle hand on her shoulder. "Why don't we let this journey be *our* re-birth? Let's just let all the angry words and hurt feelings be shed like that snake's skin?"

"I'd really like that," said Saraea, her dark eyes filling. "But ..."

"But what?" asked Aradia.

"You'll be angry - I lost the Sword of Artemis," said Saraea. "I mean *really* lost it."

"I know," said Aradia. "But we'll find it."

Saraea shook her head. "No," she said, wiping away her tears. "I - I hid it under a rock and when I went back for it, it was gone."

Aradia sighed. "Saraea ... we'll find it, okay? Let's just put all this stuff behind us now and start fresh. When we get back to the village, you show Thraso where you hid it and we'll start there to search for it, okay?"

Saraea nodded, then hugged Aradia. "I'm sorry I've been such a pain," she said.

"Yeah, I know - but I've been assured that you'll grow out of it," said Aradia with a chuckle. "Come on, we have a big day tomorrow. Get some sleep now." She got the girl settled into her bedroll and then made her way over to where Mhari sat, staring into the flames of the campfire, her eyes glazed over and her lips moving soundlessly in some chant. Aradia sat quietly, waiting for the trance to end.

The queen gazed into the flames as she waited, wondering what Mhari saw in their dance and shadows. At last Mhari blinked and spoke.

"Yes, Child?" Aradia could tell by the way the shamaness continued to gaze into the flames that the trance was still with her, despite her acknowledgement.

"Mhari, can you see the Sword of Artemis?" she asked, softly.

The old woman shuddered. "Oh, yes," she said. "And its guardian."

"Mhari, who has the sword?" asked Aradia, her desperation coming through her whispered words like a hiss.

"A fell creature, born of and greed and betrayal," said the shamaness. "A creature who will never cease to mourn."

"Athtar? Mhari, does Athtar have the Sword of Artemis?" asked Aradia.

"Athtar is no more," said Mhari.

"She's dead?" asked Aradia.

"No, not dead; just no more," said Mhari. "I do not know how we will defeat the guardian - or *her* guardians, the Graii ..." Her voice trailed off as she came fully out of the trance.

"Aradia, how long have you been listening to me ramble on?" she said with a chuckle.

"Only a moment or two," said Aradia, with a sigh. Mhari did not remember what she saw in trance afterwards. Aradia knew that it would be pointless to question the older woman any further. She patted Mhari's shoulder then walked the perimeter of the camp, checking the sentries once more before lying down on her own bedroll to sleep.

Aradia slept well that night; for the first time in a very long time, her sleep was free of the dreams which usually tormented her. She arose early, resisting the temptation to kiss the very earth upon which she had slept.

Ah, the 'Motherland', thought the queen. *I can certainly understand why these women are so attached to it, why they want to come back here. This is home ... and yet it is not; not anymore.*

She woke the others and called in the sentries to help strike the camp, then they started the arduous climb to the Amazons' old home, stopping only once for a water break. Saraea hung back, helping Mhari up the rugged incline. Aradia watched with interest, her pleasure at the girl's kindness mixed with concern for Mhari's apparent frailty. Then Mhari looked up at her and winked. Aradia grinned at the older woman's ruse, then resolutely pushed on. *Saraea will make a good Amazon,* she thought. *Mhari is wise, finding ways to show that to both of us.*

For most of the way, Aradia led the women until they were near the top of the first rise. A sense of anticipation and apprehension filled the women. None of them had returned in the decade since the land had been taken from them by Yarg and the Kaskans and they were afraid to see what was left of their home. As they approached, a small group of warriors caught up to their queen.

"Your Majesty," said one of the warriors, halting the climb. "As much as we want you to have the honour of being the first to see it, this may be a trap. The Romans might be expecting you to return here - as indeed you have."

Aradia nodded. "Of course," she said. She waited with the others as ten warriors - those who had been the most vocal about returning here - topped the first rise. The stood in a line, each grasping the hand of the sisters next to her. They stood perfectly still like that for a moment before continuing on, one by one through the overgrown trail to the lower town. Aradia waited with the others until two of the women returned, tears in their eyes.

"It's ... there are no Kaskans or Romans about," said one, her voice breaking slightly. "The lower town is almost completely destroyed. We haven't ascended to the upper town yet."

"Very well," said Aradia. "Let's press on."

The group made the rest of the difficult climb to the hilltop fortress which lay in devastating ruin. The paved streets were torn up and overgrown. The fortress which had been built by the first Amazon Queen, Lysippe so many millennia ago was now little more than rubble. It had withstood thousands of years of war and the elements; now it lay crumbled to pebbles and dust.

"What's up there?" Saraea whispered, pointing to a steep staircase. The bottom of the staircase had been viciously hacked, but it was still climbable.

"The upper part of the town," said Aradia, quietly. "This

lower part was our first line of defense. We believed that even if anyone managed to make the climb, no one could penetrate past this point. We were obviously so wrong."

"How ... how did the Kaskans get this far?" asked the girl, looking back over the climb the Amazons had just made.

"Ah, there was a hidden path - like those stairs to the upper town," said one of the warriors. "It was very well hidden and very well guarded - that is until those Gorgon bitches led Yarg and his men right to it. The Gorgons fought the guards, knowing that a *true* Amazon would never be able to bring herself to harm another Amazon. That was our downfall. The guards should have realised that no true Amazon would betray her sisters, either. The Gorgons were no longer Amazons, but it was so ingrained into us to never a strike a sister ..."

"And that is as it should be still," said Aradia. "That is one of the first laws of the Amazon Nation, Saraea - you never strike a sister Amazon in anger."

"I have seen the warriors drilling - they strike one another all the time in practise," said Saraea.

"That's different," said another warrior. "We're not angry with one another - well, most of the time." The women chuckled.

"Those practice blows are delivered with love - learning to ward them off could save a sister's life in a real battle," said another warrior. "But you'll learn all that after your Initiation."

Saraea looked thoughtful for a moment, but said nothing. Aradia took her arm and led her to the steps, which had been carved into the rock. "Come on," she nodded to the others to follow them up the stairs.

"But my Queen, the scouts haven't come down yet," protested one of the warriors. "We don't know that it's safe."

"Never mind that," said Aradia. "If you're that worried about it, you can go first. The light is failing and we need to get up there."

A group of warriors preceded their queen and the shamaness to the upper town. Saraea was quiet, gazing at the rock wall on either side of the stairs. "Sure would be close fighting here," she whispered.

"It was," said Aradia, grimly remembering the battle. "But we managed to keep the Kaskan bastards at bay until ..."

"Until what?" asked Saraea, her eyes wide.

"Gorgons," spat out one of the warriors. "They were in the upper town - had been for weeks. We didn't think anything of it - at that time, the Tribes were always mingling. We fostered their daughters, trained their warriors and their healers - we did so amongst all the Tribes in the Nation. They came pouring down from the top of the stairs and began to fight us. They and the Kaskans boxed the warriors in on the steps."

Aradia shuddered as the memory came upon her, despite her valiant efforts to hold it at bay.

She and Thalia fought side by side. Suddenly, she felt a blow to her head from behind. She whirled around and saw a Gorgon warrior, a fierce sneer upon her face. She moved behind Thalia and the two fought back to back, as did the other Amazons. But it was no use. They were trapped. Briefly she turned her head and saw Thalia was battling one on one with Yarg himself. She saw that Thalia's Amazon sword did not have the reach of Yarg's long sword, putting her Second in Command at a severe disadvantage. She could only spare momentary glances at Thalia, but it was enough to see that her friend was being hard-pressed as were all the Amazons. Frantically, Aradia tried to think of a way out of this trap before ... Suddenly, she felt Thalia slump against her. She whirled around to see Yarg pulling his sword from her breast with a sickening wet, sucking sound. With a howl of pure rage and agony, Aradia flew at Yarg, her sword raised. Her eyes saw only his blood all over her hands as the way to wash away the grief she felt at the loss of Thalia, but that was not to be. In her blind fury and battle lust, she saw only Yarg. She faced him, her face expressionless. Twirling her sword above her head, she made the first move. Yarg parried with a bored yawn, antagonising the Amazon Queen. She ran at him and he hit her with the flat of his blade, knocking her to her knees. Aradia slowly arose, her head buzzing like a hive of bees. Her arms felt numb and her face burned. Aradia moved on Yarg, tense and focussed, scoring hit after hit, yet the giant warlord seemed impervious to her blows. His expression flitted from feigned boredom to outright amusement. Suddenly Aradia was on the ground, stunned from a blow to the back of her head. Before all went dark, she saw Athtar standing over her her, grinning in triumph as she reached down and ripped Aradia's amulet from her neck, dropping it to the ground and crushing it with her foot. When she awoke, she was on a Roman slave ship, bound for the Gladiator Arena ...

"Your mother died here," she said softly to Saraea.

"I thought she was captured and crucified?" said the girl, startled at the revelation.

"Not all the Amazons on those crosses were captured, little sister," said one of the warriors, sympathetically. "The Kaskans hung some of our fallen sisters - to make it look more like a victory. It's far easier to kill an Amazon than to capture one and keep her alive long to hang her."

"Well, in most cases," said Aradia, a rueful smile gracing her lips.

"Your Majesty, that was a Gorgon who took you down," said another of the warriors. "It would take an Amazon to capture another Amazon like that. Most of the captives were taken by the Gorgons - which is what makes it even more heinous."

The women made it to the top and Saraea was silent the rest of the way, contemplating the revelation about her mother. They saw the scouts going from building to building. The upper town was remarkably untouched, except by time and the elements. Most of the stone and mudbrick buildings still stood, including the Temple. There was no evidence of any living creature larger than Saraea's cat who had accompanied them up the stairs. The cat now ran off to Aradia's old home which still stood next to the Temple. The queen decided to investigate the larger building first and made her way to the Temple with Mhari and Saraea in tow. The three entered reverently and Aradia made her way to the front of the building where the altar still stood, though the large marble statue of the goddess lay in three pieces over it, the rope apparently used to topple it still tied around the waist. On the altar was a loaf of bread, long ago turned to stone and flowers which were now dust. A flagon held dust the colour of dried blood which had once been wine. Aradia approached cautiously, shoving Saraea quickly behind her at the sight of a skeleton behind the altar.

"Mhari, it's Leilë," she said, hiding the sight of the long-dead priestess from the young girl with her own body. Saraea resisted her attempts.

"Aradia, I've seen dead bodies before," said the girl, impatient with the protectiveness of her guardian.

"You want to repeat the experience?' asked Aradia, one eyebrow raised at the girl, who reluctantly backed away.

The heavy pediment of the large marble statue which had once stood behind the altar now lay over the crushed bones of the priestess who had died to protect the sacred artefacts it had once held in its marble hands: The Sword of Artemis and a *bipennis* - a double-headed battle axe - which had once belonged to the ancient Amazon Queen, Hippolyte. A broken arrow showed how she had died before the statue had crushed her. The axe lay beneath the skeleton.

"Saraea, go and bring the rest of the Amazons in here," said Aradia and the girl rushed off to comply. Mhari approached the altar and shook her head slightly at the loaf, flowers, and wine.

"Poor Leilë - this must have been one last desperate cry to the gods for help," she said.

"Yeah - lot of help *they* were," Aradia muttered. "Still, let's get this place cleaned up."

The Amazons arrived and very shortly had the Temple put back in some semblance of order. Leilë's body was committed to the flames of a makeshift pyre and her ashes placed in the crypt below the Temple along with the ancient queens of Amazonia, including Lysippe herself. Aradia kept her amulet in a pouch on her belt to add to the ones in the basket at her house in the tree village. The statue once again stood proudly behind the altar, the *bipennis* in its accustomed place in her right hand, though the left remained empty, as if waiting for the return of the Sword of Artemis. The seams where it had been broken were all but invisible.

The late afternoon sun streamed through the open windows and the building once again felt serene and peaceful as it had before the battle so long ago. Aradia led Saraea behind the altar and pointed to the legend inscribed upon the pediment below the feet of the statue.

"Can you read that?" she asked the girl.

"Of course! Mhari taught me," said Saraea, proudly. "It says, 'An Amazon bows to no man, be he king or god.'"

"Never forget that, Child," said Aradia, quietly. "That's the first lesson every Amazon learns. It's a part of what it means to be an Amazon."

"Aradia, we had better set up camp," said one of the warriors, eyeing the sinking sun through the window.

"Why camp?" said another of the warriors. "Our houses still stand. We can sleep indoors tonight."

Saraea looked alarmed for a moment as Aradia nodded. "The houses are in good condition?" she asked.

"Yes, the ones we checked were, anyway," said one of the warriors.

"I wonder why this part of the town wasn't destroyed, too?" the queen mused.

Mhari spoke slowly, her eyes taking on a far away look. "The Kaskans feared this place," she said. "Yarg came and took the Sword from the Temple, but that was all. They camped in the lower town, then destroyed it when Yarg was killed. They have returned to their own land, all but a few." The shamaness blinked and smiled at them, once again aware of the present.

"Very well," said the queen. "We'll sleep indoors - I want at least four to a house, though." She led Mhari, Saraea, and two warriors to her old home. Saraea hung back a bit and Mhari looked at her with concern.

"What's wrong, Dear?" she asked.

"I know why the Kaskans were scared of this place," she said softly, her dark eyes wide. "It's haunted. There are ghosts here, Granny - lots of them. I can feel them all around me."

Mhari smiled and patted the girl's shoulder. "Of course there are, Child," she said. "This is an ancient and most sacred place to the Amazons. All of our ancestors' spirits reside here. Not to worry - they mean *us* no harm. They are here to guide and protect us."

"How ... how do you know they don't mean to harm us?" asked Saraea.

"Talking to spirits is what I do," said Mhari, smiling. "Trust me, Saraea, I've been doing this all my long life. Even if they did mean mischief - which they don't - they are spirits and are physically incapable of hurting anyone."

"If you say so, Granny," said Saraea, moving closer to the older woman.

"I am curious, though," said Mhari, looking at the girl with interest. "How long have you seen spirits?"

"Always," said Saraea. "Especially at the crossroads where ... well, you know. They aren't there now, though."

"Interesting," said Mhari, bringing the girl through the door of Aradia's old home. Saraea's cat ran to greet them.

"Hekau!" the girl cried as she bent to pick up the tabby. "What have you been doing? Huh? Kitty things?"

"Very much so," said Aradia emerging from one of the bedrooms. "Making very short work of the mice who nested in the mattresses. The beds are a mess because of the mice, so we'll just build a fire in here and put the bedrolls out."

"Oh, Hekau," said Saraea, cuddling the cat close. "You are the very best cat in the world."

"Saraea, you and Prothoë go and bring in some wood for the fire," said Aradia, nodding to the warrior. The girl set the cat down and went with the warrior to do as Aradia asked. The cat followed. Aradia strode over the hearth and looked up the chimney.

"Amazing - it's clear," she said, smiling in delight. "So as soon as they get back with the wood, we'll have a fire - nights are cold here this time of year as I recall."

"I'll go for some water - the cisterns are full," said the other warrior, leaving.

"Now, if we just had a rabbit for the pot, it would feel like home again," said Aradia, wistfully. *A rabbit and Thalia to share it with, that is,* she thought.

"Would it, Aradia?" asked Mhari, softly. The queen turned to her and the shamaness saw tears in the violet eyes.

"I just don't know," said Aradia.

"We could re-build here, you know," said Mhari, looking around the house.

"Yes, we could," said Aradia. "I just don't know ... the tree village has begun to seem more like home than this place."

"Has it, Child? Or are you still hiding?" said the shamaness.

"From whom?" said Aradia, frowning at the older woman.

"From your memories," said Mhari. "The tree village is very defensible - so long as the trees stand."

"Yes, but now we can learn from our mistakes and make this place truly impenetrable," said Aradia. "Believe me, I have thought about it; I spent the last decade replaying every move in that battle. At the time, it seemed that I was doing all I could to protect my people. Now I see where I could have done so much more. That lesson came at a terrible price."

"All lessons have a price, Aradia," said Mhari. "You did what was in your power to do - you are mortal, after all."

Aradia said nothing, contemplating the older woman's words for a time. Her reverie was interrupted by Saraea and Prothoë's return with armloads of wood - and a rabbit, which Saraea had snared and presented with a shy pride. The other warrior, Aëlla, followed shortly with two buckets full of water from the cisterns.

"The water is clear and good," she said, happily. Soon the women were seated on the bedrolls before the fire, sipping tea from their packs and waiting for the rabbit to cook. The scent of roasting meat filled the house. Mhari entertained them with stories of the Amazons' glorious past, long before the battle which had nearly decimated the Nation.

At last, the rabbit was eaten and the dishes washed. The women lay down to sleep, Aradia taking the first watch. She didn't think she would be able to sleep in this place, so filled with bittersweet memories. Slowly, the women's breathing deepened and Aradia settled back in her old favourite chair which she had moved in front of the door. She sat, thinking about the stories Mhari had told this evening. *Tales of magic and of gods*, thought the queen. Thalia had loved those stories and her daughter no less so. Saraea had sat enthralled by the spell the shamaness wove with her words and voice.

Aradia believed them to be just tales, allegories at best, which made the mundane magical to make the tale entertaining. Despite her encounter with Artemis and witnessing Silas's resurrection, the queen could not bring herself to believe in magic. The gods were, at best, distant and uncaring about the mortals who served them, save perhaps, Artemis. At worst, they were meddlesome and capricious, playing with mortals like pieces on a game board. Ares was the worst, Aradia thought. He not only used mortals for his own ends, he had absolutely no compunction about destroying, then discarding the mortals along the way.

Suddenly Aradia was startled by a movement in the shadows. She arose and checked the fire, which she intended to keep burning. It did get cold here at night, she remembered, shivering. Hekau, Saraea's cat was the author of the movement which had startled Aradia and the queen chuckled to herself, willing her heart to slow its beat to a more comfortable pace. Hekau had been curled up beside Saraea, but now arose and sauntered slowly into the bedroom.

"Stupid mice never learn," said Aradia to herself. She heard the cat make a chirping sound in the other room, then it emerged, keeping to the shadows outside the boundary of firelight; Aradia could only make out a dim outline of feline proportions as the cat slowly made her way back to Saraea's bedroll.

"Oh, no you don't," said the queen. "Though I have no doubt your intentions are honourable, I doubt your young mistress will appreciate any gift you leave in her bed - " She stopped as she saw the cat emerging from the shadows. She saw that no dead rodent was in its mouth, but even more amazing was the cat's eyes. Normally emerald in colour, the firelight reflected back a familiar sky blue. Aradia blinked and the eyes were normal again.

"I'm just jumpy," she said to herself. "It's this place. It's home and yet ... the familiarity is gone somehow."

Suddenly, the crackling blaze in the hearth sank to mere glowing embers and the room became very cold. Aradia shivered.

"I'm going to have to reprimand myself for falling asleep on watch," she muttered, blinking rapidly in the sudden blackness of the room, trying desperately to deny the fine hairs on her arms and the back of her neck rising and prickling.

"Ari', you're not asleep," said a familiar voice behind her. Aradia squeezed her eyes shut as her own shadow appeared against the wall before her, cast by a bluish glow behind her.

"No," said the queen through gritted teeth. "This isn't real. It isn't possible."

"It's both possible and real, Aradia," said the voice. Gasping for breath, the queen turned to see the glowing figure of Thalia, smiling gently at her. The apparition went to the sleeping Saraea and knelt beside the girl. The cat seemed unconcerned with the spirit's presence and lay back down beside the girl as Thalia gently brushed a lock of dark hair from her daughter's face before bending and kissing the child's forehead. Saraea smiled in her sleep and turned, cuddling the cat close to her. Thalia rose and walked over to Aradia.

"Thalia," Aradia whispered, reaching out to the apparition. Thalia extended her hand and Aradia felt her touch as a whisper of wind on her arm. "How is this possible? Are you trapped ... here?"

"No, Ari', I am free now - thanks to you," said Thalia, smiling.

"Then why are you here?" asked Aradia. "Why now?"

"Because you are here now," said Thalia. "And this is where your memories of me are the strongest." She looked around the room which was now illuminated by the glow she cast.

"So this is a memory," said Aradia nodding. "And I have finally become as mad as Athtar, talking to myself."

"I am no mere memory, Aradia. And you are neither mad nor talking to yourself," said Thalia. "I am very real. When I felt you here and my daughter, I had to come. I had to let you see me."

"Why?" asked Aradia, tears welling in her eyes.

"Because you must stop feeling guilty," said Thalia. "You are not responsible for what happened."

"I am queen," said Aradia. "That makes me responsible."

Thalia sighed. "Still the same Aradia," said the apparition. "This place is a graveyard now. It is home to the dead, not to the living. Will you try to move back here?"

"I don't know," said Aradia. "Should we?"

"Perhaps," said Thalia. "It is not for me to say. It matters not where you dwell, Beloved Aradia. I am wherever you and Saraea are now. She sees me, though she knows me not. Nor did you tell her that Yarg killed me."

"She killed Yarg after she saw him kill Silas," said

Aradia. "It ... was not good for her. I had no desire to bring that pain back to her."

"My daughter avenged me," said Thalia, smiling proudly. "Yet I have no wish for her to be a warrior."

"I doubt you need to fear on that count," said Aradia. "She doesn't seem to wish that either."

"No," said Thalia. "She will be your successor, though. And she will be High Priestess of the Amazon Nation as well."

"Priestess? Thalia, what do you mean?" asked Aradia.

"The Goddess claimed her a long time ago, Aradia. She has the gift of sight; she can see and will soon hear the spirits of her ancestors. Mhari will teach her, but she will indeed be the spirit healer of the Amazons, even as Mhari is now," said Thalia. "But first she must overcome her fear."

"Thalia, no priestess or shamaness has ever been queen of the Amazons," protested Aradia. "If what you say is true and the goddess has claimed her for that path, then I shall have to seek elsewhere for my successor."

"On the contrary, Aradia, there have been many priestess-queens, trained by other priestesses and shamanesses, in our history," said Thalia. "Look to the Temple; under the altar, you will find scrolls which chronicle our history, I would have you take them back to your new village of trees."

"As you say," said Aradia, doubtfully, part of her still believing this a dream or more likely, a hallucination.

"I must go now, Ari'," said Thalia, smiling. The glow around her began to dim as she faded.

"Wait!" cried the queen, reaching out for her.

"Aradia, I am always with you," said Thalia. "Stop mourning me as if I weren't. And please, take care of my daughter."

The apparition disappeared and the fire again rose up in the hearth. Aradia shook her head, then glanced out the window. The greyish half-light of dawn was creeping through the cracks in the shutters. The queen sighed and woke the others, making ready to start the new day.

Chapter Four: Champions of the Sword

Aradia left the others in the house and went alone to the watchtower on the summit and gazed out over the rich valley which had once belonged to her people. She could just make out the sea through the early morning mist which would later wet the grass as dew.

It was just as the sun turned from pink to a blazing golden glory that Aradia sensed Saraea's presence behind her. Without taking her eyes from the scene before her, Aradia reached back and drew the girl beside her.

"Oh," said Saraea, taking in the view. As the sun rose, it caught the mist, making tiny rainbows which bounced about before the lemony rays began to burn it off.

"This was our valley once," said Aradia. "It could be again."

"Are you thinking of moving from the tree village, Aradia?" asked Saraea, leaning into the queen. Aradia wrapped one arm around the girl's shoulders and felt her shivering in the damp chill of the early morning.

"I am thinking of it, yes," said the queen. "But it really isn't all up to me. When we get back, we will report to the Amazons what we've found here and then put it to a vote."

"Mhari said that this was an ancient and most sacred place to the Amazons," said Saraea.

"It is indeed," said Aradia. "But it is also a place full of ghosts from the past."

"Mhari also said that the ghosts were here to protect and guide us," said the girl. "I love the tree village, but I think that this place is home. The dead walk here, but we could fill it with life."

"You are very wise for one so young, Saraea," said Aradia. "We will see what happens. Our first priority, though, is to deal with the threat of Rome."

"Yes," said Saraea, her dark eyes narrowing as she spoke the hated name. "Rome."

The two went back down to the house where breakfast was ready. They ate and then Aradia took a few warriors to the Temple. They pushed the heavy altar aside and there they found a slight depression in the floor of the Temple, covered with a wooden lid. Aradia lifted the lid and there were the scrolls, just where Thalia had said. Aradia looked at them in wonder before lifting them one by one out of the well.

"What do you know?" she said, looking at them.

"What do we do with them, my Queen?" asked Prothoë.

"We're taking them back to the tree village," said Aradia, standing and dusting off her hands. "And I suspect, I will be drafting a few younglings who know how to read and write to make some copies." She looked at Saraea and grinned. Saraea grinned back; the girl couldn't wait to get back to the tree village and begin reading this treasure.

They left later that morning. The group was a great deal quieter on the way back, each woman lost in her own thoughts. It was an uneventful journey and they arrived at the tree village, welcomed by the Amazons with shouts and cheers. Immediately the queen stepped up onto the dais, and addressed the village.

"The old lower town has been demolished," she began. "But the upper town is nearly untouched. The Kaskans have abandoned it, and presumably returned to their own land. It's ours for the taking back. I see immense potential for re-building, but I will leave that decision to you. I will have all who accompanied me on this journey tell their own tales of what they found there and in three days, we will meet back here at noon to vote."

The Amazons murmured amongst themselves for a few moments. Aradia looked at them, puzzled. "Are there any questions?" she asked.

"My queen," said one Amazon, stepping forward. "Why wait? We all know what we want - to go home."

"Wait," said another, younger Amazon stepping forward. "This village is the only home I have ever known. I don't want to leave it and start over with re-building some ghost town."

The murmurs grew angry in tone and Aradia raised her hands for silence.

"That is why we wait the three days before putting it to a vote," she said, smiling. "I want everyone to have a chance to think this through and to speak with those who made this journey. It will not be easy to re-build, but it can certainly be done."

"Your majesty, what about the Romans?" asked another Amazon.

"The Romans are a priority," said Aradia, nodding. "We must deal with the threat they pose before any thought of moving back to the town can be entertained."

"Then why don't we attack them?" asked another woman. "We outnumber them, surely."

"We outnumber the Legion camped around the village - slightly," said Aradia, drily. "We do not, however, outnumber the entire Roman army. If we dispatch this Legion, be assured that Rome will send more troops - *many* more troops."

"So how do we defeat them?" asked the Amazon.

"I don't know yet," said Aradia. "For now, at least, it must be enough to keep them from defeating *us* until we figure that out."

The women weren't happy with that, but it was the best she could do for now. Aradia stepped down from the dais and stopped at the bottom, hearing Saraea arguing with another younger Amazon girl.

"Shut up! You don't know what you're talking about!" Saraea cried. She didn't see the queen watching her.

"What would you know about being an Amazon?" asked the other girl. "You were raised by a *man*. I have spent my whole life in this tree village and I don't want to leave it."

"I know plenty about being an Amazon," said Saraea, her nostrils flaring in anger. "My mother was a warrior. She died in battle, trying to save the Amazons."

"Your mother was captured and strung up on a cross by

the Kaskan pigs," said the other girl.

Saraea pulled back her fist then stopped. "Never strike a sister Amazon in anger," she said, softly. She dropped her fist. "You're wrong about my mother. Aradia was there. She told me my mother died in battle."

The other girl looked down, then took Saraea's hand and smiled. "I'm sorry - you're right - never strike a sister Amazon - I guess a person can strike even harder with words sometimes," she said. Saraea looked at her, her smile spreading wider. "Hey, you want to help with something really important?"

"This is how you recruit volunteers?" said Aradia, smiling at the girls as she made her presence known.

"Um, Aradia, this is ... my friend, Momi," said Saraea. "She can read and write, too. I was going to ask her to help copy the scrolls."

"Excellent," said Aradia. "Come, Girls. We might as well get started right away."

The two girls followed Aradia to her tree house where the warriors had delivered the scrolls. They lay in a chest Aradia had retrieved from her old house. The chest had held clothing, now rotting and eaten by insects. Aradia had emptied the chest of the clothing and the insects and it now held the precious parchments.

"You two, go ahead and sit down at the table," said Aradia. "I will bring you parchments and quills. I would suggest that you read the scrolls through first - they must be *exact* copies to preserve the integrity of the contents - no embellishments or, conversely, editing out anything - that includes misspellings and bad grammar."

"The ancient Amazons didn't know how to spell?" said Momi, her bright blue eyes wide.

Aradia chuckled. "It isn't that - they just spelled words differently than we do now," she said. "Saraea, I will be back in a few hours. Please stay here?"

"I promise," said the girl, grinning as she gazed at the

scrolls.

"Be careful with those - I have no idea how old they are or how well preserved," said Aradia, nodding toward the scrolls as she left.

Thraso had set up the meeting with Silas and Aradia walked briskly to the meeting place, taking Thraso and a couple of other warriors with her. Silas emerged from the trees and Aradia greeted her friend with a hug, shocking the other warriors. Thraso merely smiled.

"Silas, it's good to see you," said Aradia.

"And you, Aradia," said Silas. Aradia looked at him with some concern.

"What's going on, Silas? You don't look well," she said.

He waved the question aside. "We don't have time to inquire about each other's health, Aradia, though I appreciate the concern," he said. "There are some things you must know, and then perhaps it's best if we don't see one another again."

"Alright," said Aradia, frowning.

"The Kaskan stragglers are not just left-behinds or deserters," Silas began, then was interrupted by a fit of coughing. Again, he waved away the queen's concern. "Some of them are, certainly, but most are bounty hunters. Aurelian has been given the authority by the Emperor to offer a bounty for you - five hundred denarii for proof of your death, or one thousand denarii if you are captured alive."

Thraso whistled. "Blessed Artemis, Aradia - five hundred - or one thousand - goddess, I'm almost tempted to turn you in myself," she said, laughing.

"Knowing Aurelian, the Emperor offered three times that much and he plans to keep the difference and call it a commission," said Aradia, smiling slightly at her Second's teasing.

"It's not funny," said Silas. "Too many in the village have been tempted. You know that the Romans have taken over the village. They are now felling trees in your own forest. Evidently, word got out that the Amazons were settled in the trees. Your village is in great danger. If the Romans cut down the forest ...."

"Then the forest and the Amazons will be lost," said Aradia, nodding. "We can't allow that. That forest is sacred to Artemis."

"Then let Artemis protect it and get out of there, Aradia," said Silas. "I am saying this to you as a friend - please, you have to get out of there. It's no longer safe for the Amazons."

Aradia looked at Thraso and nodded to her, grimly. "I think we have just had that decision made for us, Silas. What about you?"

"What about me?" said her friend, coughing again.

"You are obviously not well," said Aradia. "Evidently the Romans are treating you no better than the Kaskans did. You need to get out of the village."

"And go where?" asked Silas.

"I don't know, old friend," said Aradia. "Just ... get out of there. There's nothing left for you in that place. Saraea is fine - she is adjusting."

"Finally," said Thraso, with a grin.

"Maybe you're right," said Silas, quietly. "In any case, I must wish you farewell, Aradia. Give ... give my love to Saraea."

"I will," said Aradia, offering one final embrace. Silas turned and left and the Amazons made their way back to the village.

"What do you suppose is wrong with him?" asked Thraso as they walked back.

"Rome," said Aradia, bitterly.

"What do you mean?" asked one of the warriors.

"They are trying to get to us through him," said Aradia, her violet eyes narrowed in anger.

"How could they know he knows you?" asked the other warrior.

"His sister was an Amazon. He raised her daughter - who is now missing, along with the old village herbwife, Mhari," said Aradia.

"But the Romans couldn't know that Thalia was his sister - and they thought that Saraea was his own daughter," said Thraso.

"No, the *Kaskans* thought that Saraea was his daughter," said Aradia. "Rome has a way of getting people to tell old village secrets."

"Okay," said Thraso, frowning in thought. "Do you think Silas would ever betray us?"

"Why do you think he said this was farewell?" said Aradia.

"I'm sorry," said Thraso after a moment of heavy silence between the women. "Silas was a good friend."

"Yes," said Aradia. "And this way, he remains so. I only hope he heeds me and leaves that village."

"Too bad he isn't a woman," said Thraso. "He could come with us."

"But he isn't - and he wouldn't anyway," said Aradia, smirking to herself at the two warriors' shocked looks. "Unfortunately, I don't know that he can find anywhere else that hasn't been invaded by Rome or Roman influence."

"Is it really that bad, Aradia?" asked Thraso.

"I forget sometimes that the Amazons have been so isolated," said Aradia, shaking her head.

"Well this news should influence a lot of votes," said Thraso.

"One way or another," said Aradia. "Some will want to leave immediately to get away from the threat and others will insist on staying to protect the forest or to keep men from taking another home from us, whether they want to stay in it or not. It's the principle."

"It's silly pride," said Thraso, frowning. "But unfortunately, I think you're right."

"We do have to stop them from desecrating this forest," said Aradia.

"What do you have in mind?" asked Thraso.

"I don't know yet," said Aradia, thoughtfully. "I wish we had the Sword."

"I'll take Saraea and a platoon as soon as we get back - " began Thraso.

"No. It's too late today," said Aradia. "Tomorrow, first thing. But something just tells me that we won't find it there anyway."

"Where do you think it is?" asked Thraso.

"Mhari said something about a 'guardian' and *her* guardians, the Graii - whoever that may be," said Aradia.

"Someone has it, then," said Thraso. "But who?"

"Well, when we find that out, we'll be much closer to finding the sword," said Aradia with a sigh. "Come on. We have a lot to do and not much time."

)O(

"Athtar."

The Guardian turned toward the sound. It was a familiar-sounding word, but the Guardian no longer recognised it. She hissed at the man who was standing there, an insipid smile plastered across his pretty face. For some reason the creature could not explain, a hot hatred arose in her cold breast at the sight of him. She clutched the Sword of Artemis tightly in her bloodless hands.

"Mine!" she whispered.

"Oh, yes," said the man, nodding. "Oh yes, I'm not here to take it from you. Quite the contrary, I just wanted to make sure you had it."

Sudden recognition flared in the Guardian's numbed mind.

"Ares," she said with another hiss.

"Very good," said Ares. "It's coming back to you, isn't it?"

"You ... you tricked me!" spat the Guardian who had once been Athtar, Queen of the Gorgons. "You knew what I would do."

"Once a traitor, always a traitor," said the god of war, his dark eyes narrowing. "Now you won't be able to deceive anyone into trusting you ever again."

"I will kill you!" screeched the creature, brandishing the sword.

Ares threw back his head and laughed. "You can't," he said. "Not even with that Sword. Athtar, look at it this way - we both got what we wanted out of this - you have the Sword and I ... well, I don't believe the Amazons will ever get their hands on it again. Not with you guarding it."

"Why?" asked the Guardian.

"Because, as long as no Amazon holds that Sword, my sister is all but powerless," said Ares. "The less she has, the more I have. I intend to be the god in charge."

"The Amazons will destroy you, Ares," said the Guardian. "I could help you."

"No, Athtar. See, Amazons mortal, Ares god - got it?" said the god, chuckling. "Mortals do *not* destroy gods - and I don't need your kind of help."

"You will pay for this Ares," said the Guardian.

"Oh, I doubt that very much," said Ares, laughing as he disappeared from the cavern. The Guardian gazed at the Sword for a bit, then slithered her way to the mouth of the cave. The serpent turned at the sound of her body scraping against the cave floor and transformed into the three old women. The Guardian approached the Graii.

"I must know if the Amazons come here," she told them.

"They've been and gone," said the first of the Graii.

"What?" said the Guardian. "When?"

"Three days past, they were here," said the Second.

"Why didn't you tell me this?" asked the Guardian.

"They tarried not, but passed us swiftly by," said the Third.

"Which way?" asked the Guardian, desperately.

"Both ways," said all three in unison.

"Both ...? Ah never mind," said the Guardian. "They will return, I have no doubt. Ares is playing with all of us. I must know of it when they do."

The three nodded and turned away from her again,

transforming back into the serpent. The Guardian slithered back into blissful forgetfulness of her former life until the Amazons' return.

)O(

Myrina had taken over leadership of the Gorgons until the queen's return. She would give Athtar until the next full moon; then she would march the Gorgon's back to their homeland of Hesperia near Lake Tritonis.

Myrina was not quite ready to give up on Athtar, even though some deep instinct told her that the Gorgon queen was never coming back. She had to weigh loyalty to Athtar against the safety and survival of the Gorgons, though. With Yarg and the Kaskans gone, there was no buffer between them and Rome and Myrina believed that if Aurelian did not manage to re-capture Aradia, any Amazon would do to take back to Rome in chains, even a Gorgon. She had no intention of allowing that to happen and she really doubted that Aradia would be caught by any Roman. There was no reason, save their missing queen, to remain here any longer.

"No reason at all," Myrina muttered aloud.

"Oh, I don't know about that," said a man appearing before her.

"Who are you?" cried a startled Myrina.

"Oh, where *are* my manners? I am Ares, god of war," he said.

"A god ...? What do you want here?" asked Myrina.

"I come bearing sad news," said the god, a mien of regret upon his face. "Athtar is no more. She will not be back."

"Did the Amazons ...?" began Myrina as the message sank in.

Briefly, Ares considered the possible benefits of allowing the Gorgons to believe that their queen was dead at the hands of their enemies. Then he decided that the deception would not fit in his plans, amusing at it might be to watch that scenario play out. No, he must forego the immediate gratification of watching the women battle each other and stick to the original plan, which had the more subtle appeal of perverse irony. In the long run, it would be worth it.

"Hm, no - snakebite," he said.

"Oh," said Myrina, remembering the Hesperian viper she had seen the other day. "Why does it take a god to deliver this news?"

"You are very good," said Ares, grinning, though he was beginning to feel chagrined. Myrina would pose a greater challenge than Athtar had; she seemed to have none of her former queen's avarice or any other self-interested qualities he could exploit. Still, Ares believed that every mortal had some fatal flaw. If he could just find out what Myrina's was, he could still use it to get her to do what he wanted. "Normally I wouldn't have bothered, but I also have a message of more personal interest. The Amazons are holding a Tournament."

"The Amazons are holding a Tournament?" repeated Myrina. "What does that have to do with us?"

"Yes, the day of the next full moon," said Ares. "I would like for you to enter it as my champion."

"Why should I represent you?" asked Myrina. "What do you have to with the Gorgons? Or the Amazons, for that matter?"

Ares felt a cold rage overtake him at the woman's impudence. Before he could stop himself, he threw a bolt of lightning at her which sent her into the wall on the other side of the room.

"How dare you question and defy me?" he roared. "I am a *god*!"

Myrina came shakily to her feet. "I bow to no man, be he king *or* god," she said, meeting the god's dark eyes with her own unwavering gaze.

With supreme effort, Ares checked his wrath and stopped himself from killing the woman outright.

"That would be the answer of an Amazon, Myrina. But the Gorgons are no longer Amazons. My sister has turned her back upon you," he said. "You did betray her, after all."

"I betrayed no one," said Myrina. "I was a child when that happened."

"Ah, yes, that was Athtar's doing," said Ares. "But you swore fealty to Athtar of your own free will. That makes you as guilty as she. My sister has abandoned the Gorgons. I am offering to take her place as the Gorgons' patron."

"What do you get out of all this?" asked Myrina.

Again, Ares tempered his anger at her impudence. "Let's just say that I am annoyed with my sister," he said, through gritted teeth. "Seeing my champion defeat hers would be immensely satisfying."

"Why don't you gods just fight your own battles instead of involving mortals in your petty quarrels?" asked Myrina, now angry herself.

"You are stretching my patience, Woman!" said Ares, his eyes blazing.

"Yeah, and if you didn't *need* me, I'd be dead already," said Myrina, calmly.

Ares looked startled for a moment, then he chuckled. Yes, Myrina would be a far greater challenge to manipulate than Athtar had been. This woman was clever and didn't have the queen's selfish streak. That might just be the flaw Ares was looking for.

"You're right, of course," he admitted.

"Why should I be *your* champion?" said Myrina.

"As I said, Artemis is no longer the goddess of the Gorgons - you could hardly expect her to be after your betrayal," said Ares. "You need a patron to worship - and to protect your interests."

"Then I will do *everything* in my power to try and re-gain Her favour – even if it takes the rest of my life," said Myrina. "The Gorgons may be exiled from the Amazon Nation, but we will still never worship a *male* god."

Ares smiled. He could use her own unselfishness and love for her people to his advantage nicely. And even after the

Tournament, the Gorgons would prove very useful, indeed. The god grabbed Myrina's arm and roughly pulled her to the door. "You need a reason to serve *me*?" he said. He threw open the door and Myrina saw that the Gorgons were all in cages, Romans guarding and patrolling the Gorgon village. "Promise to fight in the Amazons' Tournament as my champion and in my name or the Gorgons will be destroyed."

Myrina gazed out and saw the Romans hammering crossbeams together in preparation of crucifying the caged Gorgons; some already hung, writhing in agony. She unsheathed her sword to rush to their rescue.

Ares grabbed her, pulling her back inside. "Are you crazy?" he said. "You can end this and make it all go back to the way it was. I'm a god - I have the power to do that - if I were your patron, that is. Just say yes."

"Great Mother Artemis - help us!" Myrina cried. She waited, watching helplessly as Gorgons were dragged from the cages and secured to the crosses. Ares smiled sympathetically.

"You see? She must have abandoned you," he said. "Something I will *never* do."

"Very well," said Myrina, reluctantly agreeing. "I will be your champion and fight in the Amazons' Tournament in your name."

Ares grinned and waved his hand and the glamour faded; the Gorgons were not captives of Rome, after all. Myrina looked at the god, her eyes narrowed.

"You tricked me," she said.

"Not at all - I merely showed you the consequences of your refusal," said Ares, fading from her presence. Myrina sighed and summoned runners to carry her message to the Amazons.

)O(

Aradia was pleased with progress of the Tournament plans. So far fifty Tribes were represented, but Aradia had no reason to doubt that many more would enter before the day of the Games. The Arena was being built in a large natural clearing which the Amazons of this village had been using for a drill field.

Mhari was kept busy with putting the Tribal marks on many of the younger Amazons. She had drafted Saraea's assistance and the girl sat looking at the parchment onto which were etched many symbols, one for each of the Tribes of the Amazon Nation, past and present.

"There sure are a lot," said the girl. "Oh, my! What's this one?" She showed Mhari a gruesomely fierce face with lolling tongue and fanged serpents spiked and writhing from the head.

"I don't think we'll be doing many of those," said Mhari with a chuckle. "That's Gorgon"

"It's ugly," said Saraea, shuddering.

"It certainly is, but powerful all the same," said Mhari.

"I still don't think I would like to walk around with thing on my skin for the rest of my life," said Saraea. "Especially now."

"Hmm, you do have a point," said Mhari.

"Which of these did my mother wear?" asked Saraea.

Mhari hesitated a moment. "I don't remember," she said. Saraea looked at the shamaness sharply, then sighed.

"It's sad. I have a feeling that the Gorgon mark isn't the only one we won't do many of. So very many of the Tribes are gone," she said.

"That's true," said Mhari. "The entire Nation is now the only size of two large tribes together now."

"Whoa - you mean that all of the Tribes were *each* half the size we are now? That's ... that's just amazing," said Saraea.

"Well some of the Tribes were no more than fifty strong even at the Nation's height of glory, but the numbers are still daunting," said Mhari.

"Yeah, they are," said Saraea. "And Aradia was queen of all of them?"

"Well, each Tribe had its own queen, some had as many three, but they all answered to Aradia, yes," said Mhari.

"No wonder she gets so sad sometimes," said Saraea, leaning down to scratch the ears of the ever-present Hekau.

"Yes, well, come along, Dear - we have about a dozen eager young warriors waiting to be marked," said Mhari, arising and gathering her equipment.

The Amazons had set up a hut for Mhari to do this work not far from the Tournament arena. Saraea spent her mornings training with other girls her age to use to the sword, axe, staff, and bow. She spent afternoons with Mhari, helping with the marks as well as learning Tribal and Amazon lore and evenings she spent with her friend, Momi, painstakingly copying the old scrolls. Aradia made sure the girl stayed too busy to get into any more trouble. The queen watched Saraea's progress with interest. Meanwhile, the day of the Tournament approached swiftly.

The masters at arms made sure they finished with the younger girls' training sessions by mid-morning so that the contest participants would have the arena to practice the rest of the day. Free time for practice or any other "leisure" pursuit was precious. The Amazons had very little and what they had, most used to hone their skills.

The deadline for entering the Tournament was three days before the Games were scheduled to begin. On that day, the Amazon sentries found two Gorgons wandering in the forest, bearing the badge of messengers. The Amazons brought the Gorgons to Thraso, who was overseeing the final preparations for the Tournament at the Arena. Thraso could see the Amazons seething; the Gorgons' messenger status protected them from the sound thrashing that the sentries clearly wanted to administer to the traitors.

"We bear a message from Myrina, in the Name of our Queen," said one of the Gorgons, thrusting a rolled parchment to Thraso.

Thraso ignored the parchment. "Why from Myrina and not Athtar? Is this message to me or to Aradia?" she asked. The Gorgons looked at one another, not knowing what to tell the Amazon Second. They were under orders to not divulge Athtar's demise unless they had no choice.

"The message is for the Amazons," said the other messenger, clearly apprehensive with the situation.

"Very well," said Thraso. "In that case, you must deliver this to Aradia."

She led them to where Aradia was watching Mhari mark a young warrior who was the last living member of her Tribe. The queen looked up, curious at the sight of the two Gorgon messengers, flanked by her own sentries, as Thraso approached her alone, bearing the parchment they had brought from Myrina.

"Aradia, these women bear a message from Myrina - in the name of their queen," she said, handing the rolled parchment to her. Aradia beckoned the Gorgons to approach as she unrolled the parchment.

"So how is Athtar?" she asked, scanning the message, one eyebrow raised. She looked up at the messengers, waiting for their reply.

The Gorgons looked at one another.

"I really wouldn't know," said one with a shrug.

"Really?" said Aradia with a chuckle. "My people know every time I so much as sneeze. Thraso, can these sentries be trusted to escort these messengers to the meal hall for refreshments while I draft a reply to Myrina?"

Thraso looked sternly at the sentries.

"Yes, they can - can't you?" she said to them.

They saluted first their queen and then their commander before escorting the Gorgon messengers away.

"Remind me to give those sentries punishment detail - what do they mean bringing them to the heart of the village?" said Thraso, shaking her head.

"They're messengers - they are not permitted to divulge our location or anything else they see here," said Mhari. "That's probably what the messengers were thinking, anyway."

"They're Gorgons," said Aradia, rolling her eyes. "I agree with Thraso - we can't trust them because they're Gorgons, yet at the same time, we can't kill them because they're messengers."

"Perhaps if we honour the pact, the Gorgons will do the same," said Saraea.

"You have a lot to learn, youngling," said Aradia, shaking her head, but she smiled at the girl. "I really hope you're right, though."

Mhari finished the mark and sent the young warrior off. "So, will you allow her to enter the competition?" asked the shamaness.

Aradia looked at her, only mildly surprised. "How did you know what - ? Never mind," she said with a chuckle. "That is what the message says, though. Myrina wants to enter the competition."

"Why?" asked Saraea.

"I don't know - Thraso, you know her. Why is she doing this?" asked Aradia.

"I *knew* her, but that was a very long time ago," said Thraso. "Your guess at her motives is as good as mine."

"Any reason why I shouldn't let her compete?" asked Aradia.

"Because it could be another Gorgon trick," said Thraso, bitterly.

"Thraso, when was the last you sent a message in my name?" asked Aradia.

"Uh ... never?" said Thraso.

"Exactly," said Aradia. "I'm wondering what's going on with Athtar. I knew her very well before ... well, I thought I did, anyway. That's partly why her betrayal was such a shock. The thing is, Athtar craves power. Power over everything and *everyone*, especially her own people. I can't believe that

Myrina would go behind her back to enter the Tournament. Athtar's people know better."

"Maybe she's dead," offered Saraea.

"No, Mhari told me in a trance that she wasn't dead," said Aradia.

"What did I say?" asked the shamaness with a small smile.

"That Athtar was 'no more' but that she wasn't dead," said Aradia.

"Interesting," said Mhari. "I said that?"

"In trance," said Aradia. Mhari nodded, thoughtfully.

"So if she isn't dead, then what?" asked Thraso.

"Perhaps incapacitated ... or she's finally crossed the line into madness," said Aradia. "And Myrina is now the Queen in name as well as fact."

"How did the Gorgons even find out about the Tournament?" asked Saraea.

"Good question," said Thraso.

"When was the last time anyone saw Julisa?" asked Aradia.

"Do you think she was a spy?" asked Saraea, her eyes wide.

"No," said Mhari.

"She may have been re-captured by the Gorgons," said Thraso.

"Yes, she may have," said Aradia. "Did she know about the Tournament?"

"When ... when you made the announcement, I felt angry - I thought ... anyway, when I came back into the house, Julisa was there at the table. She asked me what was wrong and I told her about the Tournament. Then she said she had to go to the privy and I haven't seen her since," said Saraea.

"That sounds very suspicious," said Thraso.

Yes, it does," said Aradia, her eyes narrowed.

"Things are not always as they appear to be," said Mhari, shaking her head.

"That's true," said Aradia. "But I have to play it safe with the lives of these women. We have to call an assembly of the Amazons immediately and tell them everything. They have to know, to prepare."

"You do realise that the decision whether to move or stay is now out of our hands," said Mhari.

"Yes, I do," said Aradia, grimly. "It's almost like .... we're being moved about like pieces on a game board. Which tells me the gods are very much involved in all of this."

"Speaking of gods, Silas said that Romans are felling trees in the sacred forest," said Thraso. "How do we protect it if we leave here?"

"By leaving," said Aradia. "Once we are no longer here, the Romans will lose interest. They fell the trees because the trees are our best defense. If there are Gorgons or any other traitors in our midst, they will leave to report back to Myrina or Aurelian after I make the announcement - that's when we'll make our move."

)O(

Ares's visit to her in this cave had awakened the memory of herself. Contact with the world outside of her prison through the serpents kept her from slipping back into forgetting everything before her transformation.

Athtar spoke with her serpent children. She was not permitted to leave her prison, but they were. Willingly, they hunted until their bellies were full, then gave their own lives to feed her. They served her well in this and other ways. They could hide almost anywhere in the Gorgon camp, the Roman controlled village, or the Amazon Tree Village. They listened well and reported back to her what they heard. It was from them that Athtar learned of the Amazons' Tournament and plans to move back to the old town. She also learned of Ares's visit and Myrina's intent to do his bidding.

She seethed at Myrina's weakness. She would never have fallen for such a cheap trick. True, she was a victim of Ares' manipulation, but that had been much more subtle than that fake vision he'd planted in Myrina's mind. As painful as it was to remember, Athtar held tightly to her identity. With the pain came a sliver of hope; if she could but leave this cave, she believed that she would return to her former self completely, taking the power of the Sword of Artemis with her. Then they would all pay.

)O(

It was the day before the Tournament, a time when the fervent preparations should have been made with happy anticipation. Instead the Amazons were on the move. They made their way through the forest. All those not competing in the Games were on their way to their new/old home.

Aradia had made the announcement immediately after speaking with Mhari, Thraso, and Saraea. The Amazons were mostly relieved; the difficult decision had been made for them. Some would grieve, primarily the younger Amazons to whom this village in the trees was home, the only home they had ever known. They all knew, however, that this move was necessary to ensure the survival of the Nation.

The queen sent Mhari and Saraea ahead with the others. She debated whether to send Thraso with them, then decided that her Second in Command had invested too much in the Tournament to be so cruelly left out at the last minute, despite the desperate circumstances. Instead, she sent several other experienced warriors and, in a flash of intuition that Aradia could not explain even to herself, she presented Saraea with Thalia's sword and charged the young girl with protecting Mhari - and the scrolls. Saraea accepted solemnly and then saluted before turning to follow the others out of the tree village.

Now, as darkness fell, Aradia found herself missing the girl. By now, the lamps would have already been lit and Saraea busily copying the old scrolls from the old town. Instead, Aradia sat in the dark at her table in her nearly empty tree house. All that was left was the table and chair and Aradia's bed. Most of the empty tree houses had been dismantled and the wood from which they were composed fed to the common fire in the centre of the village. Fewer houses would help to conceal from Myrina and her Gorgon entourage the true number of the surviving Amazons, now making the journey to the ancestral home of the Amazons.

Aradia puzzled over Myrina's motive for entering the competition. She didn't know how the Gorgons had even heard of the Tournament, which had been an impromptu affair at first, a friendly competition honouring the memories of the fallen Amazons with their amulets as prizes. Such sentimental treasures were of immense value to the Amazons, but Aradia couldn't see what Myrina would want with such a prize. In her heart, she worried that this was merely an opportunity for the Gorgon to challenge her as Queen of the Amazons. Aradia had no intention of entering another arena as a contestant or combatant for the rest of her days on this earth. Yet she could think of no honourable way to refuse if she were challenged by the Gorgon warrior.

Another thing she feared was the fact that the Amazons were no longer in possession of the Sword of Artemis. If Myrina found that out, the Gorgons would start looking for the artefact themselves. Aradia had no doubt that she would have heard something if the Sword had been found by anyone, especially the Gorgons. No, Mhari had said some "Guardian" had it. Aradia didn't know if that was a good thing or not; the Sword of their goddess had been entrusted to the Amazons and they had failed in their task to keep it safe. Fortunately, Artemis apparently didn't hold that against them. What could they have done against both the Kaskans and their own sisters, the Gorgons? Evidently just what they did. Nothing.

That wasn't true, either, Aradia admitted to herself. She had been captured, her Second in Command, Thalia, killed by the Kaskan leader, Yarg. Amazons were falling all around her, mostly in shock at the betrayal of the Gorgons. If she was completely honest with herself, there was nothing she could have done to stop it at that time. Now was different. She was older and a lot wiser and she would die before allowing any such thing to ever happen to the Amazons again. She thought especially of Saraea. Saraea was fourteen now. Nearly all the girls who had been about that age at the time of the Battle of Chadesia had died fighting. At least, Aradia hoped they had. She couldn't imagine being that young and captured by Romans or even worse, Kaskans. It had been bad enough at her age to be enslaved, in chains, and sold like a loaf of bread or a pair of sandals. In her heart, Aradia vowed that would never happen to Saraea, even if she had to kill the girl with her own hands to prevent it.

"That's not going to happen," she said to herself, startled at the echoing sound of her own voice in the empty house. She chuckled. "Yep, going just as mad as Athtar - talking to myself and then answering as well." The queen shook her head and arose from her chair, making her way in the dark to her room and lying in her bed. She hoped sleep would find her soon.

)O(

The Amazons made their way through the deep forest. It was a very different trip from the first one Saraea had made with Aradia and Mhari and a platoon of fifty or so warriors. Strangely, these women seemed to look to the girl as a sort of leader. She had killed Yarg, the leader of their enemies. That alone would have conferred their respect to the young girl. She carried her mother's sword and was proficient enough in its use, thanks to the morning training sessions, that the Amazons believed she could take care of herself. Still, as Aradia's heir, she wouldn't have to; every warrior in the group was there to protect her. Aradia had made it clear: avoid trouble, but if trouble came to them, they must let Saraea fight for herself. They were only to bail her out if she was in over her head. Aradia expected the trip to be uneventful, but just in case she made sure herself that Saraea could handle the sword before she gave it to her.

They walked through the tall trees and as night fell, they were near the heart of the forest. It was already dark here, for the trees were so tall and thick that they blotted out the twilight. Saraea wanted to keep going, but there were many elders among them who couldn't go another step, Mhari included. Saraea remembered the spooky cave from the last trip and had been hoping to get as far past it as possible, but it wasn't going to happen. She stopped the group shortly before they reached that point when she saw Mhari leaning heavily upon her walking staff.

They made camp and the hunters went out to catch some small game for the cook fires dotted about the clearing before the cave. The small fires offered the only illumination in the clearing as the moon was hiding her face that night.

Saraea shared a fire with Mhari and her friend Momi. The cat, Hekau, stayed close to Saraea until the hunters returned empty-handed.

"No game," said one of the hunters. "In fact, there's no sign of any living creature here besides us."

"Just like last time," said Saraea, grimly. Hekau jumped from Saraea's arms and ran toward the cave. "Hekau, no!"

Saraea jumped up and started to run after the cat, but Mhari held her back with a surprisingly strong grip for one her age. "No, Child, stay far from there," said the shamaness. "That's a very bad place."

"But Hekau - " began the girl.

"Never mind her - she can take care of herself," said Mhari, firmly.

Reluctantly, Saraea sat back down and gazed into the darkness toward the cave.

Suddenly, the Amazons heard a loud squealing and screeching. Immediately, Saraea and the warriors were on their feet, swords drawn.

"Princess, stand back," said the one of the warriors as a small group moved towards the eerie sounds in the dark.

Briefly, Saraea was startled by the appellation, but only very briefly as another howling screech pierced the darkness and chilled her. The girl's heart pounded uncomfortably in her chest and her breath came in short gasps. She worried about Hekau even as she instinctively put her own body and her still-drawn sword between the terrifying sounds and the old shamaness entrusted to her care. One of the warriors looked at her then nodded her approval before running after the others. The remaining warriors formed a shielding circle about the rest of the group.

Suddenly, the Amazons heard shouts and screams of fear and pain and more of the screeching. Briefly, Saraea remembered her pledge to Aradia to protect Mhari, then rushed toward the sounds, grabbing up a thick burning stick from the cook fire to use as a torch.

She came upon a horrific scene. Many of the Amazon warriors were dead. The rest were all trying to battle a creature from a nightmare. A three-headed serpent was rearing back, striking at any Amazon who came near them. Saraea saw Julisa, briefly. The other girl met her eyes for a moment before slipping into the cave while the monster was distracted.

"What ...?" said Saraea, then turned her attention to the monster. She looked about at the Amazons who were fighting the thing, then saw an opening and rushed in, just as she had been taught in the training sessions. Granted, this was a bit different than fighting a human adversary, but still Saraea had learned well. She managed to stab at one of the thing's eyes, blinding it on one side. It reared back and hissed again - that was the first time it had been blooded since this battle began. Turning its attention to the young girl with the scarred sword, the thing lunged. Saraea managed to take one of the heads off with a swipe of her sword before jumping back, narrowly missing its massive jaws snapping closed upon her arm.

"Princess, get back to camp!" cried one of the warriors. Three Amazons converged upon the creatures, but none could wound it.

Saraea frowned and shook her head, looking for another opening. She found one and lunged, slicing away the jaw of another one of the remaining heads. Another warrior got close enough to swipe at the other head, cleanly separating it, but almost instantly, another grew to take its place. Saraea got in one more hit, piercing the scaly hide just below the new head, and then the creature began to slither back into the cave. Saraea, realising that Julisa was still within, started to go after the creature again, but one of the warriors grabbed her and pulled her back.

"No - never go after an enemy who has retreated or surrendered - there is no honour in that," said the warrior. "Let it go."

"That is no mere enemy," said the girl. "And the others may have to contend with that ... thing when they come this way." Saraea struggled free of the Amazon's grip, then saw Julisa, moving through the trees towards camp. Reluctantly, she allowed the mortally wounded monster to crawl back into the inky blackness of the cave.

The girl bent to clean her sword in the grass, then rose and looked about at the remaining Amazon warriors. She glanced down at the fallen warriors then back up at the Amazons, standing in a circle around her.

"Let's get them back to camp - and then we need to get everyone out of this place," she said, grimly.

They gathered their fallen sisters and made their way back to the camp. Saraea saw Mhari standing with Hekau in her arms and a dead viper at the shamaness's feet.

Mhari looked about at the group as they returned, carrying their fallen sisters.

"What in the Four Hells happened out there?" asked the shamaness.

"I'll tell you on the road," said Saraea, grimly. "Let's pack up and get out of here. Mhari ... what do we do with the dead? There's no way we can give them proper pyres here."

Mhari nodded. "No, we can't," she said. "But in the ancient time of our people, when we were constantly moving from one place to another, we had other ways of freeing the souls of our fallen sisters."

The shamaness gathered the elders of the Tribes who were travelling with the group and they began to prepare the bodies as the rest of the group packed up the camp. Mhari burned the incense, smudging both the living and the dead in the camp while the elders washed and oiled the bodies and chanted. They melted the candles they had brought with them and encased the bodies in the beeswax, then sewed each of them into a linen cocoon.

When they were finished, their amulets and weapons were placed safely in packs to take to the Amazons' new/old home. Then the younger, more agile Amazons put their fallen sisters high up in the trees, securing them to the limbs with rope while Mhari and the elders chanted and danced about the fires. Saraea watched the Rites, becoming caught up in the chanting; though she didn't understand the words they chanted, she *felt* their meaning. She found herself joining the dance. Mhari saw her and smiled, and the elders welcomed the young girl into their midst. Soon, others joined them until the entire group was dancing and chanting the souls of their sisters to the Great Mother of them all.

All of a sudden, Saraea sank to her knees and her eyes took on a far away, glazed sort of look. The dancing and chanting ceased as Mhari rushed over to the girl, and knelt beside her.

"Where are you, Child?" asked the shamaness.

"I go with the sisters - they travel to the Womb of the Great Mother to await re-birth," said Saraea. "They are free now and we must leave this place before ..."

"Before what, Child?" asked Mhari.

Saraea shook her head, then looked up at Mhari, fear in her eyes. She raised her hands before her eyes and saw blood there. Blood seeped from her breeches and Mhari smiled.

"What ...?" began the girl.

"It's alright" said the shamaness. "It's just the Moon-Blood - do you know what that means?"

The fear was replaced by a touch of pride. "Oh, yes - Silas told me - it means that I'm a woman now," said Saraea.

Mhari chuckled. "Not quite, but you are on your way to preparing for that," she said.

"But - " Saraea began to protest.

"Listen, Dearie, just because a girl's body can create life does not mean that she is prepared to care for and protect that life," said Mhari. "Trust old Mhari, you are not yet a woman by Amazon standards, but like I said, you are indeed on that road. Come now, let's get you cleaned up so we can be on our way."

The shamaness helped her to clean up and the Amazons happily buried her soiled clothes in the earth. There was a festive air to the proceedings and Saraea saw Momi and some of the other girls her age looking enviously at her.

"This sure is different than in the village," Saraea commented after she was dressed and ready to go. "When a village girl begins to bleed it's all secret and scary."

"Why scary?" asked Momi.

"'Cause that means it won't be long before she's tossed into some man's marriage bed," said Saraea, shaking her head. "When Yarg killed most of the women and girl children, that left a shortage of marriageable women so as soon as a girl was capable of conceiving, she was married off."

"Against their will? How awful!" cried Momi.

"Yes it is," said Saraea with a sigh. "Silas said that would never happen to me, though."

"Damn right," muttered one of the older Amazons. "Thalia's daughter would never be sold to some man. We'd have been there, weapons drawn before allowing that."

Saraea looked down. "Silas wouldn't have allowed it," said Saraea. "Even if it meant trouble with the Kaskans."

"No he would not have allowed it, Saraea," said Mhari placing a gentle hand on the girl's shoulder. "Thalia's brother did well with her daughter."

That silenced the Amazons on that subject. They began to move forward, skirting the cave widely.

"Mhari, where did that dead snake come from?" asked Saraea as they walked.

"Hekau pulled it out of your bedroll and killed it," said the shamaness, grimly. Saraea shuddered. "Now what happened out there?"

Saraea told the shamaness about the Amazons' battle with the three-headed serpent. "Mhari what was that thing?" she asked.

"Graii," said Mhari, grimly. "A guardian entity, very hard to kill or even to wound."

"Well it can't be *that* hard - *I* managed to wound it pretty badly," said Saraea.

"On the contrary, Child, I don't know how you managed it, but it usually takes magic - like a magical weapon - to wound a creature like that."

"Like the Sword of Artemis?" asked Saraea.

"Perhaps," said Mhari, nodding.

"It still isn't dead, though," said Saraea. "Aradia and the others may have to have to face it when they come through here in a few days. I would have finished it off, but it crawled back into the cave and the others stopped me from going after it. Told me there was no honour in following and killing an enemy who has retreated. That was no ordinary enemy, though."

"No, indeed - and while those warriors were absolutely correct when it comes to *human* enemies," said Mhari. "I don't think honour has anything to do with not following that thing; in this case, following anything like that into a dark cave does not seem wise to me; it could have been a trap."

"Like a spider drawing a fly into its web," mused Saraea, nodding. "I hadn't thought of it that way. Still, Aradia should be warned."

"Aradia can take care of herself," said Mhari.

"But you said that those things can only be killed by magic," Saraea protested. "Does Aradia have any? Magic, I mean."

"She has what she needs," said Mhari.

"I still think someone should go back and warn her," said Saraea.

"We can't spare anyone, Saraea," said Mhari. "Let it be."

Saraea sighed, but remained quiet. The rest of the journey was uneventful, though the women were exhausted by the time they reached the end of the forest. It was there they made camp to rest before crossing the great open fields to their home.

)O(

Aradia waited near the new arena. It was far smaller than the Roman amphitheatre in which she had been forced to fight her hapless opponents. Still, even being in the vicinity brought back unwanted memories of that time. It had been as if Aradia moved in a dream, a nightmare from which there had been no awakening until that night her mysterious saviour appeared.

"I need you elsewhere ...." The words haunted her. The Amazon Queen felt that a reckoning was not afar off and she would soon pay for her freedom. She felt things once again spinning out of her control. The gods must certainly be playing with her and the Amazons and Aradia didn't like it one bit. The Gorgons were coming. The Amazons had been forced to abandon yet another home. Rome was felling the trees of Artemis' sacred forest. Why didn't the goddess herself step in and stop them? Aradia shook her head.

"One minute I'm annoyed about gods interfering, the next I'm asking for that interference," she said to herself. "Better make up my mind." She sighed, then gazed back out at the arena.

It had originally been a large natural clearing where the Amazons who had settled here in this place had drilled with one another and taught the Amazon children entrusted to their care the rudiments of fighting. Now, a wooden wall had been built all around and seats for spectators had been built. Not that there would be many spectators; Aradia had sent anyone not competing on to the old town. She herself would not be in the games. She'd had enough of all that to last for several lifetimes. She dreaded the games, in fact, but as queen, it was her responsibility to be here. She hoped that the Gorgon, Myrina, wasn't coming here with some challenge for her, but she knew that was almost too much to hope for.

"What did she mean, she *needed* me?" mused Aradia aloud, then the queen shook her head. "Yep, definitely on the road to madness, talking to myself. Pretty soon, I'll be as bad off as Athtar, wherever she is."

"No you won't," said a figure materialising before her.

"Blessed Artemis!" Aradia cried, almost falling to her knees before the goddess.

"Yes," said the goddess, smiling slightly.

"Lady, what ...?" began Aradia.

"I would ask a boon of you," said Artemis.

"My Lady, what do you require of me?" asked the queen.

"Myrina will offer a challenge in this Tournament you have planned. I want it accepted," said Artemis.

"With respect, my Lady, but no," said Aradia, bowing her head slightly.

"What do you mean, 'no'?" asked the goddess, a frown beginning to mar her perfect brow.

"I mean no, I have done with the arena," said Aradia.

"I can certainly understand your reluctance," said Artemis with a small sigh. "But hear me out before you refuse."

"As you wish," said Aradia, though she had no intention of complying no matter what the goddess might have to say. "But I will promise you nothing."

Artemis smiled. "I could ask no more of one of my daughters - Amazon Honour prevents you from making such blind promises and I would have it no other way," she said. "Ares has chosen Myrina to be his champion."

"Ah, I see - so this is really more of a competition between the two of you," said Aradia, eyes narrowing.

"Yes, it is," said Artemis with a small shrug. "Sorry, but that's just the way it is."

"Well, at least you're honest," said Aradia.

"I have no choice - gods cannot lie," said Artemis, a small smile playing about the corners of her mouth.

"What do you mean?" said Aradia. "Gods can't lie? There really are 'god-rules'?"

"Not so much rules - we are not physically capable of lying," said Artemis. "We can deceive and twist the words about and not tell the entire truth, but we cannot tell a lie."

"That's good to know," said Aradia. "So, what are the stakes? What do you get if I beat Myrina?"

"This isn't about what I get - it's about what Ares doesn't," said the goddess, impatiently. "He wants Rome."

"He can have it," said Aradia with a derisive chuckle.

"You don't understand," said Artemis, sternly. "With the armies of Rome, Ares could take over the entire world. Only the Amazons and some of the Tribes of Keltia in Britannia stand between him and his goal: to be the only god worshipped in all the world."

"And war would never cease," said Aradia, her voice barely above a whisper as she took it in.

"Yes. Peace would be forgotten," said Artemis. "Fighting and destruction would be the ultimate form of worship until mankind utterly destroyed itself."

"Blessed Mother of us all," said Aradia, sitting quickly on a large rock. "But what does the rest of the world have to do with us? I can only see this a boon to the Amazons. If the rest of the world destroys itself, there will be no more armies trying to destroy *us*."

"Do you think you can separate yourselves from the world so easily, my Daughter?" asked the goddess, sternly. "You know better than anyone how the world encroaches upon you - even now. You will not be immune to the destruction. The Amazons, too, will destroy themselves from within, just as before when the Gorgons betrayed you."

"You're right, of course," said Aradia with a sigh. "That cannot happen. But how does competing against Myrina stop Ares from this world domination?"

"He believes he has a powerful ally in Medusa and in return for her assistance, he has offered her the Gorgons," said Artemis. "If Myrina is defeated, that lessens the appeal of the Gorgons as a 'prize'."

"And are the Gorgons such a prize?" asked Aradia, one eyebrow raised.

"If Ares believes that Medusa wants them, whatever her reasons may be, they are," said Artemis.

"But if she wants them regardless, it won't matter if I defeat Myrina or not," said Aradia, thoughtfully. "No there has to be more to it than that. I think Myrina - or even Ares wants your Sword. The trouble is, I don't have it."

"Ah yes, the Sword," said Artemis, smiling at her. "Do you know what powers the Sword conveys upon she who wields it?"

"I have heard stories," said Aradia, her voice taking a reverent hush. "I have heard that the Sword has the power to kill creatures no other weapon can touch. I have heard that the Sword bestows battle skills upon those who are not warriors. I have heard that it can cut through any armour like a knife through cheese and that so long as it is in the Amazons' hands, it protects *your* power."

"All of those things are true," said Artemis. "The Sword is a living entity in and of itself. But it is so much more. You, Aradia, *do* have my Sword."

"What do you mean?" asked the queen.

"Saraea holds the answer for you," said the goddess, smiling. "I want you to find it for yourselves and I have told you too much already. Only know this, my daughter - the magic which you doubt is real; it exists and it is within you and all of the Great Mother's children. Stand up for me against Ares, and you will find it."

As the goddess faded from her vision, Aradia realised that Artemis had neither waited for her answer to her request, nor had she given Aradia a real answer about the Sword.

Chapter Five : Visions of the Sword

With a sigh, Aradia stepped into the arena, taking up a wooden practice sword as she went and began drilling against a practice dummy.

Thraso arrived and watched her for a few moments. The queen moved with deadly grace and precision, "killing" the straw mannequin many times over. Thraso noticed that Aradia's eyes were empty of all life and spirit. It was as if the queen's body was a puppet and Aradia herself controlled the strings from somewhere far away. Her face held neither the passion nor the determination of the other Amazons in the arena, all involved in their own practice drills. Aradia moved as if by rote, though she made her killing strokes with a graceful flick or flourish.

The Second in Command waited until Aradia took a water break before approaching.

"I thought you weren't entering the competition?" she said, wiping the queen's face and neck with a linen towel.

"I wasn't, but I have it on excellent authority that Myrina is coming to challenge me," said Aradia, her voice quiet and devoid of emotion. She shook off her Second's ministrations with an annoyed sigh. "Sorry, Thraso, I'm not very good company right now. In fact, I'm downright lethal to be around." Aradia left to her treehouse. Thraso watched her walk away, then shook her head and picked up her practise sword to spar with some of the others who were practising in the arena - and to do a little strategic rumour control.

Aradia climbed the rope ladder and sat down at her table. The Tournament was tomorrow and she didn't want to fight. As soon as Artemis had asked her, though, her decision had made, despite her refusal. She had just needed the goddess's explanation to justify that decision.

"What am I?" she said to herself. "Do I really enjoy fighting and killing?" She put her head into her hands. "By the gods, what have I become?"

She wished for Thalia, but knew that her dead Second in Command would not come to her, not here. Perhaps in the old place, but not here where she had returned after becoming a monster. Rome had created her in its image - a murderer.

You don't have to kill her. Thalia's voice spoke in her head. Aradia jumped, looking around the treehouse. Thalia was nowhere to be seen.

"No surprise there," Aradia muttered to herself. Still, whether the words came from Thalia's spirit or from somewhere deep within her mind, buried there long before she had been tainted by Rome, they were true words.

The Tournament was intended to build morale among the Amazons. Already with the sudden forced re-location of the majority of the women, that goal was thwarted; yet Aradia still felt obligated to go through with hosting the games. She could not cancel them now, especially since sending the message which allowed Myrina to compete.

Aradia arose and began to pace. "I don't have to kill her," she said. "I wish I knew that were true. I just don't know if I can stop myself once I step into that space. Oh, Thalia, how I wish you were here with me! You could always make me see what I needed to see. You could always show me the light even in the darkest of situations. I need your vision and guidance now - oh, gods, I just need *you!*"

Aradia felt hot tears making her eyes and throat ache terribly. She sat down again and again lowered her head into her hands, holding the weeping at bay until the ache passed. Aradia dropped her hands from her hot face and went to bed feeling completely drained. She was so exhausted she was asleep as soon as her eyes closed.

The queen found herself walking through the forest. She looked down and saw to her mild surprise that she was completely naked. Still, she kept walking. The trees loomed huge and ancient over her head, creating a living canopy through which the light filtered, casting a greenish glow over everything. Small unseen creatures made their presence known to Aradia with their furtive hiding sounds in the brush and leaf covering and in the leafy tree tops above.

As she walked, Aradia became aware of the cool breeze caressing her skin like a lover. She smelled the gentle decay of the fallen leaves under her bare feet and the rich earth beneath the fallen leaves. She could hear the wind singing through the living green leaves high above her. She heard the twittering of birds and the buzzing of insects all around. Then she heard another sound that was not of the forest, but was still a part of this place. It was Thalia's voice singing a lullaby.

Aradia came upon her sitting on a rock. In her arms, she cradled the Sword of Artemis and crooned. She looked up as Aradia approached and smiled.

"Thalia, what are you doing?" asked the queen. "What is this place? Am I dreaming?"

"Perhaps you are, Aradia, but what are dreams?" said Thalia arising and approaching her.

"Leftover garbage from the waking day?" asked Aradia, shrugging.

"Sometimes, maybe," said Thalia with a chuckle. "Dreams are sometimes messages from our deeper mind, messages which our waking mind cannot always comprehend. Sometimes they are messages from the spirit realm or even the gods at times."

"So, are you here to give me a message?" asked Aradia, frowning.

"What do you think?" said Thalia.

"I think I would like a straight answer, Thalia," said Aradia impatiently.

"Dream messages aren't like that, Aradia," said Thalia, shaking her head slightly. "Haven't you ever noticed how distorted things are in dreams? And yet, within the dream, it all makes sense, even distorted."

"Only to be forgotten or confused again when the dreamer awakens," said Aradia, nodding in agreement.

"I'm sorry, Ari'; the answers you seek must come from within *you*. I cannot just tell you," said Thalia.

"What is the point of this dream?" asked Aradia, frowning.

"Perhaps I just missed you and needed to see you again," said Thalia.

"Thalia, I ..." began Aradia. She looked down and saw that she was wearing the tattered rags she had worn on her flight from Rome. "I miss you, too. A part of me died the day you did."

"I know Aradia, but that part must be resurrected - for my daughter's sake, if not your own," said Thalia. "You are her guardian now. I'm counting on you to help her realise her destiny."

"What destiny is that?" asked Aradia.

"That is yet to be written," said Thalia with a smile. "But I believe she is to be great."

"Of course," said Aradia, returning the smile. "She is your daughter."

"And now she is yours as well," said Thalia, handing the Sword of Artemis to Aradia. As soon as the Amazon Queen's hand touched the hilt, the Sword turned into a silver key.

"What ...?" said Aradia, turning the key over in her hand.

"Remember, Aradia - the symbol is the language of dreams, but the reality is life itself," said Thalia as a silver chariot drawn by a winged dragon appeared behind her. Thalia turned and walked toward the chariot then stopped and turned back to Aradia with a wistful smile. "Ari', please ... don't forget me - and please don't let my daughter forget me, either."

"Never," Aradia whispered, tears streaming from her violet eyes. Thalia turned again and stepped into the chariot which then flew off.

Aradia sat up in the dark of her treehouse, tears still flowing from her eyes, the key clutched in her left hand. She looked at it in wonder.

"What does it all mean?" she whispered into the dark.

)O(

Saraea felt her frustration with the Amazons growing. They had arisen just before dawn and she had been struggling with them for the better part of the morning. The Amazons were apprehensive about leaving the cover of the forest for the wide open fields which stood between them and their home.

"And I thought the hard part would be the climb," she commented to one of the warriors. "Does Initiation confer such cowardice?"

"Don't be so hard on them, Saraea," said the warrior with a sympathetic smile. "Most of them have been through all four of the hells since the battle of Chadesia. They have found their Amazon selves again and they are terrified of losing it."

"Amazons aren't afraid," said Saraea.

"On the contrary - most of us have known nothing but fear for the last ten years," said the warrior. "Fear of discovery by the Kaskans, mostly. But also fear of betrayal by a sister after the Gorgons' treachery. Fear of being abandoned by the goddess - they have known such fear and despair over the years. They have lived through it, though, and the last thing these women are is cowardly."

"I didn't know," said Saraea, quietly. "In the village, the Kaskans were terrible - and I think Silas was more afraid than I that they would learn who I really was, but I have never known such fear as they have. I'm sorry I judged them so harshly. But we still need to get moving - we'll never make the town before nightfall otherwise."

"I wonder what Aradia would do?" mused the warrior.

"Or even Thraso - she can always get the Amazons to do what needs to be done," said the girl, thoughtfully. "I'll go and talk to Mhari. We have to figure something out fast." The girl walked over to the shamaness, who was strapping a pack on her back. She stood amidst the elders, who were already packed up and ready.

"Ah, Saraea," said the older woman, smiling in delight at the sight of the girl. "We thought it might be easier if we went in groups - the elders are volunteering to go first."

"Artemis bless you, Mhari," said Saraea, relieved.

"Well, we thought if someone went first, it might help the others," said one of the elders. "And since we have the least to lose ..."

"Don't say that," said Saraea. "Nothing is going to happen to you - I won't let it. I'm going with you."

"Saraea, you - " began Mhari.

"No, I promised Aradia I would look out for you, Mhari - I'll come back and make the trip with each group, but I am going with you," said Saraea.

"As you wish, Child," said the shamaness with a sigh. "But by the end of the day, you will probably regret it."

Saraea moved swiftly through the Amazons, putting them in groups of one hundred and assigning a platoon of warriors to escort each group.

"There are groves of trees growing wild at the foot of the hills," said Saraea. "I want everyone to wait there until all the groups have come across the fields. We'll make the climb together."

Saraea stayed close by Mhari as they led the group of the elders, flanked by the platoon of warriors, across the wide open fields. The elders spoke rarely during their trek. They looked around the familiar surroundings with a quiet joy. They were coming home.

Saraea saw the group safely to the grove of hazelnut trees at the foot of the steep hills they must later climb, then returned for the next group. She looked back at the women and was struck with the thought that this was the last time most of those women would make the impending climb. She thought of Mhari and realised that the old shamaness would never again leave the town. Quickly, she brushed away the tears which sprang to her eyes before the warrior who had insisted upon accompanying her could see them.

The young girl made the trip back and forth seven more times. As Mhari predicted, she was utterly exhausted by the time all of the groups were in the trees, waiting to make the climb. By consensus, the Amazons decided to wait until dawn to climb the steep hills to their home and Saraea was grateful. It was dusk and they would have been foolish to try it in the growing darkness as tired as they all were. Instead, the women made a cold camp just below the hills. No fires were lit and most of the women were sleeping at least two to a bedroll. Saraea snuggled down next to Mhari, Hekau purring between them, sharing her feline warmth with the two.

Suddenly, Saraea was startled awake. She sat up and looked around, seeing the sentries patrolling the perimeter. With a sigh, she lay back down, but could not go back to sleep. Something was still not quite right. She sat up again and felt Mhari's chest. The slight rise and fall of her breathing eased the young girl's mind somewhat. Still, something was amiss, Saraea could feel it. She arose and walked over to one of the patrolling sentries, a woman she didn't recognise, which was strange.

"Princess," said the sentry, smiling at her.

"Just call me Saraea, please," said the girl.

"Very well. What are you doing awake?" asked the sentry.

"I don't know," said Saraea, frowning. "Something woke me, but I don't know what ..." She looked to see another sentry whom she didn't recognise approaching.

"Never mind - we're watching over you," said the first sentry, softly. "You will be safe. Right, Anu?"

"Very safe," said the second sentry. "Absolutely no one will pass by us."

"So you can rest easy, Little One," said the first sentry, gently brushing Saraea's hair out of her eyes.

"Okay," said Saraea, feeling suddenly very sleepy. She went back to her bedroll and curled up next to Hekau. The cat was sitting up, staring at the sentries on patrol with some intensity. Then she yawned and stretched. She walked over to the sentries, sniffing, then looked back at Saraea who was once again fast asleep.

"Hm, nice disguise, Lady," said the first sentry, bending to pet the cat. Hekau stretched once again, then stood up as the woman who had freed Aradia from the Gladiator barracks.

"Don't *ever* pet me, Thalia," said the woman, glaring. Then she broke into a grin. "It's one thing for those who know no better, but you do."

"Sorry, Lady," said Thalia returning the grin with a shrug.

"You Amazons," said the woman, shaking her head. "I love the way your reverence is so tempered with your mirth."

"You made us this way, Lady," said Anu.

"Yes, I did, though my reasons at the time escape me now," said the lady, smiling fondly at the two. "Dawn is near. I think they are safe enough now - you may go."

"Mother," said Thalia, glancing at the sleeping Saraea.

"Of course - go ahead, Daughter," said the lady, kindly. Thraso went to her daughter's bedroll and knelt, gently brushing the girl's dark hair away from her face and kissing her forehead. Mhari sat up, startled, then smiled.

"Careful - she'll see you," said the shamaness.

"She already did," whispered Thalia, looking wistfully at her daughter. "She just didn't recognise me. I thought she might but ..."

"She's young and untrained, Thalia," said Mhari.

"I know - but I'm sure you'll remedy the last," said Thalia, smiling.

"Perhaps," said Mhari, frowning. "If there is time. But as always, that will be for the goddess to decide."

"Of course," said Thalia. She arose and looked to the pinkening east. "I must go - good-bye, Mhari - I will see you again."

The warrior walked towards the brightening sky and disappeared from Mhari's sight. The shamaness sighed and lay back down to sleep, dreamlessly, until morning.

)O(

Aradia arose from her fitful sleep, unrested and unready for the day. Still, she got up, splashed water on her face and dressed in fighting leathers. Then she made her way to the armoury. Thraso intercepted her.

"Aradia, are you alright? You look terrible!" she said.

"Thanks," said Aradia, continuing on to the armoury, which was located next to the Tournament Arena.

"I'm sorry - I didn't mean it like that," said Thraso.

"I know," said Aradia, hefting a sword and swinging it experimentally. She set it down and picked up another. "Have the Gorgons arrived yet?"

"Not yet, but I have assigned a special group to greet them and escort them to the arena when they do," said Thraso.

"Good," said Aradia, testing yet another blade.

"Aradia are you alright?" asked Thraso. The queen sighed and looked at Thraso for a moment, then cast her attention back to choosing a weapon.

"I just want this over with," said Aradia, wearily. Thraso looked down quickly.

"Yeah, I know," she said with a sigh. "This isn't turning out like I thought it would - not at all."

Aradia blinked once, then looked again at her Second in Command. "I'm sorry, Thraso," she said.

"No, it's okay - I'm sorry this has become so screwed up," said Thraso. "Damn Gorgons - I hope we kick all of their collective asses - especially Myrina's."

"Well, I'll do my best," said Aradia hefting another sword and swinging it, just barely missing the messenger who came through the armoury door.

"Whoa, your majesty," she said with a slight chuckle. "Myrina's out *there*."

"They've arrived, then," said Aradia, nodding once.

"Not 'they', *she*," said the messenger.

"Myrina came alone? No honour guard? No Second?" said Thraso, frowning.

"Nope," said the messenger. "She's warming up now. We'll be starting soon?"

"Yes," said Aradia, nodding to Thraso.

"Right, let's get going," said the Second in Command, leaving the armoury with the messenger.

"Blessed solitude," Aradia whispered as she finally found a sword to suit her. "Alright Artemis - if I have to fight, so be it; if not, that would be even better."

The queen emerged from the armoury and made her way to her seat on a dais at the end of the arena. Aradia kept her disappointment to herself, knowing Thraso must be even more disappointed than she as she gazed out over the empty spectator seats. She scanned the faces of the few hundred remaining Amazons, all of whom were competing in the Tournament. There, standing a little apart from the rest of the women stood Myrina. Aradia looked appraisingly at the other warrior. She felt Thraso come up beside her and spoke without taking her eyes from her probable opponent.

"So that's Myrina," she said, admiring the woman's long, thick, wavy black hair and copper-coloured skin which sheathed the well-defined muscles of her limbs.

Thraso followed the direction of her queen's gaze and swallowed hard. She dropped her own eyes and spoke very quietly.

"Will you announce the games, my queen?"

Aradia looked at her, one eyebrow raised.

"Why don't you do the honours, Thraso? You've earned it," she said smiling at her. Thraso returned the smile and stepped forward. She raised her arms, calling for silence.

"Let us begin!" she cried and the Amazons cheered - all but Myrina. With a quick, business-like nod she took her place to the side to hear the contest rules and to await the calling of the first match.

She's going to make me wait for the inevitable, thought Aradia, grimly staring at the Gorgon. She saw Myrina looking at the dais as Aradia, the only spectator, took her seat. Thraso took charge of the games, announcing each match. All Aradia had to do was hand out the prizes to the winners. She glanced at the parchment in Thraso's hand on which she had written the roster of participants, including the Tribal mark of each, inscribed next to the names. Myrina was not yet paired up in a match.

"Thraso, what's going on?" asked Aradia, pointing out the discrepancy on the parchment.

Thraso frowned. "She hasn't declared a challenge against any of the others yet," said the warrior. Aradia sighed.

"She's counting on one of the Amazons to call her out on the basis of the betrayal," said Aradia, shaking her head.

"The Amazons know better," said Thraso. "They've all been ordered to be on their best behaviour around her - and especially since there seemed to be no Gorgons accompanying her."

"You think there's a trap? An ambush of some kind?" asked Aradia.

"What else can I think," said Thraso, quietly. "Sure wouldn't be the first time."

"No, it wouldn't," said Aradia, grimly. "Well, we are prepared for that, but I hope it doesn't come."

"So do I, Aradia," said Thraso, looking at Myrina. Aradia couldn't read what that look meant, but she believed that Thraso meant those words with all her heart.

As the day progressed, Aradia found her focus wandering from the contests before her to the sisters on the road to the old town. She worried for the elders and began to regret that she had made Saraea responsible for Mhari. If anything happened, the girl would be sure to blame herself. Aradia was waiting patiently for Myrina to make a move - something, anything to tell the queen why she was even here. *As* Ares's *champion, no less - what is she up to? And what does she hope to gain from Ares?* Aradia thought.

So far, the Gorgon had simply stood by the side, a little apart from the others, and watched the competitors critically.

"What is she doing, gauging our fighting strength so that she can attack us in the future?" asked Aradia.

"Maybe," said Thraso, grimly. "Though I would have never thought it of her - it's far too obvious."

"Hm," said Aradia, watching the Gorgon. "So, what do you think we should do? She came here to compete."

"Well, the way the Tournament is set up, she has to offer a challenge to one of the victors of the preceding matches," said Thraso.

"Why don't you go down there and talk to her," said Aradia. Thraso looked at her as if the queen had slapped her. "What? What's wrong? You said knew her before."

"I - I did," said Thraso. "But ... there's history between us. I don't think she'll tell me anything."

"You might be surprised," said Aradia. "Go and talk to her - consider it an order from your queen, Thraso," said Aradia, troubled. She couldn't have her Second in Command intimidated by a potential enemy - no matter what the history between them.

Thraso met Aradia's violet eyes with her own dark brown ones for an instant. Aradia read defiance there, as if Thraso was considering refusing the order from her queen. Then Thraso looked away towards Myrina, her jaw setting in determination. "As you wish - my queen," she said and left Aradia, making her way to where Myrina stood. Aradia felt bereft at that moment, as if she had just lost something precious and irretrievable, though she couldn't say what - or why.

As Thraso made her way from the dais to where Myrina stood, her heart pounded and her ears burned. She felt angry with Aradia, though she couldn't say just why - maybe it was the not so subtle reminder of their respective ranks. It wasn't like Aradia to just throw it around like that. Thraso sighed. Aradia was right. She was the queen and Thraso her Second in Command. There was more at stake here than Thraso's personal feelings. Hadn't Aradia just made that painfully clear?

Painfully - yes, Thraso was hurt, stung by Aradia's apparent disregard for her feelings, but the queen was right - they had to find out why Myrina was here and the Gorgon would be far more likely to reveal her purpose to Thraso than to Aradia.

As Thraso neared, Myrina looked up, her honey-coloured eyes unreadable. Then the Gorgon grinned at her.

"I was beginning to think the Amazons weren't going to acknowledge me until they dragged me down there to tear me apart," she said, chuckling. Thraso smiled back.

"Nah," she said, stopping a few feet away. "We won't tear you apart - at least not until we're sure that your warriors aren't waiting in the trees to attack as soon as we make a move."

Myrina raised an eyebrow, not sure if her old friend was kidding. "Is that what you think?"

"Of course not," said Thraso. "We already scoured the area - you're the only Gorgon around for miles."

"Figures," said Myrina, shaking her head.

"What did you expect?' said Thraso, stepping a bit closer. "Why are you here, Myrina?"

"To compete," said the Gorgon with a shrug.

"With whom?" asked Thraso, producing the roster and unrolling it. "You haven't declared a challenge against any of the victors."

"Yet," said Myrina, scanning the contestants who had ceased for a water break.

"So who do you like?" said Thraso nodding towards the circle of warriors, milling around the water carrier.

"You want to wager?' asked Myrina.

"No," said Thraso. "That's hardly fair - I know these women. You don't. I just want to know who you're planning to fight."

"I don't know yet - I haven't seen anyone who can offer me a challenge," said Myrina with a shrug.

"Blessed Artemis, Myrina - your *hybris* hasn't shrunk an iota," said Thraso, angrily. Her only reply was another shrug. "Aradia could kick your ass from here back to Hesperia."

"But Aradia isn't competing, is she?' said Myrina.

"Say the word," said Thraso, hotly.

"Fine, 'the word'," said Myrina.

"Oh, you are impossible!" said Thraso, calming a bit.

"Does Aradia really want to fight me?" asked Myrina, looking intently at Thraso.

"No, she doesn't - Aradia doesn't want to fight anyone in the arena again," said Thraso with a sigh. "But she will if she has to."

"What about you?" asked Myrina. "What do you want?"

"I - me?" said Thraso, frowning. "I never thought about it."

"Yeah, I know," said Myrina. She gazed off into the trees. "All I want is to go home. I miss Hesperia. I've been here since I was a kid and all I can ever think of is the lake."

"Why don't you, then? Go home, I mean?" asked Thraso. Myrina looked at her with a sad smile.

"I would - but the Romans stand in our way," said Myrina. "They are determined to take Amazons back to Rome - it isn't safe for any Amazon or Gorgon on the road."

Thraso frowned, thinking of the Amazon exodus to the old town.

"What?" said Myrina.

"Nothing," said Thraso. "I - I hope you get home safely." She turned to leave.

"Wait." Myrina placed a hand on Thraso's arm to stop her. Thraso felt her skin tingling under the Gorgon's touch. Her face flushed and she kept her eyes down.

"For Goddess's sake, Myrina, let me go," said Thraso, not looking at her. Her voice was the merest whisper.

Myrina nodded and took her hand away. She watched Thraso walk back to Aradia.

"I already have," she said, too softly for Thraso to hear her.

"Usually when the god of war chooses a champion, it's because she's a fighter - not a lover," said Ares, materialising behind the Gorgon. "Which are you, Myrina?" The Gorgon started and turned around.

"What are you - ?" she began. The god put up one hand.

"Don't worry - you're the only one who can see or hear me," he said.

"There's no one here worth fighting," said Myrina, looking pointedly at the group of contestants who were playfully fighting over the drinking gourd.

"Aradia is sitting right there," said Ares, pointing to the queen on the dais, watching the Amazons in amusement. "Challenge her now - your patron commands it." Ares disappeared. Myrina rolled her eyes and turned towards the dais. "I saw that," she heard behind her. Myrina turned swiftly, but Ares was not to be seen. Still, she could sense him watching her.

With a sigh, Myrina stepped into the centre of the arena before the next match was called. The Amazons, warned not to confront her except in competition, watched in silence, waiting to see what she would do. All that could be heard was the wind through the trees. Myrina looked up at the dais, her eyes meeting Thraso's for a moment before she turned her attention to Aradia.

"I offer a challenge," she said. Aradia arose and stood in anticipation of the Gorgon's next words.

"Name your opponent," said Thraso, stepping forward. A slow grin spread over Myrina's face.

"I choose you, Thraso," she said.

Thraso's eyes widened and Aradia stepped back, chuckling.

"What the hells is so funny?" whispered Thraso.

"Nothing - it's just pure relief," said Aradia, sitting back down.

"What am I supposed to do?" asked Thraso, still whispering.

"Go kick her ass - in my name and with my blessings," said Aradia, still smiling in amusement. "To the glory of Artemis."

Thraso set her lips in a grim line and unsheathed her sword, flipping it upright in a swift, practiced move.

"You got it, Aradia," she said, then raised her voice and called out to Myrina, "In the name of Aradia, queen of the Amazons and to the glory of Artemis, I accept your challenge."

The Amazons cheered as Thraso stepped down from the dais and entered the arena. She joined Myrina in the centre of the arena and turned, saluting the queen. Aradia returned the salute and Thraso turned to face her opponent.

"Are you absolutely sure about this?" she asked Myrina. The Gorgon replied with a curt nod and unsheathed her own sword.

"In the name of Ares, I am pledged to fight," she said.

"Ares?" said Thraso, wrinkling her brow in puzzlement. "What has Ares to do with anything?"

"I'm his champion," said Myrina, circling.

"What?" said Thraso as Myrina lunged, thrusting her sword at her. Thraso stepped neatly aside, evading the sword by a wide sweep. "What are you talking about?"

"Ares said if I would enter this Tournament as his champion, he would see that the Gorgons got safe passage back to Hesperia," said Myrina. "Now would you please try and make this look good?"

"I can't believe you!" said Thraso, angrily. "You sold out!" She went in, slashing and lunging. Myrina evaded every strike, smiling at her.

"That's more like it," she said, causing Thraso to fight even more fiercely. Myrina had to concentrate just to parry her blows. Finally Thraso found an opening in Myrina's defence and opened a wide gash across the Gorgon's cheek, ending the match by drawing first blood.

"I hate you!" Thraso cried, throwing down her sword and running out of the arena. Myrina watched her go. She raised her hand and felt the blood dripping down her neck.

"Well, this scar should just about match the one I gave you - on your heart," she whispered after the retreating warrior. She turned to the dais and bowed to Aradia, conceding her defeat before leaving the arena and the village of the Amazons to return to the Gorgons.

Chapter Six: The Sword Comes Home

Aradia watched her Second in Command leave the arena in tears. She fought the impulse to run after her. Instead, she ran the rest of the Tournament. Myrina left, escorted by two sentries to the boundary of the tree village. She had refused Aradia's offer to have a healer look at her wound and left without another word. Aradia sighed in relief at her departure. The Tournament ended shortly after that match. All of the Amazon amulets were distributed amongst the contestants - all except Thraso and Myrina. As soon as she was able to leave, Aradia sought out her Second.

"Hey," she said, entering Thraso's tree house.

Thraso was sitting at her table, staring down at her hands which were folded in front of her. She looked up, startled. Her travelling gear was packed and sitting on the table before her.

"Oh!" she said. "It's over then?"

"Yes - after your match with Myrina, the rest of the matches were rather anti-climactic."

"I'm sorry," said Thraso, casting her eyes back down at her hands. Aradia sat at the table across from her Second in Command.

"What you did out there was very brave, Thraso," she said.

"Not really - I got angry," said Thraso, not looking up. Aradia gently lifted her chin and looked into her eyes.

"Yes, really," said Aradia. "I know that was hard for you, even being angry. You fought your heart for your integrity."

"She sold out - to Ares," said Thraso bitterly. Tears sprang to her deep brown eyes and Thraso struggled to keep them from spilling over. "That's bad enough, but then she just ... expected me ... to take a fall for her! I can't believe her! How could she do that?"

"But you didn't, Thraso," said Aradia.

"How could I?" asked Thraso. "I was fighting in *your* name and for the glory of Artemis."

"You are an Amazon - you couldn't," said Aradia, simply. "By the way, you forgot your prize."

"I don't need - " began Thraso as Aradia opened her tunic and removed her own amulet, placing it over Thraso's head.

"I can't take your amulet," said Thraso looking at her in surprise.

"Yes you can," said Aradia, firmly. "Please, I want you to. This isn't actually my Initiation amulet - that one was lost in the Battle of Chadesia. This was a replacement I made on my way home from Rome. Besides, I have Thalia's - and I have this." She showed Thraso the silver key which she now wore around her neck on a thin silken cord.

"What is that?" asked Thraso.

"The Sword of Artemis," said Aradia.

"I - I don't understand," said Thraso frowning as Aradia put it back inside of her tunic.

"Neither do I really," said Aradia, placing her hand over Thraso's and looking hopefully into her eyes. "But I was hoping maybe we could work for that understanding ... together?"

Thraso smiled slightly and nodded, wiping tears from her eyes. "I'd like that," she said. Aradia squeezed her hand, then rose. "I see you're packed and ready - let's get the rest of them ready to go - I want to be on the road before the sun moves much more."

"Sounds great - it will be good to get home," said Thraso looking wistfully about her tree house.

"You built this village, Thraso," said Aradia, understanding.

"Yeah - but it never felt like home," said Thraso. She looked at Aradia, understanding dawning in her eyes. She smiled and shook her head. "That's what Myrina was fighting for - to go home. She said Ares promised her and the rest of the Gorgons safe passage through the Romans back to Hesperia if she would be his champion in this Tournament."

"She doesn't need Ares for that," said Aradia with a frown.

"She thinks she does," said Thraso. "I guess I just expected her to be an Amazon instead of a Gorgon. I was hurt and disappointed when she showed me otherwise."

"I'm proud of you, Thraso," said Aradia. "Insight like that shows wisdom."

"Not really," said Thraso. "I'm more disappointed in myself than in her. And tonight, when I'm lying in my bedroll under that vast, empty black night sky, I will be feeling guilt for not helping her. She has no one."

Aradia looked thoughtful for a moment.

"Perhaps that's why she's more Gorgon than Amazon," she said, feeling the silver key growing warmer between her breasts. "Can you believe I'm only just realising this?"

"What?" asked Thraso.

"The Amazons - Goddess love 'em - they're always around," said Aradia with a chuckle. "Even when they're not here, they're here. I haven't been truly alone since I got here."

"I don't think I understand," said Thraso.

"Because you've *never* been alone - you kept the heart of the Amazon Nation alive, right here," said Aradia. She went out to the porch and looked over the wooden railing at the Amazons all walking about, preparing for the journey to the old town. "The hub of the wheel, right here."

"I'm still not sure I'm getting you, Aradia, but I know we better get on the road," said Thraso, lifting her pack to her shoulder. "Myrina did say that Romans were all over and the road was safe for no Amazon or Gorgon. I'm worried about the others. We have no way of being sure they've made it to the old town."

"Have a little faith," said Aradia, feeling giddy for some reason. "They did. But there is more danger on this journey than Roma. Be sure of that."

"Like what?" asked Thraso, alarmed. She could think of no greater danger than Rome now that the Kaskans were gone.

"I don't know - just be prepared for anything," said Aradia.

)O(

Saraea looked about at the Amazons as they prepared to make the climb to the old town. Warriors had already unpacked ropes and other climbing equipment. The morning was cold and after a night out, sleeping on the ground, Saraea noticed some of the elders leaning more heavily upon their walking sticks. After her exertions the previous day, she could empathise.

"Well, Princess - sorry, I mean Saraea, how do you propose we get that lot up there?" asked a warrior approaching.

"I'm not sure, Anaea," said the girl. "What do you think? Mhari made the climb a couple of weeks ago. Perhaps the others are just as capable."

"Not after spending the night in this chill," said Anaea, shaking her head. "Even I'm stiff and I'm less than half as old as most of them."

"Yeah, I know what you mean," said Saraea, frowning.

Anaea chuckled and slapped her on the shoulder good-naturedly. "Multiply that by every day for as old as those women are and you'll have a pretty good idea how they're feeling right about now," she said.

"Okay," said Saraea, thoughtfully. "How about this - we send two platoons of our strongest warriors up first - that way, they can make sure the coast is still clear. Then we rig the ropes into some kind of ladders or nets or something and carry them over the roughest bits?"

"Pretty good - but they won't have it," said Anaea. "They are still Amazons, after all."

"Well, of course they are, but ... oh, I think I see what you mean," said Saraea as she saw several of the elders pulling ropes and other gear out of their packs. "Well, they're not stupid - surely they can see the sense of not climbing when we can all help them."

"Sure they can, Princess," said Anaea, laughing. "I wish you luck - the elders are a fractious lot when you get their backs up. I'll get the warriors moving. We'll have a couple of platoons in place by mid-day. By then maybe the elders will be a bit less stiff."

Anaea left to organise the warriors as Saraea sighed and made her way over to Mhari.

"Are we ready, Youngling?" she asked Saraea with a smile.

"Not yet - a couple of platoons are going up first - to scout around and then to help everyone else up," said Saraea, pointedly.

"Ah, I see," said Mhari, her eyes twinkling. "You think older bones are more fragile."

"Aren't they?" asked the girl.

"Of course they are," Mhari declared. "Unfortunately, so are older egos."

"That's what Anaea was saying," said Saraea, troubled. "What do we do, Mhari?"

"We argue and fight until the old hens see the reason behind being carried up the mountain," said Mhari, drily.

"There has to be a better way than that," said Saraea. "The warriors will be in place by mid-day. I have to find a way to convince them by then."

"Well, I'll do all I can, Child, but by mid-day, the older bones will be a bit less stiff and the older egos just the opposite," said Mhari.

"Can they make the climb?" asked Saraea.

"Probably, but it isn't worth the risk, just for pride - if the warriors are willing to carry me up, then by Artemis I am willing to be carried," said Mhari.

The Amazons milled about until Anaea sent the signal that all was clear in the lower town. They rigged up ropes into ladders and slings and Amazons began the climb. Saraea hung back with the remaining warriors until it was time to bring up the group of elders. Several opted for the ladders, but many did allow themselves to be hauled up in the slings, including Mhari. She stood by Saraea, waiting until all the other elders were safely up in the lower town.

"Wish me luck, Dear," said Mhari with a kiss to Saraea's cheek. The young woman sighed with relief as she watched Mhari's ascent, then gasped. The anchor rope was dragging over a sharp outcropping and the strands began to fray, then snap.

"No!" Saraea screamed as suddenly the old shamaness fell. The girl ran to her, clambering down into the grassy depression in which Mhari had fallen.

"Mhari, are you alright?" she asked as several of the warriors who were waiting until everyone had made it to the lower town followed her.

Mhari lay still and unmoving. Saraea stood frozen with fear not knowing what to do. She knelt beside Mhari, tears rolling down her cheeks, afraid to touch the older woman.

"Mhari, please, *please* wake up!" she cried until the shamaness stirred slightly.

"Saraea," she whispered. "My herb pouch, please."

Saraea, her heart pounding in her chest, rushed to where the pouch had fallen and handed it to Mhari. Mhari reached in, hands trembling, and pulled out a pinch of something which she placed under her tongue. Then the shamaness lay still again.

Saraea turned to the warriors.

"We need to get some of the branches from the trees over there and make a litter," she said.

"We'll need to immobilise her first - we can't risk any broken bones being jarred or moved about any more than necessary," said one of the warriors.

"Oh, okay," said Saraea, biting her lip as the warriors took over, first immobilising the shamaness with branches and ropes, then building a litter and rigging it securely to lift Mhari up the steep incline into the lower town.

"You next, Princess," said one of the warriors.

"I can climb it," said Saraea.

"I know, but this is faster and she'll be wanting you close, Little Sister," said another of the warriors.

"Alright," agreed the girl. She allowed the warriors to tie the ropes into a kind of sling and hoist her over the sharp rocks and steep drop-offs. Saraea made the ride with her eyes closed most of the way until she felt her feet bump the ground and several of the warriors already in the lower town untied her. Saraea thanked them and ran to Mhari's side.

"Mhari, are you alright?" she asked, worried.

"Don't pucker your brow so, dear - it isn't becoming," said Mhari, smiling at her. "I'll be fine. Just get me to my house so I can be comfortable."

"Of course," said Saraea, signalling to two warriors. She directed them to carry the litter up the steps to the upper town.

"In a minute - we haven't got the all clear from the scouts yet," Anaea told her.

"What are they doing, walking through every building up there?' asked the girl impatiently.

"As a matter of fact, yes," said Anaea.

"We are Amazons - surely we can handle any threat ourselves - let the women go up and check out their own houses," said Saraea. "We can't let ourselves be scared and hide behind our warriors for every little thing."

"You're right," said Anaea nodding in approval. "Well spoken, little sister. But I will check the shamaness's house for her myself, alright?"

"Yes, of course," said Mhari, smiling. "Since I am a trifle incapacitated at the moment."

"Yes, of course," said Saraea nodding as Anaea ran up the steps to the upper town.

"Mhari, why don't you stay in Aradia's house with me - just until she gets here?" asked the young girl.

"Still afraid of ghosts?' said the shamaness with a chuckle.

"Yes, but I'm more afraid that *you'll* be a ghost if you are alone right now," said Saraea, troubled. "I'm so sorry - I promised Aradia I would watch out for you - I let you both down."

"Oh, Great Mother in Heaven!" exclaimed Mhari.

"What? Are you in pain?" asked Saraea, worried.

"Yes a very great deal, but that is not the point - this isn't your fault - that was a brilliant idea, with the ropes Child," said Mhari. "If you hadn't carried those you did, there would have been a lot more injuries. I think Aradia will be very proud of you."

"But you got hurt, Mhari," said the girl.

"Child put that right out of your mind - I will be fine," said the shamaness. "Just as soon as I get settled in."

"Alright, Mhari," said Saraea. "But will you stay with Aradia and me - just until you're well?"

"I will stay with *you* until Aradia comes - then you will come over and help me out every day in my house until I am able to get around again," said the shamaness. "I didn't come all this way to live with others. I am coming home - and that means *my* home."

"As you wish, Mhari," said Saraea with a sigh.

Anaea joined them then.

"Mhari, we're going to carry you up the stairs - if you have anything in your herb pouch to help you with the pain, I suggest you take it now," she said. "The stairs are in good shape, but it may still be a rough trip up."

"Just make it quick," said the shamaness, closing her eyes.

"Alright," said Anaea, signalling to a group of warriors. They hefted the litter up on their shoulders and started up the stairs. Saraea followed. The carried the shamaness to the queen's house and gently set her before the cold hearth.

"The beds are in pretty bad shape - rodents and bugs, you know," said Anaea.

"Yeah, but Hekau will take care of that for us," said Saraea. "Hey, where is Hekau?"

"The cat?" said Anaea, frowning. "I don't know - she was in the lower town a few minutes ago. She's around."

Saraea nodded. "Okay - in the meantime, I'll get some wood for the fire," she said.

"We can do that for you, Princess," said another of the warriors. "We're already bringing your packs and bedding up from the lower town."

"I can get the packs and things," said Saraea, frowning.

"They're already on the way," said Anaea. She winked at Saraea. "Get used to it, Princess - we're home now. Things will be getting back to normal for us, but your life will never be the same again. No one here has forgotten that it was you who killed Yarg. Defeating the Kaskans is what has allowed us all to come home here."

"It wasn't like that," said Saraea, quietly. "I'm not really a princess. I'm just Saraea ..." *And I'm still not even sure I want to be an Amazon,* she finished the thought silently.

"I'm only telling you how the Amazons feel," said Anaea. "You'll get used to it in time."

"If you say so," said Saraea, doubtfully. "Does everyone have a place to sleep tonight?"

"Yes," said Anaea, nodding. "We're six to a house for now, but after we rebuild the fortress in the lower town, we'll have a lot more space."

"You really think you can re-build that pile of rubble?' asked Saraea.

"Of course - the foundation is of stone and it's still in place," said Anaea. "The bricks are easy to make. We have the craftswomen here and as soon as we clean out the kilns, we'll be ready to go."

"Sounds like a lot of work," said Saraea.

"Nah, not if we all pull together," said Anaea. "We can have it ready to move in by the next full moon, weather permitting."

"When will you start?" asked Saraea.

"Soon as the craftswomen get the kilns fired up - why, you want to help, Little Sister?" said Anaea.

"Sure," said Saraea. "You said if we *all* pull together, it'll be less work, right?"

"I sure did," said Anaea, smiling and putting an arm around Saraea's shoulders.

"Saraea," said Mhari from the litter. "Go find your friend Momi and go exploring - Anaea, I'm sure we can find a couple of warriors to escort the girls, right?"

"Of course," said Anaea, releasing the girl.

"Mhari, I can't - " began Saraea.

"Go!" Mhari ordered. "Just be back before sundown."

"Alright, Mhari, if you're sure," said Saraea, turning to leave.

"I am - can't breathe with you hovering over me," said the old shamaness.

"I'll just go assign some warriors to - " began Anaea starting to follow the girl out the door.

"Wait a minute - would you mind going and bringing Alkaia to me here?" asked Mhari, for the first time allowing the terrible pain she felt to show in her eyes.

"You want Alkaia? The - " began Anaea, concerned.

"Yes, please," said Mhari, closing her eyes, wearily.

"Of course, Mhari," said Anaea. "Let me just get a fire started for you - "

"No, you'd better hurry, Anaea," said Mhari, quietly.

"Damn! Of course I will," said the warrior leaving her.

Mhari lay on the litter, immobilised, but still in agony. She had heard the bone crack when she hit the ground and knew that something was broken. She only hoped her old friend Alkaia could help. Alkaia was one of the elders. She had begun training in Ephesus to be a priestess, but had to cut that training short when the city of the goddess fell to the Persians. Still, she was the closest thing to a healer besides Mhari herself the Amazons had.

"Damn is right," said the shamaness, grimacing in pain. She saw Hekau enter the house through the window. "Ah, there you are. Your young mistress was looking for you - have you come to keep me company, then?"

The cat meowed and lay down next to Mhari, gently pressing her warm furry body next to the old woman's and began to purr. Mhari felt a sensation of warmth begin to spread throughout her body as she stroked the cat's long, soft fur. The shamaness drifted off to sleep.

That was how Anaea and Alkaia found her later when they entered the house. Hekau arose, stretched and left her soft sleeping place atop Mhari's chest. She walked over to the hearth, looked pointedly at Anaea, then began to wash.

"I guess the cat wants a fire," said the warrior with a chuckle. "Let me get that going." She left the house to gather some wood and returned to see Mhari sitting up, Alkaia next to her, shaking her head.

"You old fool - you just sprained your back," said Alkaia, pulling Mhari to her feet. "Hurts like all four of the hells, I know, but you'll be fine a couple of weeks. Anaea, after you get that fire going, will you bring water down from the cistern for some tea? Going to be a cold night."

"Of course," said Anaea. "It's going now, so I'll bring some skins." Sensing the elders wanted to be alone, she left swiftly and dawdled on her way, checking in with the sentries she had posted earlier.

"What is all this foolishness?" asked Alkaia as she helped Mhari into a chair before the hearth. "It's that girl, isn't it?"

"What do you mean?" asked Mhari.

"Too much coddling on her part," said Alkaia shaking her head as she tucked a shawl around Mhari's lap. "You need to teach her that age does not detract from the Amazon Spirit."

"It isn't coddling," said Mhari, gently slapping Alkaia's hands away. "She's always been very respectful, even in the village."

"Yes, Silas did very well with her in that respect," Alkaia said, taking the chair across from the shamaness.

"Silas did very well with her in every respect," said Mhari.

"Yes, given the circumstances," admitted Alkaia, grudgingly. "If only the Kaskans had never come."

"But they did," said Mhari.

"Yes, they did, indeed," said Alkaia, shaking her head. "But if they hadn't, how different things would be. The lost potential of that child ..."

"What do you mean?" asked Mhari.

"I mean, who she is - or rather could have been," said Alkaia.

"We don't talk about that," Mhari warned. "She is who she is - Thalia's daughter and Aradia's protégée."

"I have no intention of talking about it," said Alkaia. "It just saddens me that there is no one left alive to train her as she should be trained. Leilë was the last Amazon priestess. It's a shame that a girl with her heritage and talent will be a warrior."

"Saraea is no warrior," said Mhari, shaking her head.

"She killed Yarg," argued Alkaia.

"That was a fluke," said Mhari. "You and I will have to train her and that's all there is to it."

"Mhari don't be a fool - I don't have the knowledge to train a priestess - and what little I did have, I've forgotten," said Alkaia.

"You said yourself that Leilë was the last Amazon priestess," said Mhari. "There is no one else. And we do have the scrolls."

"You do?" said Alkaia, her eyes wide. "Wherever did you find them? I risked life and limb to carry those through the Persian lines, but I haven't seen them since I gave them over to the old priestess for safekeeping."

"Aradia found them below the altar in the Temple - she's had Saraea and her little friend copying them for a while. By now I should imagine that the girls have read through almost all of them," said Mhari.

"Blessed Mother, but that's wonderful!" said Alkaia, her eyes shining.

"So, with the scrolls, do you think you could train an Amazon priestess?' asked Mhari, her own blue eyes twinkling.

"By the Sword of Artemis, I would certainly like to try," said Alkaia. "When do we start?"

"We already have, my dear friend," said Mhari, chuckling. "Or should I say Saraea has already begun her training?"

"Yes, having read the scrolls will certainly help," said Alkaia, relieved. She looked to the shamaness and smiled. "We're really doing it, aren't we, Sister? We're really going to re-build the Nation, one Amazon at a time."

"Oh, yes," said Mhari, wistfully looking off into the distance. "We'll begin it, anyway."

"What do you see, Mhari?" asked Alkaia, softly. She recognised the look as the beginning of a trance.

"It will be long in coming, but the Amazons will rise again," said the shamaness. "We won't live to see the great glory days to come, but we will be part of bringing it about."

"And that is enough, my old friend," said Alkaia, gently patting Mhari's hand.

Just then, Saraea and her friend Momi came into the house.

"Mhari! You're up!" the girl cried with delight. "Oh, and there's Hekau!"

She set down a basket she had been carrying and went first to Mhari, kissing her cheek, then to her cat. She picked up the tabby and cuddled her.

"What's in the basket, Youngling?" asked Alkaia.

"Pomegranates," said Momi, lifting one out of the basket. "There's a whole grove of them in the lower town. The warriors promised to keep the trees even when they re-build the fortress."

"Pomegranates and hazelnuts," said Alkaia, shaking her head. "Well, we won't exactly starve."

"Actually, the women who worked the fields before answering the call back said that much of our grain crop is still growing wild," said Saraea. "So eventually we'll have bread as well. And there is still plenty of game - in fact, I was going ask if I might go out and try for a rabbit for the stew pot?"

"No, Child," said Mhari, her eyes clearing. "It's too close to dark. The days when our younglings could gad about at night are gone, alas."

"They will come again," said Alkaia, nodding.

"Hm, in the meantime, the pomegranates will add a nice break from the journey bread," said Mhari, looking at her old friend sharply. "You may hunt tomorrow if you wish, but only if a warrior goes with you."

"How long do I have to have a babysitter following me around?" asked Saraea, glumly.

"How does forever sound?" said Aradia, entering the house.

"Aradia!" cried Saraea, running to her guardian.

"Hey, what's all this?" asked the queen, nodding towards the abandoned litter still on the floor.

"That was my fault," said Saraea, looking at the floor. "Mhari was hurt."

"Nonsense," said Mhari, rising from her chair to greet Aradia with an embrace. "I'm fine."

"Hm," said Aradia, looking around her house. "It's cosier than I remember."

Anaea came in with the water skins. "Oh! My queen - how did the Tournament go?" she asked, surprised to see her.

"Don't ask," said Aradia, shaking her head. "Just be glad you weren't there."

"Damn Gorgons make trouble?" asked the warrior, her eyes narrowing.

"Nothing Thraso couldn't handle," said Aradia, setting her gear down on the table next to the basket of pomegranates.

Alkaia arose. "Well, I'm off," she said. She looked around. "It's good to be home."

"Yes, it is," said Aradia. "It'll take a bit of work, but I think once we're all settled, things will be good here."

"Indeed they will," said Alkaia with an enigmatic grin to Mhari as she left the house. "Come, Momi, walk me back to my house."

The girl waved good-bye to Saraea. "See you tomorrow," she said, following the elder out of the house.

"What did Alkaia mean by that?" asked the queen.

"I've no idea," said Mhari, sitting back down wearily.

"Are you sure you're alright?" asked Aradia, kneeling next to the chair and looking at the shamaness with concern. "What happened, anyway?"

"It was my idea," said Saraea, quietly looking down at the floor. "I had the warriors rig up the ropes to help the elders over the worst part of the climb. One of the ropes broke and Mhari fell."

"But it's just a sprain - I'd have had a lot worse if I tried to climb it myself," said Mhari, smiling at the young girl.

"Well, I think that's a brilliant idea, Saraea - how did you get the rest of the elders to go along?" asked Aradia, rising to her feet.

"I - I don't know - they just did," said Saraea, shrugging.

"Oh, no they didn't," said Mhari, chuckling. "This youngling had those old hens tying rope ladders, then she had warriors stationed along the cliff tying anchor ropes to the elders as they climbed - those who were foolish to refuse the sling ride, that is."

"I - I just wanted to make sure they all made it without hurting their pride," said Saraea. "They are still Amazons, after all."

"Well, if we don't make a queen of you, Saraea, at the very least, we'll have an excellent diplomat on our hands," said Aradia, smiling. "Come on now, I'm hungry. Anaea, come out hunting with me."

"It will be my pleasure, my Queen," said the warrior, smiling. They left the house and Saraea began to put the water on to boil.

"Can I make you some tea, Mhari?" she asked.

"That would be very nice, Saraea," said the shamaness. "Then why don't you light some lamps?"

"I don't think Aradia has any," said the girl, doubtfully.

"Well, look about before it gets dark. There's lamp oil in the packs," said Mhari.

"Okay," said Saraea, going to do as Mhari bade her. She went into the largest bedroom and looked around. There was a large square, clean of dust where the chest Aradia had emptied to carry the scrolls had sat for the last decade. In the room were several other chests and a wardrobe. Saraea decided to check the trunks first.

She began rummaging through one of them, then jumped back with a squeak as she put her hand into a nest of baby mice.

"Ew, ick!" she said, wiping her hand on her trousers, though there was nothing on that hand. She could still feel the squirming naked little vermin, though. "Hekau, where are you?" she muttered eyeing the chest with a look of disgust.

"Hey," she heard and looked up at the window. It was open just a crack and Saraea went to it and opened it all the way.

"Julisa! What are you doing here? How did you get away from the Graii?" asked the girl.

"Long story. Listen, the Sword of Artemis is in that cave - the Graii are guarding it, but it's there," said Julisa, climbing in through the window and brushing the grime from her clothes.

"You need to talk with Aradia," said Saraea.

"No," said Julisa, shaking her head. "Aradia doesn't trust me. It has to be just you and me, Saraea."

"Are you crazy? No way," said Saraea.

"Saraea, listen to me," said the other girl. "You wounded that thing - no one else could get a hit in - doesn't that tell you something?"

"Yeah - I'm lucky to be alive," said the girl. "There's no way I'm going back there, Sword of Artemis or no Sword of Artemis."

"Hey, fine," said Julisa, shrugging. "I just thought since you're the one who lost it in the first place, you might want to be the one to get it back. You know that no matter what Aradia tells you, she's going to be mad at you for losing it until it's back where it belongs."

"Saraea!" Mhari called from the other room.

Saraea froze.

"Make up your mind Saraea," said Julisa, hands on her hips.

"I'm coming Mhari," Saraea called back.

"What's it going to be?" asked Julisa.

"Wait here a minute, will you?" said Saraea, grabbing a clay lamp from the small table beside the bed.

"I can't," said Julisa. "I can't be seen here - the Amazons will kill me. After what Myrina did at that Tournament, all Gorgons are fair game to the Amazons - but you could change that, Saraea."

"How?" asked Saraea.

"Bring back the Sword of Artemis - don't you see? It's the only way to make the Nation whole again," said Julisa, pleadingly.

"Saraea, what are you doing?" Mhari called.

"I - I'm looking for lamps," Saraea called back. "Alright - meet me in the Temple at moonrise."

She ran out of the room before Mhari could come looking for her.

"Oh, I'll be there alright," said Ares softly, dropping his disguise. The god threw back his head and laughed as he faded from the house.

Saraea ran back to Mhari with her one clay lamp.

"This was all I could find," she said, breathless.

Mhari frowned. "Why are you out of breath, Child?' she asked.

"Oh, there were these baby mice - they startled me," said Saraea, not meeting the shamaness's sharp eyes with her own.

"Were you bitten?" asked Mhari.

"Oh, no - they were just - icky, you know," said Saraea, carefully pouring the lamp oil from the small flask into the clay lamp and lighting the wick.

"Very well, why don't you take that one and go look for more - I know Aradia had more than just the one," said Mhari, shaking her head.

"Well, they *are* made of clay, Mhari - maybe they got broken," said Saraea.

"Saraea, will you please just go and look," said Mhari, exasperated.

"Alright," said the girl with a sigh. She picked up the lamp and went to a smaller bedroom next to the largest. She couldn't help but peek to see if Julisa was still there, but wasn't surprised to see the other girl had left.

In the smaller room, there was only one chest at the foot of the tiny bed.

"That's weird," said Saraea to herself. "That's like a little kid's bed." She shrugged, assuming that it must have been there from before Aradia became queen.

Maybe it was Aradia's bed when she was little, the girl thought, opening the chest.

She looked very carefully before putting her hand inside of this one. Finding no "beasties", she began to gingerly move things around. The trunk was filled with baby clothes, everything from swaddling strips and moth-eaten little blankets to toddler-sized little trousers and tunics. At the bottom of the trunk, under a stack of diaper cloths, Saraea found *her*. She pulled the doll out of the trunk, gazing at it in recognition.

"Julisa," whispered the girl. Until this moment, she remembered nothing of her life before Silas. Now she was assaulted by a barrage of images from her past. "No!"

Saraea saw the faces of both Aradia and her mother, Thalia leaning over her cradle, smiling at her. She remembered wearing some of the clothes she had just handled in the trunk and sleeping in this little bed, her doll Julisa tucked in close beside her. She remembered crying in her uncle's arms for her mother as Thalia rode off, blowing her a kiss.

"I - I saw her die," Saraea whispered, still gazing at the doll. In a flash, Saraea remembered being very tiny in her bed in Silas's house, waking up and screaming from the nightmare of Yarg killing Thalia. Her uncle couldn't comfort her. It had taken old Mhari and her nasty-tasting brews to settle the little girl back down to sleep. After that, Saraea remembered no more of anything that had happened to her before she came to live with her uncle.

"Saraea, the lamps are in the - oh, you found your old doll," said Aradia, poking her head into the room. "I can't believe we left *that* behind. You never went anywhere without her. What was it you used to call her?"

"Julisa," Saraea whispered, never looking away from the doll.

"That's right," said Aradia, nodding in remembrance. "How funny that ... Saraea, are you alright?"

Saraea turned and Aradia saw tears streaming from the girl's eyes.

"I saw Yarg kill my mother," she whispered.

"No, Saraea, you couldn't have - you were miles away, in Silas's village," said Aradia, going to her and kneeling beside the girl.

"I thought it was just a bad dream, but it wasn't, was it?" said the girl looking up at Aradia, her eyes pleading for the truth.

"No, it wasn't," said Aradia, drawing the girl close to her. She looked back into the past, re-living it all over again as she told the girl the story. "The scouts reported that the Kaskans were marching. We knew there would be trouble, but we never expected ... well, anyway, Thalia took you to Silas to keep you safe."

"Why me and not the others?" asked Saraea. "The other children were just hidden in the forest. Why was I taken to the village?"

"We had our reasons," said Aradia, her eyes narrowing. "We never expected the Kaskans to go to Silas's village - I don't even know how they knew to look for you there."

"Why were they looking for *me*?' asked Saraea.

Aradia was silent for a moment. "I guess you're old enough to know it all, Saraea," she said finally. "Come on - Mhari can tell you better than I can."

The two arose and made their way into the common room where Mhari was lighting the clay and bronze lamps she had found in the kitchen.

"Ah there you are - oh, dear!" said the shamaness, seeing the doll still clutched close in Saraea's arms. She sat quickly in her chair before the warm hearth.

"Yeah," said Aradia, guiding the girl to a chair before pulling a third chair close to the other two. "Mhari, we need to tell her."

The shamaness nodded slowly, then closed her eyes and leaned back in her chair. "Yes, it's time - Alkaia and I were just discussing this today," she said.

"What?" asked Saraea, her eyes sharp and bright with more unshed tears.

"When you were born, the priestess Leilë said that you were to be her successor," said Mhari. "She told your mother that you were to be the 'salvation' of the Amazon Nation, but only if you lived long enough to complete your training as a priestess. And according to Leilë, the chances of that were very poor."

"Why?" asked Saraea.

"Maybe she foresaw her own death," said Aradia with a sigh. "There is now no living Amazon priestess in the whole Nation."

"That we know of," said Saraea. "Maybe all the Amazons didn't - or couldn't answer the call when it was first made."

"Maybe," said Aradia, doubtfully.

"So how was I supposed to save the Amazons?" asked the girl.

"Who knows?" said Aradia with a shrug. "You were just a baby at the time - a cute one, but still, just a baby."

"Really? You thought I was cute, Aradia?" asked Saraea, grinning.

"Yeah, you were cute," said Aradia, returning the grin. "But cute doesn't win wars."

"I'm not a warrior," said Saraea, quietly.

"No," Aradia agreed.

"You didn't believe the priestess, did you, Aradia?" asked the girl looking intently into Aradia's eyes.

"No," said the queen, shortly.

"Then why did you hide me with Silas?" asked Saraea.

"Thalia believed her and you were everything to her," said Aradia, softly. She gazed into the fire, crackling in the hearth. "And she was everything to me."

"And now?" asked Saraea.

"Let's just say, there's more evidence for the theory than against now," said Aradia with a sigh.

"Like what?" asked Saraea.

"Like the fact that you killed Yarg - which has allowed us to return to our ancestral home," said Mhari, softly.

"There has to be more to it than that," said Saraea, to no one in particular.

"For now, that's enough," said Aradia, rising and stirring the pot. "Who's hungry? Anaea and I got a rabbit and this should be just about done."

"Oh, I am," said Saraea, brightly. She went to the table and took a pomegranate from the basket. She cut into it. Bright red juice flowed across the table, and Saraea was mesmerised by it. "Looks like blood."

She watched the pattern of juice form into a face - the face of the girl Julisa, and suddenly Saraea knew how she was supposed to save the Amazon Nation.

"I have to bring them together," she whispered.

"What's that, dear?' asked Mhari.

"I, uh, have to wipe this up," said Saraea, cleaning the juice from the table. "These things are really messy."

She cut three pomegranates and handed two of them to Mhari and Aradia. Aradia ladled up some rabbit stew for all of them and they sat down to eat.

"So, what happened at the Tournament, Aradia?" asked Mhari.

Saraea watched Aradia's face with interest.

"Oh, well, nothing much," said the queen with a shrug. She spooned another mouthful of stew in before continuing. "Poor Thraso - she worked so hard, only to have Myrina spoil it all."

"How did she do that?" asked Saraea, almost breathless with anticipation of Aradia's reply.

"Well, she waited until the last possible moment, then challenged Thraso - in the name of Ares," said Aradia, swallowing her stew.

"Ares? Why Ares?" asked Saraea, frowning in puzzlement.

"According to Thraso, Ares promised the Gorgons safe passage back to Hesperia through the legions of Rome if she would enter the Tournament as his champion," said Aradia. "But that's not the worst of it - she expected Thraso to take a fall so she, Myrina, could win."

"But Thraso didn't, did she?" said Saraea.

"Of course she didn't," said Aradia, setting her empty bowl down. "Thraso is an Amazon, with honour and integrity - unlike the damn Gorgons."

"Why would Myrina think that Thraso would do such a thing for her?" asked Mhari, calmly.

"Thraso said there was some 'history' between them," said Aradia with a sigh. "That and the fact that Myrina is a Gorgon who couldn't possibly expect anyone to act any way other than she would herself, I suppose."

"But Ares only said she had to *enter* the Tournament, not win it - isn't that what you said, Aradia?" said Saraea, gathering the empty bowls to wash.

"Yeah, Thraso never said anything about Myrina having to win it - and Myrina, when she declared the challenge said she was 'pledged to *fight*' - she didn't say *win*," said Aradia. "Curious."

"Maybe she was just testing Thraso - to see if Thraso would do it or not," said Saraea, thoughtfully.

"Hm, maybe - but the bottom line is that Thraso did the right thing," said Aradia. "No Gorgon is to be trusted."

"What if they - ?" Saraea began, troubled.

"Ever, Saraea - remember that," said Aradia, sternly. Then she softened. "Leave those for the morning. Come on - we've all had a long day - and tomorrow promises to be longer. We have a lot of work to do."

"No," said Saraea, shuddering. "We have enough vermin to fight - I don't want to tempt them."

She washed up the dishes, taking her time as Aradia and Mhari lay down to sleep. By the time she was finished, the women's breathing had deepened and Saraea knew they were asleep. She grabbed her sword, tucking it in her belt, and her pack from beside the door, then slipped silently out of the house.

Chapter Seven: Battle for the Sword

Athtar clung tightly to the sword as she slithered to the mouth of the cave. The Graii had been severely wounded in the battle and Athtar was hoping that they would be too weak to stop her from leaving the cave. She looked at them, three old women now, with only one eye and one mouth between them. The sight mortified her and she grimaced.

"What's wrong, Guardian?" sneered the one with a mouth.

"You are," she said. "What happened to you? I thought you were impervious to steel?" The three hags melded into one being, more grotesque than before, limbs sticking out all over the body, but with only one head, encompassing the mouth and eye they shared, but displaying three noses and six ears.

"Steel yes, but the wielder now, that is another thing," it said.

"Must you make yourselves into this thing?' said Athtar, averting her eyes.

"Yesss ..." it said, changing again, though Athtar could not bring herself to look at what it had now become.

"To accommodate each of us," it said. "We must be as water poured into different vessels. We cannot re-generate what we have lost."

"Why not?" asked Athtar, still not looking as she heard the wet sort of sucking sound of the creature changing again.

"Are you so squeamish?" it said and Athtar heard a horrible chuckle at her expense.

"Squeamish, no - you disgust me," said Athtar, shuddering as she heard the sounds yet again. "Why can't you re-generate? Quit doing that and answer me!"

There was laboured, wet breathing for a moment, then a sigh.

"We were wounded ... by the Sword of Artemis," said the voice with difficulty.

Shocked, Athtar looked up, then quickly looked away at the terrible vision before her.

"That's impossible," said Athtar, brandishing the sword in her hand. "*This* is the Sword of Artemis - and I tried to kill you with it. It didn't work."

"It is the wielder, we told you," said the thing she couldn't bear to look at.

"I am the only wielder of this Sword," said Athtar, angrily.

"No," said the thing, wheezing. "You are but its Guardian."

With a howl of rage, Athtar swung at the thing the Graii had become, but to no avail.

"You see?" It wheezed a chuckle at her attempt. "You will never be permitted to wield the Sword of Artemis. You will never learn its secret."

"What secret?" demanded Athtar, frustrated.

The Graii became the three old women again, two with gaping holes where there should have been eyes and mouths. That Athtar could bear to look at long enough to get her answer, but it was not forthcoming. Instead, the Graii turned its back on her and remained silent.

Athtar once again attempted to attack the Graii, but it turned and bit her with its mouth, changing into something even more horrific than before. With a scream of pain, rage and frustration, Athtar began to slither back into the cave.

"Be prepared - the Sword that wounded us will come for you next," said the Graii.

Athtar, grasping her wounded sword arm, ignored it and continued back to her lair.

)O(

Saraea walked silently to the Temple. It wasn't far from Aradia's house, but the night was dark. The moon which had begun to rise was waning and not yet completely risen. Saraea imagined that the ghosts which haunted this place were all around her, yet she still kept to the shadows, unwilling to be seen by the sentries she knew were posted all about.

She arrived at the door of the Temple and swallowed hard, remembering that the body of the priestess had lain within until just a week or so ago.

"I shouldn't be afraid of *her*," Saraea whispered to herself, jumping at the sound of her own voice. "Technically, she should approve of what I'm doing, since it's sort of her own idea." Resolutely, she began to open the door, then jumped with a little squeak of fear when a strong hand clamped down on her arm. Saraea recognised the owner of the hand as the sentry from the other night, the one she hadn't recognised then.

"Oh," she said, her breathing coming in short gasps as her heart slowed its pounding. "It's you."

"Yes - what are you doing here, Saraea?' asked the sentry, sternly.

"I - I ... um," Saraea stammered, unable to bring herself to lie to the woman.

"Yes?" asked the sentry, one eyebrow raised.

"I was, um," Saraea looked down at the ground, trying to think of what to say.

"You were going to meet someone here," said the sentry, softly. "But I am here to tell you that you mustn't do that - I want you to go back to Aradia's house and go to bed."

"I can't," said the girl. "There's something I have to do - to save the Amazons. Only I can do this - the priestess said so."

"That's not what - " the sentry began, then stopped. Suddenly Saraea looked at her, peering through the shadows and seeing her clearly.

"Mother?" the girl whispered, her eyes filling with tears. Her vision blurred and she shook her head to clear it. There stood the sentry, but her face was not Thalia's. "I'm sorry. I thought you were - "

"Saraea, your mother is dead," said the sentry, smiling sympathetically. "I know the Amazons tell tales of ghosts in this place, but really, they are just tales."

"No, I know that they are not - but I can see that you're not my mother," said Saraea, chuckling.

"So, what are you doing here?" asked the sentry.

"I ... um, I couldn't sleep - I have a lot on my mind," said Saraea, not quite lying. "I thought I could find some sort of ... something, anyway, in the Temple."

The sentry nodded, sadly and Saraea suddenly felt sick to her stomach for the half-truth she had told.

"Well, I won't stop you," said the sentry. "But you know it isn't safe yet for girls your age to be out and about at night. Make your prayers quick, then get home, alright?"

Saraea nodded and stepped past her into the inky blackness of the Amazon Temple.

As soon as the door closed behind the girl, Thalia stepped out from the shadows.

"You let her go in?" she said. Hekau appeared from the open window of Aradia's house and ran toward the two standing outside of her Temple. "Anu, what were you thinking?"

"What could I do?" asked Anu, shrugging as Hekau arrived, standing to stretch into the goddess. "We're not allowed to interfere with them, Thalia, you know that."

"Well, maybe not *directly,"* said the goddess, her eyes glittering as she looked pointedly towards Aradia's house.

)O(

"Julisa?" whispered Saraea. She felt her way to the front of the Temple where the altar stood before the statue of Artemis. Suddenly, there was a flare of light and Saraea saw Julisa standing behind the altar, a lamp in her hand.

"I didn't know if you'd come," said Julisa, smiling at her.

"I had to," said Saraea, grimly.

"I know," said Julisa, holding out her hand. "Come - we have to go to the cave now."

"Wait," said Saraea, frowning. "You're a Gorgon - how do I know that I can trust you?"

"You don't," said Julisa, shrugging. She held out her hand again and smiled. "You just have to have faith. Come on Saraea. Don't you want to heal the Amazon Nation? Come with me - bring back the Sword of Artemis. It's the only way to fulfil your destiny."

"How did you know about that?" asked Saraea, frowning. Julisa hesitated, her smile faltering.

"I ... I was listening, Silly - how do you think?" she said.

Saraea took her hand and the two girls made their way to the Temple door. Saraea stopped and listened.

"What is it?" asked Julisa, impatiently.

"Sentries," said Saraea. "One stopped me on my way in here."

"Oh," said Julisa. "Well, they're gone now."

"How do you know?" asked Saraea, looking sharply at the other girl.

"They're patrolling, aren't they? They won't be back this way for a while," said Julisa, pushing open the heavy oak door. "You couldn't have heard them through this door anyway. Come on before they come back."

With a sigh, Saraea followed Julisa down the stairs to the lower town.

)O(

Aradia stirred in her sleep. Something was not quite right. She opened her eyes. Saraea's bedroll was neatly made between hers and Mhari's, but Saraea wasn't in it. The fire had burnt down to its embers. Aradia sat up quickly and looked around the room. She rose silently and padded into the kitchen. The bowls, cups, and spoons from dinner were clean and neatly stacked on the shelf. Rubbing her sleepy eyes, Aradia went from room to room, but found no sign of the girl. She saw that Saraea's pack and Thalia's sword were missing from beside the door where Saraea had neatly set them.

Aradia swore under her breath and pulled her boots on. Suddenly the room grew very cold and a bluish light appeared before the Amazon Queen.

"Thalia?" she whispered.

"Aradia, you have to stop her - she's going to the cave in the forest," said Thalia, materialising before her.

"What?" said Aradia, shaking her head, only half convinced she wasn't still asleep and dreaming.

"It's a trick - Ares is going to get our little girl killed," said Thalia, desperation in her voice.

"Why would she go with Ares? That doesn't make sense, Thalia," said Aradia.

"He's disguised as Julisa," said Thalia. "Please, you have to hurry!"

"The doll?" asked Aradia, still half asleep.

"No! Julisa, the girl," said Thalia, trying to be patient. "The gods chose an image from Saraea's deepest mind and altered their appearance to meet it and gain her trust. That doll was Saraea's most trusted companion from a time when she felt the safest. The Sword of Artemis is in that cave - Ares has convinced her to go and try to get it back, but the Graii are there - and so is Athtar. She has the Sword."

"Athtar has - never mind - I know the cave," said Aradia, standing. "I'll go and get her - don't worry."

The apparition nodded once and left.

"Aradia, what's going on?" asked Mhari. Aradia looked up to see the shamaness standing in the doorway.

"Ares has Saraea and is leading her to her death," said Aradia, shortly as she strapped on her sword. "I'm going after her."

"So am I," said Mhari, pulling on her boots.

"No, Mhari - it's too dangerous," said Aradia.

"I'm going, Aradia," said Mhari, firmly. She donned a woollen cloak against the night's chill.

Aradia simply nodded, knowing from long experience that there was no arguing with the older woman.

The two left the house and made their way to the steps leading to the lower town.

"Mhari, are you sure? That climb is bad enough in daylight, but at night - and especially since you're already injured - " began Aradia, but the firm set line of Mhari's mouth stopped her.

With a sigh, Aradia went to the warrior camp in the lower town and roused Thraso. Briefly, she explained to her Second in Command and Thraso awakened a platoon to accompany them to the cave.

"I'm going, too," said Thraso, strapping on her sword-belt.

"Alright, but one of us has to survive this, okay?" said Aradia, chuckling coldly.

Thraso's only reply was a curt nod which conveyed the message that they would both make it out alive if she had anything to do with it.

The group made their way cautiously down the incline, the warriors helping Mhari over the worst of it and began to march through the woods, watching for signs that the two girls had been there before them.

"She's not leaving a trail," said Aradia, frowning in frustration. "How is that possible?"

"Ares," said Mhari, grimly. "He's trying to hide her from us. Little does he realise that night belongs to his sister - all things are revealed by her shining face." The shamaness pointed to a blur in the brush. Aradia looked and saw Hekau, leading them. She nodded and followed the cat's trail, motioning for the warriors to follow.

)O(

Saraea followed Julisa through the trees, tripping and stumbling. The other girl set a fast and furious pace through the trees, pulling on Saraea's arm when she felt Saraea wasn't moving swiftly enough to suit her.

"Hey, slow down!" Saraea said with a hiss of pain as a branch flew back and slapped her in the face.

"We have to hurry," said Julisa, looking up. "They'll miss you soon and come looking - we have to make it far enough that they can't interfere."

"Interfere ... ? What are you talking about?" said Saraea, stopping.

"Come on Saraea," said Julisa, her nostrils flaring in anger. Saraea had never seen the girl like this before.

"No," she said, setting her pack down and crossing her arms. "I'm not going another step. I'm tired and I want to rest for a minute." She sat down on the ground and glared at Julisa.

"Saraea get up," said Julisa with a growl. She walked up to Saraea and grabbed one of her arms, yanking the girl to her feet. "Get your pack and let's go."

Saraea fell back to the ground, defiantly crossing her arms again, still glaring at Julisa.

"What did you mean, 'interfere'? If I'm doing such a great thing, why would the Amazons try to stop me?" she asked.

Julisa took a deep breath, gathering patience, then smiled. "You tell me," she said. "Did you tell Aradia you were going? Of course you didn't, because you know she would have stopped you - or at the very least, tried to send a couple of platoons with you."

"I'm beginning to think a couple of platoons - or even the whole Amazon army - might not be such a bad idea," said Saraea with a sigh.

"But the Amazons couldn't touch that thing, remember?" said Julisa. "Only you could hurt it - and you have to, Saraea. That thing is standing between you and your destiny."

"My destiny," said Saraea, as she rose to her feet. She picked up her pack with a sigh. "Okay - I'm rested. Let's go, Julisa."

With a feral grin, Julisa grabbed Saraea's hand and began to move quickly through the thickening trees. The forest grew darker as the trees blocked out the moonlight. Saraea was growing more weary with each step. She stumbled and almost dropped her pack. Quickly, she felt for her sword and relaxed as her fingers brushed the cold metal hilt.

"Julisa, I can't see where I'm going - we really do have to slow down a little," said Saraea, pulling her arm away from the other girl.

"It's okay - we're here," said Julisa, as the girls emerged into the clearing where the cave sat like a great black maw, ready to swallow them.

Saraea looked at the cave and took a deep breath. The moon was shining down upon the clearing, bathing it with a silvery, ethereal light. Saraea swallowed hard and took a deep breath. She drew her sword and flipped it, almost absently, in a swift, neat move. Julisa saw that and raised an eyebrow, but led her to the mouth of the cave.

"In there," she whispered.

Saraea set her jaw and stepped into the inky blackness of the cave. Suddenly a horrible creature rose up, howling and roaring at her. She recognised the wounded serpent and raised her sword, backing quickly away from it at the same time. Julisa shoved her back inside.

"Get it - Saraea, the Sword is in there - you have to get past this thing to get it!" yelled the girl.

Saraea began fighting in earnest. The creature got in one slash of its claws, but Saraea lunged and swung, finally taking all three heads from its shoulders. Her shoulder hurt where the thing had clawed her. Sweat dripped from her brow, stinging in her eyes, and she was covered in blood - both the creature's and her own. The thing lay at her feet, dead, but still wriggling in a mass of jelly-like stuff.

"Ew!" Saraea cried, holding her nose at the stench of thing's dying.

"Saraea, the Sword is back there," said Julisa, taking her arm and pulling her deeper into the cave.

"Julisa, wait," said Saraea, looking around for something to clean her sword. With a grimace, she grabbed a corner of her cloak and swiped off her blade with it before tucking it back into her belt.

"Wish we had a torch," said Saraea, shivering in the dampness of the cave.

"It's okay - I know where we're going," said Julisa.

"How do you know?" asked Saraea, slowing her steps.

"I've been in here before, remember?" said Julisa.

"Yeah, I do remember," said Saraea, quietly. "Why?"

"Because ... because the Sword is here," said Julisa.

"But how did you know that?" said Saraea, slowing to a stop. Julisa reached back and grabbed her arm, but Saraea pulled away. "Stop doing that! My arm hurts from that thing cutting me."

"Oh, sorry," said Julisa. "I just did, okay? Now come on - you're almost finished."

Saraea sighed and followed Julisa, one hand on the other girl's shoulder as they made their way through the dark caverns. Suddenly Saraea heard a noise.

"What's that?" she asked, stopping again.

"Nothing," said Julisa. "Come on, let's get that Sword."

"No, I heard ... something," said Saraea, fear causing the goose bumps to rise on her arms as much as the cold dampness of the cave. "Oh, no - Julisa! Something just moved over my foot! I felt it!"

"Would you be quiet?" said Julisa with a hiss.

"Julisa - there's something in this cave besides us," Saraea whispered as once again the other girl pulled her deeper into the cave.

"Like what?" asked Julisa, a slow grin spreading over her face.

"I don't know - it's too dark to see," said Saraea, straining her eyes to try to see anything. She felt something glide over her foot again and struggled not to scream. She felt another something, cold and smooth brush across her cheek, then her shoulder. She heard a plop as whatever it was fell to the cave floor. Nausea roiled in her middle.

"Blessed Artemis," she whispered, cringing.

Julisa reached back and slapped her. The crack echoed through the cavern and the sharp sting brought tears to Saraea's eyes.

"Oh, sorry," said Julisa. "I thought there was something on you there."

Saraea rubbed her cheek. She was cold and tired. Her shoulder ached, though her cheek was now numb and tingling where Julisa had hit her. Something was scaring her, though she didn't know what; the creature which had guarded the cave was dead.

"Julisa, something is not right here," she said, turning her head and trying to see anything in the absolute darkness of the cavern. She could hear a dripping sound and something else, as well; a slithering of sorts just under the echoes of their footfalls. Saraea felt a slow panic rising in her chest. Her throat felt like it was closing and her chest was heavy. Her breath was coming in short gasps and she felt dizzy.

"Julisa, I can't breathe," she whispered through her constricting throat. "I think maybe that thing had poison in its claws. I'm scared, Julisa."

"Don't be such a baby," Julisa said, impatiently. "There was no poison - the Graii doesn't need it to kill. Now come on."

The cavern opened up and suddenly Saraea could see a little. There was a rocky shelf, similar to an altar in the centre of the chamber. Behind the shelf was a creature almost as frightening as the Graii, half woman, half snake. Suddenly Saraea heard laughter. She looked at Julisa and gasped. Her "friend" had transformed into a man and stood there grinning at her.

"Saraea, daughter of Thalia, meet Athtar, Guardian of the Sword of Artemis," he said, disappearing from the cave.

Chapter Seven: Sword of Artemis, Sword of Truth

Aradia and the Amazons tracked the cat through the trees. They could only catch glimpses of her white fur in the darkening forest. The moon was no longer visible as the trees grew closer and closer together, their trunks gaining width as they approached the oldest part at the centre of the forest. Still, they could see Hekau despite the darkness. They came to the clearing of the cave and stopped.

"This is where that three-headed serpent was," said Anaea.

"Saraea blooded it - that would make it even more dangerous," said Aradia, grimly. "Though it didn't leave the cave when we passed through here earlier; it's possible that it died of its wounds."

"Oh, the smell," said Thraso, grimacing. "It didn't smell this bad here before."

"No, but listen," said Aradia. Night birds, tree frogs, and crickets could be heard chirping their individual songs in the night.

"What?" said Thraso. "I don't hear anything."

"Ah, but you do - listen again," said Aradia, smiling.

"Just ... crickets and stuff?" said Thraso.

"Exactly - this place was completely silent when we passed through here before," said Aradia. "Come on."

The Amazons followed her to the mouth of the cave. "Oh, Goddess!" cried Anaea, holding her nose. "The smell is a lot worse in there."

"We need torches - Thraso, Prothoë, grab some dead fall and get a fire started," Aradia ordered. "I'm not going in there in the dark."

"Saraea did," said Mhari, her eyes glassy in trance. "She's in there now - the Graii is no more, but the Guardian ..."

The shamaness shuddered and her eyes cleared. "I am not permitted to see any more," she said.

"That's alright," said Aradia, patting her shoulder gently. "We'll get her back. Are you alright?"

"Yes, of course," said Mhari. "Just worried, naturally."

"Naturally," said Aradia. Thraso and Prothoë got a fire burning and approached with blazing torches. "Are we ready?"

"As we're going to be," said Thraso. "That stench though - agh!"

"Well, then you wait here," said Aradia, taking a torch from her.

"No way," said Thraso, shaking her head. "Anaea, Prothoë, and I are going with you - we've already decided it."

"Oh, really?" asked Aradia, one eyebrow raised.

"Yes, really," said Anaea, bringing another torch to the group.

"What is this, mutiny?" asked Aradia, chuckling.

"No, your Majesty," said Anaea. "On our journey home, Saraea told us many tales she had read in the Amazon Scrolls - she also told us about a very old law, which we are invoking now."

"What law is that?" asked Aradia.

"No mother whose child is in danger may lead the mission to rescue her," said Thraso. "If the daughter or other family member of a queen is in danger, her lieutenants may temporarily relieve her of command in order to make the rescue."

"You just made that up!" said Aradia.

"No, they didn't," said Mhari, shaking her head. "That law was written very long ago. It was a tragedy - one of our ancient queens had a sister, Antiope, whom she raised as her own daughter after the death of their mother. When Antiope was kidnapped, Oreithyia led the entire army across the continent to 'save' her sister and left the elders and children behind with no one to protect them. That was almost the end of the Amazon Nation."

"What happened to her?" asked Aradia.

"That's not important right now - someday I will tell you the story of Antiope - or Saraea will," said Mhari. "For now it is enough to know that after that, it was felt that a mother was not capable of thinking clearly enough to act rationally."

"Since I spent the better of my childbearing years dealing death rather than life, I hardly think I qualify as anyone's 'mother'," said Aradia, wryly.

"It's not the bearing that makes a mother, Aradia," said Mhari, gently.

Aradia looked thoughtful for a moment, then nodded once. She hefted the torch with one hand and drew her sword with the other. "Very well - lead on," she said, inclining her head towards the cave. Anaea, Prothoë, and Thraso raised their torches and stepped gingerly into the entrance of the cave. Mhari began to follow, but Aradia stepped in front of the shamaness.

"Whoa, Old-Mother," she said. "Where do you think you're going?"

"Saraea may be hurt," said Mhari, patting her healing herb pouch. "I'm going, too, Aradia."

"Alright, alright," said Aradia, exasperated. She looked towards the platoon of warriors, standing by. "Anyone else? Never mind." She held up one hand as the entire platoon started towards the cave.

Aradia followed Mhari into the mouth of the cave, holding her torch aloft. She found the others a few yards into the cavern all looking at a gooey-looking puddle on the cave floor. One tooth and one eyeball floated atop the mess.

"Artemis! Is that where the stench is coming from?" asked the queen, poking about the stuff with her sword.

"Yes - the remains of the Graii," said Mhari.

"Come on," said Thraso. "This ... stuff doesn't pose any danger to us now, does it Mhari?"

"Only the danger of losing our suppers," said the shamaness, holding a bit of her cloak over her nose and mouth.

"Look here," said Prothoë, holding her torch closer to the floor of the cave and pointing.

"What is it?" asked Aradia, leaning in to look.

"Blood - not a lot, but still, I think maybe that thing may have gotten one good hit in before Saraea killed it," said Thraso, grimly.

"Damn!" said Aradia, panic rising in her chest. "Come on." She tried to move ahead of the others, but Thraso held her back.

"Hold it there, 'Mama'," said her Second in Command.

"Damn it, Thraso, that's not funny!" said Aradia.

"I didn't mean it to be," said Thraso. "But we need to slow down. There's not that much blood. *If* Saraea's wounded, it's a small one. For all we know, this isn't even her blood. Something's not right here, though, and I don't want to go rushing in before we know what that something is."

"Alright - your point is taken," said Aradia, calmly. "Can we get moving now?"

The Amazons made their way slowly through the passageway from the cave's entrance. The smell of the dead Graii faded as they got further away, but was replaced by another smell more sinister. None of the Amazons could really identify the odour, but it still made them edgy and nervous. Worse than the smell were the sounds which grew louder as they went further through the passageway. A sibilant, dry sound, almost like a host of whispering voices echoed through the cave. Bringing up the rear, Aradia heard Thraso utter a quiet curse.

"What? What is it?" asked the queen, peering through the darkness.

"Bloody snakes!" said Thraso, disgusted. "Must be hundreds ... thousands of them."

"Alright," said Mhari, stepping up to where the others had stopped. She looked and her eyes widened. "Blessed Artemis! This is where that smell is coming from."

Aradia shouldered her way through the group gathered around the opening to a cavern. She held the torch aloft and saw them. Like Thraso said, there were hundreds of snakes all over. They carpeted the floor of the cave and hung from natural shelf-like formations along the walls and ceilings of the chamber. Aradia took a deep breath, then blew it out slowly. She did this three times, then looked around at the serpents.

"Okay," she said, quietly. "It's cold, so they're nice and slow."

"Yes, but not slow enough," said Mhari, taking a pouch from her belt. "This should do it."

She set about making a paste of the herbs and some water from her waterskin. Moulding the stuff into a ball about the size of her fist, Mhari threaded a piece of twine all way through the ball and lifted it to one of the torches, setting the twine alight.

"Now," she said. "Toss one of those torches to the floor there."

Prothoë complied with the shamaness's demand. Instantly, the serpents moved away from the blazing wood.

"Quickly now," said Mhari, moving toward the flame and setting the ball of herbs next to it before lifting the torch once again. The ball began smoking as the wick burned down to the paste. A thick, white, aromatic smoke filled the chamber and the sound of the snakes ceased.

"Mhari, what is that stuff?" asked Thraso.

"Just a mild sedative," said the shamaness "Mild for us, that is. For them, well, they will sleep as if dead for some time. Still, we should hurry now."

The elder looked worried and the Amazons forged ahead through the chamber into a narrower passageway.

"Do you think there are anymore inhabitants of this cave?" Anaea whispered to Aradia.

"I don't know," said the queen, grimly. "I can't even be certain that *those* were inhabitants of this cave. We just have to keep our eyes and ears open." Anaea nodded.

Thraso led them through the passageway, but stopped just short of the next chamber. She lifted a finger to her lips, then moved them all back a bit.

"There's a light in that one," she said, her brow furrowed with concern. "I don't know who - or what - is in there."

"There's one way to find out," said Mhari, pulling a small, silver mirror out of another pouch.

"Great Goddess, Mhari, what else do you have in your bag of tricks?" asked Aradia, grinning at her.

"Hopefully whatever we need," said the shamaness, turning around and holding the mirror over her shoulder towards the opening. Slowly she lowered the mirror and turned.

"Mhari, what is it? You're pale as the moon," said Aradia. Mhari shook her head and handed Aradia the mirror.

The queen took the same position as the shamaness had. Then with a curse, she dropped the mirror, drew her sword and sprang into the chamber before any of the others could stop her.

)O(

Saraea saw the creature behind the altar and drew her sword.

"Y-you're Athtar? Q-Queen of the Gorgons?" she stammered. The creature glared at her and hissed, brandishing the Sword. "That's the Sword of Artemis!"

"Yesss," said Athtar, slithering closer. "Mine!"

Saraea backed away, holding her sword before her. "No, it isn't," said the girl, swallowing hard. "I've come to take it back to the Amazons where it belongs."

"You'll die in the attempt," Athtar spat, coming ever closer. "You will die in any case." Saraea backed away until she hit the cave wall behind her. Her eyes narrowed and she held her sword before her in a warding gesture.

"Then I have nothing to lose," said the girl, lunging at Athtar. Athtar laughed and evaded the girl at the last moment. Unable to stop herself, Saraea fell. Carried by the momentum, she hit her head on the stone shelf which resembled an altar and fell unconscious to the cave floor. Athtar loomed over the prone girl, grinning. She raised the Sword of Artemis over her to make the killing blow. Aradia burst into the chamber, the other Amazons following close behind.

"Come on Athtar - pick on someone your own size!" cried the angry Amazon queen.

Athtar hissed angrily and slithered over to Aradia. "With pleasure!" she said, swinging.

The blades clashed once. The Sword of Artemis sliced Aradia's sword in half, but before Athtar could recover and parry, Aradia sliced off her sword-hand with the bottom half of her broken blade. The hand, still clutching the Sword of Artemis fell to the ground.

"Noooo!" Athtar howled, falling to the ground. Her lower body began to undulate and move of its own volition and Athtar screamed in pain as it split into two legs. Scales merged into skin and then Athtar grabbed the hilt of the Sword with her other hand, rising up with a triumphant yell.

The blood stopped spurting from her wrist as the hand grew back. Her legs once again merged into a scaly snake's tail. Aradia and the Amazons looked on in awe and revulsion. Athtar swung the Sword of Artemis at Aradia, but missed, though Aradia stood only inches before her. Athtar frowned and swung again; again, she missed.

"What ... what - that's not possible!" she howled, swinging yet again. Aradia felt the silver key growing warmer between her breasts. She dropped her broken sword and pulled the key out of her tunic. Suddenly, the silken cord from which it hung around her neck snapped and the key grew into a sword - the Sword of Artemis. The Amazons looked at it in wonder - it was identical to the one clutched in Athtar's hand. Athtar stared in amazement, looking from one Sword to the other.

"It's a fake!" she cried, lunging with the one in her hand at Aradia.

"No, it isn't," said Aradia, suddenly understanding. "Athtar, the Sword in your hand - it *is* the Sword of Artemis - and so is this one."

"There is only one Sword of Artemis - and it is *mine*!" cried Athtar.

"No, Athtar, the Sword of Artemis - the *true* Sword of Artemis isn't a sword at all - don't you see?" said Aradia.

Saraea sat up, rubbing her head and looked wide-eyed all around her. As quickly as she could, she grabbed her mother's sword and ran to the other Amazons behind Aradia.

"Don't be a fool, Aradia - it's right here in my hand - and it *is* a sword," said Athtar advancing again upon the Amazon Queen. "It holds the power of the Amazons and their goddess and it is all mine now."

"Athtar, the Amazons are more than just our weapons and our goddess doesn't need steel to be powerful. You can't hurt me with that blade, Athtar," said Aradia, calmly sheathing her sword. "You can only harm yourself by holding on to it."

"It's a trick," Athtar spat. "Get me to drop it so you can take it from me - it's *mine*!"

"Athtar, that sword is what keeps you ... the way you are," said Aradia. "Just now, when you didn't have it, you had legs - you have to let go of it, Athtar."

"Never!" Athtar cried, clutching the Sword to her breast. "I have sacrificed too much - it is mine. I will never let it go, do you hear me?"

"I do hear you. You are a fool, Athtar," said Aradia, sadly. "Keep the Sword. The Amazons have no need of it. We are the *true* Sword of Artemis."

She turned to leave and motioned for the others to follow her. Saraea glanced back to see if Athtar would try to follow them, but the Guardian was cradling the Sword like a baby, crooning some lullaby to it. The girl caught up to Aradia.

"Um, I - " she began.

"Don't talk to me right now Saraea," said Aradia. "Right now, I'm done with being scared for you and on my way to very, very angry."

"Um, okay," said the girl, dropping her head and falling back to walk beside Mhari. "Are you mad at me, too?

"No, not mad," said Mhari. "Just puzzled. Why did you do it, Saraea?"

"Julisa told me that to fulfil my destiny and save the Amazons, I had to retrieve the Sword of Artemis," said Saraea, quietly. "Only that wasn't Julisa."

"No, it was Ares," said Mhari.

"Ares? Why would he want me to retrieve the Sword?" asked Saraea.

"He wouldn't," said Mhari looking at the girl sharply.

"Oh," said Saraea, looking away.

"Ah, Child, who knows why the gods do anything," said Mhari, patting the girl's shoulder. "And don't worry about Aradia; she'll be done with being angry with you soon. Then I suspect that she'll be terribly proud of you."

Saraea looked between the straight shoulders of her foster-mother walking ahead of her and somehow doubted that statement. She remained silent the rest of the way out of the cave.

They emerged from the cave to be greeted by an anxious Amazon platoon, all clamouring to hear what had transpired in the cave. Aradia raised her arms for silence and received it before she spoke.

"Saraea killed the creature guarding the cave - the Graii - and led us to find this - " She unsheathed the Sword of Artemis and held it aloft. The Sword shimmered in the moonlight. It seemed to draw the light of the moon into itself until it shone with a light all its own. The Amazons were silently reverent as Aradia handed the Sword to Saraea. The girl gazed at the glowing blade, feeling power thrumming down to the hilt. Her fingers tingled with it and she handed the Sword back to Aradia. The Queen sheathed it, smiling at her.

"Now let's take it back where it belongs," she said, one arm around Saraea's shoulders.

Dawn arrived at the steep incline leading to the lower town of the Amazon city just as the Amazons did. As weary they were, all were excited to get home and spread the word that the Sword had been retrieved.

"Aradia," Saraea whispered. "Shouldn't we tell them that's not the real Sword?"

"Saraea, weren't you listening to what I told Athtar?" said Aradia, smiling enigmatically. "This *is* the real Sword of Artemis. Didn't you feel it when you touched it?"

"Yes, I did," said Saraea, frowning. "But I just don't understand how there can be *two*."

"Look around, Little One," said Aradia, as they ascended into the lower town. The warriors who had preceded them had already spread the word to all the warriors who were camped around the ruins of the fortress which would be their barracks as it had been in the "old days". They went up the steep staircase to the upper town where the warriors were pounding on doors and shouting to all the Amazons that the Sword was back. Women came out of the houses and began to gravitate to the Temple. Soon, the entire Amazon Nation was gathered there, spilling out of the doors, yet hovering as close as they could. They parted to allow Aradia, Mhari, and Saraea to enter. The three walked to the front of the Temple and turned to gaze upon the Amazons.

"I'm looking - gosh, there are a lot of us, aren't there?" said Saraea.

"Yes, though not nearly as many ..." began Aradia. She shook her head. "Yes, there are. But look, Saraea - try to understand because this is important. *We*, the Amazons, are the Sword of Artemis."

"That's hard to understand, Aradia," said Saraea, frowning. "You also told Athtar that the Amazons were much more than our swords."

"Together, we are," said Aradia, smiling at the throng of women.

"I still don't get it," said Saraea with a sigh.

Aradia unsheathed the Sword and held it aloft for all to see. The sun, streaming through the open window hit the blade, casting a dazzling brilliance throughout the Temple. As Aradia gazed at it, tears welled up in her eyes.

"Oh, Thalia, how right you are," she whispered. "The symbol is nothing but a dream compared to the reality of life." She turned to Saraea and handed her the Sword. "Put it back where it belongs, Little One."

Saraea turned to the statue of the goddess and carefully fit the hilt into the marble hand. She stepped back and waited with the rest of the Amazons, holding her breath to see what would happen. She released it after a moment and turned to whisper to Aradia, then saw the cat Hekau from the corner of her eye, jump up onto the altar. Her eyes widened and she turned.

"Hekau, no! You can't ..." she began, then stopped as she saw a beautiful woman standing where the cat had been.

"You," said Aradia, staring at the woman. "You're the one who released me from the gladiator's cell. Who are you?"

"I am the one you Amazons call 'Great Mother', though I have as many names as there are souls who call upon me," said the Lady.

"You are the One to whom even Blessed Artemis must answer," said Saraea in a reverent whisper.

"I *am* Artemis, Little One," said the Goddess, smiling and laying a gentle hand affectionately on the girl's head as she transformed into the more recognised face of Artemis. Then her smile faded and her expression grew grave. "Aradia, you remember when I told you I needed you elsewhere?"

The Queen bowed her head and nodded once.

"This is the elsewhere," said the Goddess. Aradia looked up quickly.

"What do you mean, Lady?" she asked.

"I mean, Daughter of Artemis, I needed you here in this place," said the Goddess. "The Romans are marching upon you as we speak. You must lead the Amazons against them."

)O(

Myrina made her way back to the Gorgon settlement. She would have the women pack up and they would leave for Hesperia this very day, whether Ares helped them or not.

"You failed." Myrina turned at the sound of the voice.

"No, I didn't," she said.

"I sent you in there to be my champion - you lost - and to the *Second* in Command! You didn't even challenge Aradia." Ares growled in rage, his eyes were flames. "You were fighting in *my* name - and I do not back losers!"

"That's not what I heard, Ares," said Myrina, calmly. "You backed Yarg."

"Where did you hear that?" asked Ares. "You were eavesdropping!" Ares grinned.

"When I hear the voice of a strange man in my queen's private chambers, it is my duty to make sure that she's in no danger - and to do it discreetly," said Myrina with a shrug.

"And I thought you had no vices," said Ares with a chuckle.

"As I said, it was my duty," said Myrina. "So what about Yarg? You backed him and he lost."

"I backed him until he outlived his usefulness to me," said Ares, growling with annoyance.

"Oh, I see," said Myrina, softly. "And Athtar? Did she outlive her usefulness, too?"

"Just about," Ares muttered.

"Well, I suppose you will kill *me* now," said Myrina with a resolved sigh. "May I ask that you at least make it quick? Or shall I merely fall upon my own sword - ?" She unsheathed it.

"Wait," said Ares, his eyes gleaming. "There may be a way you can redeem yourself and gain back my favour."

"Why does this not surprise me?" said Myrina, re-sheathing her sword. "My mother warned me to never bargain with the gods. I should have listened. What do you want of me, Ares?"

"Actually, I think you may find this task mutually beneficial," said Ares, stroking his beard thoughtfully. "How would you like to retrieve the Sword of Artemis?"

)O(

Aradia stationed four platoons of foot soldiers around the perimeter below the lower town. Another two platoons of foot and two of archers were positioned in the lower town. She placed the remaining warriors in the upper town at both ends of the steep stone staircase and an elite squad of swords-women were assigned to protect the Temple where those both too old and too young to fight would be sequestered until after the battle.

Saraea stayed by Aradia's side, watching her foster-mother go about the business of planning a war. Although the old forge had been located in the ruined fortress in the lower town, the smiths were hard at work in the upper town, arming all of the Amazons in the city. Craftswomen, planters, animal breeders - all were preparing to stand with their warrior sisters and defend themselves and their home.

"I'm more convinced than ever that I don't want to be a warrior," said Saraea. "I'm scared, Aradia."

Aradia looked at the girl and sighed. "Truth? So am I, Kiddo." Saraea's eyes widened. "But we *all* are, Saraea. We don't fight because we like it."

"I know," said Saraea, quietly. "So do I fight this time?"

"Only if you have to, Saraea," said Aradia. "I want you to stay in the upper town, though."

"Do you think the Romans will get that far?" asked Saraea. Aradia was silent and thoughtful for a long moment.

"I just don't know," she said, looking off into the valley towards the approaching Legion of Rome.

)O(

Ares led Myrina to the clearing in the centre of his sister's sacred forest. He pointed to the cave. "It's in there."

Myrina looked around the clearing before cautiously stepping out of the trees.

"Are you sure the Sword is still there? Someone has been here - many someone's by the look of things," she said. "There was a fire and at least four torches." She pushed some charred bits of wood with the toe of her boot.

"What?" said Ares, swiftly stepping into the clearing, his nostrils flaring. "Amazons! Damned Amazons!"

"Judging by the way the fire was built and put out, yeah, I'd say it was Amazons, alright," said Myrina, squatting to examine the remains of the fire more closely. "There was at least one platoon out here - looks like they stood watch around the fire for at least an hour - maybe longer. The ground under the dirt they used to smother it is still warm, too."

"So it's been what, a couple of hours?" asked Ares, anxiously.

"I'd guess they left a few hours before dawn," said Myrina, standing and brushing off her hands.

"Get in that cave and make sure the Sword is till there," said Ares. "Now!"

Myrina looked at him, her face expressionless. "And if it isn't?"

"You'd better hope that it is," said Ares, his voice quiet, but dangerous.

Myrina walked across the clearing to the cave, her head high and shoulders straight. There was a faint odour of something rancid and a dark stain on the floor of the cave just past the opening. She skirted the stain and went on. As she proceeded deeper into the passage, she thought longingly of the remnants of the discarded torches outside. Daylight permeated the passage only a few feet, then Myrina was in complete darkness. Keeping one hand on the hilt of her sword, the warrior felt along the rough rock wall with the other, shuffling her feet across the uneven cave floor.

The passageway opened into a larger chamber, dimly lit by a small flickering flame on the floor. The room was sweetly scented and Myrina had an eerie feeling that she was not alone in the chamber. She frowned and shook off the feeling, continuing swiftly through the room and into the next dark passageway on the other side.

Once again, she felt her way along the wall. She continued that way for some time until it felt as though she had been walking in the dark for days; the concept of time no longer had any meaning for the warrior. Again she tried to shake off the feeling. She began to count her heart beats and re-gained her focus as she walked. Finally, she saw the end of the passage opening into a lighted chamber. A flash at her feet caught her attention and she bent down to pick up a piece of polished silver.

Amazons were here, alright, she thought. *And not just any Amazon - this is a scrying mirror. A shamaness's tool, or perhaps even a priestess's.* She slipped the mirror into her belt and stepped into the chamber, shocked by what she saw there.

"Athtar?" she whispered, then swiftly drew her sword as the Guardian turned and hissed at her, baring sharp fangs. She was cradling the Sword of Artemis in her arms as though it were an infant.

"Begone, Traitor!" said the creature. "The Sword is *mine*!"

"Athtar, I thought you were dead," said Myrina. She looked at the thing her queen had become and felt sick. "I think ... I think maybe you had better come with me, Athtar. You need a healer."

"All I need I have right here," said the Guardian, raising the Sword. It dazzled Myrina's eyes.

"Yes, that is beautiful, indeed, Athtar," said the warrior. "So beautiful it seems a shame to have it hidden away in this terrible place, don't you think?"

"You just want to take it from me - like Aradia and that girl," said Athtar, hissing again.

"No, I really don't," said Myrina. "I just want you to come back to the Gorgons with me - they need their queen. Was Aradia here, Athtar?"

"Yesss...." said the Guardian, her eyes narrowing suspiciously at Myrina. "Don't you know that already, Myrina?"

"No," said Myrina, shaking her head as she moved her eyes about the chamber, looking for a way out past the Guardian.

"I know you are with Ares," said Athtar, slithering slowly closer. "What did he offer you, Myrina?"

"Protection for the Gorgons from Rome," said Myrina.

"You fool!" spat Athtar. "You didn't need him for that."

"The Romans - " began Myrina.

"The Romans are marching on the Amazon city as we speak," said Athtar. "Ares set it up - he played you for a fool, Myrina, just as he did me."

"Ares did this to you?" asked Myrina.

"No, not Ares - Medusa," said Athtar. "Ares tricked me into this cave - she was waiting here for me."

"Who is Medusa?" asked Myrina.

"The new goddess of the Gorgons," said Athtar, again baring her fangs.

"I don't understand," said Myrina.

"It doesn't matter - we will both die in this place," said Athtar, lunging at Myrina with the Sword.

Myrina stepped swiftly aside, evading the blade, but narrowly. Quickly, the Guardian recovered and swung. Myrina jumped back, feeling the wind brush across her middle. With a growl, Athtar again sliced forward and Myrina sidestepped the blow. She reluctantly swung her sword at Athtar, cutting the creature's scaly hide where her thigh would be if she still had legs. A thin red line appeared as blood welled up out of the wound. The creature screamed in pain and anger. Again she lunged. Myrina tried to block, but missed. Again she felt only the wind following the blade as it barely missed her throat.

"What is this? Why can I not score a single hit with this Sword? Is it not the best blade ever forged by the gods' hands?" Athtar cried out in frustration. Taking advantage of Athtar's distraction, Myrina swung her sword upward in a short, chopping move, catching the hilt with the edge of her blade and flipping the Sword up out of the Guardian's hand. Myrina whirled around and stepped into the Sword's descent, catching it neatly with her empty hand, before finishing the revolution and facing Athtar with both swords raised.

"Give me back my sword!" said Athtar. She fell to the floor of the cave, writhing in agony. Myrina watched in horror as her scaly snake's body split into legs, one bleeding profusely from the nasty gash delivered by Myrina's sword.

As Myrina looked upon Athtar, writhing and undulating in a tantrum worthy of a spoiled two-year old on the dirty cave floor, she realised that the Gorgon Queen truly was no more; Athtar had finally completed her descent into absolute madness.

Sadly, Myrina turned and walked out of the chamber, unnoticed by Athtar. The light in the chamber dimmed as she carried the Sword out. Holding it aloft in front of her, Myrina found it illuminated her way better than any torch. She almost screamed when she came to the sweetly scented chamber and saw its inhabitants; thousands of serpents, drugged into a stuporous, somnolent sleep. Instead, she pressed her hand against her mouth to forcibly hold in the scream and swiftly made her way across to the final passageway.

It was a much quicker journey through the cave with illumination and Myrina emerged from the cave with the Sword of Artemis still held aloft, her own sword sheathed at her belt. Ares appeared before, grinning.

"I knew you could do it," he said, though Myrina detected a false note behind the forced cheerfulness.

"Yeah," said Myrina, looking at him through narrowed eyes. "Here. Now we're done, Ares." She thrust the Sword of Artemis at him. Ares jumped back, fear in his eyes.

"Ah, um, no - you hang on to it, Myrina," said the god, placing both hands in front of him in a warding gesture and backing away.

A slow, sinister smile spread across the Gorgon warrior's face. "Don't tell me the god of war is afraid of a sword," she said, playfully thrusting the blade at him.

"Stop it!" cried Ares. "I'm not afraid."

"Is that so?" said Myrina, twirling the blade ever closer to Ares's face. Then quickly, she reached around and slapped his backside with the flat of the blade. Ares became pale and dropped to the ground.

Myrina frowned and poked at him with the blade. Ares groaned and then lay still, but he was still breathing. Myrina laughed.

"Of course," she said to herself. "Artemis' sword is Ares's bane - that's why he couldn't get it for himself - for him, one touch of the blade is like being hit by lightning for a mortal." Briefly, she considered simply killing him, then decided it wasn't worth the repercussions. As long as she held the Sword, she believed Ares would avoid her and the Gorgons.

She turned and walked away from the clearing back into the trees, glancing back only once at Ares, who still lay unconscious on the ground.

"I must be getting soft," she said, shaking her head, then continued on back to the Gorgon settlement. They would have to move swiftly if they wanted to get home to Hesperia before the Romans finished with the Amazons.

Chapter Eight: Secrets of the Sword

Aradia watched the Romans' advance from the summit watchtower. They bore the standards of Aurelian and the Emperor. Aradia felt her stomach sink at the sight of the Imperial Eagle. The Legions were still at least a day away, but Aradia felt a sense of urgency. She just wanted this over with, one way or another. The thought of being captured again almost threw her into a panic.

"No way," she whispered to herself. "I will fall on my sword first." Then she felt a cold fear wash over her at the thought of Saraea in Roman hands, Roman chains. "I will kill her myself before I will ever let happen to her."

"Aradia."

The queen turned to see Thraso standing there. Her hair was tousled and her face was flushed by exertion.

"Yes, Thraso?" said Aradia.

"We have surprise for you," said Thraso, beaming. "Can you come with me?"

"Of course," said Aradia, frowning in puzzlement.

She followed her Second in Command down to the lower town where she was greeted by a platoon of Amazon Warriors on horseback.

"What ... how did you ...?" began Aradia, stunned almost speechless.

"Saraea told me that the Kaskan patrols were mounted," began Thraso, almost breathless with excitement. "I started thinking. The Kaskans were never horsemen - not like their neighbours, the Scythians. They must have stolen the Amazon horses. I went to the old stables and just beyond the paddock, I found a trail, mostly hidden by trees and brush. It led down and into the valley to where these were running wild. A cavalry unit should give us a bit of an advantage over the Romans, shouldn't it Aradia?"

"It will help indeed," said the queen. "Thraso, this wonderful - except for one thing."

"What's that?" said Thraso, worried.

"That trail you mentioned is a breach in our defences," said Aradia. "No matter how well hidden."

"I've already thought of that," said Thraso, grinning. "We need to keep it open to move the horses from the stables to the battlefield, but I have posted a squad to defend it. I kept it small enough for the women to keep hidden, so they won't draw attention to the trail itself, though."

"You are incredible, Thraso," said Aradia, smiling at her proudly. "I am so happy I chose you for my Second."

Thraso blushed and grinned happily. Then she signalled to the mounted warriors and they rode off towards the old stables.

"I would like to see this hidden trail," said Aradia as they watched the horses ride off.

"Of course," said Thraso, leading her. "Saraea was there when we got the horses. She wants one."

"Naturally," said Aradia, chuckling. "What did you tell her?"

"To ask you, of course," said Thraso.

"Of course," said Aradia. "I think when this is over, I will let her try for one of the wild herd. If she can train and ride it, she can keep and care for the horse."

"Thalia was a rider, wasn't she?" asked Thraso.

"Yes," said Aradia. "Leader of the cavalry."

"You were a rider, too, as I recall," said Thraso.

"That was a long time ago," said Aradia, shaking her head.

"For them, too," said Thraso, nodding in the direction the horses had gone. "But they said the body never forgets. Oh, Aradia, you should have seen them! They just vaulted on the backs of the wild herd and rode like the wind. It was like magic!"

"It *is* magical - the feeling of riding is incredible," said Aradia, thoughtfully. "Maybe I will take Saraea to get her horse before the battle - and get one myself. Perhaps I should lead the Amazons on horseback."

"Oh, Aradia, that would be a sight to see," said Thraso, wistfully.

"You think so?" said Aradia, one eyebrow raised.

"Oh, yes - the Amazons would love it," said Thraso. "Aurelian is mounted, isn't he?"

"Yes," said Aradia, shortly. "Where is Saraea?"

"With Mhari," said Thraso, quickly looking away from Aradia.

"Doing what?" asked the queen. Thraso shrugged. "Am I going to be annoyed by the answer to that question, Thraso?"

"It's not for me to say," said the warrior.

"Why not?" asked Aradia.

"I was asked not to," said Thraso.

"I see," said Aradia. Unwilling to ask her Second in Command to betray a confidence, she kept silent the rest of the way to the hidden trail.

Suddenly, Thraso stopped and pointed. "There," she whispered. She let out a peculiar whistle and the Amazons set to guard the trail emerged from their hiding places and saluted their queen.

"Thraso, that's not like any bird I ever heard around here," Aradia said with an amused chuckle.

Thraso grinned and shrugged. "There's the trail," she said, pointing again.

"I don't see it," said Aradia, walking closer. She had to push vines and brush away to see a faint trail leading down to the valley. It was only slightly less treacherous than the climb up the steep rock wall to the lower town, but it was, indeed, a trail. Aradia made her way down it, followed by Thraso. Again the Second in Command whistled and the Amazons guarding the bottom stepped out and saluted.

Aradia looked around at the bottom of the trail and saw the valley opened wide before her. Tall grasses waved and the scent of the water from the river came to her, bringing bittersweet memories from that time before. She caught another scent, as well, the scent of horses. Aradia looked to see a great herd, still grazing riderless. Then one in particular caught her eye. Tears sprang up and Aradia whispered, "It can't be."

"What's wrong?" asked Thraso, alarmed.

"That mare - the black one," said Aradia.

"Oh, yes," said Thraso. "She can't be caught - believe me, the others tried. Magnificent, isn't she?"

"More than magnificent," said Aradia, never taking her eyes from the midnight black mare. "She's either my horse or a descendant of her. Bring Saraea to me - now, please."

Thraso signalled to a couple of the guards who swiftly made their way up the trail. "Do you want a bridle?" she asked.

"No - not necessary," said Aradia, watching the mare prance among the herd, a queen in her own right. It was only a few moments before Saraea arrived, escorted by the sentries, but for Aradia, time froze.

"Did you want me, Aradia?" asked the girl, breathless from her swift descent down the trail.

"Watch - and learn," said Aradia, slowly approaching the herd.

"Wait," said the girl, reaching into her pocket and pulling out a large red apple. Aradia looked at her in surprise and nodded approvingly before taking the apple.

The queen walked among the horses, unafraid of the huge beasts looming all around her until she came close to the black mare. The mare saw her, watching warily, looking for a bridle or something like the other Amazons had carried into their midst. The other horses, scenting the apple in Aradia's hand, gathered close to the Amazon queen, but the mare, the object of the queen's focus, tossed her head and sidestepped away.

"Come on, Beautiful, you know you want it," Aradia crooned, holding the red fruit out to her. "Been a long time since you've had one of these, hasn't it? Come on, Sweetheart, take it."

The mare looked at the queen's offering, then sidestepped away, whinnying a warning.

"Come on, Kalika, take it from me," whispered Aradia, skilfully manoeuvring the mare away from the rest of the herd. Saraea watched, tensely silent, both fists clenched tightly down at her sides. She closed her eyes, willing the horse to come to Aradia. For what seemed like hours, Aradia stood, her arm outstretched, the apple resting on her open palm. Finally the mare bowed her head and lipped the apple into her mouth. Aradia smiled widely and stroked the long neck, allowing the mare to finish her treat before swinging herself up onto the horse's back. The mare reared up, trying to toss the burden off of herself, but Aradia clung tightly with both knees pressed into the black flanks. Horse and rider sped across the open field in a mad ride They circled both herd and Amazons several times before the mare finally tired and came to rest at the foot of the trail. Aradia still clung to her back. Her hair was wild, her eyes sparkling and she smiled brightly as she rode up the narrow trail to the stables.

Thraso and Saraea followed her on foot and watched as Aradia crooned gently to the mare, walking her back and forth in front of the stables for a bit before dismounting to lead her within. Saraea watched as Aradia led the mare to a clean stall and began to rub her down, speaking softly all the while.

"Saraea, find a brush," said Aradia. "And bring some more of those apples."

Saraea nodded and ran off. She returned with an armful of supplies, all given to her by the other riders. Aradia grinned and plucked a brush from the top of the pile. "You can set those things on the shelf over there," she told the girl. Saraea did as Aradia told her, then stepped up beside her foster-mother to watch.

"What are you doing, Aradia?" she asked.

"Watch and learn - again," said Aradia. When she was finished, the black mare shone in her stall, munching sweet oats and apples.

"Thraso said that she might be your old horse, Aradia," said Saraea. "Is she?"

"No," said Aradia, shaking her head a bit sadly. "No, she's too young to be Kalika, but I believe she must be one of her daughters. I think I'll still call her Kalika, though."

"She sure is beautiful," said Saraea, looking at the mare, wistfully.

"Yours will be just as beautiful to you, Little One," said Aradia.

"Really, Aradia?" said Saraea, excitedly. "You mean I can have a horse?"

"If you can catch and train it, then yes, you may ride and care for it - but always remember that she will be your friend and battle companion - not your property," said Aradia.

"Oh," said Saraea, nodding. "Yes, I know what you mean - like Hekau. I know that she's ... well, Who She is, but I miss her as a cat."

"So do I," said Aradia, giving the mare a final pat. "Damn rodents are all over the place."

"No, it's not just that," said Saraea. "I could tell Hekau anything. She made me feel warm ... and safe. I can't explain it."

"I know what you mean," said Aradia, looking up at Kalika and stroking her velvety face. "You can still tell her anything, you know - it's called 'prayer'."

"It's not the same," said Saraea, looking down.

"I know," said Aradia, turning to the girl and putting an arm around her shoulders. "You will feel that way again, Saraea."

"I know, but right now, I feel pretty much alone, Aradia," said the girl, quietly.

"Well, small comfort that it might be, you do have me," said the queen.

Saraea looked down. "Unless of course, you would prefer otherwise," continued the queen.

Saraea looked up at her and shook her head. "Oh, no Aradia!" she said, quickly. "It isn't that. I'm afraid."

"Of what?" asked the queen.

"Of you dying in battle," said Saraea. "That scares me more than anything - even dying in battle myself." Aradia pulled the girl into a hug.

"I wish I could promise you that won't happen," she said, quietly.

"I know you can't," said Saraea. "You never make promises that you don't know for sure you can keep."

"Not anymore," said Aradia, grimly. "Come with me, Saraea."

She took the girl's hand and led her to the summit watchtower. "Look. There they are," she said, pointing to the Roman army, marching ever closer.

"Oh, Sweet Artemis," Saraea whispered, clutching the rough stone rim of the watchtower. Her eyes widened at the sight of the eagle standard. Suddenly, in a wave of dizziness, Saraea felt herself carried back in time.

Long before the Amazons became a Nation, before the Goddess had any name save, "Mother", Her people were children of the Earth. They lived as one with their mother, the Earth and with one another, as well as Her other children. Above all, they honoured the mothers as the source of all life.

Then Saraea saw a cloud of dust rising on the horizon, beaten from the earth by the hooves of a hundred or more horses. Their riders came and attacked the gentle people, slaughtering them and conquering the land which had been their mother. They prayed to the male gods of the sky and did not honour the Mother at all. They hunted those who had escaped, but the people who fled took refuge in the caves, the womb of their mother. There, they left a record of who they had been before the raiders came. Then they were re-born as warriors from the earth. They rose and fought their conquerors, but still they were pushed north to the frozen steppes.

Saraea saw them, now mounted as were their mortal enemies, then a voice came to her, whispering in her ear, "No, my Child - that is enough. You are too young to be burdened with this knowledge ...." And the images faded from before Saraea's eyes.

"Saraea, are you alright?" asked Aradia, alarmed.

Saraea looked up at the queen and nodded. She looked at her hands, knuckles white, clutching the rim of the watchtower and slowly released them, welcoming the burning ache as sensation returned to her hands.

"I'm sorry - there's just so many of them," said Saraea.

"Yes, there are," said Aradia. "There must be at least three legions down there - they outnumber us, two to one. But that's not the worst - look there - at that wagon they're pulling. Do you see what's on it?"

"Some kind of ... machine?" said Saraea.

"That is a siege engine - or catapult, if you will," said Aradia, her lips pressed together. "We are hardly prepared for that."

"They wouldn't have gotten that through the trees if we were still in the tree village," said Saraea.

"No, but they would have felled every tree in Artemis' sacred forest if we had stayed there," said Aradia.

"What are we going to do? We haven't had time to store enough food for a siege," said Saraea. "The three cisterns are full and they can't reach them - even with that catapult thingy - but we won't have enough to feed all the Amazons."

"They know that - see the extra supply wagons?" said Aradia. "They think we will surrender when we get hungry enough - that's how Aurelian works. Bastard."

"How did they even know we were here?" asked Saraea.

"Well, it was only a matter of time before they figured it out - remember, we almost expected them to be here waiting for us both trips," said Aradia.

"You don't really believe that, though," said Saraea, looking intently at the queen.

"No, but it's far preferable to the alternative," said Aradia with a sigh.

"That we were betrayed again," said Saraea.

"Yeah," said Aradia, quietly. "Come on - we have things to do."

"What can we possibly do against *that*?" asked the girl, looking again at the Romans, marching inexorably towards the Amazon city.

"I'm about to show you," said Aradia, grimly.

The two made their way down the upper town, stopping briefly to collect Mhari. They descended the steps to the lower town and Aradia brought Mhari to the paddock to show her the horses.

"How splendid!" cried the shamaness. "That should even the odds a bit."

Saraea looked at her, then shook her head.

"What is it, Child?"

"Aradia took me to the summit tower," she said quietly.

"Ah, I see," said Mhari, her eyes twinkling. "And you think we'll need more than a few mounted warriors?"

"They have a catapult," Saraea told her, her eyes wide.

"And we have this," said Aradia, scooping up a handful of fresh horse manure.

"Ew, Aradia, that's gross," said Saraea, wrinkling her nose.

"Oh, no - it's beautiful," said the queen, her eyes gleaming.

"It is?" asked Saraea, doubtful.

"Yep - and I think it will affect the length of the siege they're planning," said Aradia, dropping the manure and wiping her hands on a rag. "I think we need to round up the rest of that herd, though - no sense in letting the Romans have access to them."

"Good idea," said Mhari, looking at Aradia and frowning in concern. She shook her head and started back up towards the upper town.

"What are you going to do with that?" asked Saraea, pointing to the lump of horse manure.

"Dip our arrows and a few darts in it," said Aradia, going to the stables and washing her hands in a basin.

"Why?" asked Saraea.

Aradia looked at her closely for a moment before answering. "Horse manure carries a poison in it," she said slowly, gauging the girl's reaction. "The poison causes a slow, painful death if it enters under the skin."

"Yes, that would shorten a siege, if all the warriors got sick," said Saraea, nodding.

"Well, not all the warriors hit with the poison arrows or darts would get sick - especially the cavalry and others who have been around horses a lot," said Aradia. "But it gives us just that much more of an edge. Obviously they are planning a siege and we are not prepared - we've not been here long enough to build up any food stores."

"We have plenty of water - the cisterns are full and inaccessible to the Romans - even by catapult," said Saraea. "Anything that can shorten the Romans' stay here, I'm for it."

"Are you sure, Saraea?" asked Aradia. "The men infected will die a horrible death."

"It isn't clean, but what they intend for the Amazons is far worse," said the girl, grimly. "Yes, Aradia, I'm sure."

"Very well," said Aradia with a sigh.

"Can I help with the horses?" asked Saraea.

"Naturally," said Aradia. The two went and gathered the other horsewomen. Aradia mounted Kalika, then pulled Saraea up behind her. "Hold on tight!"

The riders made their way down the trail to the valley below. Aradia rode into the centre of the herd of wild horses and deposited Saraea in their midst.

"Aradia, wh- what are you doing?" asked the girl looking at the horses, rearing up all around her.

"No fear, Saraea - they'll smell it on you and run away," said Aradia, flashing her a grin before riding off.

Saraea took a deep breath. She looked at all the horses surrounding her until her eyes locked on the soft, liquid brown eyes of a beautiful chestnut mare with a gold mane and tail. Saraea released the breath with a sigh of pure delight.

"Oh," she whispered, enraptured by the sight. Aradia saw the object of Saraea's attention and smiled. The mare stood a little apart from the rest of the herd. Aradia signaled to the other riders and they began the gather the rest of the herd to drive them up the trail to the paddock.

Saraea began to slowly walk towards the mare, oblivious to all else. "Oh, please come to me," she whispered as she approached. She pulled a shiny red apple from her pocket and held it out, just as she had seen Aradia do. The mare saw the girl and her offering and watched Saraea's approach warily.

Slowly, horse and girl approached one another. Saraea's focus narrowed until only those two existed. She heard both hearts beating in harmony, like a shamaness's drum. Saraea saw herself on the back of this exquisite creature, the two of them riding across the open fields. She smelled the fresh grass as it turned up under the mare's hooves. She felt the wind in her face, blowing through her hair.

At last the mare bent her head and gently took the fruit from Saraea's hand, allowing the girl to stroke her neck as she ate it.

"Stand by, Princess," said one of the riders, approaching with bridle and halter in hand. Saraea raised one hand to her.

"No, she doesn't need that yet," said the girl, never taking her eyes from the horse. Aradia rode up to them.

"Saraea, you do not yet have the skill or the strength to ride her without those," she said.

"Kaiyanta doesn't want that thing on her head - at least not yet," said Saraea, looking up at her foster-mother with pleading eyes.

"Kaiyanta?" Aradia raised one eyebrow, but motioned the others to back off away from the mare and the girl. Saraea moved closer, rubbing the mare's neck and gazing into her eyes. Finally, the mare knelt, allowing the girl to climb upon her back. Saraea's eyes shone as the horse rose back up.

"Isn't that the damnedest thing!" said another rider called Tuva as Aradia put the halter and bridle on the mare for Saraea. "You ever seen anything like that, Danaela?"

Danaela, an older cavalry member who had survived the Battle of Chadesia chuckled. "Sure," she said. "Her mother Thalia had that way with horses. That's how she came to be cavalry leader and finally, Aradia's Second."

"Heh, *I* heard Thalia became Aradia's Second on the merit of her *other* skills," said a younger rider, smirking.

"You shut your disrespectful mouth, Dosa," said Danaela, sternly.

"Well that's what I heard," said Dosa, sullen at her scolding. "I heard that Thalia caught the queen's eye and - "

"Dosa, will you *shut up*?" said Tuva through clenched teeth, looking past her. Dosa turned to see Aradia standing behind her, one eyebrow raised.

"Oh, no - by all means, Dosa, pray continue," said the queen. "I'm terribly interested in what you heard - and from *whom*."

"I ... I ... it was really nothing," said Dosa, looking down.

"Really? Nothing? So why repeat it? You know, in the old days, an Amazon convicted of causing harm by her gossip was sentenced to drink a scalding brew of tongue-bane - rendered the gossip mute for about three days. The Gorgons are a bit more harsh in their punishment. They take a wooden pin about so," Aradia held finger and thumb a few inches apart to indicate the size, "and they use it to pierce through the tongue and both lips. Then they fasten it by a means even I don't want to know about. They leave her that way for, oh, I don't know, a few months, feeding her through a hollow tube until she is left with a permanent hole in her tongue and lips. They feel that any gossip will fall through those holes before it falls upon the ears of others."

Aradia looked at Dosa for a moment to gauge the young woman's reaction to her words. Dosa looked at her, eyes wide.

"I - I didn't mean to -" she began. Aradia held up one hand, silencing her. She was aware of Saraea listening behind her.

"I, on the other hand, believe that the best way to dispel gossip is with the truth," she said. "Thalia was my Second in Command because she was the very best one to lead the Amazons after me. That's the plain simple truth of it. Anything else we were to each other is nobody else's business. Are we clear on this, Dosa?"

"Yes, your majesty," said Dosa, dipping her head in a quick bow.

"Good - come on, we have work to do - I want these horses in the paddock before sundown," said Aradia, motioning for the women to get moving. She waited until she and Saraea were alone at the foot of the trail. "You okay, Kiddo?"

"Yeah, I'm fine," said Saraea, gently patting Kaiyanta's flank.

"Listen, Saraea, what Dosa said about your mother and me - " began Aradia.

"Like you said, it's nobody else's business - not even mine," said the girl, smiling up at her foster mother. "We should probably get up there, huh?"

"Yeah, you okay to ride?" said Aradia.

"We're fine," said Saraea, starting up the trail. Aradia followed, shaking her head.

)O(

Aradia oversaw the horses being settled into the paddock outside of the stables. Then she made her way up the steps to the upper town. The Queen was exhausted after the day's work; she wanted nothing more than a hot bath, a warm supper, and a soft bed.

"I suppose I will have to settle for leftover rabbit stew and the bedroll in front of the hearth again," she said to herself with a sigh.

Wearily, Aradia made her way through the crowded streets of the upper town, raising her hand in greeting several times. She opened the door of her house to be greeted with the smells of baking bread and roasting fowl. There was a large wooden bathtub in front of the hearth and Aradia could see the steaming buckets of heated water waiting for her. Mhari was bustling about and greeted Aradia with a wide grin.

"Saraea wanted to surprise you," said the shamaness.

"She did all this?" asked Aradia.

"Most of it," said Mhari. "Remember, she took care of Silas from the time she was little."

"Yeah," said Aradia, allowing Mhari to lead her to her chair before the hearth and hand her a steaming cup of tea. "Listen Mhari, about Silas - "

"You think he betrayed us to the Romans," said the shamaness, sitting in the chair beside Aradia with her own cup.

"I think it's a good possibility," said Aradia with a sigh. "How do I protect Saraea from that if it's true?"

"Aradia, we don't know that it *was* Silas," said Mhari, shaking her head. "What's wrong with you these days? You have never been one to worry so about what *might* be."

"Maybe if I had, things would have been different," said Aradia, looking down into her cup.

"Oh, for crying out loud, stop it," said Mhari, sternly. "If you are going to keep undermining yourself, maybe you should just step down and let Thraso lead the Amazons."

"Mhari, what - ?" began a bewildered Aradia.

"I will not listen to you whine about how it was all your fault, or if only you had done this or that, things would be different," said Mhari, rising and taking both cups to the kitchen where she continued her scolding of the queen. "Do you really have the *hybris* to think that you were solely responsible for what happened? Blessed Artemis, Aradia, you are not that key a piece in the great game the gods play with us mortals. 'Maybe ... if only ...' - I'm sick of your whining. Get over yourself, Aradia; you are not that important. All you can do is your best and if you keep wondering if that's going to be good enough, then it won't be."

She emerged from the kitchen to see Aradia, red-faced, almost choking, with tears streaming down her face.

"Oh! Oh, my, Aradia!" said Mhari, rushing over to her. "Oh, dear, I didn't mean to sound so harsh! It's just that ...." Then the shamaness realised that the queen wasn't weeping; rather, she was struggling to not burst into laughter. Mhari stood and glared at her until Aradia, wiped her eyes and regained her composure.

"I'm sorry," she gasped. "It's just that .... you're absolutely right. My goodness, Mhari, you haven't scolded me like that since I was Saraea's age."

"You haven't needed it since then - until now," said Mhari.

"You are right, though," said Aradia, with a sigh. "I need to do *something* to change this feeling that no matter what I do, I will fail."

"Yes, you do," said Mhari, pouring the steaming buckets of scented water into the wooden tub. "Tell you what, why don't you have a bath now? I know those horses might possibly be the salvation of the Amazons, but the smell ... "

"Okay, Mhari," said Aradia with a chuckle. "I get it." She looked at the shamaness for a moment. "Some privacy, if you don't mind?"

"Oh, please, Aradia - I use to change your nappies," said Mhari.

"That was a long time ago," said Aradia. "Fine. Stay - just don't say anything."

"About what, Dear?" asked Mhari, as Aradia began to disrobe. Mhari gasped at a series of horrible scars laced all over the queen's torso.

"Not a word, Mhari," warned Aradia as she slowly descended into the tub. "Life as a Gladiator is not all glory and acclaim. There are certain punishments if one doesn't perform as expected."

"I see," said Mhari, nodding. "Well, I'll just leave you to your bath and collect Saraea. No doubt she'll not mind the bath house for her wash up."

"Just hurry - that dinner smells wonderful and I'm starving," said Aradia, leaning back and closing her eyes as Mhari left the house.

Aradia relaxed, breathing in the aromatic scent of the steaming bath. She felt the soreness in her limbs begin to ebb.

"Must be some herb Mhari put in the water," she murmured to herself. There was a pleasant tickling sensation at the back of her neck as the water gently rose and fell in rhythm with her breathing. Her skin tingled and her breathing grew slower and deeper. Aradia felt herself being just at that place before sleep took her, not quite awake, but aware.

Images of every battle she'd ever fought replayed before her closed eyes several times. Every possible outcome based upon Aradia's actions was shown to her. She watched with detached interest until the Battle of Chadesia replayed itself. Aradia felt her body grow more tense, then consciously, she eased it; this was the one battle she needed to see all the way through.

She and Thalia fought side by side. Suddenly, she felt a blow to her head from behind. She whirled around and saw a Gorgon warrior, a fierce sneer upon her face. She moved behind Thalia and the two fought back to back, as did the other Amazons. But it was no use. They were trapped. Briefly she turned her head and saw Thalia was battling one on one with Yarg himself. She saw that Thalia's Amazon sword did not have the reach of Yarg's long sword, putting her Second in Command at a severe disadvantage. She could only spare momentary glances at Thalia, but it was enough to see that her friend was being hard-pressed as were all the Amazons.

Frantically, Aradia tried to think of a way out of this trap before ... Suddenly, she felt Thalia slump against her. She whirled around to see Yarg pulling his sword from her breast with a sickening wet, sucking sound. With a howl of pure rage and agony, Aradia flew at Yarg, her sword raised. Her eyes saw only his blood all over her hands as the way to wash away the grief she felt at the loss of Thalia, but that was not to be. In her blind fury and battle lust, she saw only Yarg. She confronted him, her face expressionless. Twirling her sword above her head, she made the first move. Yarg parried with a bored yawn, antagonising the Amazon Queen. She ran at him and he hit her with the flat of his blade, knocking her to her knees. Aradia slowly arose, her head buzzing like a hive of bees. Her arms felt numb and her face burned. Aradia moved on Yarg, tense and focussed, scoring hit after hit, yet the giant warlord seemed impervious to her blows. His expression flitted from feigned boredom to outright amusement. Suddenly Aradia was on the ground, stunned from a blow to the back of her head. Before all went dark, she saw Athtar standing over her, grinning in triumph as she reached down and ripped Aradia's amulet from her neck, dropping it to the ground and crushing it with her foot. When she awoke, she was on a Roman slave ship, bound for the Gladiator Arena ...

)O(

Again, she and Thalia were fighting side by side. She moved behind Thalia and the two fought back to back, as did the other Amazons. But it was no use. They were trapped. Briefly she turned her head and saw Thalia was battling one on one with Yarg himself. She could only spare momentary glances at Thalia, but it was enough to see that her friend was being hard-pressed as were all the Amazons. Suddenly, she felt Thalia slump against her. She whirled around to see Yarg pulling his sword from her breast. With a howl of pure rage and agony, Aradia saw only his blood all over her hands as the way to wash away the grief she felt at the loss of Thalia.

Four Gorgons stood between her and her quarry. One at a time, as was the Amazon way, the Gorgons attacked and one by one, they fell to Aradia's crimson-slicked blade. The first approached, her face a mask of grim determination. She swung wide and rather than parry the blow, Aradia slipped past her defences and hacked off her sword arm at the elbow. She fell, clutching the spurting limb and the next Gorgon stepped over her, tripping in her eagerness to get a chance at the Amazon Queen. Aradia merely extended her sword and the Gorgon fell upon it. Bright red blood spouted out of her chest where the blade cleaved her heart, bathing Aradia in bright scarlet.

The remaining two Gorgons hesitated, weighing their strategy. They came at Aradia together. Shoulder to shoulder, they attacked the Amazon Queen, beating her back but a few steps before Aradia growled, low in her throat and leapt upon one, ignoring the other for a time. She wrapped her arm around the warrior's thigh, then turned the blade of her sword, slicing swiftly through the tendons of both legs. The Gorgon fell and Aradia rose quickly and raised her sword in one graceful and flowing move. The remaining Gorgon could only watch in horrified fascination as the sword neared, then sliced her head free of her neck.

Aradia then turned her attention to Yarg. She confronted him, her face expressionless. Twirling her sword above her head, she made the first move. Yarg parried with a bored yawn, antagonising the Amazon Queen. She ran at him and he hit her with the flat of his blade, knocking her to her knees. Aradia slowly arose, her head buzzing like a hive of bees. Her arms felt numb and her face burned. Aradia moved on Yarg, tense and focussed, scoring hit after hit, yet the giant warlord seemed impervious to her blows. His expression flitted from feigned boredom to outright amusement. He grinned at her, then brutally kicked Thalia's body away from him. That was all Aradia needed. As one possessed, she went after him with a strength like she had never known before. She turned her sword and punched him in the face with the hilt, knocking his teeth down his throat. Choking on them, Yarg fell to his knees, grasping his throat. Aradia planted one foot on his chest and knocked him flat on his back. He stared up at her, unable to move as she twirled her sword around, the point poised over his chest and plunged it downward, running the blade all the way through him, pinning him to the ground. Suddenly Aradia was on the ground, stunned from a blow to the back of her head. Before all went dark, she saw Athtar standing over her, grinning in triumph as she reached down and ripped Aradia's amulet from her neck, dropping it to the ground and crushing it with her foot. When she awoke, she was on a Roman slave ship, bound for the Gladiator Arena ...

)O(

Aradia fought alone, having left Thalia and Saraea with Silas. One on one, she battled the Kaskan chieftain, Yarg. Suddenly, she heard a familiar voice uttering a blood-freezing battle cry.

"Thalia, no!" Aradia screamed as from seemingly nowhere, her Second in Command appeared, fighting at her side.

"You didn't really believe I'd stay away from this and let you have all the fun did you?" asked a grinning Thalia. They moved into position, fighting back to back until Aradia felt Thalia slump against her. She whirled around to see Yarg pulling his sword from her breast. With a howl of pure rage and agony, Aradia turned and began to fight Yarg. Her eyes

saw only his blood all over her hands as the way to wash away the grief she felt at the loss of Thalia, but that was not to be. She saw herself, run through by Yarg's sword, her lifeless body being dragged away and hung on a cross beside Thalia ...

Over and over, the scene replayed itself, but always with the same result; no matter what Aradia did differently in each instance, the result was the same: either defeat and capture or defeat and death. Finally, she saw herself hanging on the cross next to Thalia, dead. She felt no sensation, but watched as the crows came and ate away her flesh, turning her body to mere bones and hair.

"That's how it should have ended," she whispered to herself. "If defeat was fated from the beginning, I should have died, too."

"You are hopeless," Aradia heard and opened her eyes to see Artemis. The goddess's eyes flashed in anger. "I thought you were stronger than this; that you would be able to overcome this self-pity and self-recrimination for what is clearly not your fault. Evidently, I was wrong. Go on back, then, to what you think you deserve."

Aradia felt cold. She shivered as the chill breeze from the flapping crows' wings beat upon her face. They pecked at her tender flesh. She tried to bat them away, but her wrists were securely fastened to the wooden cross-beam.

All of a sudden the crows wore human faces. At first, Aradia saw the faces of all the Amazons who had fallen in the Battle of Chadesia. They cawed at her, harsh recriminations for their deaths. She saw Athtar, cackling madly as she pecked out one of Aradia's eyes and flew off with it. A crow wearing Yarg's face buried his beak in her belly and tore out her entrails, dragging them along the ground as he flew away with them.

A large, glossy black crow wearing Aurelian's face peered at her for a moment, as if it were looking at a particularly revolting insect before fluttering towards her and tearing at her throat. One by one, she saw all those who had fallen before her sword in the arena, friend and foe alike, tearing bits of her off and flying away until there was almost nothing left but her bones.

She turned her head, the bones in her neck creaking and grinding, and looked over to the cross next to her where Thalia hung, dead. Only Thalia was gone. A large crow wearing Thalia's face was perched on top of the wooden cross, glaring at her with one yellow eye. She flew at Aradia, perching on her bony shoulder.

"You failed," she rasped at Aradia. "You failed my daughter." Then the crow who wore Thalia's face swung down and pecked away at Aradia's heart, pulling it through the bare ribs before flying off with it.

Then came the wolves. They leapt up and tore her bones down from the wooden cross, grabbing them and worrying at them until every shred of meat was gone, then carrying the dry bones away to the centre of the crossroads. The huge flock of crows awaited them. Aradia somehow continued to see what was happening. The Great Mother stood in the centre of the crossroads, waiting. She gathered the bones from the snarling wolves first and arranged them in their proper order. Then she motioned for the crows, who rose up in the air and descended *en masse*, covering Aradia's skeleton in a blanket of black feathers. They rose up in the air and flew away, leaving only Aradia's re-formed, though still lifeless body and the Goddess in the centre of the crossroads.

The Goddess held up her hands and the crow who was Thalia flew down and deposited the heart in them. She perched on the Goddess's shoulder to watch.

"I am the Circle of Re-Birth," she said, bending and placing the heart inside of Aradia's chest. "Your soul has been reborn, my daughter; let its wounds and scars be healed so that it may move on and do what you are destined to do."

Aradia sat up with a gasp. The bath water had grown cold. Her skin was wrinkled and water-logged.

"A dream," she whispered, allowing her heart to slow. Then she scowled. "Or a drug-induced nightmare. What in the four hells did Mhari put in the water?"

She was out of the tub and dressed when Mhari returned with Saraea.

"Did the bath soothe you, Dear?" asked the shamaness, smiling. Aradia merely glared at her. "No? That's odd. Ah well, are you hungry?"

"Yes, actually, I'm starving," said Aradia, her mood lightening a bit.

"Me, too!" said Saraea, her hair still damp from her bath. "I never knew riding was so hard - I thought the horse did all the work. I ache in muscles I never even knew I had."

"It'll pass," said Aradia, smiling proudly at the girl.

"That's what Danaela said - she served under my mother," said Saraea, serving up the food. "She said that I have my mother's gift with horses - what did she mean by that, Aradia?"

"Your mother had a way with all animals, but especially horses," said Aradia with a wistful smile. "When Thalia rode, it was as if she and the horse were one being. When she worked with the horses, they would do anything she wanted them to - you could almost imagine that she was asking them nicely and they were responding to that. She loved them and they returned that love. You could just *feel* it."

"With that gift, Thalia could have followed the path of the shamaness - or a priestess," said Mhari, sadly. "Instead, she chose to be a warrior."

"And died for that choice," said Aradia, bitterly. "She wouldn't even hunt - how ironic is that? She could kill a man with a smile on her face, but she wouldn't hunt an animal for food. Said it wasn't fair to use her gift to lure a creature to its death."

"I think I understand," said Saraea, quietly looking down. "I'm pretty tired. Is it okay if I just go to bed?"

"Sure," said Aradia, smiling at the girl. "Tell you what, I'll do the washing up; you go ahead and get the bedrolls laid out

... What?" She looked at Mhari and Saraea who were grinning at her.

"No need for the bedrolls," said Mhari. "This girl of ours cleaned the bedrooms and managed to procure fresh, clean mattresses and bedding. And tomorrow, she offered to do the same at my house so I can move back in there."

"You ... my, you did have a busy day didn't you, Kiddo?" said Aradia, obviously pleased. "Go on to bed, then. I'll take care of everything out here."

Saraea rose and wearily made her way to her room.

"Mhari, what did you put in that bath water?' asked Aradia.

"Just some relaxing herbs, a little rose and lavender for scent," said the shamaness. "Why?"

"I dozed off and had a ... a troubling dream," said Aradia, frowning.

"Well, moon-dark approaches; it is a time for dreams of omens and portents," said Mhari.

"Why must you always be so cryptic?" said Aradia. "As a shamaness you can interpret dreams, can't you?"

"That's what I do, Dear," said Mhari, with a smile. "That and talking to the spirits, of course. What did you dream?"

Aradia recounted the dream with as much detail as she could remember. Already the images were fading from her memory and she struggled with them. Mhari smiled and gently patted her hand.

"The experience of seeing one's body torn apart and put back together is unsettling, isn't it?" she said.

"You could say that," said Aradia. "What does it all mean?"

"Well, if you were younger, I might say that the spirits were calling you to the vocation of a shamaness - and it may be that they are. It sounds like an Initiation. But I think the beginning of the vision is equally, if not more, significant. What do *you* think that part means?"

"That no matter what I do, if the Amazons are fated to lose this battle, then they will no matter what I do," said Aradia, quietly.

"Hm, I don't think so," said Mhari.

"Then what?" asked Aradia.

"You did not see the outcome of battles to come, only battles of the past," said Mhari. "Unlike the past, the future is infinitely changeable."

"Oh," said Aradia, her eyes widening slightly. "I think ... I think I see. I can't change what happened; the Battle of Chadesia was lost and will remain so, no matter how many times and different ways I re-fight it."

"And the other part?" asked Mhari, smiling in encouragement.

"Part of me died that day," said Aradia, her eyes taking on a far away look as she remembered. "And more of me continued to die, little pieces at a time during my captivity. Now it's up to me to pull myself together - so to speak - and be fully alive again, no matter how painful that may be."

"Well?" said Mhari. "What will you do?"

"I think it should be obvious, Mhari," said Aradia, smiling slightly. "It wasn't only instinct and reflexes that made me fight for my life in the arena; I want to live."

)O(

Saraea lay down and was almost instantly asleep, despite the fact that her feet hung off the end of the small child's bed. She had indeed had a busy day - *and a busier one to come*, Thalia thought as she gazed at her sleeping daughter. Still, Saraea's work was not done. Thalia waited until she knew that both Mhari and Aradia were asleep in the other rooms, then bent and gently shook the girl awake.

"What ... ?" began Saraea, sleepily. She rubbed her eyes and looked at the glowing blue figure standing beside her bed. "Wh - who ...?"

"It's alright - don't be scared, Saraea," said Thalia.

"Mother?" said the girl.

"Yes," said Thalia. "I want you to come with me - it's important, Saraea."

"Okay," said the girl, pulling on her leather breeches and boots.

"We must be very quiet - don't wake the others," said Thalia, leading her to the window and boosting her out to the soft ground.

"Where are we going?" asked Saraea, not quite convinced that she wasn't still asleep in her bed.

"To the Temple," said Thalia. "I must show you something."

"Will you be there with me?" asked the girl, slipping her small hand into Thalia's larger one. Saraea could feel the rough sword calluses on the warrior's palm. "Are you really dead?"

"Yeah," said Thalia. "But I'm still with you; I always will be."

Saraea smiled and the two walked hand in hand through the quiet dark streets to the Temple. Thalia pulled open the heavy oak door and ushered Saraea into the absolute dark stillness of the Temple.

"What did you want to show me?" asked Saraea, shivering a bit. It was a trifle unnerving to her that the only illumination in this sacred place was the bluish glow emanating from her mother's ghost.

Thalia moved along the walls of the Temple, lighting the lamps which hung at intervals along the length of the Temple on either side before replying. In the warm flickering lamplight, she stopped glowing, appearing as real and as solid as Saraea herself. She beckoned her daughter to the front of the Temple where the altar stood.

"Do you remember where Aradia found the scrolls?" she asked.

"Yes - in fact, I put them back there myself," said Saraea. "Just in case the Romans ..."

"Yes, the Romans," said Thalia, grimly. She held out her hand and the altar slid away to reveal two wooden trap doors, side by side. Thalia stepped up and pulled open the one Saraea hadn't seen before. "Come here, Saraea."

"Wait - the last time I came here with someone I thought I knew in the middle of the night, it turned out to be Ares in a disguise he pulled from my own memories," said Saraea. "How do I know that you're really my mother?"

"I am very pleased that you learn from your mistakes, Little One," said Thalia with a small chuckle. "Unfortunately, I can offer you no proof that would make you believe what I say. You just have to have faith."

"Okay - what is that you want me to do?" asked Saraea, warily.

"Under the Temple is a tunnel which leads to a chamber," said Thalia. "Only the priestesses remembered it. In that chamber is something which will help Aradia against Aurelian and the Romans. I want you to get it and give it to her."

"That's it?" said Saraea. "Why me? Why not lead Aradia to it instead?"

"Because only a priestess is permitted to enter this chamber," said Thalia.

"I'm not a priestess," said Saraea. "I'm not really even an Amazon yet."

"Oh, but you are," said Thalia, smiling at her. "You were destined for the Temple since you were born."

"What if I refuse?" asked Saraea.

"It is your choice, Saraea," said Thalia.

"It is?" said the girl.

"Of course - the Goddess does not want unwilling servants," said Thalia.

"But if I don't do Her will, the consequences will be terrible, right?" said Saraea.

"That depends on your definition of 'terrible'," said Thalia. "I think if you choose another vocation, you will spend the rest of your life feeling unfulfilled because you're not doing what you are best suited to do, but I don't see any great catastrophe befalling you or the Amazon Nation just because you exercised free will."

"Well, I know you're not Ares now - he uses a lot more pressure - and guilt - to convince people to do what he wants," said Saraea with a sigh. "But how did you know about this secret chamber that only priestesses can enter?"

"No, Saraea, I am not Ares," said Thalia, smiling gently. "It isn't a secret. At one time all the Amazons knew about it. Only priestesses are permitted to enter it, but that's because it's a consecrated place; if anyone else were to step foot there, it would lose its magic. I think when you see what is in the chamber below, you will understand more."

"Okay," said Saraea, stepping up to the trap door. She looked down into the inky blackness, then back up to her mother's face. The girl leaned up and kissed Thalia's cheek, brushing a tear from her own. "I sure do miss you."

"I know," said Thalia, tears welling in her own eyes.

"Um, I don't suppose you can come with me?" said Saraea.

"Of course I'll be with you, Saraea," said Thalia. "I always am - remember that; but it takes a lot of energy to manifest this way and I've about used mine up."

"Okay," said Saraea, nodding. She climbed down into the tunnel.

"Wait," Thalia said, reaching over and taking the Sword of Artemis from the statue's hand. "You'll need this." Saraea's eyes widened a bit, but she took the Sword. Thalia smiled. "No, not to fight."

Remembering how the Sword had illuminated Athtar's dark cave, Saraea nodded, relieved and began to make her way through the narrow tunnel. It sloped downward in a gentle incline and Saraea walked, holding the Sword like a torch. She noticed carvings on the walls, strange symbols and pictures which told stories. She would have lingered to study them, but she was filled with a sense of urgency.

She walked until the she came to a wooden door at the end of the tunnel. She tried the door, but found it locked.

"Now what?" she whispered to herself. Suddenly the Sword shimmered and vibrated in her hand. It changed into a small silver key which Saraea fitted into the lock. The door swung open.

"Stop!"

Saraea looked to see a woman standing before her, blocking her from taking another step. She was tall and dark. She wore black silk robes with long scarlet and flame-coloured feathers trailing from a magnificent headdress and cape. "Who are you, Youngling? Do you not know the prohibition against anyone besides a priestess entering this sacred place?"

"I do know, but I was told that I was permitted," said Saraea, hesitant before the Guardian of this place.

"Who told you this?" asked the Guardian.

"M...my mother - or her shade, really," replied the girl. "I am Saraea, daughter of Thalia."

"By what sign do I know you are to be permitted?" asked the Guardian.

Saraea held up the silver key, which transformed back into the Sword. The Guardian smiled and stepped aside.

"It is the Goddess Herself who permits you, then," she said, fading from Saraea's sight.

"This just isn't possible," said Saraea, stepping gingerly into the huge chamber. "I have to be dreaming ... or something. This isn't possible!"

"Have faith," Saraea heard Thalia's voice in her mind. "Suspend your disbelief, Little One - remember how you believed in this magic and this place when you were small."

She looked around, hearing the sound of running water somewhere. Giant bins, spilling over with various types of grain stood along the far wall of the chamber. Empty grain sacks were neatly folded in front of each bin, waiting to be filled. Other wooden chests lined the other walls and Saraea eagerly went to them, slipping the Sword into her waistband since the chamber was illuminated by some source Saraea could not see.

She wandered about, peering into chests and bins and cabinets. She found lamp oil, dried fruit and meat in addition to the grain. She also found chests of scrolls she hadn't read yet. Checking her eagerness with some difficulty, Saraea looked around for the item she was supposed to bring back to Aradia, promising herself she would return to explore further.

Then she saw another wooden door at the far end of the cavernous chamber. Quickly she walked over to it, but found it locked. She pulled out the Sword, but it remained a Sword, so Saraea slipped it back into her waistband with a shrug.

"Saraea, in this place, time stands still," she heard. She turned to see Thalia, translucent and wavering. "But outside it does not. It is nearly dawn. You must get what you came for and go back."

"But what is it I'm supposed to bring out?" asked the girl, bewildered as Thalia faded before answering. Saraea sighed. Then her eyes caught a chest, smaller than most of the others. It had the Queen's mark carved upon its lid. "This must be it."

Saraea picked up the small chest and carried it back with her through the tunnel and into the Temple.

Chapter Nine: Memories of the Sword

Aradia was awakened by clamouring outside of her house shortly before dawn. She arose, grabbing for her sword, then remembered that she had not yet replaced the one broken in Athtar's cave. She threw on trousers and boots and ran out to the front door, Mhari close behind her.

"What's going on?" asked the shamaness, clutching a shawl about her shoulders.

"I don't know - " Aradia began. She was interrupted by a knock on the door. It was her lieutenants, Anaea and Prothoë.

"Your Majesty," said Anaea, offering a hasty salute. "The Romans are camped about below the lower town. They're just beyond the first perimeter, but they've not attacked the platoons there."

"Yet," said Prothoë. "But even worse, the Sword of Artemis is gone!"

"Worse?" said Aradia, raising one brow and shaking her head. "Okay, okay - where is Thraso?"

"She's in the lower town, positioning the archers and mobilising the cavalry," said Anaea.

"Good," said Aradia. "Let me just get my gear and - damn! I need a Sword!"

"Never mind about that," said Mhari, emerging from the back of the house. "Saraea's gone."

Aradia closed her eyes and took a deep breath. "Okay," she said. "You two go to your posts. I will find Saraea. Mhari, assemble the elders to the Temple - please."

"Wait a minute," said the shamaness, moving past her. The others followed her gaze to the Temple. A bright silvery light spilled out as the door opened and Saraea emerged, the Sword of Artemis glowing at the girl's waist. She carried a wooden chest in her two hands and she started, then quickened her step when she saw the women gathered outside of Aradia's house.

"Anaea, Prothoë, let the Amazons know that the Sword isn't gone, then report to your posts," said Aradia. The two women nodded and left to obey the orders.

"Aradia, don't scold her," said Mhari.

"Why not?" asked the queen, one brow raised.

"Because she has the 'look'," said the shamaness. Aradia looked at her puzzled. "She's been doing the work of the Goddess this night and I think you would regret any harsh words to her."

"Very well - I'll control myself," said the queen, drily.

"Aradia - you - you're awake," said a dirt-smudged Saraea. "Looks like the whole town is, actually."

"Saraea, what is this?" asked Aradia, arms folded across her chest.

"I don't know," said the girl, handing the chest to her. "It's for you."

Aradia took the chest and looked in wonder at the mark carved into its lid. "Where did you get this?" she asked.

"Aradia, what would you say if I told you there was huge hidden room beneath the Temple?" said Saraea, smiling, her eyes shining.

"I'd say you inherited your mother's imagination," said Aradia, guiding the girl into the house. Mhari followed and the three sat before the hearth. Aradia rested the wooden chest in her lap. She spoke as calmly as she could, containing her annoyance with the girl. "What were you doing in the Temple, Saraea?"

The girl looked down at her grubby hands for a moment before answering. "My mother sent me there," she replied, not expecting to be believed.

"Thalia was here?" said Aradia, her brow slightly furrowed, her voice soft.

Saraea looked up and nodded. "She took me to the Temple and moved the altar aside. You know where the scrolls were hidden?" Aradia nodded and the girl continued. "Well, if you push the altar a bit further, there's another trap door which goes into this long tunnel."

"And at the end of the tunnel?" asked Mhari, her eyes shining with excitement.

"There's a wooden door - and you're not going to believe this, but the Sword of Artemis is the key," said Saraea, her voice hushed, scarcely believing her own words as the night's excursion slipped into a dreamlike memory.

"I do believe you, Saraea," said Aradia, quietly. "This huge chamber is beyond that door?"

"Yes - Aradia, you wouldn't believe what I saw there!" said Saraea, her eyes widening at the memory. "There's so much food stored there, the Romans could lay siege on the towns for a hundred years and we'd never go hungry!"

"Saraea ... now, I believe that there's a secret chamber below the Temple," said Aradia, slowly.

"It's not really a secret - it's just been forgotten," Saraea interrupted.

"Even so," said Aradia, frowning. "This room could not be as big as you describe - why, the whole town would collapse if the integrity of this mound was so compromised. Further, even if there is some food stored there, the latest it could have been put there was before the Battle of Chadesia ten years ago; what the rodents and bugs didn't get to would be rotten."

"I saw it with my own eyes," said Saraea, firmly.

"Okay, look - I don't have time to argue with you, Saraea," said Aradia, wearily. "The Romans are camped below the lower town, and - "

"Already?" Saraea cried out in alarm.

"Yes," said Aradia, rising and setting the chest on the floor.

"Wait, Mother said that whatever was in that chest could help you against the Romans," said Saraea. "Open it - please, Aradia?"

Aradia sighed and sat back down, lifting the chest to her lap again before lifting the lid off of the chest. The queen grew pale.

"Saraea, where did you get this? The truth!"

"In the chamber below the Temple - I swear it, Aradia," said Saraea, solemnly.

"I - I have to believe you," said Aradia, lifting her amulet, destroyed so long ago by Athtar, out of the chest.

"Oh, that's beautiful!" said Saraea.

"That's not all," said Aradia, her voice barely above a whisper, She reached in and pulled out a leather sword-belt covered with silver plaques and decorated with the same Triple Moon and *labrys* design as the Sword of Artemis. "The Girdle of Sovereignty - this has been lost to the Amazon Nation for hundreds of years. And this - " She pulled out a silver circlet with the same design centred where it would rest on the brow.

"Is that the queen's crown?" whispered Saraea in awe.

"No - it was worn by the last High Priestess of the Amazon Nation," said Mhari, reverently. "It was believed lost with her - so long ago, no one can even remember her name now."

"I'll bet it's recorded in the scrolls I found there, too," said Saraea.

"There are more scrolls?" asked Aradia.

"At least one whole chestful - I didn't have time to look at everything in there," said Saraea.

"Blessed Artemis," whispered Aradia. "I must see this place!"

"You can't," said Saraea, sadly. "Mother told me that if anyone who is not a priestess sets foot in there, the magic will disappear."

"That's nonsense," said Aradia, frowning.

"No, I think not," said Mhari, thoughtfully. "It's a sacred place; it makes sense that only consecrated servants of the Goddess would be permitted there."

"Saraea isn't a priestess," Aradia argued.

"She is much more than a priestess, Aradia," said Mhari, softly. The shamaness moved to the girl, gently lifting her sleeve to expose a new tattoo. The Triple Moon and *labrys* which graced the "royal regalia" was now and forever etched into Saraea's skin. "Thalia was Artemis's own daughter."

"We are all Daughters of Artemis," said Aradia, feeling a growing unease at the shamaness's words.

"Aradia, search your heart," said Mhari, her eyes staring far off. "The truth is written there. Thalia was born of the goddess, her avatar, the divine made manifest in flesh and blood."

"That's not possible," said Aradia, shaking her head. "Thalia *died* - if she were Artemis's own daughter, wouldn't the goddess have saved her?"

"Thalia gave her life willingly to save you, Aradia - to save the Amazon Nation," said Mhari. "Her mortal death was necessary to free her spirit that she might do the work of her mother."

"No!" Aradia cried as Saraea watched both women, her eyes wide. "How could she? How could she leave me? How could she leave *Saraea*?"

"She hasn't left us, Aradia," said Saraea, calmly. "She's just ... different now. But she's still here. She's *always* here with us - can't you feel her?"

"The Gorgons' betrayal and the Amazons' defeat was foreseen yet unpreventable," said Mhari. "Thalia was born in the flesh in order that she might bear a mortal daughter to ensure the Amazons' survival after the Battle of Chadesia. You were chosen to be that child's guardian and protector."

"I see," said Aradia, coldly. "So I was nothing more to Thalia than a babysitter in the great scheme of destiny. And what about Silas? She lied to me - how he could be her brother? Is he an avatar, too?"

"Aradia," said Saraea, softly. The warrior looked up and saw the girl, surrounded by a bluish light, Thalia standing behind her, tears streaming from both mother and daughter's eyes. Saraea reached out to the warrior, brushing the tears which also flowed from Aradia's eyes away. The anger in Aradia's chest melted away in the warmth which filled her.

"Silas *is* my brother; he was born to the mortal woman who raised me - just as you will raise Saraea," said Thalia.

"Thalia, *why*?" she said.

"Because I love you," said Thalia. "I love you and I trusted no other to protect and care for our daughter."

Aradia looked from Thalia to Saraea and her heart was filled with such love and fierce pride as she had never known before.

"I can't fight against love," Aradia said, embracing Saraea, holding her closely for a moment before releasing her. She looked to Thalia. "I love you both so much ... it hurts."

"I know," said Thalia, smiling. "It hurts me, too. But I must do what I was born to do - and so must you two. Be safe and well and know that I am always with you, even now."

"I'll try," said the queen, as Thalia faded from their sight. She arose, fastening the girdle around her waist and placing the Sword of Artemis in the sheath attached to the belt; it was a perfect fit. The amulet Aradia lovingly lowered over Saraea's head until it rested in the hollow of the girl's throat. "I want you to have that, Saraea - I didn't have a chance to make one for you before your Initiation."

Tears welled in the girl's eyes and she hugged the queen. Gently disengaging herself from the girl, Aradia quickly kissed Saraea's forehead, then left the house without another word.

)O(

Ares arose, dazed. Except for the sounds of birds and the wind in the trees, the clearing was silent. Myrina was long gone, with the Sword of Artemis.

"Ares." The god of war turned to see Artemis standing behind him.

"If you've come to gloat - " he began, annoyed.

"Hardly," said Artemis.

"Good. Because the Amazons are doomed," said Ares, grinning at her. "Their sworn enemy has your Sword now. It's only a matter of time - "

"Oh please! Don't insult my intelligence by pretending you had this planned all along," said Artemis, shaking her head. "You really don't get it any more than that pathetic creature did."

Ares looked to see Athtar stumbling out of the cave, blinking in the brightness of the clearing.

"Get what?" asked the god. "As I see it, it won't be very long at all before I am the Supreme God, the one and only, the Alpha and Omega - "

"This is just a game to you, isn't it, Ares?" said Artemis. "'He who has the most followers, wins' - well, it isn't a game to me, Ares, and it isn't one to *Her* either."

"Oh, *Her*," said Ares, rolling his eyes. "Please - at the end of all this, I will be even bigger than She is, so don't try to scare me off with that threat."

A slow smile crept across Artemis's face. "You think so?" she said, softly.

"Oh, yeah," said Ares with a grin. "You still want to play - I can see it in your eyes, Artemis."

"Ares, this ceased to be a game when you started on the Amazons," said the goddess, severely.

"Aw, did I pick on your pet mortals?" Ares taunted.

"You have no idea what you're doing, Ares," said Artemis. "I'm warning you - "

"You're warning *me*?" Ares laughed. "Artemis, the Amazons are as good as extinct. And when they are, you will be answering to *me*. You might want to think about that a while before you say another word to me."

"Well, Ares, let me just give *you* something to think about," said Artemis, smiling. Suddenly, she changed before Ares's eyes and before him stood Medusa.

"What ... that was *you*?" he said, incredulous. Artemis changed back before replying.

"Yes, it was," said Artemis. "So you see, you 'played' yourself right out of the Gorgons. They are still mine. *And* they have the Sword." Chuckling, she faded from his view.

"Yeah, well I still have one move left. This isn't over by a long way, Artemis," said Ares, glaring at the space she once occupied before disappearing with an audible "pop".

)O(

Aradia made her way down to the lower town and found Thraso. She had put aside the revelation of who Saraea was for a time and was now focussed on what she had to do to ensure the survival of the Amazons.

"Aradia, I have everyone in position," said the Second in Command, grimly. She looked around at the troops, all armed and in their places. "Romans ... Sweet Artemis, are we ready for this?"

"Is anyone ever ready for war?" asked Aradia. "More importantly, we don't have a choice."

Thraso nodded. "So, what do we do now?"

"We wait," said Aradia. "Let them make the first move. Have the archers ready to back up the platoons at the perimeter - do they have the new arrows?"

"Aradia, those are repulsive!" said Thraso, grimacing. "The whole lot smells worse than stable offal. But yes, I have followed your orders to the letter."

Aradia chuckled. "That smell may be just the edge we need to survive this," she said.

"Well, don't expect me to bathe in it, despite all of that," chuckled Thraso. Then she grew solemn. "Aradia, Silas is with the Romans. I saw him down there on horseback, right next to Aurelian."

"I had a feeling it was he who betrayed us," said Aradia with a sigh. "I didn't want to believe it, for Saraea's sake, though."

"No, Aradia, you don't understand," said Thraso, shaking her head. "I don't think he's there by choice."

"What do you mean, Thraso?" asked Aradia, frowning.

"I mean, he looks terrible," said the Second in Command. "Come."

She led the queen to a hidden lookout where they could see the Roman troops without themselves being seen. The Amazons crouched down low in the brush.

"Look - there," Thraso whispered, pointing.

Aradia felt a quiet rage rise up within her. She had to consciously restrain herself from rushing down the hill and grabbing Silas, killing any Roman who got in her way.

Silas sat on the back of a horse. His head hung down as if he hadn't the strength to hold it up. His hands were tied in front of him and a gaping wound in his temple still oozed blood. Other wounds on his face and limbs were crusted over with dried blood, leading the Amazons to think that his ordeal at the hands of their enemy had been a long one. Suddenly Silas looked up and turned his eyes to look directly at the hidden Amazons, giving the women a start, but his eyes were glassy and vacant.

Silently, Aradia arose and started back towards the ruined fortress where the troops were mobilised and waiting, Thraso right behind her.

"Aradia, we have to get him out of there," Thraso said. "They'll kill him.

"He's already dead," said Aradia, continuing to walk.

"But Aradia - "

"Thraso, we can do nothing for him," said the Queen. "Let it go."

"If it were an Amazon down there - "

"He isn't an Amazon," said Aradia, stopping and whirling to face her Second in Command.

"No but he raised one," said Thraso.

Aradia closed her eyes for a moment. *He raised more than just an Amazon,* she thought, then again, put away the knowledge until she had the leisure to think about it. "I take your point Thraso," she said. "But I really don't believe you have any idea what we're dealing with here. These are Romans, not Kaskans."

"I don't see any difference, except that there are more of them than there were Kaskans," said Thraso.

"You don't understand - you don't know what Aurelian is capable of," said Aradia, her eyes taking on a far away, haunted look.

"I suppose you do," said Thraso, quietly.

"Unfortunately, yes," said Aradia, coming back with a sigh. "Yarg was a brute. He could fight well enough, but he was not cunning, not outright ... *evil* like Aurelian. He could never have overcome the Amazons without the Gorgons' betrayal."

"And Aurelian could?" asked Thraso, quietly.

"Yes, he can," said Aradia, troubled. "But that's not for general knowledge, Thraso."

"No, of course not," said Thraso. "Can we stop him?"

"Yes, we can," said Aradia, smiling. "You see, the other side of knowing what he is capable of is knowing his weaknesses. I will not lead the Amazons into battle against an enemy if there is no hope of winning - not ever again."

"You're talking about the Battle of Chadesia," said Thraso. "But you couldn't know that we would be defeated - could you?"

Aradia was silent for a moment. "No, I didn't know - I didn't believe it," she said, quietly, the haunted look back in her eyes. "I had been given certain ... warnings, which I ignored because I didn't consider the source reliable."

"What source was that?" asked Thraso.

"The old priestess, Leilë - she was having visions; told me to take the Amazons and leave our home," said Aradia. Thraso looked down and hesitated a moment before speaking.

"Aradia, I'm not sure what I would have done in your place," said Thraso. "It's easy to look back ten years down the road and say what we should have or have not done. I know that all those years, hiding and being hunted like animals, it would have been such a relief to burst out and confront the enemy once and for all."

"Thank the Lady you had the sense I didn't have at the time or none of us would be here," said Aradia.

"Now that we are, what are we going to do about this?" asked Thraso. "I mean, I see the problem about rescuing Silas. I just can't stand to think of him down there like that - and what about Saraea?"

"Saraea is not to know of this," said Aradia, firmly. "If I see an opportunity to rescue Silas without risking the Amazons, I will take it - that's all I can do, Thraso."

Thraso nodded, then turned to the troops. "How long do you suppose we'll have to wait?" she asked Aradia.

"Aurelian will want to make absolutely certain that we see him," said Aradia. "I'm sure that he has already sent scouts this way."

"We saw them - they did not see us," said Thraso. "What's more, they've not yet reached the perimeter where our warriors are. It's entirely possible that he's not certain we're here, after all."

"Oh, he knows we're here - don't underestimate Aurelian," said Aradia.

"What did he do to you that makes you so afraid of him?" asked Thraso.

Aradia remained silent, but the memories of that time after her capture assaulted her with a vengeance.

Aradia woke up in the dark hold of the ship bound for Rome. The captured Amazons were packed, side by side and shackled to one another, unable to move in any way. Sickened by the movement of the seas, they lay in their own vomit and filth. Their miserable and pathetic moans went unheard by any, save the occasional guard who, holding his nose against the indescribable stench, opened the door to the hold from above to throw down food and water which lay there mostly untouched until it rotted.

How long the journey lasted, Aradia did not know, but at the end, of the fifty or so Amazons captured, only Aradia and three others survived. The last day of the journey, they were pulled roughly from the hold below the deck and Aradia saw the bodies of her dead sisters thrown into the sea. The four survivors, too weak to protest, were taken to a place where they were bathed, dressed in thin gauzy veils and their hands were chained with links of gold.

Aradia at last felt the vestiges of this nightmare begin to pierce through to her soul. With a feral scream, she broke the golden chains and attacked the guards. It took several of the Roman soldiers to subdue her. She was then chained with heavy iron, beaten where the bruises and lash marks would not show through the filmy and revealing Greek chiton *and marched with her sisters through the streets of Rome.*

Aurelian rode ahead of the Amazons, proudly waving to the masses who were lined up along the streets, alternately cheering the General and screaming obscenities at the "unnatural" women. Aradia kept her head up, hissing to the others to do the same. They were marched before the emperor's palace and there the procession ended. Aradia glared defiantly upward at Gallienus who stood above them in the balcony. He had taken great pains to hide the ravages of both time and debauchery before appearing to the citizens who worshipped him like a god. His face was painted and powdered, his purple robes hung on his gaunt frame like draperies over a skeleton. The Amazon could find no mercy or even nobility in his cold black eyes which reminded her of a snake's eyes. She glared up at him until she was roughly pushed to her knees, her head shoved down in a sign of obeisance she certainly did not feel ...

"Aradia ... Aradia," Thraso said, gently pulling her away from the memory.

"I'm sorry, Thraso," said the Queen, shaking her head, trying to shake the images which still haunted her dreams.

"What happened to you in Rome?" asked her Second in Command.

Slowly at first, Aradia began to tell Thraso the story, the images again coming to her in such a way, it was as if she were back there in that hell all over again.

"What happened after you saw the Emperor?" asked Thraso, gently pulling the memories to the surface.

"We were taken to the auction block to be sold as slaves," said Aradia. "Aurelian and the Emperor were done with us. That's why they took such care to bathe, perfume, and paint us like whores - that's where they figured we'd end up anyway. And we almost did ..."

It was far too cold for the revealing garment. Aradia stood on the auction block along with the other three Amazons. All four shivered in the chill, damp wind waiting to be bought. The Romans' language was starting to be understandable to the women.

"A hundred denarii!" cried one bidder.

"Each!" cried another, trying to outbid the first. The two men began to argue with one another. Aradia's violet eyes rested on the man who had put her in this nightmare. Aurelian stood outside of the throng, watching coldly, waiting to see the outcome of his expedition to Amazonia. Then he would be finished with them.

Aradia heard the hushed voices of other women, awaiting their turn to be bought.

"Huh, my old master wouldn't give 'em one denarii - unnatural women! What could they know about serving in a

brothel? Like as not, they'd rather do each other than paying customers."

"There'd be plenty who'd pay a fortune just to watch that," chuckled another.

The other Amazons looked to Aradia, panic in their eyes, silently begging their queen to save them from this fate.

"Sold! To Amor for three hundred and twenty denarii - each!"

The brothel owner stepped up, grinning, to take possession of his newly acquired property. Aradia looked at her sisters, tears welling in her eyes, praying they would understand. Then, with a furious howl, she grabbed a dagger from the unsuspecting man. So fast it was a blur to the watching crowd, Aradia whirled about, and sliced the throats of her sisters in one flowing move. Their blood flew and splattered all over the flimsy garment she wore before the three fell dead at her feet. Aradia completed the revolution with the point of the dagger at her own chest. Just before she could plunge it into her heart, Aurelian was there. He grabbed her long hair in one hand and the dagger with the other, shoving the Amazon Queen to her knees.

The brothel owner stood, shaking as Aurelian handed the bloody dagger back to him without a word. The auction announcer stammered ... "S...sale cancelled." Aurelian dragged her away from the auction block by her hair. As she passed, she saw the women who had been talking earlier, one looking at her with a smug satisfaction and the other with an almost wistful mistiness to her expression.

Aurelian took her to a cell - really a hole in the ground - and threw her in it. It was so small, Aradia could not stand or even sit up. She was forced to crawl about on her knees just to get to the door where her daily ration of thin gruel, mouldy bread, and stale water were left. She didn't bother; Aradia was haunted by her deed, though it was what she would have wished for in her sisters' place. She hoped that they understood, wherever in Eternity their souls rested now.

Aurelian left her there for three days before he came and pulled her out. She was taken in the back of a cart to a large estate just outside of the city, then permitted to bathe and change into, by Aradia's standards, more suitable clothing. She was still in the heavy iron chains though and shackled about her ankles as well as her wrists and now the chains had been considerably shortened.

She was escorted to Aurelian who awaited her in his study. He was sitting on a padded bench, reading a roll of parchment. She stood, staring dully at him until he dismissed the escort and the two were alone in the room.

"You cost me a fortune and I should take it out of your flesh," he said, awaiting her reaction. There was none. "Don't pretend like you can't understand me - I know better."

Still the Amazon Queen stood, silent and waiting. Aurelian arose and began to pace. "I should, but I have managed to salvage something out of this fiasco. The whole expedition was a waste of resources, but I have a feeling, my dear Amazon Queen, that you will make all of that up to me."

Despite the fact that Aradia still said nothing, simply staring vacantly at the Roman General, he continued. "You are going to fight in the arena for me. An Amazon should bring in quite a revenue in wagers alone."

That's what you think, *Aradia thought to herself, though she remained silent. Aurelian whirled around and looked at her.*

"Oh you will *fight, Aradia," he said, grinning at her. The only indication that she was aware of his words was a slight , involuntary shiver. "If you do not, I will find another use for you, one you may not like as well."*

Aradia tried to still her mind, seeking that oblivion which had been eluding her since this nightmare began on the battlefield of Chadesia.

"You may even come to enjoy it, Aradia - many do," said Aurelian. "Unfortunately, I cannot allow you the luxury of an

income to one day buy your freedom as the others are permitted, but there will be rewards, I assure you."

"And were there?" asked Thraso.

Aradia snapped out of her reverie at the sound of Thraso's voice.

"No, not really," she replied. "Only those the citizens found amusing or entertaining were rewarded. I did neither."

Aradia stood in the centre of the ring, listening to the roaring from the stands. From both doors at either end of the arena came her opponents for this match. The retiari *ran at her from behind, net trailing, trident extended. Before her, a Samnite approached more cautiously, hiding behind his long shield, only the bright quivering plumes of his helmet were visible above the top.*

The Amazon tried to stand her ground. Oh, please, Sweet Lady Artemis, if you love me, you will let them kill me this time, *she thought. Almost against her will, Aradia twirled her sword over her head. She was not permitted anywhere near this weapon or any other except when she entered the arena, but at least they had ceased to keep her chained between matches. The Samnite hesitated, allowing the* retiari *to approach her first. He yelled and ran at her, raising the net to throw it over Aradia's head. With a bland expression, Aradia merely extended the sword and in as small a swing as possible, took the warrior's net hand off at the wrist. He staggered back, dropping the trident to hold his spurting wrist. Aradia stood her ground, aware of the Samnite creeping slowly up behind her. She heard his metal armour clink as he shifted his shield to strike at her. Suddenly, she whirled around, swinging the sword with the momentum of her turn and sliced through the exposed neck of the Samnite. He fell to the ground, already dead. The crowd booed, clamouring for the death of the* retiari, *but Aradia was done. She threw down the sword and walked off, back to her cell, knowing that she would pay later for her lack of showmanship.*

Aurelian awaited her in the tunnel which led to the Gladiator cells. Aradia stopped and waited for him to produce the metal-tipped whip, but this time was different.

"I can no longer afford you, Aradia," he said, shaking his head with a sigh. "If only I could trust you, you would be the perfect warrior in my Legion."

"I would never fight for Rome," Aradia said, her eyes flashing in rare emotion.

"No you would not," said Aurelian, signalling to the guards. They stepped up and clamped the shackles and chains on Aradia's wrists and ankles. "I could, however, try to breed you - what kind of warriors would an Amazon and Rome's elite produce, I wonder?"

"I will kill any man who tries to touch me that way, if I have to rip out his throat with my teeth," said Aradia through clenched teeth. "Failing that, I will strangle the thing as it comes from the womb."

"Yes, I know that, too," said Aurelian. "I don't have the time or patience to see that experiment to that end, anyway. So, I am sending you to the Provinces. They are not as jaded as the citizens as Rome; they won't expect such spectacular kills."

"I suppose being shipped out of Rome and out to the Provinces was a reward after all," said Aradia, breaking out of the memory. "Aurelian was right - they didn't mind as much if I wasn't entertaining when I fought; if they saw blood, they were happy."

"These Romans, they are like animals," said Thraso, incredulous.

"No, animals are more honourable," said Aradia. "They kill only to survive, not for sport. I thought I would spend the rest of my days in the arena, waiting to die. At first, I was kept chained all the time, touring the Provinces. Some of those places didn't even have an arena, just a dirt ring scratched out in some farmer's field. Those were the worst."

"Why is that?" asked Thraso.

Aradia closed her eyes against the memories. "Because every young peasant boy wanted to take down the Amazon Queen in battle," she said, softly. "Stupid. Such a waste of young life."

"Did you ... Didn't you ever ... um ..." Thraso stammered, unable to stop herself from asking the question. Aradia's eyes gazed unwavering at her.

"What?" asked the queen, gently. "Try to escape?" Thraso nodded. "At first, many times. Every time, Aurelian was there, stopping me and punishing me for the attempt. I even tried to fall on my own sword in the arena almost every time they put me there the first several times. Each time, Aurelian stepped in and stopped me. It was almost as if he read my thoughts before I even thought them. He *always* knew what I was going to do even before I did sometimes. It was uncanny."

"How did he know?' asked Thraso. Aradia shook her head.

"I just don't know," she said, her voice barely above a whisper. "But he did - and something tells me he still does."

"No, Aradia - no mortal has that power," said Thraso.

"I keep trying to tell myself that until I believe it," said Aradia with a wry chuckle. Then she looked around at the fortress ruins and all the bustling activity of her Amazon troops as they prepared for war. "Here, I almost can believe it."

"Aradia, he will never hurt you again," said Thalia. "By coming here, he has pretty much signed his own death papers."

)O(

Aurelian sat in his tent. He hated this place and never expected to have to return here.

"Aradia," he snarled, then arose pacing. The Emperor didn't feel the Amazons were a threat to the Empire - they were so fragile, most hadn't even survived the journey to Rome. Except Aradia had proven to Aurelian that they were not fragile, not at all.

It had been a mistake to send her from Rome. Aurelian realised that now. Up until she reached Thracia, he knew her every thought. The general had studied Aradia carefully. He knew what she was likely to do with any opportunity. Even after so many years, he never let his guard down. If she had been planning her escape, he would have known it and been there to prevent it.

"She must have had help," the general muttered to himself.

"Of course she did."

Aurelian whirled around to see a stranger in his tent. He almost called for the guards, then stopped himself. There was something familiar about this man.

"Do I know you?" Aurelian asked.

"Oh, yes. Around here, I'm called Ares, but you probably know me as 'Mars'," he said.

"A god - that explains how you got in here without me knowing," said Aurelian, going to the wooden table he used as a desk on campaign. "Would you care for wine?"

"Thank you, no," said Ares, pleasantly surprised by the offer.

"What did you mean when you said she had help?" asked Aurelian, pouring a cup for himself. "Do I need to be concerned about a traitor?"

"No, nothing like that," said Ares. "One of my kind. There's really nothing you could have done once Aradia stepped foot in Thrake - uh, Thracia."

"I should have left her in Rome," said Aurelian. "But I was losing too much money on her."

"Why not just kill her?" asked Ares.

"No," said Aurelian, shaking his head. "Letting her escape into death before I figured her out would have been a terrible waste."

Ares stroked his beard thoughtfully. "I see," he said. "And what is it that you need to figure out?"

Aurelian laughed bitterly. "I don't know," he said. "She's like a wild beast, you know - unpredictable. And yet I knew her every move before she made it, her every thought and feeling before she even thought or felt it."

"Yes," said Ares, smiling. "Of course you did."

"That was you, wasn't it?" asked Aurelian absently before sipping from his cup of wine. "You got inside both our heads and let me know what she was up to."

"As a matter of fact, yes," replied Ares, surprised. "It was my pleasure to torment one of Artemis's Amazons. I couldn't control her any more than you will ever be able to - you cannot break an Amazon. They usually die before allowing that to happen, but we came close with Aradia until Thracia ... damned interfering goddesses!"

"Why didn't she die?" asked Aurelian.

"Because they wouldn't let her," said Ares with a shrug.

"But why?" asked Aurelian.

He thought back to that day on the auction block. What had it taken for Aradia to kill her own people? Yet she had done so to protect them from what they would have considered worse than death. Aurelian had seen her fight and kill hundreds of times in the arena, always with that same dull look of bored disgust in those strange eyes of hers. Yet when she had killed the Amazons on the block, there had been something else there; fear, certainly, but love and passion, too. A certain spark of life that had afterwards been lacking in the Amazon Queen had flared, brilliantly in that moment, then gone out.

"If these goddesses truly cared for her, they would have let her die," said Aurelian.
"Why didn't they?"

"They needed her," said Ares. "In the Amazon city, there are thousands of Amazons, young and old, warrior and not. And there is one young girl. She is the reason Aradia was brought back here."

"A young girl? Of what importance could that be?" asked Aurelian, frowning.

"She is very important," said Ares. "I have seen your destiny, Aurelian; you are fated to become emperor and Rome's influence and power will expand to encompass the entire world under your command. Imagine it, Aurelian." He paused a moment to allow the general to absorb his words.

"What has a young Amazon girl to do with all that?" asked Aurelian.

"The Amazons are all that stand between you and all that power - and wealth," said Ares. "And Saraea is the one the goddesses have chosen to be the Amazons' salvation."

"A young girl? Forgive me, but I find that hard to believe," said Aurelian, shaking his head.

"She killed Yarg," said Ares.

"Yarg was a pig who needed killing," said Aurelian, his lip curled in disgust. "He was probably intoxicated and the girl got a lucky hit."

"She also dispatched the Graii and retrieved the Sword of Artemis from Athtar, the Gorgon Queen," said Ares. Aurelian raised an eyebrow.

"Indeed?" he said. "Well, then she will bear watching. Aradia and this girl must be brought back to Rome - alive. Tell me, Mars are they any more like these two amongst the warrior women?"

Ares hesitated a moment. "That remains to be seen," he said, cryptically, then disappeared.

Chapter Ten: More Memories of the Sword

Saraea made her way to the Temple, carrying the circlet of the High Priestess in the wooden chest. Aradia's amulet fit comfortably in the hollow of her throat, but Saraea remained aware of its presence. It comforted her in a way, though she was still terribly afraid. The Romans were too close for comfort.

"*Rome* would still be too close," she muttered to herself, then shook her head, grinning. "Now I'm talking to myself, too."

She arrived at the Temple and entered. Looking around, she could scarcely remember the previous night's journey here, but the evidence of the lamps still burning showed her she was.

"Aradia would tell me that lamp oil is scarce and to be conserved," she said to herself. "Of course, *I* know where to find more."

The girl set down the wooden chest and began trying to push the altar aside. She wanted to hide the circlet with the scrolls. The altar wouldn't budge and Saraea was just about to go and try to find some help when she felt her arm tingling, just where Mhari had etched her mark. Absently, the girl started to scratch, then remembered. She pushed up her sleeve to look at it again.

"It's still there," she heard. Saraea looked up, startled, to see the woman who had been guarding the hidden room.

"Oh!" she said. "Wh - who are you?"

"I am Jaiel. I was the last High Priestess of the Amazon Nation," she said. "I've come to help you."

"You're a ghost," said Saraea, her eyes wide. "You're not supposed to be here in daylight."

The priestess laughed. "I see we have some work to do," she said. "You have much to learn. Come."

She pointed at the altar and it slid away from the trap doors. The woman led Saraea to the second one and through the tunnel to the hidden room. She pointed and the wooden door swung open.

Saraea looked around, again amazed by what she saw.

"If the Romans do try a siege, the Amazons will not starve - at least not for a while," she said.

"That's true - unfortunately, you'll be on your own when it comes to lugging sacks of grain up there," said the priestess. She walked over to the chest of scrolls. "You've read the others, I assume?"

"And copied them," said Saraea, proudly.

"You will do the same with these," said the priestess. "You must begin as soon as possible."

"I understand," said Saraea. "Mother said that time does not move in this place. I could be here for what seems like a few hours, yet days or even weeks may pass up there. I should work on them someplace besides here."

"Your point is well made, Little Sister," said the priestess. "You are permitted to take them up to the Temple, but they must not leave the consecrated space."

Saraea nodded and bent to lift the chest.

"Oof!" she cried, unable to budge it. She frowned as the priestess chuckled. "You see what I mean about the grain. Take a few scrolls at a time - you will be permitted to return to this room at will - but remember, *only you*."

"I will remember," said the girl, solemnly. She took three scrolls from the chest and turned, but the priestess was gone.

Saraea walked swiftly through the tunnel up to the trap door. She pushed at it, but it wouldn't budge.

"Oh, no! she cried, panicky. She set the scrolls down carefully and pushed at the door with both hands, but it was firmly shut. "Someone must have pushed the altar back!"

Saraea began pounding on the door with both fists, crying out to whoever might be on the other side, but the altar was made of heavy stone. It was dark in the tunnel. Saraea sat down on the floor and put her head in her hands, trying to think of a way out.

"Someone will come looking for me," she whispered to herself. "Mhari and Aradia know of this place; one of them will surely figure out where I am and come for me. They have to!"

)O(

Mhari and the rest of the elders assembled in the Temple as Aradia ordered; it was the safest place in the upper town as it was the most easily protected. They were escorted by Anaea and another warrior whom Aradia had assigned to guard them there - just in case.

"Thank you, my Dear," Mhari told Anaea as she guided her to a chair. The warriors had set up chairs and sleeping mats for the elders. They had also moved the altar back over the trap doors - wouldn't do for one of the grandmothers to fall in there, after all. The warriors settled them in, then took their posts at the doors.

"Let us know if you need anything else," said the other warrior. She was eager for this watch to be over so she could go down to the lower town; she wanted to be there when the Romans made their move.

Mhari settled down in a chair next to her friend, Alkaia. Alkaia sighed and poured tea for both of them.

"What's wrong?" asked the shamaness.

"Ah, I'm just being an old fool," said her friend. "Regretting things which are long past changing. I was just thinking of how much I wish I had completed my training."

"It's being in the Temple that brings that to the surface," said Mhari, nodding her understanding. "What would you have done differently?"

"I'd have finished, of course," said Alkaia.

"What stopped you?" asked Mhari.

"Well, the Persians, to start with," said Alkaia. "Then the Scythians, and then ... oh, I see what you're saying."

"Sometimes things are out of our control," said Mhari with a sigh.

"Yes," Alkaia agreed. The two sat in companionable silence, sipping their tea for a while.

"Where's that girl?" Alkaia asked suddenly.

"Saraea? I don't know," said Mhari. "I imagine she's with the other girls, guarding the top of the steps to the lower town.

"Like the Romans will even get that far," said Alkaia, shaking her head.

"They may - we didn't think the Kaskans would get as far they did, either," said Mhari.

"They wouldn't have if the Gorgons hadn't betrayed us," Alkaia said. "Never would have seen that coming."

"No, we didn't," said Mhari.

"Leilë did," another woman interjected.

"Asteria, you hush now," said Mhari.

"Well, she did," Asteria grumbled. "If Aradia had listened to her, we'd never have been in exile for ten years."

"That's not true, Asteria," said Mhari. "Leilë was telling Aradia to take the entire city of Amazons and go into hiding - that simply wasn't practical."

"Not to speak ill of the dead, but Leilë spoke in so many riddles, how could anyone know what she was *really* telling them to do?" said another of the elders. "No, I stand behind Aradia. She did what she had to at the time. And she will again this time around."

Asteria grumbled a bit more, but quietly and to herself.

"Who else knows about Leilë's visions?" Mhari said quietly to Alkaia.

"Most of the women in here," said Alkaia. "But most of them stand behind Aradia. Besides, Leilë didn't predict Athtar's treachery. And she did speak in such riddles. Not like you when you have your visions, Mhari."

"No, I just don't remember them afterward," the shamaness said with a chuckle.

"No, but as long as you have someone there to remember for you, you do alright," said Alkaia with a smile.

An ally will come to us from an unexpected place ... and perhaps an enemy from one we trust ...

Mhari heard her own voice speaking those words, but couldn't remember the images which had produced them or when they had come to her. She had a feeling it was important, though, so she closed her eyes and drifted off. Nothing came to her and she sighed.

This getting old is way over-rated, thought the shamaness. *I can't even control these things anymore - not that I ever really could, but it's even harder to try now.*

Instead of the vision she was trying to recall, she kept seeing Saraea's face, smudged with dirt and streaked with tears. She opened her eyes with a start and arose quickly, walking to the doors of the Temple. Alkaia, alarmed at her friend's actions, followed.

"Anaea, have you seen Saraea this morning?" Mhari asked.

"Not since she came out of the Temple before dawn, why?" asked the warrior.

"I need her - can you please send someone to look for her?" said Mhari, her brow furrowed in worry.

"We don't have many to spare, but I can go," said Anaea. "She should be with her age-mates at the top of the stairs to the lower town."

"If not, try the stables - she's pretty excited about her horse," offered the other sentry with a smile.

"Right," said Anaea. "I'll be right back." Mhari returned with Alkaia to their chairs to wait. The shamaness closed her eyes and sighed.

"What's wrong?" asked Alkaia.

"I know she isn't in either of those places," said Mhari. "The trouble is, I don't know where she *is*."

)O(

Saraea sat at the trap door for a while. Finally, she could bear it no more; she had to get out of here. For all she knew the Romans had already attacked and she wasn't where she was supposed to be when that happened.

She picked up the scrolls and started walking back towards the hidden chamber. The wooden door was closed and Saraea sighed in frustration before remembering that the priestess had given her permission to return to the room whenever she wished. She reached out and pushed open the door, stepping into the chamber.

"Okay," she said to herself. "I have to be careful here - remember, time stands still here." She set the scrolls in her arms back into their chest and walked around the room, counting her heartbeats so she wouldn't lose track of how long she had been here. It was then she remembered the door that had been locked.

"Well, it's worth a try, anyway," she said, startled by her own voice. The only other sound in the chamber was running water, as if from a stream close by. Saraea walked to the wooden door and tried it, but found it locked.

"My daughter, what is that you seek?"

Saraea looked around to see Artemis standing behind her.

"Lady, I need to get out of here," said the girl, desperately.

"I'm sorry, Child, but that isn't a way out - it will only take you deeper," said the Goddess. "You are not yet ready for that place."

"Lady, you know that I must get out of here - the Romans are coming! They're here. I need to - " began the girl.

"To what? Fight?" asked the Goddess.

"I need to be there to stand by my sisters and to do whatever I can," said Saraea, solemnly. "Can you help me to get out of here?"

The Lady nodded. "You know what is kept in this room, My Child?" she said.

"Food, scrolls ... stuff?" said Saraea, frowning.

"All of the treasures of the Amazons, past, present, and future, are kept here and in the rooms beyond," said the Goddess.

"Rooms? Are there more?" asked Saraea, her eyes widening in excitement.

"Yes, but they are for another time," said the Goddess. "You, my dear Saraea, are the most precious of treasures for the Amazons right now. Perhaps that is why you are unable to leave this chamber."

"And maybe someone just put the altar back where it belongs because they didn't realise I was down here," said the girl, both hands on her slim hips.

The Lady threw back her head and laughed heartily. "You are indeed a treasure, Little One," she said.

"So does that mean that you're going to keep me down here? Or help me back to where I need to be?" asked Saraea.

"I'm tempted to keep you here where I know you'll be safe, Saraea," said the Lady. "Then again, if I could, I'd have the whole Amazon Nation tucked away someplace safe."

"Then why don't you?" asked Saraea. "Or better yet, make the Romans and everyone else just leave us alone?"

"If only I could," said the goddess.

"Why *can't* you? Aren't you the Great Mother of All?" asked Saraea, worriedly. "I mean, you're supposed to be able to *anything* – otherwise …."

"It doesn't work that way, Saraea," said the Lady, gently. "Somewhere inside you, you knew that already. I suppose it's appropriate that you receive your first 'priestess lesson' from Me – though this isn't your first lesson, is it?"

Saraea looked at her, puzzled, for a moment. Then a long-forgotten memory came back to her and she was transported back in time, to a day long ago …

Leilë still haunted by the dream from the previous night, walked up to Aradia's house from the Temple. Saraea watched her approach from her bedroom window, bouncing excitedly on her little bed. She liked the priestess; Leilë always had a sweet tucked in her pocket for Saraea and she told really wonderful stories. It was Leilë who had given Julisa to Saraea. Julisa, who was tucked safely under Saraea's arm, was more than just a dolly; she was Saraea best friend.

Something was different about Leilë today, though. Saraea could sense that the priestess was worried about something. She said as much to Julisa.

"She's worried about you, *Saraea," said Julisa.*

Saraea always saw her as a girl her own age or maybe a little older.

"Why? " asked Saraea.

"She has to warn Aradia about the bad thing that's going to happen," said Julisa.

"Bad thing?" said Saraea, her little face started to screw up in preparation for the impending tears. "What's going to happen, Julisa?"

"You're going away," said Julisa, sadly. "So's Mama and Aradia."

"And you, too," said Saraea.

"No I have to wait here for you and Aradia to come back," said Julisa.

"And Mama," said Saraea.

"Mama isn't going to come back," said Julisa, shaking her head.

Saraea started to cry in earnest and ran from the room to find her mother.

"Mama! Mama! No go!" she cried as Thalia bent and lifted her up, drying her tears.

"What's this?" asked Thalia, hugging her close. "Where do you think I'm going?"

"J'lisa said," said Saraea, sniffling and tucking her head into her mother's neck.

"Ohhh, Julisa told you something?" asked Thalia, smiling as she cuddled her little girl. "Come, Leilë is here to see us."

"No, Mama, see 'Radia," said Saraea, solemnly.

Thalia blinked in surprise.

"Yes, she did come to see Aradia, too, this time," said Thalia. "But Aradia is at the Fortress this morning."

Thalia brought the child to the main room where Leilë sat with a cup of tea before the hearth. She smiled when she saw Saraea, but her smile faded swiftly when the child began to cry at the sight of her, though she did go to the priestess and snuggle.

"Thalia, you must tell Aradia to get the Amazons to safety," said Leilë

"No!" cried Saraea, looking at her, stricken.

"No Mama no go! Mama stay, me stay right here!"

"She knows something," said Leilë looking at the child intently. "Come, we must bring her to the Temple; there may not be time later."

"We should wait for Aradia," said Thalia, frowning.

"There's no time," said Leilë ...

Then she smiled. "Besides, you know Aradia; she won't deny you anything, especially where the child is concerned."

"That's true; though I think she thinks me silly for spending so much time in the Temple," said Thalia.

"No doubt she does," Leilë chuckled. "Since Aradia's gods are a good sword in the hand and a good horse under her butt."

Saraea rode to the Temple on her mother's hip. She leaned over, reaching for the shiny pommel of the sword on Thalia's other hip.

"No, Saraea, ouch," said Thalia, gently moving the little girl's hands away.

"Me save Mama from bad thing," Saraea declared, again reaching for the sword.

"What bad thing?" asked Thraso.

"Bad thing - J'lisa said bad thing take 'Raea's mama away," said Saraea.

"Julisa said that?" asked Leilë, looking at the child with keen interest. Saraea nodded and stuck a finger in her mouth then hid her face in her mother's neck.

"Julisa is what she calls the doll you made for her," Thalia explained.

"Yes, I know," said Leilë, absently. "Saraea, may I see Julisa?"

Saraea handed the rag doll to her maker.

"She just talks to me," said Saraea. "Mama 'n 'Radia can't hear her."

"Oh, I see," said Leilë, handing Julisa back to Saraea. "You must be very important for Julisa to talk to you then."

Saraea squirmed proudly, causing her mother to set her down. "Come on Saraea. You really are getting too big to carry," she said, extending her hand for the little girl to take.

They entered the Temple and Leilë led them to the altar. She held out a hand and the altar slid over to reveal two trap doors. Leilë lifted one and motioned for Thalia and Saraea to precede her into the dark tunnel. Leilë came up behind them, carrying a torch.

"Just walk forward, follow the tunnel to the door," she said, softly.

The three made their way through the tunnel in silence until they came to a wooden door. Thalia tried it, but found it locked. Then Saraea reached out with her tiny hand and pushed it open.

"H - how did she ...?" began Thalia, looking to Leilë.

"She will be a strong spiritual leader for the Amazons - if she lives long enough," said Leilë. "You and Aradia must ensure that she does live long enough."

"Naturally we want the same thing, Leilë," said Thraso. "We'll do everything in our power to protect her and see that she grows up."

"That's not enough - if Aradia will not take the Amazons into hiding, you must at least hide Saraea," said Leilë.

"'Radia not hide from nobody," said Saraea, shaking her dark curls before toddling through the door.

"Saraea!" called her mother, starting after her. Leilë stopped her with a hand on her shoulder,

"No - this room is forbidden to all but the priestess-born," she said.

"You mean Saraea ...?" said Thalia, trying to see into the chamber.

"Yes - but you must take extra care for her, Thalia, and convince that stubborn warrior, too," said Leilë, desperation tingeing her plea.

Saraea looked about the huge chamber in awe. She wandered over to the wooden door on the other side of the chamber and pushed it open ...

Saraea was jolted out of her memory.

"Blessed Lady - how long have I been here?" she asked. She ran back through the tunnel to the trap door leading up to the tunnel.

"Okay, now what the priestess did was this - " Saraea said softly to herself. She raised her hand towards where the altar sat over the trap door. "And the altar slid over - "

She was interrupted by a scraping, grating sound and the trap door opened, spilling light down into the antechamber of the tunnel.

"Saraea, are you alright?" Mhari cried, reaching down to help the girl out.

"Yeah, I'm fine," said Saraea, climbing out through the trapdoor and into the bright Temple. She glanced out of the window and sighed with relief; it was still only about mid-day.

"Yeah, but of what day?" she muttered.

"What was that, Dear?" asked Mhari, brushing the dust off of the girl.

"Mhari, how long was I down there?" asked Saraea.

"Well, I haven't seen you since you left this morning - oh, my! Have you been down there that long? You must be starving," said the shamaness.

"Yeah, a little," said Saraea as Mhari led her to a table, set up by the warriors, laden with food and drink. "Mhari, how did you know I was down there?"

"Because you weren't anywhere else we looked," replied the shamaness. "I remembered you were coming here to put the crown back for safekeeping and I hadn't seen you since, so it was logical you were still there."

"Oh," said Saraea. "I thought that maybe ..."

"What?" asked the shamaness. "That I'd had a vision?"

"Yeah, something like that," said Saraea, wearily scrubbing her face with her palm. "I'm going up to the summit watchtower - I think guarding the steps is just busy work anyway."

"Saraea, be careful," Mhari called after her. She stopped at her house and retrieved her mother's old sword, carefully sheathing it at her hip. Then she climbed the trail to the summit.

Four Amazons stood watch there and they saluted Saraea in greeting before moving aside to allow her to climb in with them.

"What are you doing here, Princess?" asked one of the sentries.

"I just wanted to have a look," said Saraea. She was becoming accustomed to the title, though it still made her feel a bit uncomfortable.

The sentries moved aside from the lookout window so Saraea could see.

"You can see where they left their trail," said another of the Amazons.

Saraea could indeed see the wide swath of trampled and littered ground left by the Roman soldiers.

"So they came up and circled 'round the mound, apparently looking for a way up ...." mused the girl.

"No, Princess, they would have sent a few scouts to do that - not the whole army," said the third sentry.

"According to Prothoë, they did send their scouts, but we are well hidden; we saw them before they saw us," said another of the sentries. "You'd better get your post, Little Sister - Aradia is very strict about following orders."

"Yeah," said Saraea, turning to go. "What are the chances of them having seen us and us not knowing they did?"

The sentries looked at one another warily, then back at Saraea. "Let's just say ... the scouts won't be a problem in any case," one replied.

Saraea frowned, but said nothing as she climbed out of the tower and began to walk down the trail to the town. She didn't want to know what the sentries meant, though inwardly she chastised herself for her squeamishness. *Any right you had to judge them left when you agreed to Aradia's plan about the poison arrows,* she thought to herself.

Still, the girl felt troubled. She decided that the steps had enough "guards" and instead passed by her age-mates on her way to the lower town where Saraea sought out Aradia.

"Hey, Princess - what are you doing here?" asked Prothoë, riding up to her; the lieutenant was in charge of the cavalry unit. "Why aren't you with the rest of the younglings, guarding the steps?"

"It's a bit crowded," said Saraea.

Prothoë raised an eyebrow. "Does Aradia know you're not there?"

"No, I was just looking for her - is she around?" asked the girl. Prothoë nodded once in the direction of the ruined fortress. Saraea waved her thanks and trudged over to where she could see her foster mother, talking earnestly with Thraso.

"Aradia," she said as she approached. Aradia looked up and saw Saraea walking towards her. The queen frowned, angrily.

"Why have you left your post?" she asked, stepping forward to prevent Saraea from advancing any further.

"I - I wanted to see - " began the girl, startled by Aradia's anger.

"Damn it, Saraea! When I order you to a post, you do not leave it until I say so - is that clear?" Saraea's eyes narrowed in anger and she nodded once, then turned and started back to the top of the steps.

"If my own daughter disobeys orders, how in the four hells can I expect the rest of the Amazons to follow them?" Aradia called after her. Tears welled in Saraea's eyes, blurring her vision even as Aradia's words blurred the anger in her heart. Aradia had a point - and she had called Saraea her daughter - how could Saraea stay angry with her? Still the scolding had stung. She bumped into Prothoë, now leading her horse rather than riding, cooling the creature from the drills the cavalry had exercised in the paddock earlier.

"She's right, you know," said Prothoë, softly. "But I could talk with her about allowing you to join with the cavalry - I imagine watching the steps is pretty ... well, dull. And dulled senses can kill a warrior."

"I'd love that, Prothoë, but I don't think Aradia will let me," said Saraea, sadly.

"She may - I'll talk with her," said the warrior, leading her horse back toward the stables. Saraea climbed the stairs and waited with the others her age until Thraso came to tell them they were relieved for the night.

"Where's Aradia?' asked Saraea.

"She won't leave the fortress until the battle now, Saraea," said Thraso. "You go on to the Temple and stay with Mhari until morning."

"Who's going to guard the steps until then?" asked Saraea, the sarcasm slipping into her voice. Thraso smiled, sympathetically.

"How do the others like guarding them?" she asked.

"They love it - it makes them feel like they're actually doing something," said Saraea with a shrug.

"But for you - there's so much more that you could be doing, isn't there, Saraea?" asked Thraso, sympathetically.

"What do you mean?" asked Saraea, startled by the question for a moment.

"I mean, you killed Yarg. You helped lead the Amazons back to our ancestral home, you killed the Graii and confronted Athtar, helping to retrieve the Sword of Artemis - and Aradia treats you like a little girl. I understand how frustrating that must be for you."

"Oh," said Saraea. "You do?"

"Yes I do," said Thraso, sitting on the top step. "I do understand, but I want you to see it from Aradia's view point - she's already lost your mother in battle; she's scared."

"So am I," said Saraea, sitting with Thraso.

"I know - we all are; well, all of us with any sense that is," Thraso said with a chuckle.

"I would feel better if I could be down there with her somehow," said Saraea with a sigh.

"I know you would, but Aradia would be so busy worrying about you that she wouldn't be able to do what needs to be done," said Thraso.

"I can take care of myself," said Saraea, stubbornly.

"I know, but Aradia would still worry," Thraso said. "Try to understand, she loves you. She thinks of you as her own daughter. It's just too bad you couldn't find a way to watch from a safe distance."

Saraea smiled. "I know - it's okay, Thraso," she said. "I really do understand." The girl rose and walked to the Temple. Mhari saw her face as she entered and sat next to the shamaness for the evening meal.

"What's going on Saraea?" she asked. Saraea merely offered a small smile and shook her head.

"I was just talking with Thraso," she said, quietly.

"And what did Thraso have to say?" asked Mhari. Her only reply was a small shrug from Saraea. Mhari sighed, but remained silent while Saraea ate very little of her dinner.

Afterwards, the girl sat in silence as the others in the Temple sat in a rough circle on the floor and began to sing and chat together in a comfortable camaraderie.

"Hey, Princess, how about a story?" called one of the women.

Saraea shook her head and started to refuse, but Mhari stopped her with a gentle hand on her shoulder.

"Go ahead, Saraea," said the shamaness. "It will be good for them - and for you."

So Saraea joined the women sitting in the circle.

"What ... what kind of story would you like?" she asked.

"Something funny with a happy ending," said Momi.

The other girl's eyes were wide with fear of the Romans camped so close.

Saraea nodded, then closed her eyes to think. Suddenly, images began to play before her closed eyes and the girl was completely unaware she had begun to speak, telling the story which played inside her head.

"Once, long and long ago there was an Amazon princess who was destined to become High Queen. Her mothers were the priestess and a warrior queens who had fought for the dragons in the Mage Wars in Themiscyreia," she began.

The women leaned in closer as Mhari watched the girl's trance with keen interest.

"Before she could take her place in the high seat of Themiscyreia, she had to prove herself to those all important allies, the Dragons. This is the story of Princess Jaiel ..."

She told the story of how the princess Jaiel honoured the old treaty between the Amazons and the Dragons by exchanging a drop of blood each year. On her way to the Dragon Queen's lair, the princess Jaiel had to face difficult trials and her own fears, but she mamanged to overcome each one of them, in the end obtaining the gift of understanding the language of animals.

The Amazons in the Temple laughed and clapped. Saraea opened her eyes and blinked.

"What?" she said.

"Oh, Saraea, that was wonderful!" said Momi, clapping her friend on the shoulder. "I don't remember that one being in the scrolls. Did you just make it up?"

"Um," said Saraea looking desperately at Mhari. The shamaness smiled.

"No, that was a true story," she said.

"Dragons and magic?" said one of the craftswomen, raising her eyebrow.

"Remember, this was a long time ago," said another of the women.

"That is a true account of a priestess initiation," said Mhari, nodding knowingly.

The women begged for another story, but Saraea declined; the trance had exhausted her and she lay down behind the altar on her bedroll to sleep.

Chapter Eleven: Prophecy of the Sword

Saraea awoke late in the night. The Temple was dark and Saraea could hear the slow, even breathing of the women asleep all around her. She felt disoriented and arose, very quietly so as not to wake the sleepers. The girl skirted around the women in their bedrolls and made her way to the Temple doors. She slipped quietly outside, nodding to the sentries posted at the door, then began to walk toward the house she shared with Aradia.

"Princess, where are you going?" asked one of the sentries.

"To my house - I forgot something," said Saraea. "Why, has Aradia ordered all to remain inside?"

"No, nothing like that - I was just hoping you could, uh ... maybe stand by while I run to the privy?" asked the sentry.

"Sure, but there are two of you," said Saraea.

"Aradia *has* ordered that there be two outside this door at all times," said the other.

"Our relief isn't due until moonrise," said the first sentry. "And that *koumiss* we drank with dinner is going right through me."

Saraea made a face at the mention of the slightly fermented mare's milk. "*Koumiss* - ugh! Go on ahead, I'll stand by," she said.

The first sentry flashed a grateful smile at the girl as the second chuckled. "Our mothers raised us on *koumiss* - they used to say it made for strong Amazon warriors," she said.

"Or maybe for Amazon warriors with strong stomachs," said Saraea, shuddering, but grinning at the woman.

"What are you doing in the Temple, anyway? I would have thought that Thalia's daughter would be in the lower town, preparing for whatever the Romans are plotting," said the sentry. Saraea looked down.

"I am not a warrior," she said, quietly.

"You killed Yarg - you fought that thing in the cave - if that's not a warrior, I don't know what is," said the sentry, some admiration in her voice.

"It's not me," said Saraea, firmly. "I - I admire warriors - my mother was one - but that is not the path for me. I will be a shamaness or a priestess."

"Ah, a magic wielder, huh?' said the first sentry.

"I suppose, though I never really of it that way," said Saraea.

"Then you will be a great priestess, Princess," said the second sentry, taking back her post.

Saraea nodded and walked to her house. She made her way through the dark into her own bedroom and opened the window. Saraea sat on her bed to gaze out at the bright moon, drinking in the tranquillity of the sleeping town.

She was startled by the cat, Hekau, jumping up on the widow sill. "Hekau ... I mean, Lady?"
The cat jumped down to the girl's lap and curled up there, purring as Saraea began to gently stroke the soft fur.

"Whoever you are, I'm glad you're here," said Saraea, lying down. Tears welled in her eyes as the cat curled up close to her. "I missed you and I sure could use a friend right now."

Together, girl and cat fell asleep.

)O(

Aradia strode through the warriors' camp in and around the ruined fortress in the lower town. The first wave of scouts to the Roman camp had returned and waited for her and Thraso to make their report.

"They're mobilising," said a scout named Peruna. "We heard them in the general's tent, blocking a wing formation. They're dividing their mounted unit to flank the foot soldiers. Then they plan to spread out and surround us."

"That will take an awful lot of warriors," said Aradia, smugly. "I don't think they appreciate the size of the mound."

"They have the warriors to accomplish this," said the other scout, who was called Anikha. "They have camped all the way to the Forest of Artemis."

"No," Thraso whispered in horror.

"Of course," said Aradia, grimly. "I should have anticipated this; they sent some through the trees. They must have found the abandoned tree village and then Aurelian would have sent word to the remaining troops to come around by the sea. Damn!"

"Yes, your Majesty," said Peruna.

"Was there any sign of Silas?" asked Aradia.

"Who is that?" asked Anikha.

"Thalia's brother," said Thraso. "The Romans are holding him prisoner."

"There were many men there - how can we distinguish one from the others?" asked Peruna, a look of distaste marring her features.

"This man is a friend to the Amazons - we have few enough of those," said Aradia, coolly.

"I'm sorry, Majesty," said Peruna. "A man who is friend to the Amazons is a little hard to swallow, though I know what you say is true."

"That's alright," said Aradia.

"Actually, we did see a man - he was not looking well, though; I doubt he'll last another day with the Roman scum," said Anikha.

Thraso and Aradia cast looks at one another. "It's up to us," said Thraso quietly.

"Thraso, I don't think - " began Aradia.

"Unless you give me a direct order otherwise, I'm going in after him," said the Second in Command.

"Wait - I'll go with you," said Anikha. "With your permission, of course, my Queen."

"How am I going to justify the loss of two warriors if you fail?" asked Aradia.

"He's a human first, a man second," said Anikha, earnestly. "And like you said, my Queen - men who are friends to the Amazons are few - we need to keep all we can find."

"Where is he?" asked Aradia.

"Tied to a post near the edge of the camp," said Peruna, with a sigh. "With your permission, I will go, too."

"Alright - what's your plan?" asked Aradia. The other Amazons looked at her, puzzled. "You have to have a plan - how are you going to get Silas out of there?"

"I hadn't thought that far ahead," said Thraso.

"A diversion?" said Anikha.

"No, we don't want to instigate them into an attack before we're ready," said Thraso. Aradia laughed. "What?"

"You don't think rescuing their prisoner will do that?" said Aradia.

"Well, maybe they'll think he escaped?" said Anikha.

"You saw him - escape? Come on," said Peruna, rolling her eyes. "The only way he will escape is in death."

"Actually, that's not bad," said Thraso, thoughtfully. "We may be able to pull that off."

"How are you going to do that?" asked Aradia.

Thraso looked at her for a moment before speaking. "The Roman scouts - we made sure they would not report back to Aurelian," she said.

"Where are they?" asked Aradia, grimly.

Thraso motioned for her to follow and the women did. They went deep into the brush where the bodies of the Roman scouts lay. One swift blow to each had silenced them and they lay, peaceful in their final repose.

"Damn!" said Aradia. "If they don't report within a certain amount of time, then Aurelian will know they're dead. He won't let this go - his troops' morale will demand vengeance for this."

"*Roman* vengeance?" said Anikha, making a rude noise. "What about Amazon vengeance? How many of our sisters fell to the Romans? To hell with Romans and their vengeance. I say we kill as many as we can."

"Anikha, I share your ... vehemence, but we must be cool-headed about this," said Aradia. "So, Thraso, you propose that we substitute one of these for Silas? And the Romans won't be able to tell the difference? To us, perhaps, one man looks much like another, but to them ... I just don't see this working."

"No, if Silas is tied to a post near the edge of the camp, we can substitute one of these for him. It may be a bit before they notice," said Thraso, chuckling. "As opposed to just having an empty stake in the ground, I mean."

"Hm, yes, but how much time would it buy?" said Aradia.

"I don't know - enough for us to get Silas away from them, at least," said Thraso.

"Okay," said Aradia. "Be back by moon set - regardless; do you understand? If you are not back by then, the Amazons will be forced to attack the camp and we are not ready for a direct confrontation."

"I understand," said Thraso, solemnly.

)O(

Aurelian sat in his command tent, resisting the restless urge to start pacing. The nagging doubts about this campaign assaulted him. The Amazons were too unpredictable, like wild animals; you could never anticipate their next move. Their motives were alien and inscrutable to the rational Roman man's mind.

He knew they were up there, hiding - they were very good at being invisible, Aurelian knew, especially here in their home territory.

"Let them wait," he muttered to himself. He could outwait them. He knew that they hadn't been here long enough to stockpile food and supplies; the tree village, left abandoned by them had betrayed signs that it was only recently vacated. It was only a matter of time before the Amazons showed themselves and Aradia would be forced to surrender.

Something still bothered him about the plan, though, something he couldn't quite pinpoint.

"Unpredictable," he muttered to himself once more, then rose and left his tent to walk the perimeter one more time before going to bed.

)O(

Aradia paced from her watching place as she awaited the return of the three warriors with Silas. That they would be successful in his rescue, the queen did not doubt, but still she worried. At Thraso's insistence, she had moved back up the trail, closer to the fortress ruins and could now only see the dotted campfires of the Roman camp. She ran her fingers over the rough and broken walls of the old fortress.

"We've really got to re-build this," she said to one of the warriors who was passing by. "You know this was originally built by Queen Lysippe, the Lawgiver."

"Really, your Majesty?" said the warrior, stopping to touch the wall.

"Yes," said Aradia with a sigh. "At one time, this fortress housed the entire Amazon Nation. But that was a long time ago."

"Yes, it was," said the warrior. "But as soon as we rout the bloody Romans, we'll re-build. Not only the fortress, but the whole city, upper and lower. We've already started. As soon as the rains are over, we'll begin making more bricks. The kilns have already been fired up."

Aradia smiled at her. "You're optimistic," she said.

"One Amazon can take twenty Romans - we'll soon send them back to Rome, my Queen - you'll see."

"I know," said Aradia, smiling with a confidence she did not feel.

Suddenly, the Amazons heard a "panic" whistle.

"Quickly - mobilise the archers - I want the cavalry mounted and in line!" Aradia began calling out orders and the Amazons leapt to obey swiftly. They had been waiting for this.

)O(

Thraso, Anikha, and Peruna made their way silently to the edge of the Roman camp, dragging the body of one of the Roman scouts with them. Anikha and Peruna signalled for Thraso to remain in the trees as lookout.

"I don't like it," said the Queen's Second. "I'm too far away to help if anything should happen."

"Never mind that," said Peruna. "Nothing will happen, but if it should, you are the Second - we have to make sure you make it back to the city. Just whistle if anything goes wrong."

The two slipped over to the stake to which Silas was tied. They released him and Anikha made her way back to where Thraso was hidden in the trees while Peruna tied the dead scout in his place.

All of a sudden, Roman soldiers were there, attacking Peruna. Thraso dragged Silas deeper into the trees, whistled the "panic" signal, then ran after Anikha to Peruna's aid.

The three Amazons were woefully outnumbered. Peruna fell to a Roman short-sword, her throat cut to the spine. Thraso caught Anikha's eye and they nodded at one another, manoeuvring until they were back to back. Together they fought off the squad of Roman sentries. The Amazons glanced down once at the Roman bodies littering the ground, then grabbed Peruna's body and hurried back to the trees before any more Romans heard the fight and came over. They dragged both Peruna and Silas up the trail to the lower town. There they found the Amazons mobilised and ready for battle.

"What happened?" asked Aradia, tersely.

"We were caught," replied Thraso. "The Romans killed Peruna."

"Damn!" said Aradia, then she called out the order, "Hold the line! We wait for the Romans to move first!"

There was some quiet grumbling, but the warriors obeyed.

"Thraso, get up to the upper town and let them know what's going on," said Aradia.

"Right," said Thraso with a brief nod.

"And bring Saraea down here to me," said Aradia, with a resigned sigh.

"Aradia, we have Silas and he's alive, though barely," said Thraso, quietly. "He's down in the trees with Peruna's body."

Aradia nodded. "I doubt many of these women would find the life of any man fair trade for that of an Amazon, Thraso - you had best leave him there for now."

"He needs attention," said Thraso. "And the Amazons will be wanting to retrieve Peruna's body. I could move him to a safer place -"

"Thraso, don't push me right now," said Aradia, sternly.

"Your Majesty," said Anikha, approaching the two. "In my other life, before I answered the call to come home, I was apprenticed to a village herb-wife. I know a bit about healing. I will help the man, Silas. Peruna gave her life for him. If he dies, then it was for nothing."

Aradia was silent for a moment, considering her offer.

"Very well," she said at last. "Thraso, make sure Saraea does not see him. His condition may make her do something foolish."

"Like trying to take on the whole Roman legion herself, I know," said Thraso, smiling.

"She's not as impetuous as she was, but yes," said Aradia, grimly.

"No she's grown up a bit, but she still has that stubborn streak," Thraso agreed, going to get the girl.

She ascended the steps and informed the sentries, alerting them to the threat of the Romans' imminent attack. Then she walked quickly to the Temple and alerted the sentries standing guard there, too, before entering and picking her way quietly through the sleeping women all about. Finally, not finding Saraea, she gently woke Mhari.

"Mhari, where's Saraea?" she asked.

Mhari sat up and looked around the dimly lit Temple. "She's not here?" asked the shamaness, feeling around in the dark.

"I can't find her," said Thraso. "And Aradia wants her - now."

Briefly, Thraso told Mhari what was happening in the lower town.

"That girl," Mhari muttered, shaking her head. "She's as much trouble as Aradia ever was at that age. Well, let's go and look for her."

They went first to the sentries standing outside the Temple.

"Did you see the princess Saraea leave the Temple?" asked Thraso.

"No Commander," said the first sentry.

"You might ask Lykopis and Pisto - we just relieved them a little while ago," said the second.

"And where are they?" asked Mhari.

"Asleep, most likely," said the first sentry. "In the guardhouse by the steps to the lower town - that's where Aradia billeted the upper town sentries."

"Thanks," said Thraso, taking Mhari's hand and walking quickly to the guard house. She opened the door and raised the wick on the lamp until the house was lit up then called out, "Everyone up!"

"Thraso, is this necessary?" asked Mhari.

"They need to know what's going on, too, Old-Mother," said Thraso as a dozen sleepy sentries arose swiftly to their feet.

"Sisters, grab your weapons and get to your battle posts - the Romans will be making a move at any moment," Thraso announced. "Pisto, Lykopis, I need to see you - you just got off watch?"

"Yes, Commander," said Pisto.

"Did you see the Princess Saraea leave the Temple?" asked Mhari.

Lykopis and Pisto looked at one another. "Yes," said Lykopis, with a sigh. "She said she forgot something at her house." Both sentries neglected to tell their commander that they had conscripted the princess to cover for Pisto on her privy-break.

"Thank you," said Thraso, clapping her shoulder. "You two, take another hour of rest since you just got off watch and sleep - tomorrow will be a busy day for us all."

Thraso and Mhari found Saraea asleep in her tiny bed, clutching the doll Julisa, close to her.

"Saraea," said Mhari, gently shaking the girl. Saraea awoke with a start.

"Oh! I fell asleep," she said, rubbing her eyes.

"Is this what you forgot?" asked Thraso, lifting the doll from Saraea's arms. The girl looked down, a little embarrassed.

"Uh ..." she began. "Where's Hekau?"

"Saraea, are you alright?" asked Thraso, frowning.

"Yeah, fine, I just ..." she began, rising to her feet. "What are you two doing here?"

"The Romans' attack is imminent," said Thraso. "Aradia wants you in the lower town - like fifteen minutes ago!"

"Goddess!" said Saraea, her eyes wide. She sheathed her sword and tucked the doll securely into her belt. "Let's go."

"Mhari, we need for you to go back to the Temple and wait for the casualties - and wake the women; let them know what going on," said Thraso. "See if you can gather any more women with knowledge of healing and prepare."

"We're going to carry all the wounded up here to the Temple?" said Saraea, doubtfully.

"We've done it before," said Mhari, with a nod. She hugged the other two then left them to return to the Temple.

Thraso escorted Saraea to the lower town. The girl's eyes scanned over the assembled, armed, and ready troops, all standing in formation, their eyes focussed forward. Saraea felt intimidated at the sight. They reeked of discipline - until the girl caught Anaea's eye. The warrior, a lieutenant standing a little apart, winked at the girl and she relaxed a moment.

"Saraea." Saraea looked up to see Aradia standing beside her, reviewing the lieutenants inspecting the warriors.

"You sent for me?" said Saraea.

"Yes. You brought your sword ... and your doll?" said Aradia, raising one eyebrow.

Startled, Saraea looked down. "I guess I did," she said, sheepishly.

"Don't worry about it," said Aradia, smiling at her. "Most warriors carry a good luck charm into battle."

"Why did you send for me, Aradia?" asked Saraea.

"I want you close to me," said Aradia as she gazed out over her assembled troops.

"Okay," said Saraea, eagerly.

Aradia's eyes snapped sharply back upon the girl. Then her expression softened.

"Saraea, there will be fighting," she said. "You will see and hear and smell things. Ugly things."

Saraea sobered immediately, instinctively reaching down to touch the doll securely tucked into her belt.

"I've seen battle before, Aradia. I killed Yarg, remember?" she said, quietly.

"I do remember," said Aradia. "I also remember how that affected you. If I had a brain in my head, I would send you right back up to the Temple."

"But?" said Saraea.

"But I need you where I can see you," said Aradia with a sigh. "I've watched you grow these past months. I'm hoping - no, I'm praying - that you've grown enough to handle what's before us. These are Romans, not Kaskans, Saraea. This will be far worse than the Kaskan battle."

"As long as I can be with you, Aradia, I will be fine," said Saraea.

Aradia felt a pang of bittersweet remembrance; Thalia had said those words to her before the battle which had stolen her life.

"You must do exactly what I say, Saraea," she said, sternly. "That means if I say run, you head for the Temple as fast as you can. Do you understand me?"

"I understand," said Saraea.

"Your majesty! The Romans are attacking the perimeter!" cried an Amazon from the watchtower just before an arrow hit her in the chest. She fell lifeless to the ground below the tower.

"Hold the line!" Aradia cried out the order as another Amazon began to climb up the tower to take the watcher's place. "Archers, ready ... find your marks ... loose!"

A volley of arrows flew towards the Roman soldiers below, most hitting their marks. Saraea watched from the wall as both Amazons and Romans fell.

The Romans outnumbered the Amazon braves, yet the Amazons managed to hold them off until, by their sheer numbers, the Romans began pushing them back, encroaching inexorably toward the city of the Amazons.

Aradia called the order to retreat, but there was no place for the Amazons to go. They couldn't climb the steep and treacherous cliff because of the Roman archers and they wouldn't lead their pursuers to the secret trail, miles around on the other side of the mound.

Mounted warriors rode out from their hiding place in the trees and engaged the Roman foot soldiers, allowing their sisters time to escape towards the hidden trail. They successfully kept the Romans from pursuing their sisters on foot until the Roman cavalry rode out against them. Again, Aradia called to the archers and again, volley after volley of

Amazon arrows flew to the Roman cavalry. Man and horse dropped to the ground in great numbers until finally, the Roman commander called for them to retreat. But they had gained ground towards their goal: the city of the Amazons.

"There are just too many of them," Aradia whispered to herself. "How are we ever going to defeat them?"

The Roman commander gestured to Aradia, calling for a temporary truce for both sides to collect their dead. Aradia nodded her acknowledgement, then gestured to the archers to cover the detail of warriors climbing down ropes to the battlefield below. She started towards the cliffs to help. She was vaguely aware of Saraea following her and turned to face the girl.

"Saraea, wait here," she said, sharply.

"You said I could stay with you," the girl protested.

"Saraea, I don't want you to see this," said the queen sadly. She turned and continued to the battlefield, aware that Saraea still followed, but she did not try to prevent her further.

They descended from the lower town and picked their way through the dead, looking for survivors. Saraea heard flies buzzing all around, their plump, black bodies already landing to feast on the plentiful blood. Crows cawed loudly as they flew overhead, the bright sun bouncing off of their glossy black feathers. Some landed and walked boldly between the bodies, casting their eyes defiantly upon the living as if daring them to deny the crows their due.

Saraea smelled coppery blood, sour vomit, and bitter bile. She bravely kept walking behind Aradia as the queen supervised the collection of the Amazon dead and kept a wary eye on the Roman soldiers doing the same for their own.

"Princess." Saraea heard a desperate whisper.

"Anaea!" she cried, kneeling beside the fallen lieutenant. "Over here! She's alive!"

"Saraea, forget it - it's too late for me," said Anaea, coughing blood. "Take ... take my amulet ... give it to ... Prothoë."

Saraea bit her lip and knelt beside Anaea. She struggled to untie the leather thong, but it was stiff and sticky with blood.

"I - I can't get it!" she cried.

"Just ... pull it off," gasped Anaea.

Saraea grasped the amulet and began to pull. Anaea's head tipped back with the girl's effort, exposing the deep cut in her throat. Blood bubbled out as Anaea released her last breath. With a sob, Saraea pulled one last tug and the amulet came free in her hand as Anaea's head came free of her body and rolled some inches to the side. Nausea roiled in Saraea's stomach and she ran for the brush to vomit, stumbling and falling over Silas who was still hidden there.

Anikha, startled, arose and drew her sword, then sheathed it when she saw it was Saraea.

"Princess, what are you doing here?" she asked.

"What happened?" asked the girl with quiet horror. Her mouth was dry and her heart pounded in her chest, as if trying to escape the confines of her flesh.

"The Romans - " Anikha began, but Saraea held up one hand, silencing her. Her expression grew grim and she drew her sword and began out to the battlefield.

"Princess! Wait - it's a truce - you can't go out there with your blade drawn!" she cried, but Saraea did not seem to hear. She walked purposefully towards the nearest Romans.

"Saraea!" Aradia screamed, running to her. "Saraea, sheath your blade before - !" She was interrupted by the arrow which suddenly bloomed from her left side, just under her arm. Aradia looked down at it, surprised, for a moment before falling to the ground. Saraea turned and saw her foster-mother wounded, then sheathed her sword and ran to her. Thraso called out to Prothoë, the surviving lieutenant and began also running to her fallen queen.

"Come on, we have to get her to the Temple," said Thraso, quietly.

"There's no time for that," said Saraea.

"Well, we have to get her to safety until Prothoë can re-set the truce," said Thraso, grabbing Aradia under the arms. Saraea bent and grabbed Aradia's legs and the two carried her into the brush and lay her next to Silas. "Stay here. I'll go and bring Mhari."

Saraea nodded, then sat between Silas and Aradia, tears flowing freely from her eyes while Anikha patrolled back and forth, guarding her three charges.

"What have I done?" Saraea whispered. She was startled to see Hekau, the cat, approaching. The cat stretched and before Saraea stood Artemis. "Lady, can you help them?"

"No, but you can, Saraea," said Artemis, bending and plucking the doll from Saraea's belt. She began to pull the cloth doll apart.

"What are you doing?" Saraea cried. She leapt to her feet and tried to snatch the ruined doll back.

"Saraea, you don't need Julisa anymore," said the goddess, sternly. "All the power she had is already within you - it always has been." She pulled a shining, purple stone from the doll's cotton stuffing. "Do you remember this, Saraea?"

Suddenly, Saraea did remember. It was that day long ago, when Leilë had taken her and her mother to the tunnel below the altar of the Temple...

Saraea looked about the huge chamber in awe. She wandered over to the wooden door on the other side of the chamber and pushed it open . She looked about the room in wonder. It was a treasure cave to the little girl. Shiny, bright, coloured stones littered the floor and were embedded into the walls and the most beautiful lady she had ever seen - except, of course, her mama - stood before her.

"Hello, Saraea," she said, smiling at the little girl.

"Hi," said the child, hugging Julisa tighter.

"Are you afraid of me?" asked the lady. Saraea nodded. "You don't have to be. Come here, Saraea."

Saraea stepped closer and the lady bent and picked her up, cuddling her close. Saraea felt the warmth and love coming from the lady and returned the cuddle, no longer fearful.

"Mama said I'm 'most too big to carry," she said.

"Not for me, Little One," said the lady

"You look kinda like J'lisa - are you her mama?" asked Saraea.

"In a way - you see, Saraea, I am everyone's mama," said the lady. Saraea frowned in puzzlement, trying to wrap her child's mind around the lady's words. She was distracted by the shimmering stones all around her.

"It's pretty here," she said. "Is this a magical place?"

"Yes it is," said the lady. "And I am going to give you some of its magic to take back with you. You will need it someday when you are almost grown up." She set Saraea back down and reached for a glowing purple pebble, no bigger than the lady's thumbnail. The lady held it out to Julisa, who took it in her cloth hands and pulled it closer until Saraea could no longer see it.

"It inside J'lisa now?" asked Saraea, her eyes wide.

"Yes, Little One - she will keep it safe for you until you need it. Just remember, when that time comes, you may only use it once ..."

Saraea snapped back to the present as Artemis dropped the pebble into her hand.

"You must choose," said Artemis. "That magic stone will only save one of them."

"No," she whispered. "Only ... one? Which one?" She looked up at the goddess with her tear-stained face.

"That is for you to choose," said the goddess.

"That's not fair!" cried Saraea, pounding both of her fists into her thighs.

"Grow up Saraea," said Artemis, sternly. Then she softened. "Surely, Child, you know by now that *life* isn't fair. You'd better hurry - they don't look like they have much time."

The goddess faded and Saraea sat there, shocked into numbness by this day's horror.

Chapter Twelve: The Sword and the Stone

Aradia floated somewhere above the pain. She watched with detachment as Thraso and Saraea dragged her body into the brush and lay it next to Silas. Then her attention was diverted by a gentle hand on her arm.

"Thalia !" she cried, embracing her.

"Aradia," said Thalia. "I have missed you so much."

"I'm here now," said Aradia. "We're together." Thalia released her and looked away. "What's wrong?" She followed Thalia's gaze and saw all of the Amazons who died, standing assembled before her. For a moment, Aradia felt a pang of fear and guilt. She swallowed hard and braced herself for their anger and recriminations at her failure to save them all. Then, as one, the assembled Amazons saluted their queen. Aradia smiled.

"Finally, Sisters, I have joined you," she said.

One by one, her sisters approached and embraced her.

"My daughter is Thraso," said the first. "Thank you for giving her the responsibility of the younglings. She has grown and learned. The day you made her your Second, I watched with pride. She will be great, thanks to you."

"My little sister is Prothoë," said another. "Because of you, she lived to grow up and now she is a great warrior. Thank you, my queen."

"My mother is Alkaia," said a third. "Thanks to you, she will live out her days in the comfort of her own home. Thank you."

"My grand-daughter is Momi. You have given her the opportunity to grow up among her own people and to learn from the old scrolls what it means to be an Amazon. Thank you."

"My sister's daughter is Pisto. Because of you, she will be a great warrior and protect our people. Thank you."

"My daughter, Anikha, heard your call to come home and answered. Now she will be a great midwife and healer among our people because of you. Thank you."

"My daughter is Lykopis. Because of you, she found the courage and strength to save herself from marriage to a man she didn't love, but had to wed to survive in the world of men. Thank you."

All of the Amazons there gave Aradia the names of the kin she had saved for them. Aradia looked out over the faces of the assembled Amazons and saw the bright eager faces she had first greeted in the tree village on that day which now seemed so long ago.

"They survived - and so much more - because of you Aradia," said Artemis, stepping forward from amidst the assembly. "Because after they thought they had lost everything, even hope, you gave it all back to them. They still need you."

"No," said Aradia, shaking her head. "I want to stay. I want to be here, with my sisters. This is where I belong."

"It is your choice," said the goddess, sadly. Aradia once again scanned the faces of the Amazons standing before her, but she couldn't separate them from the faces of those she had brought home to their ancestral city. She was torn between her desire to stay and her responsibility to those who still lived.

"Our daughter still needs you, too," said Thalia, gently. She waved her hand and Aradia could see Saraea, sitting between her body and Silas, weeping. Aradia thought her heart would break at the sight. She saw Saraea raise her head and lower her hands. The girl's eyes widened.

"Oh," she whispered as the vision of Thalia and Aradia standing together, arm in arm, faded from her sight.

Saraea sniffed, then leaned over and kissed Aradia's cheek.

"Okay, I know what to do now," she said. "I need to let you go - you're with my mother now, which is where you want to be. I have to let you be happy with her."

She placed the purple stone on Silas's chest. It began glow brightly, then it stopped and was merely a pretty, shiny pebble. Saraea picked it up. It felt warm to her fingers as she slipped it into a pouch on her belt.

Silas groaned and stirred. His eyes fluttered open.

"Saraea? What are you doing here? What am *I* doing here?" he asked, struggling to sit up. Anikha rushed over to them.

"Just lie back," she said, gently. "You took quite the beating."

"That's not the half of it, but I feel okay," said Silas, pulling himself to a sitting position. "Gods! Aradia! What happened?"

"I killed her," said Saraea, dully.

"What?" said Silas.

"I - I went out on to the field with my sword drawn - I broke the truce," said Saraea. "I saw you, Uncle and I just felt so ... angry. Walked out to ... I don't know, I guess I just wanted to hurt the people who did this to you. Aradia tried to stop me and took this arrow that was meant for me."

"Don't flatter yourself, Kid," said Aradia. "It could just as easily have been meant for me. Could someone please get a healer? This hurts."

"Your majesty, I have had some training, but I'm afraid this a bit beyond what I can handle," said Anikha. "Thraso went for Mhari; they should be here soon. Just try to relax until they get here."

Aradia closed her eyes and nodded.

"Aradia?" said Saraea.

"Yeah," said the queen, her eyes still closed.

"I'm sorry," said the girl.

"My fault - don't beat yourself up, Saraea," said the queen. "I should have ... I don't know, tied you to a tree or something to keep you from following me down here."

"Wouldn't work - I can get out of any knot you tie," said the girl. "I've been practising. Anaea said ..." the girl choked back a sob, then bravely continued, "Anaea said it was a good skill to have."

Aradia sighed and opened her eyes. Weakly, she patted the girl's hand. "I'm sorry, Saraea," she said, softly. "I know that you loved Anaea."

"I've only just realised how much you loved all the Amazons who died," said Saraea, sniffing back tears. "I thought you would want to stay with them."

"I thought so, too," said Aradia. "But I love all the Amazons who still live just as much. My time will come soon enough, but for now, I'm not finished here. Not yet, anyway."

"I'm really glad, Aradia," said Saraea.

"Your majesty, you should really stop talking and rest now," said Anikha, though she was looking sternly at Saraea. "I need to go and report to Prothoë. Saraea, can you stand watch over them until Thraso gets here?"

Saraea rose to her feet. "Of course," she said.

"Good girl," said Anikha, smiling encouragingly to her and patting her shoulder before peering carefully through the brush. "Good - the truce is back up. And I see Thraso and Mhari - they'll be here in a few minutes."

Saraea nodded as Anikha left them. She looked around and saw a pale blur in the brush approaching her charges. Saraea whirled around to see Hekau approaching. The cat looked at her then at Silas, then lay down close to Aradia and began to purr.

"Hey, it's a cat," said Silas.

"Yes - she came to us in the tree village and followed us here," said Saraea, smiling. "Aradia let me keep her."

"You always wanted one, I remember," Silas chuckled. "Even went so far as to catch field mice and plant them in the house, remember?"

Saraea laughed. "Yeah, I do remember that," she said. Silas looked at her sword.

"Is that ...?"

"Yes, it's Mother's," said the girl, quietly.

"You know how to use it, I suppose," he said with a sigh.

"When I have to," said Saraea. "Remember how mad I was that day?"

Silas shook his head. "I should have just let you keep it," he said.

"No, you were right," said Saraea. "You made me put it back where I found it because you were afraid of what the Kaskans would do if they caught me with it. Actually, it was the best place for it to be until Aradia came and taught me when to use it."

"You mean how to use it," said Silas.

"No, I could learn that anywhere," said Saraea, thoughtfully. "That day I brought it home, I thought having a sword in my hand was the answer to everything. Aradia taught me differently. Actually, until today, I thought I had learned that lesson pretty well, but when I saw you ... the way you were, I just ..."

"And I thought you just wanted it because it was Thalia's," said Silas.

"No, that was most of the reason," said Saraea. "There were swords all over out there - until the Kaskans went and picked up all the ones that were usable. I didn't care if it was broken or not - it was my mother's. I couldn't reach her amulet, so I took her sword."

"Oh, Saraea," said Aradia, quietly. "I understand now."

"What?" asked Saraea.

"Why you were so angry that day," Aradia gasped with a weak chuckle. "I had taken both the amulet and sword. You couldn't know that I always intended for you to have both - when you were ready."

"I think ... I think you should keep the amulet," said Saraea. "I have yours - and I have her sword."

Just then Thraso, Mhari, and Anikha arrived.

"Well, what happened here?" asked the shamaness.

"What does it look like?" said Aradia, crossly.

"Well, well, you seem alright to me," said Mhari, chuckling. She began to kneel beside the queen. Saraea rushed over to help her and Hekau arose, stretched and sauntered off a little way away from the group. The cat sat and began to wash. Mhari placed both hands around the wound and felt a bit.

"Can't you just pull the damn thing out?" grumbled Aradia.

"Hush," said Mhari. She felt a bit more around the shaft and the wound. "Hm, it didn't penetrate very far."

"Lucky for me it wasn't an Amazon arrow; damn Romans don't know how to properly string a bow," said Aradia.

"Anikha, Thraso tells me you were apprenticed to a healer?" said Mhari, rising with assistance.

"Yes - well, actually, they called her the village 'witch'," said Anikha. "No one would have anything to do with her until they were injured or sick - or wanting a love potion. She took me in - one outcast to another, I suppose."

"You're not an outcast anymore, Anikha," said Aradia. "You're home now."

"Thanks to you, your majesty," said Anikha, solemnly. "Glauke wasn't much older than me, but she was very wise in the old ways. She taught me a lot. Then one day, I was attending a very difficult birth. I heard the call. It was all I could do to not just run out of there and make my way home, but the woman would have died without a midwife. Then all of a sudden, there was Glauke, her medicine bag in one hand and my travelling pack in the other. She kissed me on the cheek and told me to remember what she taught me - and to think of her every so often. That was it. She took over assisting the birth and I left and came home. I miss her, but I'm glad I'm here."

"When this is over, Anikha, you go find this Glauke and bring her here," said Aradia.

"I don't think she would accept initiation, my queen," said Anikha.

"Doesn't matter," said Aradia. "She will still be welcome."

"I'd like that," said Anikha, her eyes shining. "And so would she, I think. I know she was lonely. I was, too, but at least I had memories of the love and companionship of my sisters. She said I was worse off than she was because you don't miss what you've never had."

"She is wise, indeed," said Mhari. "Now, Anikha, take a look at that wound."

Anikha knelt down and felt around. "Oh, the arrowhead is lodged between the ribs!" she said. "Wedged in there pretty tight, too."

"Okay, so can you pull it out?" said Aradia with a hiss of pain.

"Oh, no, not without cracking one - or both - ribs," said Anikha, frowning. "Unless ..." She looked around until she found a small wooden stick. "Here. Bite." She placed the stick between Aradia's teeth and began to work the shaft of the arrow back and forth, gently at first, then a little faster until it came free. Then Anikha placed an herb-laden compress over the wound.

"There," she said, looking to Mhari for approval.

"That was wonderful, Anikha," said the shamaness. "You learned that from a midwife?"

"Well, it's the same principle when a woman's pelvic bones don't open enough to allow the baby's head through. Actually, our bones aren't set as rigidly as they seem," said Anikha. "You just have to work them loose a little."

"Okay, great, tape me up and let's go," said Aradia, struggling to sit up.

"Aradia, we can carry you -" Saraea began.

"No, tape me up - I'm walking out of here," said the queen, pulling herself to a sitting position.

"The wound is pretty superficial," Anikha said, as Mhari handed her strips of linen. "The herbs should prevent infection from setting in - at least until we can clean it and dress it properly."

"Great - let's do it," said Aradia. "Silas, look somewhere else, huh?" She lifted her tunic off over her head. Saraea gasped at the scars. Aradia closed her eyes. "Saraea."

"The Romans did that to you, didn't they?" asked the girl, quietly.

"Yep," said Aradia. "Don't get it into your head to take on the whole Roman army, though, okay?"

"I won't," said the girl defensively. "Just the ones who did this to you."

"You stay away from him," said Aradia, fiercely. "Come on."

She led them out of the brush. She looked over and saw Aurelian and another man she didn't recognise though he looked familiar, watching them. Saraea turned and followed her gaze. The girl felt the man's eyes rake appraisingly over her and she suppressed a shudder and looked quickly away.

"Aradia, is that ...?" she whispered, as if he could hear her even from that great distance.

"That's Aurelian," said Aradia, casting one defiant glance back at him before turning and striding purposefully away.

Mhari turned. "So that's Aurelian, huh?" she said. Then she stopped walking and glared at him, waving her arms about in an elaborate gesture.

"Mhari, what are you doing?" asked Aradia.

Mhari turned so the mounted men couldn't see her chuckling.

"Ah, Aradia, he isn't spit," she said. "I just made the 'evil eye' at him and you should have seen his face!"

"Mhari, there's no such thing as the evil eye," said Saraea, quietly, glancing back at the men who still watched, though she could see that the general had grown a bit pale.

"He doesn't know that," said the amused shamaness.

"Perhaps not, but I'd be willing to bet that his companion does know," said Aradia. Saraea looked back again and gasped.

"What's wrong Saraea?" asked Aradia. She turned to look at the girl and saw that Saraea was very pale and sweating.

"That man ..." she whispered. "I've seen him before."

"Where, Saraea?" asked Mhari, gently.

"That's ... that's Ares," said Saraea. "That's who Julisa turned into in the cave where
Athtar ..."

"It's alright, Saraea," said Mhari, gently. "He won't harm you. He can't."

"I'd say leading a little girl into a cave against the Graii - not to mention that thing Athtar has become - is pretty harmful," said Aradia.

"Exactly," said Mhari. "If he was capable of doing it himself, he would have already."

"Hm," said Aradia. "Alright, you have a point. However, he's still helping the Romans."

"And Artemis is helping us," said Saraea, quietly. "She's just not as visible as he."

"On the contrary," said Mhari, looking back at Hekau still following them. "She is quite visible, to those of us who know her."

Aurelian sat astride his horse, complacent and smug - until the old hag hexed him, that is.

"Relax, she's playing with you," said Ares.

"Playing ... does the old woman make light of me, then?" said the general.

"Yes, she does," said Ares, slightly amused at Aurelian's outraged surprise.

"Then the Amazons do not fear me," said the general with a growl.

"Aradia still does - and the girl; did you see her?" said Ares.

Mollified, Aurelian frowned and nodded. "Yes, but she looks just like any other young girl, nothing special about her that I could see."

"She is more special than you can ever know," said Ares slowly, his eyes narrowing as he watched Saraea walk with Aradia, Mhari and Silas, the cat, Hekau following them. "Even *I* wasn't aware of just how special until now."

"So far your plan is working," said Aurelian, turning to see the god had disappeared from the back of the horse. Aurelian shook his head and turned back to watch the group walk into the trees.

It had been Mars's - or Ares, as he was known in this part of the world - idea to take the man from the village and to make sure the Amazons saw him in Aurelian's company. The god had assured him that the Amazons would attempt a rescue, though Aurelian didn't quite know why; everyone knew the Amazons were man-haters. Why would they risk themselves to save an enemy? Yet they had and, against all of even Ares's predictions, they had succeeded, three of them taking out an entire patrol of soldiers! Still, they had gotten one of the damn women and Aurelian waited for them to attack ... and waited. Finally, the general had been forced to make the first move by attacking the Amazon perimeter.

"I knew that was a mistake - that's the price I pay for my impatience," Aurelian said to himself with a sigh.

The skirmish had not been the wholesale massacre Aurelian had had in mind. He had wanted to destroy as many of the warriors as possible, leaving the Amazons defenceless and unprepared for the long siege he planned. He wanted Aradia to know just how hopeless her situation was so that she would surrender herself - and her ward - to him in order to save what was left of her people. He had no idea that the Amazons were mounted! Lucky for the scouts that the Amazons had killed them before he could get his hands on them.

"Still," Aurelian muttered to himself. "I can outwait them. I have the men and the supplies. Aradia *will* surrender - and when she does, that girl of hers will be just the insurance I need to make sure that she never gets away from me again."

)O(

Aradia assembled the Amazons in the lower town before bringing Silas into their midst. She explained to the women that Silas was a friend and ally to the Amazon Nation. Grudgingly, the Amazons accepted Silas's presence, mostly for Saraea's sake, and on the condition that he remain in the lower town. Silas was given sleeping space among the warriors camped around the ruined fortress.

Escorted by Thraso, he walked around the ruins. "Amazing," he said.

"What?" asked Thraso.

"This building - well, what's left of it," said Silas. He eyed the freshly-made mud bricks awaiting the kiln. "You're re-building it - that's wonderful."

"Well, of course," said Thraso. "Our traditions say that this was built by Lysippe, the - "

"The Lawgiver," said Silas, nodding. "Thalia told me of her - and the rest of the queens who made history. Saraea has a proud heritage."

"So do you, Silas," said Thraso. "Didn't you and Thalia have the same mother?"

"That's quite a stretch for an Amazon," said Silas, smiling. Thraso shrugged. "I guess we did, though I never thought of Areto as my mother. She gave birth to me, then gave me to the woman who raised me. My father taught me carpentry and stone masonry - I used to be a builder before the Kaskans came."

"So how would you re-build the fortress?" asked Thraso, aware of the Amazons listening to them.

"Well, the foundation is still in perfect condition - even this newer part here," said Silas, pointing.

"What do you mean 'newer part'?" asked an Amazon named Aeda stepping forward.

"Well, here, you can see it yourself - they must have added on after the fire - " began Silas.

"Fire? What fire?" asked Aeda. Silas bent and began to dig around the foundation a bit. He held up a charred sliver of wood.

"You can still see scorch marks on some of the stones," he said. "See, originally there were wooden beams for support as part of the first structure. After the fire, they added on and the new walls added the necessary support."

"That's amazing," said Thraso. "So, how would you do it, Silas?"

"Well, you can build on the existing foundation, but I would add the wooden beams again and expand it ..." Silas looked around until he found a stick, then began sketching in the dirt. The Amazons gathered around to watch.

Aradia found them later, all sitting around on the stone foundation, drinking *koumiss* and laughing together.

"Uh, isn't there a war going on?" asked the queen, one eyebrow raised.

"Aradia!" said Thraso, jumping to her feet. The other Amazons followed, looking around at one another guiltily.

"Sorry, it's my fault," said Silas, rising. "We were just discussing the re-building once the Romans are gone."

"Uh, huh," said Aradia. She motioned with one hand and the Amazons dispersed, leaving her, Thraso, and Silas alone. "Silas, I'm glad you're making friends here. That's something I wanted to discuss with you. Obviously, you can't stay here forever, though if Saraea had her way you would. I don't think it's safe for you to return to the village, either -"

"There is no more village," said Silas, quietly. "The Romans destroyed it the night they came and took me away."

"Silas, I'm sorry," said Thraso. Silas shrugged.

"Well, actually, that sort of fits what I had originally had in mind," said Aradia. "I wanted to bring the villagers closer to the Amazons. I was actually thinking of building another village over on the other side of the mound. We could offer protection to those who lived near us. There are fields for crops, hazelnut and pomegranate trees, the sea and the river are full of fish - "

"That's very generous of you, Aradia," said Silas. "But won't the Amazons have a problem with that? This is their - *your* land, after all."

"If the Amazons are to grow and thrive, we need the villagers," said Aradia. "Besides, there aren't enough of us to work the land now. Everything that lies fallow is potentially dangerous if an enemy to the Amazons decides to take it. This way, our neighbours are also our friends and allies."

"I can see that," said Silas, thoughtfully. "I can talk to them, but I can't promise anything. The Kaskans had us working the fields and - "

"Amazons are not Kaskans, Silas," said Aradia, gently.

"No, I know," said Silas, shaking his head. "But it may be hard to convince the villagers that one group of warriors isn't much the same as another."

"That's still in the future, though," said Thraso. "We still have the Romans to deal with - and they have Ares."

"I know," said Aradia. "But I have to believe that we will be victorious over them. The Amazons need me to believe it so that they can. Otherwise, what is the point?"

What is *the point?* said the old pessimistic voice in Aradia's head. Aradia sighed and pushed the voice away. "Never again," she muttered aloud.

"What?" asked Thraso.

"Nothing," said Aradia. "Come on Thraso. Let Silas get some sleep. We have a lot to do - are the watches set?"

"Of course," said Thraso, frowning.

"Good, then let's go," said Aradia. She and Thraso walked to the command tent she was occupying.

"Aradia, is something wrong?" Thraso asked her.

"No," said the queen, shortly.

"Look, I'm sorry about the warriors and me sitting around talking with Silas, but - " began Thraso.

"No," said Aradia. "That was better than I had hoped for, actually. They need to get know more people like Silas if my plan for the new village is going to work out. I was thinking of populating it with Amazon kin at first - and I still may at least partially. No, Thraso, that was fine. I didn't mind that."

"Then what is it?" asked Thraso.

"Who says it's anything?" said the queen. "Blessed Artemis, Thraso, we're at war - isn't that enough?"

"You're right - I'm sorry, Aradia," said Thraso.

"Do we know how many ...?" asked Aradia.

"Not yet," said Thraso. "I'll give you a count when the healers are done. We'll probably lose more throughout the night. How is Saraea?"

"Not so great," said Aradia, grimly. "I sent her to escort Mhari back up to the Temple. I'm hoping she decides it's too much for her and stays there."

"Don't count on it, Aradia," said Thraso. "She's scared and sick about what happened to Anaea, but she's also really, really pissed."

"That's the natural progression - until you start to get numb, that is," said Aradia with a sigh.

"That numbness can be fatal," said Thraso. "I remember, I fought against it for so long. We were in a constant state of wariness. During the day we were so busy, hiding and trying to find food and shelter and doing what we could to protect the children entrusted to our care, but at night ... I would lie awake, too tired to sleep. We were just waiting, though at the time, I didn't know what we were waiting for. Now I know; we were waiting for you to come back."

"I was waiting too - waiting for death to finally take me," said Aradia, wearily. "Or so I thought at the time."

"I guess you were waiting to come back, too," said Thraso.

"Yeah - I guess so," said Aradia, smiling. "Seriously now, get some rest - tomorrow is going to be another rough day."

Thraso nodded and left her. Aradia was startled by a shadow outside the tent, then Saraea entered.

"You're back," said Aradia.

"You sound surprised," said Saraea, frowning.

"N – okay, I thought maybe today would be too much for you," Aradia admitted.

"It almost was," said Saraea, nodding. "But I still want to be here - with you. I - I thought I lost you today, Aradia."

"Nah - not even close - arrow just sort of knocked the wind out of me for a bit," said Aradia, not quite managing to look at the girl.

"I saw you ... with my mother," said Saraea, quietly. She reached into a pouch on her belt and pulled a small, purple stone.

"Pretty," said Aradia.

"It was inside of Julisa - my doll," said Saraea. "I remember Artemis putting it there when I was really, really small. She told me then that it was magic, but I would only be able to use it once when the time came. I ... I used it for Silas today."

Aradia remembered vaguely seeing Saraea sitting between her body and Silas, crying.

"And you feel bad because you didn't choose me?" she said gently. Saraea nodded. "Don't. It was always my decision to stay or to come back. I chose to come back. I have all of eternity to be dead and only a few years here in the greater scheme of things. I saw that my work here wasn't finished."

"I thought you were with my mother and your sisters, whom you miss so much; I thought you were where you wanted to be," said the girl.

"My sisters are here, too - they showed me that," said Aradia, smiling at Saraea. "And my daughter is here - I really don't want to miss you growing up - I've missed enough of that as it is."

Saraea broke into a huge grin and hugged the queen tight. "So, what comes next?" she asked.

"We fight - again," said Aradia.

"And we win," said the girl.

"I hope so," said Aradia. "I won't lie to you, Saraea. They outnumber us by a lot. It won't be easy to defeat Aurelian."

"But it's not impossible," said Saraea.

"Almost, but no, not impossible," Aradia agreed.

"Will the poison arrows help?" asked Saraea.

"Maybe," said Aradia. "But that takes time. We don't have much of that."

"Why not?" asked Saraea.

"Well, first, Aurelian can send for re-inforcements and supplies and have a couple of legions here in a few weeks," said Aradia. "Second, the rains are coming; I don't want our sisters battling in the mud. And finally, we have only limited stores and no fresh food."

"And mostly, having Romans this close seems like desecration," said Saraea, quietly.

"Yeah," said Aradia. "It really does."

"So, why don't we send out the cavalry and push them back some?" asked Saraea.

"Saraea, they outnumber us," said Aradia.

"I know, but we're better than they are," said Saraea. "Surely that has to count for something. They pushed first. Now we need to push back."

"Saraea, I don't want to lose any more Amazons in a petty shoving match," said Aradia, irritably.

"It isn't petty," said Saraea. "We need to let those Romans that we aren't going to give ground so easily."

"Easily?" said Aradia. "Do you have any idea what the cost in Amazon lives was?"

"No, but neither do you - not yet, anyway," said Saraea, defiantly. "I just want them gone."

"We all do, Saraea, but we can't afford to lose any of our sisters to impatience," said Aradia. "We have to work fast to get the Romans out of our space, but not so fast we sacrifice more lives than necessary."

"If only I could bring us all into the room under the Temple - time stands still there," said Saraea. "We could easily outwait the Romans there and they'd never even know where we went."

"Yeah - if only," said Aradia. "Alright - get some sleep. We have a long day tomorrow."

"Sleep?" said Saraea, sitting on the cot upon which her bedroll was laid out. "How are we supposed to sleep? Romans are practically right outside the windows."

"Trust me, Saraea, no Roman is getting up here tonight," said Aradia.

"What about Ares?" asked Saraea, lying down on the field cot as Aradia sat at the table the Amazons had set up for her inside of the tent.

Aradia gazed out of the open tent flap for a moment and allowed her hand to rest on the pommel of the Sword of Artemis, sheathed at her waist. "I don't think he will come up here, Saraea," she said. "Go to sleep."

The girl lay her head down and closed her eyes, drifting off though not quite to sleep. She watched Ares watching Hekau as the cat stretched into Artemis. It was as if Saraea was there, though it seemed neither god could see her.

"Artemis," said Ares. "You cheated - you brought Aradia back."

"No, I didn't," said Artemis. "Saraea - and Aradia herself - did."

"Oh, come on - how can a little girl bring a spirit back from the dead?" said Ares. "Without a little 'divine intervention', that is. And Aradia has had a death wish for over a decade now. You really think I believe you didn't interfere?"

"I don't honestly care what you believe, Ares," said Artemis. "I didn't bring Aradia back from the dead."

"Then it must have been the girl," said Ares. "So who is she?"

"She is Saraea," said Artemis with a shrug.

"You know what I mean," said Ares. "I know that she is supposedly the 'Salvation' of the Amazon Nation. What is her role?"

"Ares, why would I tell you that?" asked Artemis.

"Suit yourself, Artemis," said Ares. "But you'll be sorry - and so will the Amazons. What would *She* say about you interfering and bringing a mortal back from the dead, huh?" asked a smug Ares. Artemis smiled.

"Again, I didn't. Why don't you go find *Her* and ask *Her*? Better yet, why don't we ask Her to come here?" said Artemis. Ares looked away.

"I suppose you expect me to believe that the Great Mother of All is at your beck call now, huh, Art - " Ares looked up as he spoke, then stopped as he saw the goddess who had freed Aradia standing where Artemis once had. He swallowed hard. "No."

"Yes," said the goddess. "I am *Her*, too."

Chapter Thirteen: Messenger of the Sword

Saraea awoke and sat up. It was morning and Aradia was not in the tent. The girl splashed water on her face and went outside.

The Amazons were once again in formation and Aradia was mounted on Kalika. Saraea's horse, Kaiyanta, was saddled and waiting.

"Come on, Saraea," said Aradia. "We've got an hour's ride around the mound to meet the rest of the cavalry in the trees before the foot warriors attack."

"Oh!" said Saraea, running and mounting Kaiyanta. "Are we really going to ...?"

"Yep - we're pushing back," said Aradia, with a grin.

"What about losing Amazon lives to impatience?" asked the girl as the two rode to the stables and the secret trail behind them.

"If we do this right, we won't lose anyone," said the queen. "Come on, a little faith here, Kiddo."

"You must have a flawless plan to be letting me ride down with you," said Saraea, checking her sword.

"No, I don't," said Aradia, soberly. "No plan is flawless, but I don't think you'll be in any danger. Our cavalry ride out and attack the wings while our foot keeps the Roman *velites* busy. You and I have a special mission. We're going to capture Aurelian's standard."

"Why are we going to do that, Aradia?" asked Saraea.

"Because it will really annoy him," said Aradia, chuckling.

"Okaaay, who are you and what have you done with my stuffy, overprotective ... uh, m-mother?" asked Saraea, stumbling slightly over the word as she tasted it, feeling it with both her heart and mouth and liking it.

Aradia, too, liked it and smiled slightly at the appellation. "We need his standard for my plan against them," said the queen.

"What plan is that?" asked Saraea,

"Diverting his re-inforcements if he decides to send for any," said Aradia.

They rode down the secret trail in silence, whistling a signal to the hidden sentries posted along the way to let them pass. They continued their silent ride , accompanied by the sounds of the birds singing and the buzzing of bees, gathering the last pollen of the autumn blossoms until they reached the edge of the hazelnut grove; there they met with the rest of the mounted Amazon warriors. They greeted their queen and princess with a salute. Aradia acknowledged them with a nod and returned the salute, then rode to the further edge of the trees. She watched as Thraso led the foot warriors into their places. They crouched behind large rocks and in the thick, concealing brush around the perimeter of the Roman camp.

Aradia waited until they were all in place. She nodded to the mounted warriors, then whistled a signal to attack. The Amazons emerged in a wave. Aradia led the mounted Amazons, bursting out of the trees with Saraea at her side. Saraea held her sword in her hand, screeching a battle cry as she rode like a missile straight into the Roman camp, knocking Roman foot soldiers out of her way with the flat of her blade. The Amazon warriors followed her, dispatching the fallen Romans. Aradia stayed beside the girl, struggling to keep up as she skirted around Amazon and Roman warriors alike, engaged in their own battles on the ground.

Aurelian emerged from his tent at the sounds of fighting, his sword drawn. He shouted orders at the Roman soldiers, getting them mobilised and ready to fight.

Gods-be- damned unpredictable *women! Where in the hell is Ares* now*?* he thought as his soldiers assembled against the attacking Amazons. They were engaged with the soldiers at the perimeter of the camp. Then Aurelian saw them, two mounted Amazons, riding straight towards the heart of the camp. He watched with fascination, as if he were mesmerised by the women. They came ever closer and Aurelian remained frozen, watching in disbelief. He could not fathom the suicidal dash - what were they after? Him? Was this an assassination attempt? Were the women mad?

He saw them stop short of his command tent. They were close enough that he could now see they were Aradia and the girl. Aradia looked at him, a slow smile spreading across her face. The girl looked over at him, grinned, and made a rude gesture just before grabbing the wooden pole of his standard and riding off back to the Amazons. Aradia shrugged, then grabbed the Emperor's standard which had stood next to Aurelian's and rode after the girl.

The realisation then hit Aurelian. No, not an assassination attempt - they had stolen the Roman standards! They were playing with him, mocking him once again as the old woman had.

"Stop them!" he yelled, but too late; the Amazons were already gone, retreating from the battles at the perimeter, leaving the Romans standing there, bewildered, as the women faded back into the trees, rocks, and brush, disappearing from sight as if they had never been.

Aradia and Saraea rode around the mound, escorted by the rest of the Amazon cavalry. The sentries posted along the hidden trail emerged and silently saluted the cavalry as they returned the horses to the stables. The foot soldiers climbed the cliffs to the lower town, Amazon archers covering their ascent.

Aradia and Saraea cooled down the horses, then brushed, watered, and fed them before taking the Roman standards to the ruined fortress where Silas awaited them. Two Amazons approached, dragging an unconscious Roman soldier between them.

"Okay, Silas," said Aradia. "Are you ready?"

"Absolutely," he said. They stripped the Roman of his armour and helm. "Are you sure more Romans are coming, Aradia?"

"Yes," said Aradia. "Aurelian wants to overwhelm us with numbers. I saw his face yesterday, watching. He was disappointed we didn't lose more Amazons than we did."

"He must be fuming today," said Saraea, grinning.

"Yeah," said Aradia, smiling. "The fact that we stole his standards right out from under three legions - with *no* loss of Amazon life, thank you very much - probably has him crazy. We'd better be prepared; Aurelian will try to regain what dignity he can by attacking. I expect more Romans within the week."

"And I'll be there to meet them and take them to what is left of the village," said Silas.

"And we'll be there to hijack the supply wagons they will undoubtedly bring with them," said Saraea.

"Which only buys us a bit more time," said Aradia. "We have to figure out how to get rid of Aurelian for good."

"We need re-inforcements like he has," said Saraea, quietly.

"Yes, that would be ideal," said Aradia. "If Aurelian thought that there were more of us than those here in the city, he would realise that he won't ever defeat us. Unfortunately, that isn't possible. We just have to find another way."

"What about our allies?' asked Saraea. "Surely we had some before ..."

"We've had no time to negotiate and renew the old treaties," said Aradia, with a sigh. "And no guarantees that our friends would side with us against Rome. They are a formidable enemy."

"They aren't so much," said Saraea. "There's just so many of them. If everyone came together and fought them, they would be crushed for good."

"That's true," said Aradia. "That's why, like any wise predator, Rome strives to separate its prey from everyone else before pouncing and conquering them. No if Rome ever falls, it will be from within."

"Yes, it will," said Saraea, a faraway look in her eyes. She shook her head. "But we can't afford to wait for that."

Silas looked at her sharply. "Has she been doing that again?" he asked with concern.

"All the time," said Aradia. "Why?"

"She did that when she was small, too," said Silas. "Woke up one night right after she came to me, screaming that her mother had been killed. Mhari gave her something and it seemed to stop. Well, mostly. She still told stories about seeing ghosts."

"Those were no stories, Silas," said Aradia. "She does see them. It's just part of who she is. Being here brings it out more, I believe."

"Yes, but ... is she okay?" asked the concerned uncle.

"Of course she is," said Aradia. "Now come - we have to get this Roman somewhere safe until our armour-makers can duplicate his armour. I don't want Aurelian getting any ideas about what we're up to. We can take him back to his camp as soon as they're done."

The drums started beating as they dragged the unconscious Roman into an unoccupied tent. Silas waited there for him to wake up.

"You!" said the Roman when he saw Silas sitting there, bound as he himself was. "What happened? Why are you tied up? Aurelian said they would rescue you."

"They think I betrayed them - that I led you to them here," said Silas, wincing at the sound of a ram's horn blaring outside of the tent. "We have to get out of here before they kill us both."

The Roman began struggling against his bonds until the tent flap slapped open and Aradia strode in, accompanied by Saraea and two Amazon warriors.

"Amazons, mercy, please!" cried Silas, his eyes wide.

"Shut up, Traitor," said Aradia, delivering a kick to his ribs. Silas fell and rolled to his side, moaning. "You." Aradia cast her eyes on the Roman. She motioned to the warriors flanking her and Saraea. They moved as one, bending and pulling the Roman to his feet.

"Take him to my tent," said Aradia. The warriors dragged him off and Aradia followed. Saraea remained behind until the tent flap closed, then she bent and untied Silas. She handed him a bundle.

"Here's the duplicate armour, Uncle," she said, quietly. "Please be careful."

"I will," said Silas. He stood as two more Amazons entered the tent. "I'll see you soon. Ready?" He bent and hugged Saraea tightly. One of the Amazons splashed rabbit blood on Silas's shirt. Then they took him by the arms as Silas made himself limp. His head lolled to one side and the Amazons carried him past the Roman who was being escorted to Aradia's tent.

Thraso waited in the tent for Aradia and the Amazons to bring the Roman soldier. As soon as they arrived, she signalled to one of the warriors who had escorted the Roman. The warrior nodded slightly and left them. The remaining Amazons shoved the Roman roughly into a chair. The beating of the drums and intermittent blaring of a ram's horn wore away at the Roman's nerves. It seemed that the noises had been going on his head forever.

"Aradia, I've sent out the call for our sister Tribes to join us against the Roman scum," said Thraso, just loud enough for Briccius to "overhear". "We can expect our re-inforcements to arrive any day - some perhaps even today."

"Very good, Thraso," said Aradia, sitting across from the Roman. "What is your name, Soldier?"

"I am Briccius Venatus Amazonum," said the soldier, hesitantly.

"'Briccius, Amazon Hunter', eh?" said Aradia. "Is this your first campaign, then?"

"Are you going to kill me?" asked Briccius.

"I don't know yet," said Aradia.

"That other man - "

"Silas was counted as a friend to the Amazons - until he betrayed us," said Aradia, coldly. "You, on the other hand, are a soldier, doing your job. The Amazons understand that. We respect it. We are still enemies, you and I, but the Amazons have honour and that honour is very important to us."

Briccius sat there. The incessant drums pounded in his head, confusing him. He was disoriented and afraid. What did these women want from him?

"Why am I here, then?" he asked.

"I want you to carry a message to Aurelian," said Aradia. "Tell him that Aradia sends her greetings and that if he will take his men and leave Amazon territory for good, I will not crush him and his troops to oblivion when our sister Tribes arrive to fight by our side against him."

"The general will kill me for bringing him such a message!" Briccius protested. Swiftly, Thraso was behind him, her knife at his throat.

"You don't seem to understand your position here, Briccius," said Aradia. "You are a man in a city full of women warriors who have every reason to hate you and none to help you - save delivering that message."

Briccius hesitated only a moment longer; bringing Aurelian the information that the Amazons were expecting re-inforcements *might* save his life if he agreed to do this for the Amazon Queen. If he refused, the Amazons would surely kill him.

"Very well," he said, swallowing hard. Thraso backed off and put her knife away, then tossed Briccius's armour to him.

"Get dressed and we will escort you to your camp," said Aradia, rising and leaving the tent with Thraso right behind her.

Briccius dressed swiftly, then emerged from the tent. The Amazons immediately placed a blindfold over his eyes and took both of his arms, leading him towards the cliffs.

"M-my sword," said Briccius.

"Not until you are out of the city and among your own people again," said Thraso.

They wound a thick rope about his chest and waist, then handed the ropes over to the sentries on the wall. The sentries lowered Briccius to the ground below the lower town while Thraso and the two warriors descended by way of the rope and pulley system they had devised first for the tree village, then adapted to use here for swifter descents and ascents. They met Briccius on the ground and led him by the ropes still fastened around him to just beyond the perimeter.

Almost Briccius didn't realise that the ropes were gone, so deftly and silently did the Amazons remove them and disappear, fading out of sight and into landscape. He removed the blindfold and looked around, blinking in the sunlight. Then he bent and retrieved his sword. He straightened and looked around. Seeing and hearing nothing but the wind blowing through the trees and tall grasses and the birds chirping in the trees, Briccius ran to the Roman camp, occasionally looking back to see if the Amazons were watching him.

Briccius was no fool; there was no way the Amazons would be able to kill him if he did not deliver their dangerous message to the general now. Aurelian, however, might not look favourably upon a soldier who withheld knowledge that might be useful to the general. Briccius was undecided. He had no way of knowing the Amazons had kept him unconscious for three days while their craftswomen replicated his armour; as far as Briccius knew, none of his comrades even knew he'd been captured.

If Aurelian found out he'd been with the Amazons and Briccius himself didn't report that ... The young man shuddered at the imagined repercussions. He didn't want to die, not like that. If his time came, he wanted it to be in glorious battle, not hanging from a tree like a traitor or a coward.

He went to the general's tent to give Aurelian Aradia's message - or at least the part about expecting Amazon re-inforcements - but the sight of the General's elite honour guard standing outside of the tent gave him pause. The sound of the general roaring inside the tent in anger at the Amazons' stealing of the Roman standards had made him turn back, the message undelivered. He decided that the best course of action was to wait and see what happened.

Chapter Fourteen: The Sword Calls Again

Aradia sat in her tent and waited for Thraso to return. The Second in Command did not keep her waiting long. Just after the drums and the horn stopped, Thraso entered the tent.

"Thank Artemis. I don't mind the drums so much, but three days of hearing that horn was getting to me. How'd it go?" asked the Queen.

Thraso smiled. "He ran to his camp as fast as he could," she said, chuckling. "Think he'll deliver your message?"

"It really doesn't matter - that was just a diversion from the real reason we captured him," said Aradia with a shrug.

"The armour," said Thraso, nodding.

"Yes," said Aradia. "I don't want Aurelian to have an idea what I'm doing. This is our one chance to buy a little time until I can figure out how to rid our land of these damn Romans once and for all. If he figures out what I'm up to, it will blow that chance and we won't get another."

"He won't figure it out, Aradia," said Thraso. "How could he?"

Aradia grew silent, withdrawing against the tight fear which clutched at her chest and had since Aurelian arrived in Amazon Territory. Resolutely, she tried to push the fear away, but it was no good; it was an old resident in her mind, well-established and nearly unevictable.

"Aradia, did he anticipate you and Saraea grabbing the standards?" asked Thraso.

A crack in the shell of fear surrounding the queen opened. "No ... no he didn't - he was completely surprised," she said, thoughtfully. "He would have certainly stopped us if he had."

"Whatever power this man may or may not have held over you, Aradia, it's gone now - perhaps being here, in the city of our Ancient Mothers, protects you," said Thraso. "Or perhaps this man never really had any power over you at all, save what he made you believe he had. In any case, you are free of this hold he had over you now."

"Maybe not free, but it's shaking loose and crumbling away, little by little," said the queen. "Thank you, Thraso, for helping me put it into perspective."

"Eventually, Aradia, you will realise fully that you have nothing more to fear from this man - other than in battle, of course," said Thraso. "Though I have heard it said that many of Rome's generals have merely bought their commission, rather than earn it in battle."

"No, you can tell by the way he moves, Aurelian is a warrior," said Aradia.

"So are you," said Thraso.

"If only we had more of an advantage," said Aradia. "If Aurelian wasn't so sure of victory against us, I could challenge him, one on one, winner decides the war. Unfortunately, there's no reason for him to believe such a match would be to his benefit in any way."

"Well, if your message is delivered, he may believe that more Amazons are on their way," said Thraso. "That may shake his confidence a bit."

"I wouldn't count on that hap-" began Aradia. She was interrupted by Saraea bursting into the tent.

"Roman ships approaching," she gasped. "Three of them"

"Where's Silas?' asked Aradia.

"He took a horse - and the standards - to meet them," said Saraea.

"Thraso mobilise the cavalry for an ambush - " Aradia began, then stopped.

"Aradia, I'm no rider," said Thraso, quietly.

"I am! Let me go!" cried Saraea. "Please, Aradia? I can lead the ambush."

"Saraea, I just don't know," said Aradia.

"Aradia, there's no one else," said Thraso, slowly. "With your wound, you can't do it."

Aradia flexed her arm and saw the bandage seeping red from underneath. "It's too soon," she said. "Even if Aurelian sent for troops during the truce, it would take over a week for them to arrive, even from the nearest Roman outpost. Something's not right about all this."

"What do we do?' asked Thraso.

"Saraea, stop Silas and Thraso, take some scouts down there to spy out the ships," said Aradia.

"Do you want me to send Mhari - or Anikha - to take a look at that wound, Aradia?" asked Saraea.

"No - just hurry and get to Silas," said the queen. "I'm fine - go, go you two!"

Saraea mounted Kaiyanta and started down the hidden trail, whistling for the sentries to detain Silas before he left the trees. She met up with him just at the bottom of the trail.

"Saraea," said Silas. "What's going on?"

"Aradia says it's too soon for the Roman reinforcements to be coming," said Saraea.

Silas dismounted and looked out of the trees at the three galleys slowly approaching the shore. He whistled.

"She's right. Those aren't Roman, they're Greek-made - pirates, by the look of them, too," he said.

"What are they doing, Silas?" Saraea whispered. "Are they coming ashore?"

"I don't know," said Silas. He looked up at the sky through the trees. "Not likely - by the time they get close enough it will be too dark to navigate the coastline."

Thraso appeared with a group of scouts while Silas was removing the Roman armour. He bundled it up and tied it to the back of the horse.

"What's happening?' asked Thraso.

"Greek-made galleys - unmarked, so they're most likely pirates," said Silas.

"Not Roman, then," said Thraso with a nod. "Aradia was right - again. Karia, go and inform the queen. The rest of you - how close can you get to those boats without being seen?"

"Let's just find out," said one of the scouts with a grin. The group moved forward, then seemed to disappear into the land.

"How did they ...?" began Silas.

"This land is our home," said Saraea "And we are a part of it."

Silas looked at the two Amazons standing before him. They did indeed look as if they risen from the land around them. Saraea's eyes were the colour of the ripe hazelnuts hanging in the trees around them. Thraso's eyes matched the green of those same trees' leaves. Saraea's long, wavy hair was the colour of the dark, rich earth from which those trees grew. Thraso's was as golden as the reflection of the sun upon the sparkling water of the sea before them. Saraea's skin was as dark as the fallen leaves all around them while Thraso's was as fair as the sand on the shore. Light and dark, both Amazons were a part of this place.

Silas heard the cry of a strange bird arising from the rocks lining the shore. "What was that?" he said.

"It can't be," Thraso whispered. "Can it?"

"Can wha-?" began Saraea as Aradia came swiftly down the trail on Kalika.

"What's going on?" asked the queen.

"Those ships," said Thraso. "Silas says they're Greek - pirate ships, most likely. But the scouts just whistled – "

The group in the trees heard the odd birdcall again. Aradia rode past the others to the edge of the trees at the bottom of the trail. She frowned and began riding faster towards the shore. A slow grin spread across her face.

"Telepyleia!" she cried, waving both arms at a small figure on the deck of one of the ships. The figure waved back enthusiastically. Aradia turned her head and called back to Thraso. "Quickly - get a platoon down here - I want torches and a huge fire on the beach to guide their ships to shore."

Thraso nodded and sent a sentry from the trail up to the lower town to carry out the queen's orders. Then she rode up to Aradia.

"Aradia, what's going on?" she asked.

"Looks like we got some re-inforcements," said Aradia, smiling.

)O(

One by one, boats were lowered from the ships. Telepyleia came in the last boat launched, leaving only small crews to bring each galley to shore. Aradia dismounted and ran to greet her old friend.

Telepyleia was about the same age as Aradia, though the sun and wind of the sea made her look at least a decade older. Her straw-coloured hair was generously threaded with silver, her blue eyes remained in a perpetual squint. Her dark, leathery skin was deeply creased with lines that deepened even more when she smiled. Her hands were rough and calloused, as was her speech.

"Aradia, how in the Four Hells are you?" she cried, grabbing the queen and pulling her into a tight embrace.

"How are *you*?" asked Aradia, deftly avoiding the question.

"Freakin' *great*," said Telepyleia, releasing her from the strangling embrace. "Now that we're all home. We heard the call a while back, but damned if it didn't stop before we found you. Then, there it was again. I told my girl, Meploeo here, to turn about and follow those drums. Shoulda known we'd find you here eventually."

"Eventually? You've been by here before then?" asked Saraea.

"Well, sure - we were just waitin' for Ari' to come back," said Telepyleia, smiling at the girl. "Ari', this isn't ... is that Thalia's little one? She can't be, can she?"

"She can and she is," said Aradia, putting one arm around Saraea's shoulders and giving the girl a re-assuring squeeze. "This is Saraea."

"Saraea, good to see you again - you grew up real nice," said Telepyleia. "I've got two girls about your age - Meploeo, Kleite, come on over here and meet your kin."

Meploeo was fair-haired like her mother, with a quick grin and an even quicker wit. Kleite was dark-haired and fair-skinned, solemn and quiet.

"Meploeo was born onboard," said Telepyleia, ruffling the girl's short-cropped hair. "And she's a born sailor for more than just that - my right hand at sea, she is. My Kleite, though, she was born right here in our city. Been studyin' in Alexandria these past few years at the Pharaoh's own library."

"Really?" said Saraea. "What is it like there?"

Kleite shrugged. "Alright," she said, quietly.

"As much as I would love to catch up," said Aradia. "We have three Roman legions camped below the lower town around the other side of the mound and I need to get back to camp."

"Point us to them," said Telepyleia, her bright blue eyes gleaming.

"Will do - when the time is right," said Aradia, smiling. "But for now, let's get you and your women settled - "

"Nah - thanks, Ari', but we'll camp here," said Telepyleia. "Need to stay near the ships just in case those Romans get any ideas."

"Well, suit yourselves, but I would really like it if you could come up to my tent," said Aradia.

"Oh, yeah?" said Telepyleia, wagging her eyebrows teasingly at Aradia. The queen laughed aloud and playfully punched Telepyleia's arm.

"Stop it," said Aradia. "We really do have some things to discuss."

"Alright," said Telepyleia. She turned to the rest of the women from the ships and ordered them to set up camp, then took her daughter Kleite by the arm and propelled her towards the secret trail as Aradia handed Kalika's reins to Saraea. "Take her up for me, Saraea, then join us in our tent, alright? Thraso, come with us."

The group went up the trail to the lower town, signalling the hidden sentries along the way. Silas followed, but went to the warriors' camp around the fortress instead of to Aradia's tent.

"Now, I have to ask you, Ari' - you allow that man among your warriors?" said Telepyleia, sitting in one of the chairs at the table in Aradia's tent. Aradia poured *koumiss* for her guests before answering.

"That's Silas, Thalia's brother," she said, sitting across from the sailor.

"And?" said Telepyleia looking intently at the queen. Kleite sat on the cot and Thraso stood behind Aradia.

"And he raised Saraea," said Aradia. "It's a long story. Just trust me, he's a valuable ally."

"Okay," said Telepyleia, with a shrug. She downed the cup of *koumiss*. "Ah, I've missed that. Now, what's going on?"

"Well, as I told you, we have three Roman legions camped below," Aradia began as Saraea entered the tent and sat next to Aradia at the table.

"Any engagements?" asked Telepyleia.

"Two - only the first held any casualties," said Aradia.

"And the second?" asked Telepyleia.

"Rome pushed - we pushed back," said Saraea, darkly.

"We, ah, captured their standards," said Aradia.

Telepyleia threw back her head and laughed. "Well done," she said, wiping her eyes. "I've been tweaking the damn Romans' noses for years, but that is priceless. Hit 'em where it hurts - the pride."

"Silas thought you were Greek pirates," said Saraea.

Telepyleia chuckled. "And well he might," she said, sobering. "We were captured by the Kaskans and sold to Greek merchants. Only about half of us survived. Those of us who did found ourselves on those very ships, bound for Greece."

"How did you get the ships?' asked Saraea, almost breathless as she listened.

"The Greeks were merchants, not warriors," said Telepyleia. "As soon as my women got their sea-legs, we took over - threw them over-board and took the ships. We removed the markings and we've been uh, 'privateering' ever since. Which reminds me, we have grain, cloth, wine, oil and other supplies on the ships. In the morning, we'll unload them. I imagine they'll come in handy."

"Will they ever," said Aradia, smiling gratefully. "Are you sure you want to camp by the water? It gets awfully cold at night this time of year."

"Yep, I'm sure," said Telepyleia. "Kleite, now, if you could find a warmer spot for her to sleep, it would be much appreciated. She's used to warm Egyptian nights."

"Of course," said Aradia, smiling at the girl. "Saraea, why don't you take Kleite to the Temple and get her settled in?"

"Sure, come on, Kleite," said Saraea, rising and taking the other girl by the hand. They left the tent and Telepyleia shook her head.

"I had to practically drag her aboard," she said.

"She didn't want to leave?" asked Aradia, pouring more *koumiss*.

"Nah, wasn't that - she hates being at sea," said Telepyleia. "Seasick the whole way here."

"Well, I can speak from experience - I don't blame her," said Aradia. "I will never get on another boat as long as I live."

Telepyleia chuckled. "Eh, Amazons are notoriously bad sea travelers, that's true," she said. "'Cept for that lot out there." She pointed back towards the sea with her thumb.

"So you've been a pirate for the last decade, huh?" said Aradia.

"That's 'privateer', if you don't mind," said Telepyleia, a twinkle in her blue eyes. "Yeah - and you've been a gladiator; I caught one of your matches. Little town called Patara - you were really out of it - did they drug you or something?"

"No," said Aradia, quietly. "At least I don't think so. It's pretty much a blur now. I don't even remember Patara."

"Thank Artemis for that," said Telepyleia. "It was a slaughter."

"They all were," said Aradia, not raising her eyes from her empty cup.

"Hey - we all did what we had to do to survive," said Telepyleia. "There's no shame in that. My women and I tried to get a message to you - we were going to try and rescue you. We couldn't get within an arrow shot. Some Roman - Aurelian, was his name - he had you guarded and locked down so tight - even had these amulet-thingies hanging outside of your cell. I suppose he thought he was using magic to keep you a prisoner as well as the locks and the guards."

"Amulet - what did they look like?" asked Aradia, frowning.

"Well, let me see," said Telepyleia, scratching her chin. She took a stick and began to draw in the dirt as Silas had earlier. "They were these clay tablets - 'bout the size of my palm - covered in wax. Under the wax, there was this symbol painted, but I couldn't really see it because of the wax. And then the wax overlaying it had another symbol scratched into it - like this. Then hanging from the whole affair were these strings with a bunch of knots tied in them."

"What does it mean?" Thraso asked, looking at Aradia.

"I don't know," said the queen, puzzled.

"I asked Kleite," said Telepyleia. "She's the scholar in the family. She said that the symbol in the wax was the Roman symbol for Mars - or Ares, we call him."

"Sweet Artemis - she couldn't find me," Aradia whispered. "She wasn't ignoring me - she couldn't hear me."

"Aradia? Are you alright?" asked Thraso.

Aradia shook her head. "What I fool I was - I should have known ... should have believed ... I'm fine Thraso," she said. "Just ... I'm fine. I need to go up to the Temple for a bit. You two are welcome to join me, but I need to do this."

"Sure, I'd love to see the old town - how'd it hold up, anyway?" asked Telepyleia.

"Almost perfect," said Thraso, smiling. "You two go on ahead - I'll stay down here and keep an eye on things."

"Are you sure?" asked Aradia. "Prothoë can handle things here for a bit - you haven't had a break since all this started."

"No, really - I'm fine," said Thraso, yawning.

"Go ahead, then," said Aradia, smiling at her Second. "Get some rest if you can."

Aradia and Telepyleia walked up the steps to the upper town and on to the Temple. Telepyleia looked about, smiling. "You're right - a bit time-worn, to be sure, but almost perfect," she said. "Ah, it's a sight to warm my heart. I can hardly wait to rout the Romans and move back up here."

Aradia smiled at her old friend. "Me, too," she said.

"So what's the game plan?" asked Telepyleia. "Oh, wait - there isn't one, is there? You're gonna play it as it happens, right?"

"No - I tried that last time," said Aradia. "That was a costly lesson. No, I'm waiting to see what Aurelian is going to do."

"Aurelian? He's here?" asked Telepyleia.

"Yeah - he's leading the legions," replied Aradia with a sigh.

"Ooh," Telepyleia whistled. "So it's personal."

"Maybe for him," said Aradia, lips pressed tightly together. "I didn't ask for him to come here; in fact, I would have been a lot happier if he had just stayed in Rome and away from me forever."

"But now that he is here, if you get the chance, you'll be just as happy to kick his ass all the way back to Rome, right?" said Telepyleia.

"If that's what it takes to make him leave us alone, then yes," said Aradia.

"That's it? You don't want revenge for what he made you do?" asked Telepyleia, brows raised.

"What are talking about?" asked Aradia.

"Killing all those people - that wasn't you, Ari'," said Telepyleia, darkly. "This Aurelian put some kind of spell on you."

Aradia grinned. "Blessed Goddess - as if the Amazons aren't superstitious enough, now we have *sea-faring* Amazons - add the sailor superstitions to the mix and we're *really* in trouble."

Telepyleia grinned back. "Okay, Ari' - maybe you're right - but I saw you out there - there was something missing in your eyes - and then those amulets," she said, shaking her head.

"Those amulets hid me from the goddess," said Aradia, quietly. "Oh, when I think how many times I cursed at her in my heart for abandoning me - and all the while, she just couldn't find me." Aradia shook her head.

Telepyleia looked at her, doubtful, then sighed. "Well if that's the case, then if it's any consolation, Ari', she probably didn't hear ya cursin' at her, either," she said.

The two women walked into the Temple. The Amazons who were settled in there for the duration of the war all arose and saluted their queen. Aradia smiled and returned the salute, then motioned for the women to go back to what they were doing. Aradia and Telepyleia walked over to where Saraea was settling Kleite with Mhari and Alkaia. Kleite was now wearing some of Saraea's warmer Amazon clothing instead of the light-weight Egyptian-style clothing in which she had arrived.

"Mhari! I can't believe it!" said Telepyleia, delighted as she grabbed the shamaness and hugged her tightly. "It is so good to see you."

"And you, Little One," said Mhari, tears oozing from her eyes. "I never thought ... I am so happy you have come home - and brought us your daughter, as well!"

"Two daughters," said Telepyleia, proudly. "My youngest, Meploeo, is down with the ships."

"Two - ah, Telepyleia, truly you have blessed the Nation and have been goddess-blessed yourself," said Mhari, speaking the ritual words of congratulation one usually said to a mother who had just given birth.

"Thank you," said Telepyleia, softly. "It is good to hear at last."

"Saraea, I need to talk with you," said Aradia, pulling the girl aside.

"Yes, Aradia?" said Saraea.

"Where is Hekau?" asked the queen.

"I haven't seen her since we came back up here," said Saraea, frowning. "Why?"

"I need to see her," said Aradia. "I need for you to take me to that room below the Temple."

"Aradia, you know that I can't do that," said Saraea.

"Just take me through the tunnel, to the door," said Aradia.

"Alright," said the girl with a sigh. She went to the altar around which the women had left a wide space, clear of bedrolls and personal belongings. Saraea pointed at the altar and closed her eyes. It shifted to the side, slowly and halting at first, then slid the rest of the way to reveal two trap doors. Saraea went to one and pulled it open. Then she and Aradia stepped down into the tunnel.

"We could use a torch," said the queen, squinting in the dimness.

"Use the Sword," said Saraea, absently as she felt along the rough wall.

Aradia unsheathed the Sword of Artemis which began to glow, illuminating the narrow tunnel. Aradia marvelled at the paintings along the wall. "This is amazing," she whispered.

"I know," said Saraea, taking Aradia's free hand and leading her down through the twisty passageway. They arrived at a wooden door.

"Here, but Aradia, you can't - " began Saraea.

"I know, but just open the door - I promise, I'll not step foot on the consecrated ground, I just need to see if - just please open the door, Saraea," said Aradia, biting her lip.

Saraea sighed and pushed opened the door. Aradia gasped. It was as the girl had told her. There stood the Guardian Priestess.

"Queen you may be, but priestess you are not," said Jaiel. "You may not pass, Aradia."

"I know," said Aradia. "I seek an audience with the Lady."

"She knows already what you would say," said Jaiel. "Think you, Aradia, Daughter of Artemis, that the Great Mother of All could not pierce through the charms and icons made by mortal man's hand?"

She held up an amulet like that described by Telepyleia and crushed it between her fingers.

"Then why ...?" began Aradia. "I don't understand."

"All that has happened has happened for a reason," said Jaiel. "The amulets did not hide you from Her - they hid Her from you. She was with you the whole time; you could not see or feel Her, but She was there, by your side, guiding your hand."

"If She could hear me, then why didn't She let me die as I begged Her to do?" said Aradia, tears springing to her eyes.

"If you could have heard Her, you would know Her reasons for making you live," said Jaiel. "You know them now - they are camped in her Temple, around the ruined fortress, and now on the shore."

Aradia nodded, slowly. "I guess I know that - now," she said. "But - "

"Aradia, the Amazons were nearly completely destroyed in the Battle of Chadesia," said Jaiel, gently. "It was necessary to wait for the Amazon children to grow up into the warriors they are now. Who are your leaders? Think, which Amazons lead your troops?"

"Living in fear and on the run, hiding like animals - this was supposed to prepare them?" asked Aradia, angrily.

"The Goddess knows what Her daughters are made of," said Jaiel. "It strengthened them; where others might have given up and died, they survived and not only that, they thrived and grew stronger still. They became part of the land of their mothers and of their goddess. The land is your ally. It is the body of the Great Mother."

Aradia shook her head. "Priestess-talk," she said. "You were making sense up to that last. I have the answers I sought and I thank you."

"Ever too impatient for wisdom, Aradia," said Jaiel, smiling indulgently at the queen. "Is it any wonder the Lady must use such extreme measures to make you see and hear Her? Go, then, Sister, and know that Great Mother goes with you wherever you may tread."

Aradia sighed and turned to leave. Saraea smiled at Jaiel.

"I'll see you later, Little Sister," said Jaiel. She raised two fingers and the wooden door swung gently closed, latching with a quiet *snick*.

In silence, Aradia and Saraea walked back up the winding tunnel and crawled out through the trap door to the Amazons waiting in the Temple. The warriors had brought in braziers and more blankets to keep them warm during the cold night to come.

Shyly, Kleite approached Saraea. "Thank you ... for the warmer clothes," she said, her voice almost a whisper.

"Sure, Kleite," said Saraea, smiling brightly at her. She looked at Aradia. "If it's alright with you, I think I'll sleep here tonight, too - it's a lot warmer in here than in the camp."

"Of course - just be down at the tent early - by sunrise; I'll have the sentries wake you. We have a lot to - " Aradia was interrupted by a loud rumbling and shaking of the earth beneath them. Cries and shouts of fear and confusion filled the Temple. Aradia strove to be heard over them.

Finally, the Temple was still. Women rushed to put out the small fires caused by the fallen lamps and tipped braziers.

"Hades' jewels! What the furk was *that*?" said Telepyleia.

"Earthquake?" offered one of the women. "They're not unknown here, remember?"

"No," said Aradia, remembering the words of the priestess, *The land is your ally. It is the body of the Great Mother.* "When in war, you attack not only your enemy, but his allies, too. Come on - the Romans are firing the catapult!"

Aradia, Telepyleia, and Saraea ran to the steps leading to the lower town, stopping briefly to cling to the walls on either side as another quake hit. Stones and gravel rained painfully down upon them until the earth stopped moving. As soon as they could, the three hurried to the warrior camp where Thraso was standing on a tall pile of rubble, calling out orders to the warriors. There was no panic here, but Aradia could see the fear in the warriors' eyes.

"Telepyleia, you may want to get down to your boats," she said, quietly. The sailor nodded and ran for the hidden trail, Saraea following.

"She hasn't learned the signal yet - I'll give it to the sentries for her and come back," said the girl, looking over her shoulder to Aradia as she ran.

"Then get back up here - fast, Saraea," Aradia called out to her, then turned her attention to her troops. She strode over to Thraso. "Thraso, that's not stable - if another quake hits, you could fall," she said so that only Thraso could hear. Thraso hopped down, her face grim.

"What's going on Aradia?' she asked, and Aradia could see the same fear in Thraso's eyes as in the rest of the warriors'. Aradia mustered a grin.

"Catapult," she said.

"Cata- ... gods-be-damned Romans!" said Thraso, her eyes now blazing in anger instead of hooded with fear.

"Find Prothoë," said Aradia, chuckling. "And we need to promote another Lieutenant - for Anaea's platoon."

"Oh ... I, um ..." began Thraso, biting her lip.

"You already did," Aradia said, her eyes twinkling. "Well done - who is it?"

"Well, not yet, not without your approval, but Pisto has been filling in - without a formal promotion," said Thraso.

"Excellent," said Aradia, her eyes already scanning the neatly assembled troops. "Give it to her - we'll have the ceremony after we kick Aurelian's ass back to Rome."

"Will do, Aradia," said Thraso, going to seek out Pisto and bring her and Prothoë to the Queen, along with the other lieutenants.

"At ease, Sisters," Aradia called out to her troops as the lieutenants approached.

There was one Lieutenant per platoon of fifty to one hundred warriors. Each platoon held a specialty; there were three of archers, one of cavalry, three of swordswomen, three of spearwomen, three of warriors bearing the *labrys* or double-headed battle axe, and four of warriors wielding quarter-staffs. There were also the scouting units and a separate platoon of sentries, specially trained to watch and observe without being seen by the enemy. A few of the platoons had warriors who expertly wielded several weapons and could change in mid-battle, especially in the cavalry unit. Aradia smiled at the two dozen lieutenants who stood before her awaiting orders.

"Tell your people not to be afraid of the earth shaking - it's just the Romans playing with their little toy," said Aradia, smiling at them. "I want them mobilised and ready - we're going down in a little while - I'm getting tired of playing Aurelian's little game - "

Suddenly, she was interrupted by a man's voice, a voice that her made her skin feel as though small creatures crawled about underneath it even as her blood turned chill and cold at the sound.

"Aradia, Queen of the Amazon Nation!"

She looked at her troops and with a grim nod, approached the lip of the wall which separated the lower town from the cliff. There Aurelian sat astride his war-horse, surrounded by the two legions and four huge catapults. Aradia merely looked down upon him and waited.

"I call upon you to surrender yourself and the girl known as Saraea to me," he said, a smug smile on his face.

"Otherwise, I will tear your mountain down out from under you."

"It will take more than you have to do that, Aurelian," said Aradia.

"I have one half dozen more of these," said Aurelian, inclining his head towards the nearest catapult. "Waiting to be assembled. You cannot hide up there forever. Surely you must realise, Aradia, that you cannot defeat Rome. We outnumber you. We have the supplies and the troops to lay siege to your city for years - of course, it will not last that long; long before we eat the last of our food, we will have brought your city - and your people - down and destroyed you."

As if to illustrate his point, Aradia saw a cloud of dust in the distance as thousands of horses and their riders approached the two armies. Still Aradia glared at Aurelian in defiance.

"If you think you will ever get your hands on me again - or my daughter, Saraea - think again," she said. "I will kill the girl with my own hands before I ever let you near her - you know I will, Aurelian."

Aurelian thought briefly back to the auction block in Rome and knew she meant it; he must not let that happen. Ares said he needed the girl to complete his destruction of the Amazons for good. Although Ares hadn't been around for a while now, Aurelian decided he couldn't wait for the god to return to make his move. He shot the catapults at the cliffs upon which sat the Amazons' city, hoping to - literally - shake the women up enough to force their queen to surrender.

"Surrender yourself and the girl to me, Aradia, and I give my word as a Roman citizen that I will leave the rest of the Amazons alone," he called to her. "What are two lives to save your Nation and your people? Are you so selfish that you would not sacrifice yourself to save the rest of your people? What kind of Queen are you, Aradia?"

Aradia felt a gentle hand on her shoulder and glanced briefly back to see Saraea standing behind her. The girl's eyes were dark and unreadable.

"Saraea, get back," Aradia said, quietly.

"No," said Saraea. "Let me stand at your side ... Mother."

Aradia sighed and tears fell from her eyes. "Saraea ... what I said ..." she began. The girl stepped up beside her and put one arm around her shoulders. "If it comes to that, I will not make you kill me," she said, softly. "I will fall upon my own sword and spare you that anguish. But Aurelian shall not have either of us, no matter what happens. The Goddess Herself and the Amazon Nation will not allow either of us to make that sacrifice." Saraea turned back and Aradia followed her gaze. As one, the troops slowly saluted them both, then readied their weapons.

On Thraso's command, the archers swarmed to their posts along the wall, flanking Aradia and Saraea and knocked flaming arrows to their bows.

"Ready your marks," said Saraea, looking defiantly at Aurelian. "Loose!"

The flaming volley hit their marks - the wooden catapults and their operators. Romans struggled to put out the flames and save their machines, but to no avail; the arrows had been made of the same resinous wood and attached to the arrows were small leather bags filled with the volatile oil of the fire blossoms. As soon as the arrows hit their mark, the bags broke open and the oil spread over the wooden catapults.

Thraso came closer and stood next to her queen. Her eyes caught the cloud of dust in the distance and narrowed.

"Aradia, is that Roman re-inforcement approaching?" she asked quietly.

"I don't know who else it could be," said Aradia.

"Are we in trouble?" asked Saraea, following the gaze of the other two. "'Cause that looks like a lot of horses coming our way."

"Yep - I'd say at least two more Leg-" began Aradia. Her eyes widened as the leading rider became recognisable.

Just then, Telepyleia approached, gasping for breath. "My women are waiting for orders," she said. Aradia turned once more to see not only the women of the ships joining the ranks of warriors, but the women who had been in the Temple, streaming down the stairs, armed and grimly determined. She nodded, then turned to look at the scene below once more.

"What in Poseidon's piss is *that*?" Telepyleia cried, pointing at the rising cloud of dust.

"More trouble," said Aradia, darkly.

"Myrina," Thraso whispered, her eyes looking stricken.

"Treacherous Gorgon bitches," Telepyleia said, seething. "Figures - well, that just gives us a chance to avenge all those they betrayed to their deaths. Say the word, Ari', and we're down there."

"No, wait!" Saraea cried, as the Gorgon army came closer and began attacking the rear Roman flank. "Look, Aradia - see? Look who's with them!"

Aradia squinted to see through the dust and the late autumn afternoon sun which was slowly sinking towards dusk. Hekau sat, perched securely on Myrina's saddle. The cat leaped gracefully down and picked her way safely through the battle raging all around her, then ran to the brush at the foot of the cliff and disappeared inside the trees.

"No, not *Roman* re-inforcements - they've come to help *us*!" cried Aradia, grinning. She thought back to that day so many months ago when Silas had brought her back to the Amazons, Mhari had prophesied, *An ally will come to us from an unexpected place ... and perhaps an enemy from one we trust ...*

Aradia wasn't quite sure who the enemy was, but she thought it might be Julisa, the form Ares had taken to lure Saraea to what he thought would be her death. Julisa, the doll, had been Saraea's most trusted "friend" when she was small. The ally from an unexpected place – it had to be the Gorgons; they were the very last ones Aradia would expect to help the Amazons, save Rome itself.

She left the wall, Saraea, Thraso, and Telepyleia close behind her. Thraso got busy, assembling the additional warriors into a tight formation.

"Sisters - the Gorgons have come - they are our allies in this battle," Aradia called to them. "We must all put our personal feeling for their former betrayal aside, at least for this battle. Do not - I mean do *not* attack them. Anyone who does will be tried for treason against a sister Amazon. Be angry with me later if you must for this decision, but for now - *Attack the Roman invaders!"*

With a collective roar, the Amazon troops swarmed down the cliff, the cavalry taking the long way around and mustering in the trees before riding against the Romans.

With the Amazons before them and the Gorgons behind them, the Romans spread out, seeking a way out around the warrior women. The Gorgon cavalry flanked the Roman camp on both sides.

The Amazons and Gorgons now closely matched the Roman legions in number. They swept across the battlefield like a swarm of angry bees following the two queens and stinging the Roman Legions painfully with swords and axes.

Aradia sought out one Roman in particular. She spied Aurelian, watching from the distance astride his horse. In determined silence, she rode as fast as Kalika could carry her towards the general, twirling her sword, the Sword of Artemis, over head. Aurelian caught sight of the battle-crazed Amazon queen riding straight for him and unsheathed his sword, bracing himself for her attack.

The two warriors manoeuvred their horses around one another, each looking for an opening. Suddenly, seemingly from nowhere, Saraea streaked by on the back of Kaiyanta, screeching a battle cry. She swung her staff hard, hitting Aurelian in the mid-section. The general flew off of the back of his horse and landed flat on his back, struggling to breath. Saraea stopped a little distance past him and grinned wickedly before riding off to assist a group of Gorgon swordswomen against a platoon of Roman cavalry.

Aradia leapt down from Kalika's back, warning away the Amazon and Gorgon foot soldiers who swarmed near, ready to dispatch the enemy.

"No - he's mine," she told them. They backed off and went on to other fallen Romans. "Get up, Aurelian." Aradia pushed at him with the toe of her boot. The general groaned and started to roll over. Aradia pushed a little harder. "I said, get *up*."

She waited until the Roman managed to pull himself to his feet and grab his fallen sword. He looked at her, his gaze intense, but Aradia showed no sign that she was intimidated as she always had before. For the first time, Aurelian began to doubt his victory against the Amazons. Still, he took his stance against her. He knew that she would kill him; he'd seen her innumerable times in the arena and knew that his death was imminent. He would die with honour and never have to endure the humiliation of his failure. To be defeated by a woman - even such a woman as he knew Aradia to be - would be the ultimate blow to his pride. Better to be dead than to face that for a lifetime. He silently made his peace with the gods and lunged, waiting for the killing blow. Aradia merely side-stepped the blade, neatly avoiding it. Aurelian checked himself against the momentum of his movement and turned again to face her.

"Why don't you just get it over with?" he said. "Go on - kill me; take your revenge out in my blood. We both know that you can without much effort."

"No," said Aradia. "That was a woman *you* created, the Gladiator. I am Aradia, Queen of the Amazons. Amazons don't kill like that. We have honour. Either fight me or run, but I will not give you the mercy of a swift death."

Aurelian saw her eyes. They were no longer the steely eyes of the gladiator, empty of all life and spirit. They held fire and passion and rage, but not the dead emptiness he was so accustomed to seeing there. Then he found hope; perhaps he could defeat her, after all. She had lost that killer inside of her. If he killed her, then the Amazons would capitulate at the loss of their queen and surrender. He might find victory this day, after all.

Aradia stood, silent and still as a statue, waiting for him to make his move against her. Aurelian did not disappoint her. He lunged again, but at the last moment pulled back and twisted to the side, his blade slicing through Aradia's leather jerkin. Aradia stepped to the side, swiftly enough that the blade merely grazed the scant flesh covering her ribs. She whirled, following the momentum of her step and dipped low, her sword slicing neatly through the muscle of Aurelian's thigh. She pulled back just before reaching the vital artery, though. Aurelian dropped to one knee, bleeding. Aradia stepped back and waited for him to rise. Before he could rally and attack, the Amazon flipped her sword, the sharp point cutting a wide path in the general's brow. It bled freely into his eyes, blinding him for a moment.

"Something to remember me by," she said, then began beating him back, hitting him repeatedly with the flat of her sword, though occasionally turning it so the sharp edge would superficially knick some exposed flesh.

Finally, Aurelian's vision began to clear. He shook the blood and the sweat from his eyes and roared, rushing the Amazon with his sword outstretched. Aradia stood her ground, then turned just when Aurelian was close enough. She extended her arm, allowing the point of her sword to catch in his side. Aurelian followed the momentum of his rush at the queen and her sword tore free of him, creating a jagged gash along his ribs. Aurelian fell to the ground and lay there.

"End it," he gasped.

Aradia stood over him, the point of the Sword of Artemis poised bare inches from piercing his heart; suddenly she flipped the Sword up in a neat, quick motion of her wrist and sheathed it.

"Live with it," she said.

"No," Aurelian gasped weakly.

He tried to reach for her, but his hands fell weakly across his chest and tears of shame flowed from his eyes. Aradia looked coldly down at him, then rolled her eyes in disgust and walked away; she signaled to two Amazons who walked over and flipped the weak, helpless Roman over his horse, then slapped the horse's backside. It ran off, jolting the wounded Roman into unconsciousness.

The Roman Commander saw his general being carried off by the runaway horse and called the retreat. The Amazons watched them go, cheering wildly, hugging one another - and the Gorgons with whom they had fought; for the moment, all old animosities were forgotten in the joy of their victory. Almost all.

Thraso wandered the battlefield, dirt and blood covering her, her hair dishevelled and escaping her tight braids. She called orders to the Amazons to collect the wounded for triage and the dead for the funeral rites, but her eyes scanned the field, searching for one warrior ...

"Looking for me?"

She started at Myrina's voice. Equally dirty and dishevelled, the Gorgon Queen sheathed her sword. Thraso saw it and gasped.

"That's - "

"I know," said Myrina.

Thraso looked up and into the Gorgon's eyes.

"Why?" she asked.

"You may not believe this," said Myrina. "No reason why you should believe anything I tell you, but it's the truth. When Ares approached me about fighting for him, I refused - at first. He told me that Artemis had turned her back on the Gorgons because of Athtar's betrayal. He got terribly angry when I told him that if that was the case, I would do whatever it took to win back her favour, even if I spent the rest of my life trying ."

"But you did fight for him," said Thraso.

"It was a mistake - a big one," said Myrina. "Or so I thought at the time. He got angry because I neither challenged Aradia nor beat you - then he told me I could 'redeem' myself by retrieving the Sword of Artemis. I found Athtar. She told me that the Romans were marching on the Amazons here. We fought and I got the Sword away from her. Turns out, the Sword is Ares' bane. I decided to keep it and take my people home. I figured as long as we had the Sword, Ares would leave us alone - and as long as the Romans were busy with the Amazons, they would leave us alone, too."

"That figures," said Thraso, angrily.

"Wait - you haven't heard the best part yet," said Myrina, smiling a bit sadly. "On our way back to Hesperia, I heard the drums beating, and then the ram's horn blew – the Amazon call for all Daughters of Artemis to come to the aid of their sisters. I thought about what I had said to Ares – about spending the rest of my life to regain the goddess's favour. I know that, forever a Gorgon's word will mean nothing to an Amazon; I know that we'll never make amends to the Amazons for Athtar's betrayal, but when I heard the call, I just couldn't ignore it and keep riding. It was like ... something inside of me was *pulled* here."

"You're right – the Amazons will never trust the Gorgons again," said Thraso, sadly. "We will never again be part of the same Nation, but we can have peace between us, at least. As sisters – we are all Daughters of Artemis."

Just then, Aradia approached the two. She smiled at Myrina and clasped hands with the Gorgon Queen. "Thank you," said Aradia.

"You're welcome, Aradia," said Myrina, solemnly. "I know it doesn't make up for ..." Myrina looked at Thraso and sighed. "You're welcome."

"What will you do now?" asked Thraso.

"I'm going home," said Myrina, softly. Thraso clasped hands with Myrina and looked into her eyes.

"Be well ... Sister," she said.

"You, too ... Sister," said Myrina before turning and calling out the order for the Gorgons to form up and begin their long march home.

)O(

Aurelian looked up from the litter his men were carrying him on. His wounds had seemed less severe before they began bumping him over the rough terrain back to Rome. He groaned at the feel of a rough hand on his shoulder, then saw the god, Mars, wearing a centurion's helmet walking alongside the crude litter.

"My life is forfeit, my Lord," said Aurelian, closing his eyes. "I failed to destroy the Amazons. I failed to re-capture their queen."

"Don't be so hard on yourself, Aurelian," said Ares, quietly. "I'm not sure anyone can defeat those women - not with their allies. But take heart. I'm sending you north - to the land of the Goths and Teutons. You will capture some of those women and take them back to Rome with you to appease the Emperor. How long can a nation of all women survive anyway? One generation, maybe two. They will die out and then, the way will be clear for us. Trust me, Aurelian, we are not defeated - not yet."

Epilogue

As Myrina stood gazing out over the waters of Lake Tritonis that spring, the first of the Amazon babies was born. Mhari joyfully announced the little girl's arrival to her mother, holding her up as the baby took her first breath, then made her displeasure known at being forced from her nice warm nest.

"Truly you have blessed the Nation and have been goddess-blessed yourself," said the shamaness as she swaddled the little one and handed her back to her joyful mother.

It hadn't been an easy winter, but the Amazons survived the snows on grain they had harvested from their ancient crops, now growing wild. The fortress had been re-built by the hands of all the Amazons. Even Mhari had hobbled to the lower town to lay a brick. It was harder for her to leave her snug little house and make the journey down to the lower town now. Saraea had spent most of the winter helping her and Alkaia in the little house the two elders shared.

Saraea at fifteen Springs old, presided as priestess over the dedication ceremony of the fortress. She blessed it, then lit the celebratory bonfire. She now sat between Aradia and Mhari, watching the Amazons dance their joy around the fire. The celebration would last long into the night; the Amazons had a lot to celebrate.

The shamaness gazed into the fire and sighed, wishing her joints were young enough to join in the dance. She had to be carried down to the ceremony. She was a full ninety birth-seasons now and she was weary. Soon, she would have to ask to be taken back up to her house so that she could rest, but for now, she was content to sit with her younger sisters.

"Tomorrow, Saraea," she said.

"Yes, Granny?" said the girl, leaning closer to hear her.

"Tomorrow you will preside over the Planting of the First Seed Ceremony," said Mhari. "Do you remember the invocation?"

"Yes, Granny, every word," said Saraea, smiling proudly. "I remember everything you've taught me."

Mhari nodded and closed her eyes. "Then all is well," she said, sighing one more time. Then she smiled and whispered, "I wish I could have just one last dance ... "

In the festive firelight, Saraea saw all the lines on the shamaness's face smooth. Her smile remained, though the gentle rise and fall of her chest had ceased.

"Aradia," said Saraea, softly. "Mhari ... she's ..."

Aradia looked over to the shamaness. "I know," she said, softly, one tear slipping from her eye. "It's okay, Saraea; she's still here. They all are."

Saraea looked up through tear-filled eyes to see Thalia, Anaea, and a younger Mhari, surrounded by a host of other glowing Amazons stop briefly to wave at the two before joining the dance around the fire.

"Will they always be here, Aradia?" asked Saraea, smiling through her tears. "Will *we*?"

Aradia looked over at the youngest Amazon, sleeping contentedly in her mother's arms then back at the whole Amazon Nation, past and present, dancing in celebration and joy. She smiled and nodded.

"Always."

L.M.Townsend
The Amazon Queen

L. M. Townsend

L. M. Townsend was born and raised in Michigan, though she now lives in California with her partner, Crow, Crow's two boys, and five cats. She is an ordained Wiccan Priestess (3rd Degree HPS) and practices a sort of eclectic/ Dianic Wicca as a solitary. She also had some brief training in shamanism. Her "day job" is doing daycare for twins - which she loves.

"I don't know if there was ever a specific moment in my life when I had the actual realisation that I wanted to be an author - writing is just what I do and what I have done almost as soon as I could read. I think it's a just a part of who I am and always has been - even before I could write them down, there was always some story running through my little head. <g> Usually it included talking animals and lots of magic - actually, most of my stories still do! ☺

"When I was about 6, my uncle took me to the library. I think I found heaven that day. (Picture the library scenes from the movie "Matilda" <bg>) I was a voracious reader even then, but the limit for a child's library card was three books a week - I ran out of stories to read and started writing my own down on paper to fill the gap between library visits. I think it may have been shortly after that I started dreaming of someday seeing a book I had written in the library."

Currently, Lisa is working on two more novels and "thinking about" a children's story book.

Limitless D2D	Order Form	
The Amazon Queen By L M Townsend	20.00	
Define Destiny By J M Dragon	20.00	
Desert Hawk, revised By Katherine E. Standell	18.00	
Golden Gate By Erin Jennifer Mar	18.00	
The Brass Ring By Mavis Applewater	18.00	
Spirit Harvest By Trish Shields	15.00	
Omega's Folly By Carla Osborne	12.00	
Up The River-out of print **...While supplies last...** By Sam Ruskin	15.00	
Memories Kill By S. B. Zarben	20.00	
Connecting Hearts By Val Brown and M. J. Walker	18.00	
Total		

South Carolina residents add 5% sales tax.
Domestic shipping is $3.50 per book
Visit our website at: http://limitlessd2d.net
Please mail your orders with a check or money order to:
Limitless, Dare 2 Dream Publishing
100 Pin Oak Ct.
Lexington, SC 29073

Please make checks or money orders payable to:
Limitless Corporation

Limitless D2D Order Form		
Shattering Rainbows By Ocean	18.00	
Kara: Lady Rogue By J. Taylor Anderson	18.00	
Mysti: Mistress of Dreams By Sam Ruskin	18.00	
A Thousand Shades of Feeling By Carolyn McBride	16.00	
The Amazon Nation By Carla Osborne	20.00	
Poetry from the Featherbed By pinfeather	18.00	
Encounters, Book I By Anne Azel	22.00	
Encounters, Book II By Anne Azel	25.00	
The Fellowship By K. Darblyne	18.00	
Total		

Limitless D2D Order Form

Cat on the Couch By Cathy L. Parker	16.00	
Up The River, Revised By Sam Ruskin	18.00	
Return of the Warrior By Katherine E. Standell	18.00	
Haunting Shadows By J M Dragon	18.00	
A Saving Solace By D S Bauden	18.00	
Passion's Phrases By Charlsie Todd	15.00	
PWP: Plot, What Plot? By Mavis Applewater	18.00	
Queen's Lane By I. Christie/J A Bard	18.00	
Total		

South Carolina residents add 5% sales tax.
Domestic shipping is $3.50 per book
Visit our website at: http://limitlessd2d.net
Please mail your orders with a check or money order to:
Limitless, Dare 2 Dream Publishing
100 Pin Oak Ct.
Lexington, SC 29073

Please make checks or money orders payable to:
Limitless Corporation